Available ... from ... Special ...

TRUSTING RYAN

"I like listening to you talk. I like how you think, too."

The words were offered slowly, softly. A declaration of admiration. At least. Or so her heart seemed to think. It flip-flopped, sending a sharp blade of desire down through her most feminine places.

What was she doing?

Ryan leaned forward. Slowly. Deliberating. Coming closer.

Audrey watched, frozen as she waited. There was no thought of action, of should and shouldn'ts, wants or not wants. No thought of any moment that came before, or any that might come after.

His lips covered hers, his hands coming up behind her, pressing her against him, and as she melted into his embrace, she knew that she was going to break her own rules.

THE BACHELOR'S STAND-IN WIFE

"I don't want to complicate our relationship, our business relationship, David."

"I know." He brushed his thumb along her jaw. "I've been wanting to do that for a long time," he said, soft and gruff.

"You have?"

"Yeah."

"Please don't fire me."

He dropped his hand. "I have no intention of firing you."

"You can't sleep with me, either. We can't go there at all. We can't kiss again. I can't lose this job, David. I can't."

His gaze held steady. "Can you forget this happened?"

"I have to."

First published in Great Britain 2009
Harlequin Mills & Boon Limited,
Eton House, 18-24 Paradise Road, Richmond, Surrey TW9 1SR

Trusting Ryan © Tara Taylor Quinn 2008
The Bachelor's Stand-in-Wife © Susan Bova Crosby 2008

ISBN: 978 0 263 87627 7

23-0809

Harlequin Mills & Boon policy is to use papers that are natural, renewable and recyclable products and made from wood grown in sustainable forests. The logging and manufacturing processes conform to the legal environmental regulations of the country of origin.

Printed and bound in Spain
by Litografía Rosés S.A., Barcelona

TRUSTING RYAN
BY
TARA TAYLOR QUINN

THE BACHELOR'S STAND-IN WIFE
BY
SUSAN CROSBY

TRUSTING RYAN

BY
TARA TAYLOR QUINN

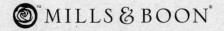

With more than forty-five original novels, published in more than twenty languages, **Tara Taylor Quinn** is a *USA TODAY* bestselling author. She is known for delivering deeply emotional and psychologically astute novels. Ms Quinn is a three-time finalist for the RWA RITA® Award, a multiple finalist for the National Reader's Choice Award, the Reviewer's Choice Award, the Bookseller's Best Award and the Holt Medallion. Ms Quinn recently married her college sweetheart and the couple currently lives in Ohio with their two very demanding and spoiled bosses: four-pound Taylor Marie and fifteen-pound rescue mutt/cockapoo, Jerry. When she's not writing or fulfilling speaking engagements, Ms Quinn loves to travel with her husband, stopping wherever the spirit takes them. They've been spotted in casinos and quaint little antique shops all across the country.

To Tim,
my own young hero who's all grown up now.
I love you more today than yesterday.

CHAPTER ONE

THE WOMAN WAS too damned gorgeous for his good. When he was with her, he couldn't focus on anything else. Including the reasons why he, Columbus Police Detective Ryan Mercedes—one of the city's youngest and newest special victim detectives—was not going to get romantically involved with anyone anytime in the near future.

Most particularly, he was mesmerized by her laughter—had been since he'd first met her six months before at the adoption of an incest victim he'd rescued. The young girl had been Audrey's client.

"What?" Audrey Lincoln asked, glancing over at him in the small living room of his one-bedroom loft condominium.

On the TV Bruce—Jim Carrey—had just been endowed with God's powers and had single-handedly taken on the gang of thugs who'd earlier beaten him up. The scene involved a birth-worthy monkey and cracked Ryan up every time he saw it.

"Nothing," he said, maintaining eye contact with the woman sitting next to him. They'd started hanging out a few months ago. Catching an occasional movie or meeting for a cup of coffee.

"I thought you liked this movie."

Bruce Almighty. He'd seen it so many times the lines randomly popped into his head. "I do."

"You said it was your favorite."

"It is."

"Then why aren't you watching it?"

Good question.

"I am."

Her brown eyes narrowed in a way that made him hungry. She stared at him a second longer, then turned back to the large screen television across from them.

They weren't dating. Weren't on a date. They were just friends. Watching a movie on a Saturday night.

So what if, the week before, they'd moved their watching from a generic theater to his home?

This was where the old movies were.

They'd watched her favorite movie, *The Mirror Has Two Faces,* the previous week. She'd said she related to the main character, Barbra Streisand's version of a university sociology professor. The woman had struggled with being ugly. Undesirable.

Audrey Lincoln had no such worries.

"What?" She was looking at him again.

Sorry, Jim, Ryan silently apologized to the actor who'd given him more hours of hilarious entertainment mixed with just a bit of life lesson than he could count. "You thirsty?" he asked his guest.

"A little."

He stood. Delilah, the cat, opened one eye from her perch on the back of the recliner. "Wine, beer or diet soda?"

"A glass of wine would be great."

He thought so, too. It meant she'd have to stay around a while. Or he'd be forced to arrest her for DUI, and they certainly couldn't have that.

AUDREY COULDN'T remember ever laughing so hard. And she'd seen most of Jim Carrey's movies more than once. Was familiar with his brand of humor. Enjoyed it. Just never this much.

Or perhaps—she glanced over at the handsome detective sitting on the other end of the couch finishing off his glass of wine—it was the company?

Credits rolled. She didn't want the evening to end. Tomorrow it was back to work—no matter that the calendar read Sunday. Audrey hadn't had a day off in longer than she could remember.

She didn't really want one.

Days off led to introspection, which led to…

Nothing that she needed to be concerned about tonight.

"Okay, so tell me why that's your favorite movie," she said, smiling at her companion.

He shrugged, leaving the remote on the table beside him, the DVD flashing its welcome screen. "It's funny."

"And?"

"How do you know there's more?" His glance was intense again—just as it had been during the movie. Her stomach tightened, whether from reaction or dread, she wasn't sure.

Maybe both.

For a thirty-five-year-old woman who spent her days trying to protect the hearts of damaged children, she was embarrassingly inexperienced when it came to matters of her own heart.

"I may have known you only a few months, Mercedes,

but for a cop who's been around long enough to make detective, you're surprisingly empathetic. That's an amazing
feat. One that only a man with some depth could manage.
So, show me the depth. Why's that your favorite movie?"

The wine was talking. Ordinarily, Audrey would never be
so bold. Especially not with a man she actually liked. More
than as just an acquaintance. A peer.

Were they actually becoming friends?

She couldn't remember the last time she'd had a
personal friend.

"I don't know." Ryan didn't look away as many men would
have when faced with a touchy-feely question. "Maybe
because I'm a control freak and the idea of having God's
power is so compelling I have to keep coming back for more?"

She studied him. Thought about what he said. Shook her
head. "I don't think so."

"Why not?"

"Because you aren't power-hungry."

"How do you know?"

"You let me handle the Markovich kid."

"You're his guardian ad litem. He knows you. Trusts you."

"And you were the arresting officer. Jurisdiction was
yours. Most cops I know would not have stepped back."

"I still arrested him."

"You took him to the station to keep him safe."

"I charged him."

"He beat up his stepfather. He had to know there were
consequences for that."

Scott Markovich was safe now. For now. He was one of
her "jobs" for tomorrow. She was making a visit to the
fifteen-year-old in detention.

"How do you do it?" Ryan's gaze was piercing. Personal.

A combination that was dangerous to her budding sense of awareness around him. The tight jeans he was wearing and close-fitting polo shirt, stretching across the breadth of his shoulders, didn't help.

Or maybe it was just that she'd always been a sucker for light hair and green eyes.

"How do I do what?" She wanted a little more wine, but didn't want to be too forward.

And she needed to go. Get home to her house. To her nice big pillow-top mattress and down pillows and lose herself in rejuvenating oblivion for a few hours so that she could get up tomorrow and start all over again.

"How do you see all the stuff you do—kids like Marko-vich who've been sexually abused by people in positions of authority over them—and be able to get close to them? To suffer with them? How do you even get up in the morning, knowing that's what you're going to face?"

How could she not? was the better question.

"How do you?"

"I don't get close. I see them for a few minutes and my job is done. And I'm not always dealing with the little ones. I work with adult victims, too." The room's dim light cast shadows over his frown.

"Still, *why* do you do what you do? Face danger every day—dealing with the toughest to handle crimes."

He seemed to give her question serious consideration. "I don't have a good answer for you. I've wanted to be a cop since I was a kid, never asked myself why. I just know that if I can make a difference, I have to try."

There was more to his story. Audrey didn't succeed at her

job without being able to read between the lines, to read people, to hear what they weren't saying as much or more than what they were. And she didn't succeed without knowing when not to push.

Ryan Mercedes was a private man. An intriguing man. A man who had the looks of Adonis and the heart of Cupid.

A man who was occupying her thoughts so often he was making her uncomfortable.

"How about you?" he asked. "*Why* do you do the work you do?"

For maybe the first time ever, she considered telling someone the whole truth. *Considered.*

"In 2003, in Ohio alone, there were 47,444 substantiated cases of child abuse and or neglect. More than seven thousand of them required the services of a guardian ad litem." Hide behind the facts. It had always been her way. People couldn't argue with facts. And win.

"I understand the need for child advocates," Ryan said. "Remember, I see the results of child abuse and know full well that there are far too many children in this city who need someone on their side, someone looking out only for them and their best interests. But that's not what I asked. I asked, why you?"

His perception surprised her. Or maybe not. Maybe her heart already knew that this man was good for her. That he was personal. In a life that was anything but.

She opened her mouth to tell him about the volunteer guardian ad litem program. The hours of training it took for one qualified ad litem to emerge. The need for legal advocates sitting alongside children in court to help clear up the confusion that stole childhoods.

And about the few of them, the paid lawyer ad litems

who, in addition to looking out for the child's best interests and supporting the child, also offered legal advocacy.

She opened her mouth and said, "I...had a...rough childhood." And in spite of the heat in her cheeks, the discomfort attacking her from the inside out, she couldn't seem to stop. "Other than my parents' divorce, things looked fine on the surface. Middle-class, well-dressed mom with a college education and respectable job. No one could see the things that went on underneath the surface, behind the closed doors of our home. And trying to get anyone to listen, when things looked so picture perfect, proved impossible."

His frown deepened. "She hit you?" He sounded as though he'd like to hit her mother back, and Audrey almost smiled. Too many years had passed, the wounds had healed, and still it felt good to have someone come to her rescue.

She was falling for this man.

"No," she said. "She suffers from depression, though she refused counseling and has never been treated. Sometimes she's fine, but when the darkness descends, watch out. She'll turn on me without warning. Her way of loving is to control. If you do something to displease her, she'll take away her love. And anything else she's providing that she knows you want."

"Such as?"

"When I turned sixteen, she gave me a car. I needed it to get to the university where I was attending class as part of a special high-school-student program. From that point on, she used that car to control me. From the classes I took, the people I chose as friends, the jobs I applied for, the clothes I wore, the church I attended, even the boys I dated. If I didn't do as she suggested, she'd take away my car. Or my college-tuition money. Or the roof over my head. She'd tell me what to think, how to act, who to love. She used to write these horrible letters, telling me how stupid I was, how I never *came to the table,* as she called it, or that I came late. Anytime anything went wrong, it was because I'd screwed up again."

"Where was your dad through all of this?"

"I'm not sure. They divorced before I was a year old. Mom told him he wasn't my real father, but there's never been anyone else in her life that I'm aware of."

"You didn't get tested, to find out if the man was your father?"

Audrey kept thinking that she'd stop the conversation. Right after the next sentence.

But something about Detective Ryan Mercedes compelled her to talk to him. She'd never met anyone like him. Such a mixture of idealism and rigid determination. He was a man you could count on to protect the tribe. But one with a heart, as well.

"He wasn't interested in proving anything," she said.

"Did you ever see him?"

"Nope. I don't even know what he looks like. I wrote to him once, when I was in high school, but the letter came back with a big 'return to sender' on the front. My mother said it was his handwriting."

"And she never told you who your father really was?"

It did sound rather fantastic, now that she heard her story aloud. Audrey was so used to that part of her circumstances, it seemed normal to her. And in her line of work, representing children whose rights were in jeopardy, she regularly saw familial situations that were much more dysfunctional than hers had ever been.

"I've always assumed that the man listed on my birth

certificate, the man she was married to, was my father. My mother has a way of changing the truth to suit her in the moment. She uses words to lash out and hurt when she's hurting, but I don't think she'd have been unfaithful to her marriage vows."

"He must have known that."

"Probably. But she uses people's vulnerabilities against them until she breaks them down to the point where they'll agree with her just to get some peace. I'm guessing she hit him where it counts one too many times."

Audrey sat forward. She'd said too much. Far too much.

"Nice guy, to leave his kid all alone with that woman."

"He paid child support, every single month, until I turned eighteen."

"Like money was going to make you happy? Protect you?"

Life was black and white to Ryan. There was right and wrong. Good and bad. You chose the right. Righted the wrongs. Served good and obliterated the bad.

A characteristic that had drawn her to him from the beginning. The world needed more of his kind of passion.

She just didn't want to need it. Not on a personal level.

"Maybe he thought, since I was a girl, her daughter, that there'd be some kind of motherly instinct that would come out in her, protect me from the emotional abuse he must have suffered."

"Or maybe he sucked as a father."

Ryan's words made her smile.

"YOU NEVER DID answer my question." Ryan wished he'd brought the wine bottle in with him. Wished he could pour another glass for both of them. Keep her on his couch with him.

At least for a time.

Long enough to get to know her well enough to get her out of his system. To dispel the strange and uncomfortable hold she had on him.

Ryan was used to being his own man. He'd been hearing the beat of his own drummer for most of his life. And walked to it alone.

He liked it that way.

He had things to do with his life—lives to save and evils to conquer—and he couldn't do that if he gave his heart away.

Or at least that was the story he'd been telling himself. If there was another reason, some deep-seated something that prevented him from living the normal life of wife and kids and family, he didn't want to know about it.

"What question?" Her big brown eyes were mysterious, pulling him into their shadowed depths, as she flung a lock of her long blond hair over her shoulder. She sat on the edge of the couch, as though poised for flight. He wished she'd relax again.

"Why you do what you do."

"Oh, I thought I had. That's easy. I spent my childhood feeling powerless," she said as though that explained it all.

And in a sense, it did. She'd been stripped of something vital as a child. And every day, when she went to work, when her work preserved the dignity and sense of self of even one child, when she protected the innocence of childhood, she took back the personal power she'd lost.

Ryan understood that. Righting wrongs was what made his past, his history, his genealogy conscionable, too.

CHAPTER TWO

AUDREY DIDN'T WAIT around for his call. And only checked her cell phone so many times Sunday evening because she gave the number to all her clients, and if a child needed her, tomorrow could be too late.

It wasn't Ryan's fault she'd bared her soul like an idiot the night before. He had no way of knowing she'd shared with him more than she'd ever told anyone.

She'd come across like some pathetic victim, instead of the strong and healthy woman she'd become.

With the hundred-year-old hardwood floors of her Victorian-style cottage shining, she put away the cleaning supplies she'd hauled out and went upstairs to the treadmill. And half an hour later, panting and sweaty, headed across the hall to her home office—the only other room upstairs—and read over her files for the next day.

When everyone else in the world was relaxing, watching television, reading, napping, Audrey worked.

The kids whose lives seemed reduced to files of unfortunate facts, whose parents, for a variety of reasons, were unable to parent effectively, called out to her. They were always calling out to her.

Kaylee Grady. Date of birth, 9/29/04. That made her four years old. Audrey looked through the documents of the new case she had an initial meeting on the following morning.

Kelsey Grady. Date of birth, 9/29/04.

Twins.

Lifting the cover page, she studied the picture underneath. They were identical. Blond. With chubby cheeks—and far too serious eyes. Their parents had been killed in a car accident during a blizzard the previous February. There'd been no will. And the family was fighting over custody. They wanted to split up the girls to satisfy members from both sides.

"Over my dead body." Audrey's voice, usually a comfort, sounded loud in the gabled room. Loud and lonely.

And she glanced at the cell phone she'd carried up with her. Nothing. No missed calls. No messages.

She didn't blame him for not calling.

The cuckoo clock in the family room downstairs of her 1920s, whitewashed home chirped eight times. Not meaning to, Audrey counted every one, and then knew what time it was. A piece of information she'd purposely been denying herself.

It was just that, last night, she and Ryan had crossed into new territory. Hadn't they?

That of friends, trusted friends. Or something. It wasn't as though they were kids, playing the dating game. They were mature adults. Getting to know each other. Sharing a moment in time.

A phone call would have been nice. That was all.

HE WAS STILL WORKING the eleven-to-seven shift. Not because he had to—no, Ryan Mercedes had all the right contacts in all the right places, whether he wanted them or not. He was on the night shift for one reason only.

A selfish reason.

Working nights allowed him to keep his distance from everyone in his life. Having to sleep when family gatherings happened, when an old school mate suggested going out for beers, anytime he was issued an invitation that got a little bit too close, he could always bow out with the excuse that he was working.

The night shift let him operate in a different world. A world where everyone slept—except those few who were working as well, or those who took advantage of others' sleep to commit crimes against them.

The downside was, when he came off shift Monday morning, he was completely exhausted and wired at the same time. He'd been awake all day Sunday having dinner with his birth parents—he hadn't seen two-month-old Marcus Ryan in over a week, and his biological cousin, Jordon, a fatherless young man Ryan had met the previous summer who seemed to gravitate to him, had been visiting from Cleveland. Then he'd visited his adoptive parents to watch the Reds game on television with his dad.

He hadn't been to bed since Saturday night. And that session hadn't contained his most restful sleep with the continuous interruptions of vivid dreams of a certain lady in the bed with him.

He'd never had a woman in his bed at the condo. Never had a woman in his bed, period.

So why was one suddenly appearing there, uninvited?

He wanted to think she was unwanted, but his body wouldn't let him go quite that far.

He settled for…uninvited.

And still, nearly thirty-six hours after she'd left his apartment, he was thinking about her.

He was on shift again that night, Ryan reminded himself as he drove slowly through the streets of Westerville, cell phone in hand. Two kids were waiting for the school bus on the corner of Cleveland Avenue and Homeacres Drive. Usually there were three. The shorter girl was missing.

Ryan made a mental note to take the same route home tomorrow. And the next day. If the girl was still missing by the end of the week, he'd stop and ask about her.

In the meantime, he had to sleep. And sleep well. He couldn't do his job on adrenaline alone. His instincts wouldn't be as sharp. Lives could be at risk.

He had to get some rest.

"Hello?"

Her number was on speed dial only because a couple of her clients were under his investigation.

"Audrey? Is this a bad time? Did I wake you?"

Seven-thirty in the morning was early to some people.

"Of course not. I've been up a couple of hours."

Well, then… "Are you at work? With someone? Should I call another time?"

"No, Ryan." She chuckled. "This time is fine. I don't have to be in court until ten-thirty this morning, and my breakfast meeting canceled."

Canceled. She was free for breakfast. Unexpectedly. The thought of asking her to meet him somewhere for a quick bite sent alarm signals up his spine. Where was the harm in two friends having breakfast?

They both had to eat.

"So what's up?" she asked, bringing to his attention the length of time he'd let lapse while he blubbered over the idea of asking her out to eat.

Shifting in his seat, adjusting the pistol digging into his thigh beneath the brown tweed sports jacket he wore, Ryan thought about the case he'd been working on for most of the night.

Focused on the life he'd chosen to live.

The juvenile who'd beaten his stepfather to a pulp, claiming that it was self-defense. He'd claimed some other pretty horrendous things, too.

Reviewing four hours of witness testimony, tapes, doctors' reports and police records had netted Ryan no more than they already had.

"The prosecutor's going to charge Markovich."

"No way." He heard the drop in her voice and felt as if he'd failed not only the fifteen-year-old boy whom he'd believed, but Audrey, too.

"The kid's testimony has too many holes," he said. "He contradicts himself on four separate occasions."

"But there's a doctor's report that proves he was molested."

"At some point in his life. Not necessarily by his stepfather."

"He nearly killed the man, Ryan. A fifteen-year-old kid, especially one as sensitive as Scott, doesn't suddenly get violent unless something pretty vile is going to happen to him."

"I know." He was missing something. He just didn't know what. "But it's not my job to be the lawyer," he reminded himself as much as her. "I check out the facts, make the arrests, collect the evidence, then I'm done."

"You aren't, though, are you?" The soft question surprised him.

And then it didn't. He'd called her, hadn't he?

"No," he admitted. "The kid's lying about something, but not about why he unhinged on his stepfather, I'm sure of it. Unless I can find out what else is going on, the kid's going back to detention. Maybe for a long, long time."

"They aren't charging him as an adult, are they?"

Ryan wasn't sure. But he'd heard a rumor that they might. He let his silence answer for him.

And because he'd called to escape the sometimes hell of his job, he asked another question that had been plaguing him on and off for more than a week.

"Why do you relate so much to *The Mirror Has Two Faces?*"

The woman was gorgeous. Not only the classic beauty of long blonde hair, long legs, great figure and big brown eyes, but also the sensitivity that shone through those eyes, especially in one so young, the job she'd chosen to do when, with her law degree, she could be making a mint, made her irresistible.

As a friend only, of course.

"I don't know."

It was one of *those* "I don't know"s. The kind that really meant, "I don't want to tell you."

"I think you do."

"Maybe."

"So tell me."

Another long pause.

"I told you why I like *Bruce Almighty.*"

"Because you have power envy."

The more commonly used *p*-word in that phrase sprang immediately to mind, and Ryan was grateful that Audrey couldn't read his thoughts.

Glad, too, that they were on the phone and not where she could see the reaction hearing her voice was having on that *p* part of his anatomy.

Turning, he pulled into the parking lot of his complex. Parked in the covered lot and headed around to his door. His place was only a one-bedroom, but it was two stories with a private patio that looked out over a golf course.

"So why do you?" Delilah, the cat he had because he was gone too much to have a dog, wrapped herself around his legs as he let himself in and dropped his keys on the table by the front door.

"Why do I have power envy?" she asked, the amusement in her voice sending another surge of blood beneath his fly.

With Delilah under one arm, like the football he'd never carried in high school, Ryan entered the kitchen, looking for the opened can of tuna in the fridge.

"Why do you relate to *The Mirror Has Two Faces?*"

"You're like a dog with a bone, you know that?"

"Yeah."

"Don't you ever get sidetracked?"

"Not often."

Delilah munched from the can. Ryan snagged a chunk of the white fishy meat, dropped it in a bowl and looked for the mayonnaise. Not bacon and eggs, but it would do.

"I'm waiting," he said.

"What are you doing?"

"Eating."

"Eating what?"

"I'm not telling you until you tell me why you identify with that movie."

"Fine." The word was clipped, but her tone wasn't nearly

aggrieved enough to convey any real irritation. "I've always thought that kind of relationship would be perfect."

"What kind? The kind where they end up dancing in the street?"

"No." Her voice had quieted. Lost the playfulness. "I'd love to have a best friend, a significant other, someone to come home to, without messing everything up with sex."

Not what he'd expected to hear. Where was his opportunity to tell her that she was gorgeous? That she had no reason to think herself anything but beautiful? It was all about what you saw in the mirror, right? The way you see yourself, as opposed to how others see you.

"So get a roommate."

"Roommates leave. Get married. I want a lifetime companion."

He couldn't believe she meant that. "A sexless one." Hell, everyone knew that part of the movie was crazy. Even the stars of the movie found that out.

It didn't work. *Couldn't* work. Unless maybe one of the parties was gay...

"At least one where the relationship isn't based on sex," she said slowly, as though choosing her words with great care. "If, after we've lived together for a while, we decide we want to do that some time, that would be fine. As long as we both want it. And it isn't a big deal one way or the other."

The woman was nuts. Sex, not a big deal? She couldn't really expect any guy with blood in his veins to live with someone as beautiful as she was and not burn up with a need to make love with her. Could she?

"So you'd do it once?" he asked, out of morbid curiosity. "Or do it once in a while?"

"I don't know." She drew the statement out. "That's the whole point. Whether we ever did it or not wouldn't matter. If we both wanted to, we could. If one of us didn't want to, no big deal. The relationship would be based on mutual respect. Trust. Great conversation. Just enjoying being together."

If one of us didn't want to. Alarms went off in Ryan's head. The kind he'd honed to perfection.

"Are you gay?"

The question was inappropriate. Disrespectful. Uncalled for. And not what he'd really wanted to ask at all. He just didn't know how to find out what he suddenly needed to know.

"No. But that's a typical guy response."

"I'm a guy."

But not a typical one.

"I'm not gay."

"But you've been abused, haven't you?" He wasn't pleased with himself, with the words. His tone had lowered enough that maybe she hadn't heard him.

"If you're asking if I was raped, the answer's no."

Thank God. Thank God in heaven. Shocked at the emotion pricking at the back of his throat, his eyelids, Ryan grabbed a carton of juice from the refrigerator and took a huge swallow.

"But you've been in a relationship where you had sex because you felt like you had to."

"That's kind of a personal question, don't you think?"

"Yeah."

"Well, I told you why I liked the movie. Now I want to know what you're having for breakfast."

Fair enough. But he figured they both knew she wasn't getting off the hook permanently. "Tuna."

"You made a sandwich?"

"No. Just tuna."

"With dressing?"

"Nope. Couldn't find any."

"You're eating tuna out of the can."

"Ate. It's gone." Thanks to Delilah. She wasn't great at sharing.

"And that's all you're going to have?"

"I'm on my way to bed," he reminded her, trying not to remember the images of her that he'd taken to his repose the last time he'd been there.

"What time do you get up?"

"Depends on the day."

"Today."

"I'm planning to crash until I wake up. No alarms. Which means I'll probably make it until around three." If he was lucky.

If not, he'd be up in an hour. Even with room-darkening curtains he couldn't lie in bed during the day if he was awake. There was always someone to see, or talk to, who wasn't available in the middle of the night.

Like the cable company that was supposed to be adding Sportzone to his monthly service—had charged him, but failed to turn on the games.

"You think you'll want some breakfast then?"

"I'm sure I will." If you could call stale bread and peanut butter breakfast. He hadn't been to the grocery store. Saturday nights were usually reserved for that because it was the only time of the week the place wasn't milling with people.

"I make a mean omelet."

Ryan's blood started to pump harder again, all signs of exhaustion taking a hike. Had she just invited him to her place?

"I'm glad to hear that."

"I have a seven-o'clock meeting tonight, but nothing after court this afternoon. If you'd like to stop by, I could show you my ham-and-cheese."

"Okay." Sure. He crossed one scuffed wing-tipped shoe over the other. Nonchalance was called for.

He just had to find some.

"If you want to, that is," she added in a bit of a rush. "I mean, you've provided dinner the past two Saturday nights. I thought I should return the favor."

He'd ordered pizza.

"That'd be great," he said with a tight rein on himself. *Don't make anything out of it, Mercedes. The woman's beautiful. And not interested in sex. Or you. Or she'd be interested in sex.*

And he wasn't interested, either. His obsession with her was a blip. Like the flu.

"It's not a big deal," she said. "I mean, I'm just offering one friend to another."

"Hey, Audrey." He added a teasing chuckle to his tone—he hoped. "It's fine. I'm a bachelor. I never say no to home-made food. No strings attached."

"Good. Fine." The confidence had returned to her voice. "Say, around five, then?"

Five was fine. That left him seven and a half hours to get his libido under control and forget that he'd ever had one intimate thought about a stunningly desirable guardian ad litem.

He was not the least bit interested in a long term relationship.

And one thing was certain. Audrey Lincoln was not a woman a good man had casual sex with. She was the type of woman he loved.

CHAPTER THREE

THE OMELET didn't happen. The phone rang, instead, and Audrey only had time to scramble some eggs and take five minutes to eat them with Ryan before running off to be at Mollie Anderson's mother's house when the confused twelve-year-old's father came to pick her up for visitation.

Neither of Mollie's parents had known she was coming because Mollie had been the one to call for Audrey's help.

Audrey talked to Ryan again on Wednesday morning. He phoned as he came off his shift to ask her about another case they'd shared—a pair of nine-year-old fraternal twins who'd initially been reported as runaways several months before. Very soon into the investigation, however, they'd realized the twins had been abducted.

Ryan thought he might have located them living in Arizona with a man who, other than the color and length of his hair, perfectly fit the description of the children's father.

She'd grieved for Darla and Danny Buford for months until she'd finally, with the help of some counseling, let them go. There'd been an obvious break-in at Mrs. Buford's well-to-do home. A ransom note.

Mr. Buford, the other half of the lengthy and ugly divorce that initially had brought Audrey into the picture, had been right beside his ex-wife through the entire ordeal. He'd paid half the ransom and cried with his ex-wife in his arms when the terms of the bargain were not met.

The money disappeared. The police didn't catch the slight figure who'd picked up the bag in the middle of the busy New York City street where the kids supposedly had been taken. And the children were never returned.

The kids were dead. Plain and simple.

And shockingly, horribly, grossly unfair.

Audrey wanted Ryan to be right about the Arizona lead, but she didn't think so.

Yet that didn't stop her from hoping. If any other detective had told her he'd located those kids, she'd have shrugged off the news without much thought. But Ryan Mercedes's track record for accuracy was impressive.

Because he didn't speak until he knew what he was saying? Or because he was that gifted at his job?

He called again on Friday morning. The Buford twins were alive.

"Turns out some psycho, who'd just lost his wife and daughter in a car accident, had taken them. He never let them out of his sight."

"What about school?" Audrey prided herself on the professional tone—glad that Ryan couldn't see the moisture in her eyes.

"He home-schooled them. They're pretty confused, but physically unharmed. The state has them until their parents can get there."

Audrey had to take a deep breath to let the emotion pass. There were so many more tragic stories in her line of work than happy endings. "Mr. and Mrs. Buford are going together?"

"They remarried more than a month ago."

Thankful that at least two traumatized children had every advantage for full recovery, Audrey listened as Ryan offered to grill a steak for her that night to celebrate a homecoming they both took personally, yet neither would attend.

"I can't." It was for the best, she told the part of herself that was disappointed. "I'm having dinner with a therapist who had a session with one of my clients yesterday."

Both she and the therapist were booked for the next week, but Audrey wasn't willing to settle for a paper report on this one. Nor could she wait a week. The family was due in court again on Monday.

Saturday night she had a fund-raiser with the Arizona Bar Association, and on Sunday she was volunteering legal services at a women's shelter.

All things she did because she loved to do them. Wanted to do them. Because they gave her life meaning. And a reason to get up in the morning.

The activities were designed to create the life she wanted. And that was exactly what she had as she hung up the phone, fully aware that Ryan thought she'd been making excuses not to see him again. Fully aware that she might never hear from him again—outside the office.

Fully aware and completely okay.

It was very unsettling, therefore, that a time or two over the weekend she almost resented those same activities. Mostly when she was thinking of the handsome detective and wondering what he was doing with his two days off, living in real-world time.

Still, a little resentment, in exchange for the ability to live her own life, was a small price to pay.

When her phone rang again Monday morning at the time

Ryan was due off shift, she picked it up with far too much vigor. And flooded with warmth when she heard his voice.

Get a grip, my girl, she admonished herself. *He's a friend. Nothing more.*

"Do you have any free time this week?" he asked after a brief hello. He sounded as impatient as she felt over the past weekend's misses. Not angry. More like…needy.

Or maybe she was projecting her own eagerness onto him?

"I have a couple of hours between court hearings tomorrow, starting around eleven, but you're sleeping then," she told him.

"I'll stay up."

"What—and get yourself killed tomorrow night?"

"I can sleep after lunch."

"Are we having lunch?"

"I think so."

"Okay."

AND THEY DID. She had a quick dinner with him on Thursday, too, before her guest lecture at the Moritz College of Law at Ohio State. They talked about work. About the weather and the Cincinnati Reds and about work some more.

She asked about Delilah.

They didn't talk about each other. And the more they didn't, the more Audrey wanted to.

What was the matter with her?

She'd never needed a man to complete her before. To the contrary, she did better, felt stronger and more capable, when she wasn't with a man.

So why couldn't she stop looking at him? Whether he was

wearing jeans and a T-shirt, exhausted and on his way to sleep, or wearing a jacket on his way to work, the man looked like an art sculpture to her. Legs that were long and lean and nothing but delineated muscle, shoulders that blocked the clouds from her view when he stood in front of her, eyes that smiled, or admired, or sympathized without guise, and a butt that—

No. She wasn't going to think about that. Wasn't going to think that way. She wanted a friendship.

She didn't want sex. Didn't want to be that vulnerable. A man might be able to join his body parts with a woman, share pleasure with her, and get dressed and walk away, but not Audrey. Nope, she'd open her heart right along with her legs, then she'd be right back where she'd been at sixteen. Craving love. Needing validation from someone who could give it, or take it away, without notice.

No butt looked good enough to risk that.

RYAN STAYED UP on Friday after work. He had two days off, plans to see Marcus Ryan—because he couldn't seem to stay away from the baby recently born to the biological parents he'd met the previous year—to go to a Reds game with the dad who'd raised him, and have some of his mom's home cooking. He needed to be on the same time as the rest of the world.

He also needed to shop and clean his place before Audrey showed up at six expecting steaks on a grill he didn't yet have. He didn't have the food, either, or furniture for the patio, but those were minor details.

Things to take his mind off the rape victim he'd watched being loaded into an ambulance at three that morning. What in the hell a middle-aged married woman had been doing out in a deserted school parking lot by herself in the middle of the night, he didn't know.

But he hoped to God she lived to tell him. One way or another, as the newest detective in the Special Victims Unit, he was going to find out.

His place was ready, new furniture assembled, grill put together, salad made and steaks marinated by five. Up in the master-suite loft, Ryan showered, pulled on some jeans and a black T-shirt, ran his fingers through his hair—then decided to shave again. Just for something to do.

Ten minutes later he still had forty minutes to kill. Avoiding the king-size bed, avoiding thoughts of his dinner guest in that bed, he checked his cell phone for messages.

Nothing from work. Good. Sometimes it was nice not to be needed.

Needed. He adjusted his jeans. Ryan wanted to be needed. Bad.

He needed his watch.

Walking around the massive bed to the nightstand where he'd left the timepiece his father had given him when he'd made detective—it had a tiny recording device built into it— Ryan glanced at the comforter.

It was clean. The browns and beiges were kind of masculine, but then, he was a guy. Guys tended to be masculine.

The sheets were light-colored. While he tried to see them from a woman's perspective, a thought occurred to him. He hadn't changed them in a while.

Never seemed to have the time.

He had twenty minutes right now.

Only because he so rarely had extra time, only because

he needed to take advantage of that time to accomplish something, Ryan changed his sheets.

He'd just finished when the doorbell rang.

HE'D SEEN HER in jeans before. Several times. Just didn't remember them fitting those long, feminine thighs quite so well. The white, short-sleeved T-shirt covered the waistband. As long as she didn't move.

"Wine?" he asked, handing her a glass as she sat in the wicker rocker he'd purchased that afternoon.

She lifted her hand to take the glass. "Thanks." Ryan had to turn away before she noticed his reaction to the thin strip of lightly tanned stomach she'd exposed.

He'd have raised his gaze to avoid that possibility, except that her breasts, which were round and full and completely framed by the tight shirt, were far too much temptation.

He was a solitary man. With a job to do. People to protect.

Maybe he should go next door. That way he wouldn't see her. Wouldn't flirt with temptation. He could cook on his neighbor's grill and courier the steaks over....

"I talked to Scott Markovich today."

The kid who'd beat up his stepdad. The bastard dad was going to live. Thank God. As it stood, Scott had been charged with assault, which was a lot better than murder.

And talking about work was a lot better than…anything else.

"And?"

"I think he's protecting his mother."

"She was out of town when the incident took place."

Audrey's hair fell forward across her shoulder as she shook her head.

"I don't think so. I think she was there. I think she'd been drinking again."

"I thought the court ordered that she'd lose custody of Scott if she went back on the juice."

"Right."

Realization dawned and Ryan blurted, "She knows what happened that night."

"I think so."

"And she won't speak up because she was drunk."

Audrey shrugged.

"She knows what that SOB was going to do to her son."

"That's my guess."

Ryan swore, his mind racing ahead—and back at the same time. Going over the reports he'd practically memorized, looking for clues he'd missed. Trying to figure out how he was going to prove Audrey's theory.

"Her sister wasn't her only alibi. There was the bus driver who took her to Detroit," he reminded her.

And maybe the guy was dating the sister. Or had lied for favors. Maybe he'd been drinking on the job and couldn't remember who he'd transported and had lied to save his ass.

Maybe…

"There was the woman who sold her the ticket, too," she added.

Didn't mean she got on the bus. "No passengers remembered her."

"It was the middle of the night," Audrey said, not that he hadn't already been thinking the same thing himself.

"There were only two of them and they were both asleep," he finished for her.

The evidence was mostly circumstantial. But Scott had openly threatened to kill his stepdad the previous year. And there was no denying that the kid had used the crowbar on the man's back. The only question was why.

"If we can get it on the record that she was there that night, we can subpoena her to testify. If her husband had been about to rape her son, any halfway-decent attorney should be able to get a self-defense dismissal out of that."

Her eyes had the fire of battle, the glow of an imminent win, and Ryan was almost a little sad that she'd opted not to practice law. She'd make a damned good prosecutor. And Lord knew the world needed them.

But she was young. Fresh out of law school, he figured, based on the fact that she'd taken the bar exam the previous year. There was time.

"As strongly as I believe you," he said, sitting down beside her, wishing he'd opted for the footed double swing rather than two chairs, "I can't put theory on report."

"I think I can get Scott to talk to you, if you're willing."

Sitting forward, Ryan almost spilled his drink. "Hell, yes, I'm willing."

"It'll have to be tomorrow. They're moving him to a facility in Dayton until his trial. Something about bed space in the non-sexual-offense unit for fifteen-year-olds."

"Fine."

The Reds game might have to wait. His dad would understand.

SHE'D HAD BETTER steak. Apparently Ryan liked them very well-done. But Audrey couldn't remember anyone whose company she'd enjoyed more.

"I like how you think," she told him, trying not to over-react as he sat next to her on the darkened patio, handing her the half-glass of wine she'd requested.

His eyes, as they stared at her, glistened with two white spots, a double reflection of the moon shining overhead. "You like how I think? What does that mean?"

"I don't know." She should go. Before she did something she'd regret. "I like the way your mind works, your take on things. You've got all these theories that are just a bit outside the norm, and yet I agree with them, you know? I like lis-tening to you talk."

And if she didn't shut up she was going to ruin a friend-ship before it had the chance to exist.

Because her next sentence wasn't going to be about liking his conversation.

"I like how you think, too." The words were offered slowly, softly. A declaration of admiration. At least.

Or so her heart seemed to think. It flip-flopped, sending a sharp blade of desire down through her most feminine places.

Without removing her gaze from his, she took a sip of wine. Moistened a throat that was suddenly far too dry. In-explicably dry. What was she doing?

Ryan didn't seem to want his wine. Setting down the glass he'd barely touched, he stared at her for a second longer, then leaned forward. Slowly. Deliberating. Coming closer.

She watched, glanced down to his lips, frozen as she waited. There was no thought of action, of shoulds and shouldn'ts, of wants or not wants. No thought of any moment that came before, or any that might come after.

And when those full, masculine lips touched hers, the shiver that went through her wiped away any last conscious thought.

She'd been kissed before. Many times. But never like this.

Ryan's mouth controlled hers, even as it asked permission. He invaded and invited at the same time, taking her on a sensual journey that consumed her entire being with the mere touch of his lips. He was tender. And confident.

And when he pulled back, Audrey couldn't let him go. Her mouth followed his the couple of inches he retreated, until her lips were once again attached to his.

He opened his mouth then, demanding more from her, his tongue finding hers, not just tip to tip, but fully engaging with her in a give-and-take that made them far more intimate than friends.

"I want to make love with you."

She wasn't sure she heard the words at first. Thought maybe she'd imagined them. And even then, her body responded, igniting every nuance of sensual feeling inside of her.

"Please."

There was no mistaking the pleading in his voice.

Or the answering desire inside of her.

Pulling back, Audrey studied those glistening green eyes. "I…"

How did she say no without turning him off? Without losing his interest? What words did she use?

"I want that, too."

She didn't just say that. Didn't just lick her lips. Her nipples weren't hard, sensitive, against her bra.

She couldn't…

Ryan's lips covered hers again, his hands coming up behind her to rest beneath her shoulder blades, pressing her against him, and as she melted into his embrace, Audrey knew that she was going to break her own rules.

CHAPTER FOUR

HE SHOULD HAVE BEEN nervous, for many reasons. Any time he'd thought about this moment in his life—and he'd thought of it plenty over the past ten or so years—Ryan had envisioned shaky hands. Some fumbling. Uncertainty born solely of ignorance.

Hesitation, at the very least, as he risked the isolation he'd so carefully concocted and guarded vigilantly.

Audrey's hands on his shoulders, her moans consuming the air around them, the light flowery scent of her perfume enveloping him, allowed no room for hesitation. Her soft, feminine skin, waiting there for him to find, to expose, to caress, created fire within him, not quivering.

He kissed her, opening her mouth wider with his, exploring her with his tongue in ways that happened naturally, as if of their own accord. With no learned or practiced moves to draw on, he lifted her body gently against him, breaking contact with her lips only briefly, as he carried her to his bed.

He'd be Detective Ryan Mercedes tomorrow. And all of the tomorrows after that.

Tonight he was a man.

He'd made the trek upstairs many times—exhausted and coming off thirty-five hours without sleep, wide awake, early, late, angry, frustrated, enervated, flying up the steps two or three at a time. He'd made it hurt, content, and even drunk once. He'd traversed them alone with a hand truck and solid pine chest of drawers, a bed, his second large-screen television. Tonight he climbed them with no thought of the journey, only of the woman with her arms wrapped around his neck, of getting her to the soft mattress that awaited them so that he could love her properly.

Reverently.

Laying her gently crossways in the middle of the bed, Ryan slid down next to her, covering one of her legs with one of his as he half lay on top of her. He was on fire, needing everything, everywhere, and was compelled to stare at her, instead, to connect, first, through the eyes of her soul, the eyes of her heart and mind, those chocolate-brown windows that gazed back at him with an intensity that matched his own.

"I've wanted this since the first moment I saw you." He confessed what he'd sworn to himself he'd never admit to anyone.

She was his match on a level much deeper than anyone ever had been. But she was independent, too. Surely there was safety in that.

"Have you?" she asked, her voice huskier than usual. The little grin turning up the edges of her mouth made him hard.

Harder.

The bulge in his pants wasn't a new thing. Its control of him was.

"I have," he told her, bending to kiss her again, opening his mouth over hers, needing to get as far inside her as he could, to join as much of him to her as was humanly possible.

And beyond.

Audrey's moan lit another flame in his groin and Ryan

rubbed his aching penis against her denim-clad thigh. He felt like a damned animal, rutting against her.

She didn't seem to mind. Lifting up, Audrey moved back and forth against his chest, pressing her upper body against him until he could clearly distinguish two hard nipples caressing him.

"I like that." He'd had no idea.

"Me, too."

"I'd like to see them." He could only give her honesty.

"Okay."

Her gaze was open, and shadowed with desire, as she studied him. The rest of her didn't move.

Which left him one choice. Glancing down at the rounded mounds of her breasts, he lifted her shirt as though he'd had a lot of experience with such things. With one hand and a smooth glide, the white cotton was bunched up beneath her armpits and the lacy, low-cut bra he'd seen only in outline was fully exposed. The soft skin of her breasts spilled over the edges of the flimsy material.

Heart racing, Ryan took his time, savoring the view. His hands itched to cover those breasts, but he couldn't deny himself the beautiful sight.

"I've never seen anything so perfectly gorgeous." His voice was mostly a whisper. It was all the breath he had to spare.

"You're pretty gorgeous yourself," she said. She'd lifted his T-shirt, as well, was staring at his chest.

She touched him, running slim fingers over the muscles in his chest, stroking her thumbs against his nipples. Flickers of sensation moved through him, straight down to his erection.

His nipples had that kind of power? He'd taken one hell

of a lot of showers, rubbed them with hundreds of bars of soap, to have missed that one.

Mary Ellen Rowe had spent the six weeks they'd dated rubbing his chest. He'd been pleasantly comforted by the touch.

Nothing more.

"That feels good," he told the awesome woman lying in his bed. "Really good."

Her smile was a sweet mixture of knowing and modesty. A woman who was, perhaps, just becoming aware of the depths of her own sexual power, as well?

What the hell was the matter with him? Analyzing, even now. He had breasts waiting before him.

Loving to do.

And still, Ryan couldn't lose his distinct awareness of every single movement, every touch.

These moments were going to be embedded deeply within his memory, his heart, for the rest of his life.

Over the next hour Ryan discovered much about himself. And about Audrey Lincoln. As much focus as she gave to her young clients, she gave to making love with him. Every aspect of her was intent on him. Her gaze. Her touch. Her responses and attention. He'd never felt so consumed—and so alive. She knew him better in an hour than anyone had ever known him.

With fingers skimming the edge of his jeans, she almost drove him over the edge.

He had to release the zipper on his fly. Get his pants off. He had to set his penis free to love a woman. This woman.

Where before he'd moved slowly, savoring, Ryan now pulled at the button of Audrey's pants with more strength than finesse. It came free with one tug. On his knees above her, he bent to her hips, grasping the jeans in both hands to tug them down over slim hips and long legs that seemed to go on and on.

Just when he'd thought it couldn't get any better.

He stared at her thighs. At the scrap of white lace panty that didn't quite cover the dark hair curling there. The thin strap of thong disappearing into her backside.

And something occurred to him.

She'd dressed for this. For him.

Looking up at her, he sought silent confirmation in the gaze that was fully on him.

"You're okay with this." It was more statement than question.

Her lips were trembling as she nodded.

With fingers that were oversensitized, he touched her, the soft skin of her legs, her inner thighs, the brush of hair at the top of her panties. He had to go slowly now, or explode before he ever got where he was going.

"I want yours off, too."

Slow down, Mercedes, he told his raging body as he stood. Unbuttoned his own jeans, stepped out of them—taking his briefs off at the same time.

And then he stood before her, his penis full and weighted down, while she looked at him.

"Okay?" he asked when her gaze finally met his.

Licking her lips, she nodded again.

Ryan was beginning to love that silent affirmation, recognizing that she gave it when she most wanted something.

He meant to take another hour with her, to put his fingers every place he wanted his penis to go, to explore her so thoroughly there would be no part of her unknown to him.

He took a moment to sheath himself with a condom from

the box in his bedside drawer—a supply that he used to replace the one in his wallet each month—and turned back to her.

Taking off her panties as he rejoined her on the bed, he made it only so long as it took him to spread her legs and settle himself between them. He didn't have to wonder what to do. His body knew. He found her opening and gave a slow nudge, his gaze glued to hers.

And he watched her eyes open wider as his penis first penetrated and then, moving gently in and out, filled her more fully.

Nothing had prepared him for the way that felt. *Ecstasy* was too bland a word. *Perfection* not good enough to describe the sensation that filled him from head to toe. Heaven couldn't be this good.

Ryan hadn't known how he'd make certain that Audrey had an orgasm, wasn't sure he'd recognize it when it happened. He only knew that he was not going to take his own pleasure without ensuring hers.

As it turned out, there was no issue. Fully inside her, he pulled out and thrust in again, and again, more quickly, feeling the pressure building in his erection, getting ready to explode, and knowing he was going to have to stop or go before she did when her moans changed, became more frantic, and then surprised-sounding as the inner folds of her body clasped him, pulsing around him. Over and over.

"Oh, my…" Her words were more cry than statement, released breathlessly before she sucked in air.

And with that breath, Ryan joined her, his body erupting with huge throbs as he came inside a woman for the first time in his life.

Highly praised and swiftly rising detective, Ryan Mercedes, had just lost his virginity.

YOU'RE IN TROUBLE, girl. Big trouble.

With Ryan's "Oh, yes," still ringing in her ears, the aftermath of his lovemaking leaving her lethargic and absolutely joyful at the same time, she tried her darnedest to rein herself in. To find reality.

She'd had sex before. Way before. And more recently than that, too. But she'd never made love.

Never felt that liquid heat devour every vein in her body, or known herself to give up control to the wild and free ecstasy he'd built inside her.

It had to be the wine. Or the fact that no one had ever taken more than an hour to have sex with her before.

It had to be how long they'd known each other without acknowledging the attraction between them.

It had to be the overdone steak.

It absolutely could not be that she'd in any way given any part of her heart to the man who was even now inside her.

Making her want to do it again.

"I'm sorry—am I too heavy?" Ryan lifted his shoulder off hers. The chilled air that drifted over her newly exposed skin was not welcome.

"No." With one hand on his backside, holding him in place, and another on his shoulder, she pulled him back down. "You feel good."

"I'm about to fall asleep."

She'd figured so. Any man she'd ever been with—not that there'd been that many—had either jumped up and thrown on clothes immediately afterward, or fallen asleep without a word.

Novel to have someone actually talk to her about doing either.

"Sleep awhile, then," she said softly, thinking she'd do the same herself.

Another first.

"But I don't really want to sleep." He raised up enough to look her in the eye. "I don't want to waste a single moment with you."

Oh, God, I am in serious trouble.

"I think that's just about the sweetest thing anyone has ever said to me." She told her new lover the unadorned truth. And lifted her head to plant a small kiss on lips that were slightly swollen.

Had she done that?

And left that love mark on his neck, too?

Was he going to be angry when he saw that?

Guiding his head gently back down to her chest, she ran her fingers slowly back and forth through his hair. It was full and thick, even for its shortness. And surprisingly soft.

So many things about this man were surprising to her. And yet, not surprising at all. He fit her so exactly, not only where they were still connected, but in all ways. He approached his job as she did, with everything he had, sparing little for any other life. He cared. He didn't give up. He saw reality and still believed.

He had unbounded energy and had found a way, in spite of the experience and time it took to make detective, to avoid cynicism.

The weight of his head grew heavier and she hoped he'd allowed himself to rest. The man had worked all night. And if she had to guess, she'd figure he'd been up all day today, getting ready for tonight.

Everything in the apartment had been perfect. He'd

dusted since she'd been there last. Vacuum marks had still lined the carpet. And the furniture outside was new, added since her previous visit when she'd peeked outside to the empty patio.

Dinner had already been prepared, other than the cooking of the steaks. Even the meat had been marinated.

It all spoke Ryan to her. Attention to every detail. Few mistakes. Dependable.

And she couldn't fall prey to the tugs he was making on her heart. Neediness had cost her part of her soul.

A part she'd never get back.

As she continued to stroke his hair, Audrey glanced around the bedroom. As pristine as the rest of his apartment, and as sparsely decorated, the room was what she would have expected of a man whose priority was not his home, but rather, in getting the sleep he needed to do his job.

A bed. A dresser. Another big-screen television—for those sleepless nights? No window treatments other than the standard white blinds that were on every window in the condo.

And in every other unit in the complex, as far she'd been able to tell.

Nothing that really spoke of the man's life. His past. No pictures of parents—or any other family. No obvious mementos from past girlfriends.

Not even a receipt on the dresser or a belt hanging from the doorknob.

He didn't put himself out there.

And that was just fine with her.

"I want to make love to you again." The words were uttered against her skin. Other than his mouth he hadn't moved.

And she was already filling up with the moist heat that

threatened to flood her lower belly. With a hand on his buttocks, she pulled him more fully inside her again.

"Then I think you should," she whispered, needing him so badly she ached for him.

But only physically.

Please, God, let it only be physical.

CHAPTER FIVE

RYAN GOT UP in time to make it to the meeting with Scott Markovich. The kid, fearing that his stepfather would hurt his mother if he was in detention and not there to protect her, admitted that the woman had been home the afternoon the bastard had come after Scott in a way a man should never come at a boy.

She'd been drinking since early morning and had been plastered enough that her husband thought he could get away with a little on the side with her son.

He'd miscalculated Scott's determination never to be touched that way again.

He'd also overestimated his wife's stupor. She'd come into the room soon enough to keep Scott from killing the son of a bitch.

And she'd promised him that from that moment forward she would never, ever let another drop of alcohol pass her lips.

Scott believed her.

Ryan didn't. As much as Scott wasn't going to like it at first, being separated from his mother was the best thing that could happen to the boy. There was a relative, an aunt on his father's side, who desperately wanted him.

None of that was Ryan's business, however. His

business here was almost done. A report to the prosecutor and he was out.

Another job done. A successful outcome this time.

Not something he ever took for granted.

Just as he didn't take for granted the woman who, on Saturday night, he was once again holding in his arms.

Not because he wanted to, but because he had to. His sudden need for Audrey was not something he was comfortable with. It didn't fit at all with his life plan. With his self-concept.

But one thing he'd learned in life—sometimes the things least understood were the most important.

"Thank you," she said now, her voice sleepy.

"For what?" They'd been talking for more than an hour, lying there naked in his bed, the covers up around their waists.

They'd been in bed almost three hours.

"For Scott."

He shrugged. "It's my job."

"Maybe."

There was no *maybe* about it.

"But there's something different about you. Something that makes you, I don't know, more accessible. I don't think Scott would have talked to anyone else. He's not very trusting of cops. As a rule, every time they've come around, his life has been painfully disrupted."

Because of his mother's drinking. And because when he'd reported his stepfather's earlier abuse, there hadn't been enough solid evidence to charge the man with anything. And now, when Scott had been defending himself from a horror that must have seemed worse than death to him, he'd been arrested and detained on charges of manslaughter.

They were all doing their jobs. Enforcing laws that were

in place to protect society, the people. So why was it so often that the victims were the ones who had the fewest rights?

With a brief flash of his birth mother, and a briefer one of his birth father—a man Ryan still struggled to accept for so many reasons on so many levels—Ryan said, "I think maybe my age helped us out this time. Most times it's the other way around."

He could say this here, to her. She'd understand. Audrey must have to fight many of the same battles he did, having so much responsibility, being capable of a maturity that was uncommon at such a young age.

Being forced into it by life's lessons.

Maybe someday, he'd even be able to tell her about the circumstances surrounding his conception.

Maybe someday. Not today. Other than a few brief conversations with the parents who'd raised him, Ryan hadn't talked about that particular case since they'd solved it the year before. Not even to the biological grandfather who was a law-enforcement icon in this state.

"How would your age have had anything to do with Scott's ability to trust you?" She turned onto her back, her head in the crook of his shoulder, pulling his hands around her to rest across the flatness of her belly.

"Maybe it doesn't. I just figured I'm probably closer to his age than any other detective he's had to deal with. I figured that might have helped him relate to me a little bit."

Her skull dug into his flesh as she turned to look up at him, grinning. "What, they give out some kind of memo at the office listing detectives' exact ages?" she asked.

"No." Suddenly Ryan wasn't feeling so good. Surely she knew…he just assumed she knew. Everyone seemed to.

Shit. What if she didn't know? His skin grew cold. Clammy. Worse than when he'd been facing that freaked-out druggie with the sawed-off shotgun the previous month.

"Then why would you say that?" she asked again. He could tell, from the frown marring her brow, the confusion in her gaze, that she was catching on to something.

And had no idea what.

Disentangling himself as gently, but as quickly, as possible, Ryan stood, skipping underwear as he pulled on his jeans and zipped them.

Surely this wouldn't be a big deal. She'd only be what, two, maybe three years older than he was, assuming she went straight from college to law school?

Suddenly the budding relationship he'd been fighting against became something he had to have. No matter what. And another one of life's little lessons became personal. Only by losing something—or facing its possible loss—did you realize its worth to you.

"You haven't heard them telling the jokes about the detective in diapers?" he asked, scrambling for words.

"Nooo." She drew the word out, sitting up and pulling the covers to her chin. "Exactly how old are you, Ryan?"

"How old do you think I am?" Now that was a mature reply. Fresh out of junior high.

"I don't know. I thought early thirties. So…what…you're twenty-eight, twenty-nine? That's young for a full detective. And I guess it could make you seem more accessible to a kid Scott's age."

Ryan didn't lie. Or prevaricate. Or play games. He lived life by the rules. All of them.

If you didn't, people got hurt.

He was also a risk taker. Came with the cop territory.

He'd just never known such stark fear before when taking one.

"I'm twenty-two."

He faced her, an unarmed firing squad of one, and knew by the look on her face as soon as he said the words that he'd risked as much as he'd feared—and lost.

AT FIRST AUDREY THOUGHT he was joking. He had to be. She was not spending the weekend in bed with a twenty-two-year-old boy. Someone had paid him to say that. Except that Ryan wasn't the type to play mean games—not even for money. Especially not for money. If there was one thing she was sure of, it was that Ryan Mercedes could not be bought.

"Say something." He wasn't laughing.

He wasn't even smiling.

Nor did he look nonchalant, as though he was playing with her. In fact, he looked about as sick as she was beginning to feel. Sick, and scared.

And young.

Oh, God, what had she done?

"You're twenty-two." How could her voice sound like her when she'd just become someone she didn't know at all?

"Twenty-three in a little over seven months."

A young twenty-two. Not even twenty-two and a half. With numbers running quickly through her head, she stared at him, horrified.

Suddenly the sparseness of his apartment was no longer admirable. It screamed at her of youth and college and just starting out. The new patio furniture didn't make her feel warm and wanted, but rather, as though she'd come to a tea party with a child.

And lying there, naked in his bed, she felt like a sex offender. What would this young man's mother think of her?

She had to get up. Get dressed. Get out. Except that she didn't want him to see her naked. At twenty-two Ryan would be used to young, nubile, completely firm and unmarked coeds.

Audrey had cellulite.

And what in the hell did that matter?

She did not want to attract this kid. Didn't want him interested in her. At all. It was gross. She was gross.

Besides, he'd already seen it all.

When tears sprang to her eyes, she wanted to die.

"Hey, Audrey, it's not a big deal." With her eyes closed against the wetness still squeezing its way out of them to slide down her cheeks, Audrey almost gave in to that voice.

It had been the highlight of her life for weeks. It had brought her to life all weekend long, speaking to her of needs and a beauty that transcended all the trash their jobs brought to them. She'd responded to it like a flower to rain.

"Sweetie…"

Her heart calmed at the word. Knew a second of peace. Everything was going to be all right.

Then the bed dipped beneath his weight.

And she waited to feel the touch of his fingers on her face. Her neck. Needed to feel his heart beating beneath her cheek, his arms around her, keeping her safe…

No!

No! No! No! No! No!

"Stop!" The scream was shrill. Not a sound she'd ever

heard come out of her mouth before. "Don't come any closer." The tone was softer, but no less foreign.

"Come on, babe, it's not as if…"

Audrey's eyes flew open. Wide open. She held up a hand, silencing him. She knew now. Couldn't get sucked in by that deep, reassuring tone. The sense of confidence. How could she possibly find emotional safety and security with a twenty-two-year-old child?

Or almost child, she had to amend as she looked at the man sitting on the edge of the bed, concern shadowing his gaze. Concern and a caring so deep she almost couldn't breathe.

She knew the breadth of that chest intimately. Knew the strength in the bones and sinews. The gentleness and passion in his…

No! What in the hell was the matter with her?

His lack of chest hair wasn't genetic as she'd assumed. It was a symptom of youth. He hadn't grown any yet!

Good thing she knew where the bathroom was. She might need to make a dash for it if the nausea attacking her got any worse.

They'd showered together in there that morning. He'd soaped her back and breasts and…

"Don't *babe* me," she said with more strength in her voice. And some venom, too.

"You're angry." He sounded surprised, was sitting there wearing the most heart-wrenching frown. Compelling her to smooth it away with her fingers, followed by a kiss…

What was she? His damn mother? Needing to take care of his woes?

"Damn straight I'm angry." Audrey swung out of bed with a heave worthy of a football team, taking the covers with her. She would not expose her old body to his young gaze again.

Ever.

How embarrassing. Humiliating.

Wrong.

"Why? I don't get it." He followed her around the bed to where her clothes were scattered all over the floor. Helped her pick them up.

She snatched her bra from his fingers with a sharp "Give me that." He shook his head.

"What's a few years' difference in age, Audrey? We're still the same people who've been making love in that bed for most of the past twenty-four hours."

How dare he remind her of that? Especially now?

"A few years?" she screamed at him. Where *had* that voice come from? Taking a deep breath, she finished a little more calmly, "That's what you call it?"

"Last time I looked a few's three to four," he said, standing between her and the door—deliberately, she suspected. "I figure at the most we're looking at five or six, so if you want to split hairs and worry about semantics, then it's one or two more than a few."

His voice had lost some of its tenderness, though she detected no anger. Just distance. He was transforming from lover to detective again. From child to man. Audrey stared at him. She couldn't help it.

She had to leave. Had to get away and pretend this weekend never happened. To somehow rescue her heart from the debacle she'd created.

She started to laugh incredulously.

"Five or six years?" she asked, her voice, shaky with tears, still sharp. "That's what you think?"

He slid his hands into the pockets of his jeans. A child his age had no right to look so damned mature doing that.

So damned sexy.

"Yeah," he said with another frown. "You just took the bar exam. On average, a person graduates from college at twenty-one or -two, then does three years of law school. That puts him at twenty-five. But as smart as you are, and being a workaholic, I figured you probably didn't take five years to do your undergrad, so there's a good chance you were twenty or twenty-one when you finished your undergrad and twenty-three or -four out of law school, which made the difference in our ages not that great."

He'd given the matter a lot of thought. She didn't really understand why the notion calmed her, but she welcomed the respite. However brief it might turn out to be.

"I graduated from college at twenty," she told him, not sure her delivery carried the power she intended as she stood there trailing sheets and a blanket over her naked torso. "At which time I followed my mother's dictates and worked for her until I had saved enough money to attend law school without any help from her. She'd told me she would disown me if I made a decision so obviously not right for me."

Ryan's shoulders straightened. Tensed. His entire body seemed to be on alert. As though he were walking into a robbery in progress. "How long did it take you to save up for law school?"

"You can't work your first year in law school, did you know that?"

His eyes narrowed. "No."

"I had to save a couple of years' living expenses, as well as tuition and books…"

"But you were working for the boss, so you made a lot." There was nothing childlike about the alert man standing before her. Nothing young or immature about the commanding tone of voice, almost as though he could will the truth to be what he needed it to be.

"My mother insisted I start out at the bottom and earn my way up just like everyone else. Character building, she said."

She almost felt sorry for him. Except that she had to stay angry to survive this. And to figure out a way to exit with dignity.

Or, more importantly, with finality.

She just wasn't sure who she was mad at. Herself or him. She hadn't known. She'd assumed.

And so, apparently, had he.

Suddenly Audrey was exhausted. Needed to get this over and done with. Needed to get outside his world and find herself again.

To reassure herself that she was still there.

Intact.

That she hadn't made a mistake that would change the rest of her life.

"I'm thirty-five, Ryan." Her words were crisp and clear. All business. "Thirteen years older than you. Almost old enough to be your mother."

CHAPTER SIX

YOUR MOTHER. Audrey's words crashed around in Ryan's brain, deafening him to whatever else she was saying. He could see her lips moving, but couldn't make any sense out of the sound. *Your mother.*

She had no idea how close she was to the truth.

Ryan's biological mother was thirty-eight. Only three years older than the woman he'd spent the past twenty-four hours in bed with.

He stood rigid. It's what he did. Remained on his feet no matter the circumstances. Met it head on. Handled it.

Did what was right.

Followed the rules.

Black and white.

What in the hell did he do with a situation that had every color of the rainbow, in every hue, all clashing with one another, surrounded by a sea of brown and a buzzing that wouldn't quiet?

"Ryan, say something." She repeated his earlier words. They got through the cacophony.

"You're thirty-five," he said, only half-aware that he, too, repeated her earlier response.

"I can't believe you couldn't tell," she said. She looked so tiny standing there in bare feet, her slim shoulders naked above the tangle of covers she clutched around her. "I mean, I'm thirty-five. Not twenty."

"And?"

"My body doesn't look twenty."

The slight bit of insecurity that slipped through her tone, more than the statement itself, brought him back to the *them* he'd been a part of all weekend. Been a part of for months.

Audrey and Ryan. Two people who were meant for each other in some form.

"I have to go."

He couldn't let her walk out of his life. Regardless of his need to live it alone.

"Your body is beautiful," he told her. "Perfect. It drives me crazy with desire, turns me on almost to the point of self-ishness, as this weekend's marathon session can attest to."

"I've never been with a less selfish man."

Her eyes had darkened, reeling him in, until her words landed. She was thirty-five years old. There had been others.

Undoubtedly with a lot more experience.

Growing warm despite the chills climbing the back of his neck, an unfamiliar lack of confidence creeping up his spine, Ryan continued to stand there. He didn't have any other method of operation.

"I've never been with another woman."

He could have kicked himself. Why in the hell had he said that? What possible bearing could it have on the current situation?

Except perhaps to seal his fate, showing himself for the kid she was making him feel like.

Damn it. He saved lives for a living. Looked after two sets of parents. Risked his life every single day.

Society relied on him to keep them secure. His superiors respected him. Trusted him. Knew he'd get the job done.

"You're kidding, right?"

Here was his chance. One word and he could get some of his pride back. *Right.* That's all he had to say.

Except that it wouldn't be right. Ryan didn't lie. He didn't shy away from tough situations. He didn't settle or compromise. He upheld black and white so that the citizens of Columbus could sleep at night.

"No."

"You're gorgeous, Ryan! And the most virile, passionate man I've ever met. There's no way you made it through twenty-two years of living without some girl offering to take care of you."

"She offered."

"And you said no."

"Yes."

"Why?" Head tilted, she watched him. "You weren't attracted enough to her?" The honest curiosity in her eyes, mixed with a bit of incredulity in her tone, compelled his answer.

"I wasn't in love with her."

"And?"

"Lovemaking, by its very definition, requires love."

He knew exactly what he was telling her. And said the words, anyway. Black and white. That's how he lived. Even if the facts staring him in the face were hard to take.

"No guy waits for love his first time. Or any time for that matter."

"I'm the exception that proves the rule, I guess."

"You didn't want her."

"Oh, I did." He nodded, remembering how physically painful it had been to turn Mary Ellen away. She'd followed him into the kitchen of his apartment one night shortly after he'd moved in. He'd intended to throw some popcorn in the microwave for the movie they were about to watch.

She'd unbuttoned her top, and the snap on her jeans....

"I don't get it."

He wasn't going to explain it to her. Not right now, at any rate. "Let's just say that I have a clear understanding of what damage can be done when one has sex for the wrong reasons. Taking a chance on hurting someone who said she was in love with me when I knew I wasn't in love with her, just for a few minutes of physical gratification, was not worth the lack of self-respect I'd have later."

"Unbelievable."

"Mine is the only face I see when I look in the mirror in the morning. It's up to me to keep it clean."

"People have sex all the time without love. *Like* is nice, but even that's not necessary in today's world."

Was she telling him something? If so, he wasn't sure he wanted to know. Not if it meant that the experience they'd shared meant nothing more to her than good sex.

"Just because I've got a penis doesn't mean that I can be irresponsible with it."

As she'd been with her vagina? As much as she might want him to believe that—and he wasn't sure she did—she could be speaking generally. He couldn't see Audrey giving herself lightly.

She'd been emotionally engaged with him. He wasn't going to accept any other version of what they'd shared.

"I've never met anyone like you." Her tone had softened distinctly.

Ryan took one step closer. "Nor I you."

Tilting her head to meet his gaze, Audrey started to speak and stopped. Age didn't erase the lost waif confusion from her eyes. Or the trembling from her lips.

She hadn't called him on his backhanded declaration of love.

"I was afraid you'd be able to tell it was my first time."

"Uh-uh." She shook her head without breaking eye contact. "You were incredible. Why would you think that?"

"I came so soon."

"The first time, but anyone would have after all the touching we did beforehand."

"You didn't just have sex with me because it felt good," he said.

"No."

"Your heart was involved."

She turned her head away, burying her face in her shoulder. And he breathed the first easy breath since the entire conversation began.

It was still there—whatever it was they were to each other. Right now he was too relieved to know that to care about the danger of losing his autonomy.

"Audrey." With a gentle finger he lifted her chin. "It's okay."

"No," she said with trembling lips, a trembling voice, "it's not okay, Ryan. I'm thirteen years older than you. A whole different generation. Nothing's ever going to change that."

"So we have some unexpected challenges we'll have to face," he said slowly, leaning toward her. Another inch and their bodies would be touching again.

Every nerve he possessed needed the contact.

"Life is full of challenges," he continued. He had to have her in his life. He had to be alone. White and black inside him at the same time.

What in the hell was he doing?

What could he do?

She licked her lips.

And he said, "We're still the same people we were last month. Last week. And last night."

What was he saying?

He couldn't possibly bring a thirty-five-year-old woman home to meet his parents.

Either set of them.

Eyes wide, she stared at him as though he were a lifeline. Her only hope out of a nightmare that wouldn't end.

That look resonated within him, knocking him off any sense of direction he might have thought he had. She was *his* hope.

And he had to protect her. Period.

"Right," she said, an unfamiliar note of bitterness in her voice. "I want children, Ryan. Tell me how we'd meet that challenge."

Children. With her. Having kids of his own wasn't something he'd given much thought to. Except to know that it was way down the road.

But having children with Audrey? It seemed natural. A given. Like he should have known all along.

Like he'd left himself and was living the life of another man.

"What?" he said, needing to take her shoulders, to hold her there right where he knew she needed to be—and sensing that if he did, he could lose her. "You think my sperm's different from some thirty-five- or forty-year-old guy's? I'm going to produce some inferior kid?" he asked, being deliberately obtuse.

He couldn't argue her point. The obstacles in front of them seemed insurmountable. He needed some time to find the way over them. Around them. Through them.

Or a way out. For both of them.

"I have to go." She glanced away.

Cupping her shoulders, Ryan said, "Audrey."

"I cannot stand here and discuss having babies with you, Ryan. You *are* a baby."

That stung. "Oh, so the guy who made you scream with ecstasy less than two hours ago, who was he?"

"Ryan."

"Or how about the one who talked Scott Markovich into saving his own ass by turning in his mother?"

"That's different."

"Oh, I get it. It's okay that I risk my life every day for the people in this city, but I'm just too young to live that life. If it ends when I go to work tomorrow night, then so be it. I wasn't old enough to live it, anyway."

"Ryan!"

"I'm grown-up enough to carry a weapon, several of them, to help protect you and everyone else in this town from the dregs of humanity. I'm man enough to take on conscienceless, drugged-out, maniacal murderers and rapists and child molesters, just not man enough to love?"

"Stop it." There was a hint of begging in her tone.

"Why? Because I'm getting too close to the truth for you to handle?" He couldn't seem to shut up. Which was so unlike him. He could hear his anger and frustration, knew he had to stifle himself before he said something he'd regret and have to atone for. "What's the real truth here, Audrey? Is it that you're older than me? Or that you've had a great weekend, maybe the best you've ever had, and you're scared? Because tomorrow you're going to have to go home, go back to the real world and face the fact that I might have been playing with you? That *you* might actually get hurt rather than being the woman who's always helping heal other people's hurts?"

Her chin rose. "I don't have to listen to that." She didn't step away.

"I think you do," he said, not budging, either. "I get that this isn't going to be a normal relationship. We're going to raise some eyebrows. And probably have an occasional generational blip—like I'm guessing you don't know who One Republic is. But in the large scheme of things, looking at life and death and happiness and love, none of that matters."

"Of course it matters!" Audrey's shoulders drooped as though the energy it took to get out that sentence was all she had left. With a couple of sloppy swooshes, she moved back to the edge of the bed. Sat.

Ryan wanted to join her. Wasn't sure he should. And this was what she'd brought him to? A man who was so unsure of himself all of a sudden that he couldn't decide whether or not to sit on his own bed?

He sat, close enough that his arm was touching hers. If he was going to do something, he was damn well going to do it all the way. If he made a mistake, he'd make it big.

"We can sit here and pretend all we want to, Ryan, but there is no way we can ignore the ramifications of a thirty-five-year-old woman taking up with a twenty-two-year-old man. Think of what people will say! And I can guarantee you, they'll be a whole lot more negative about me than about you."

"So? We're going to let strangers' opinions determine our lives?"

"They'd call you my boy-toy."

"And?"

"It's disgusting."

"So? It hurts us how?"

"I don't want people thinking things like that about either one of us."

"I'm not that bad-looking, Audrey," he couldn't keep from reminding her. "Some folks might actually envy you. Hell, they're probably going to think you're an amazing woman to catch the attention of a young stud like me."

A smile started at the corner of her mouth, then she looked at him. Studied him. And her face fell.

"Yeah, and follow that one through," she said softly. "How attracted to me are you still going to be when I'm forty-five and menopausal and starting to sag and you're thirty-two and virile and some twenty-five-year-old beauty is falling all over you?"

"If I'm with you, I'm not going to be close enough to any other female for her to have the opportunity to fall all over me."

"You're human, Ryan."

"I'm also *me*. I don't cross those lines."

"You don't know that!" With her fists still clenched in the covers, she pounded her thigh. "This is my point, Ryan. You're only twenty-two. You haven't lived long enough yet, haven't had enough experience yet to know how you'd react in a situation like that."

"Oh, so there's some magical chart that tells when a man's lived long enough to know himself? To know what kind of choices he makes in life? Do I need to live longer to know that I'm not going to rape a woman? Or rob a bank? Or murder my next-door neighbor?"

"Why do you keep doing this?" Her eyes were moist as she looked at him again. Those naked shoulders were making it hard for him to keep his hands to himself. He needed to pull her into his arms. Comfort her until she was smiling and energetic again.

Hold her until she was happy.

"I'm not letting you walk out of my life," he told her simply. "I don't see a reason worthy of how wrong that would be."

"Ryan. Go call your parents. Tell them that you're seeing a woman who's thirty-five years old. Go on. Do it."

Thinking of his adoptive parents, Harriet and Glen, their simple lives, he blanched. They knew him. Protected him where they could. Accepted his aloneness. What in the hell was he thinking?

Then he looked at Audrey and his heart took over once again. Putting him on a course he didn't choose, didn't understand, but couldn't deny.

"In the first place, I can't call them," he said. "It's midnight and they'll be asleep." At least the parents who raised him would be. Mark and Sara, his biologicals, tended to be late-night people. Ryan liked to think it was because of the baby, but knew it was more than that. Mark still had problems sleeping at night.

Came from spending too many years in a prison cell.

"In the second place, no matter how hard you try, you are not going to make me into a little boy. I'm of age, Audrey. I do not have to call my parents for permission for anything. Nor am I in the habit of doing so."

Standing, Audrey reached for her clothes, stepping into the pants she'd changed into earlier that day when they'd stopped by her home on the way to see Markovich. "Look, Ryan, I know you mean well, but—"

"Don't humor me," he interrupted, standing, as well. "I'm still Detective Mercedes. You know, the one whose capabilities you respect?"

His tone stopped her, midway through fastening her bra. "I know you are," she said, looking him straight in the eye. "And I know I'm confused," she continued. "I just need to go home, try to sort all this out. I need to get some sleep."

"You think you're going to sleep?"

"Honestly?"

"Of course."

"No. But I'm going to lie in my bed, like I do every other night of my life, and try."

"I'm not giving up on us," Ryan said, holding her blouse for her as she slipped her arms inside. This would not be the last time he saw this woman's skin, the last time his knuckles brushed her stomach.

"There is no *us*."

That stung. "You're the one who mentioned babies."

"I was speaking hypothetically." Bending, she slipped into the high-heeled sandals she'd left at the end of the bed. "Pointing out the impossibilities."

"You never actually got around to doing that," he reminded her, fully aware that he was being somewhat irascible at the moment. Acting like the brat she thought him? "Tell me why I'm not capable of fathering your child."

"There's a whole lot more to fathering a child than impregnating its mother." Audrey's voice sounded weary as she headed for the stairs. "Do you have any idea how awkward it would be for a child to have to live with peoples' exclamations every single time he introduced them to his parents?"

"Oh, we'd be wearing signs, then? With our ages scrolled across our chests? Just like Hawthorne's scarlet *A*?"

"No, but—"

"But what, Audrey?" His stomach knotted as he followed her down the stairs. What if this was it? What if he couldn't get her to come back? "When you were a kid, did people ask you how old your mother was?"

"No!"

"Did either of us notice a difference in our ages by looking at us?"

"No."

"And we even saw each other naked." He just had to bring that up. Had to remind her who they were, what they'd done together. Created together.

"But with time—"

"I'll dye my hair gray if it'll make you feel better. Or you can keep yours blond. We'll exercise and eat right. I'll spend more time in the sun so I wrinkle prematurely."

They were downstairs and she wasn't stopping. She grabbed her purse without missing a step and turned to the entryway. He had to do something.

Had to stop this from happening.

"Think about this," he said, scrambling for anything that might help. "The average life expectancy of men in the United States is seventy-something. That skews younger if you have a job like mine. For women life expectancy is eighty-something. That's where the buck stops and puts us just about even."

At his front door, her hand on the knob, Audrey turned to him. "Ah, Ryan, why do you have to be so determined?"

Several smart remarks sprang to mind. Mostly along the lines of *That's what I'd like to know.* But the words came from someplace inside him. "Because this matters. You matter."

He knew he'd scored—at least a chance—when she nodded. "I'll call you tomorrow."

"Call me tonight." When it looked as though she was going to argue, he continued, "I won't pick up, I promise. Just leave me a message letting me know you're home safely."

At her acquiescence, Ryan walked her out, saw her safely into the front seat of her blue Acura.

He bent to kiss her, fully expected her to turn her head, and was thrilled when she didn't. The effect of her lips on his rent through his entire system.

Body. Mind. And heart.

He had it bad.

"And by the way," she offered, starting her engine as he was pushing her door closed.

He stopped midway.

"One Republic hit number four on the pop rock charts last October with a song called 'Apologize.' They were big news because their debut album wasn't out until November. Even us old folks, hard of hearing as we are, listen to the radio occasionally."

With that, she pulled her door closed, put the car in Drive and sped away.

Ryan missed her already.

CHAPTER SEVEN

SHE CALLED as she'd promised she would. And as he'd promised, Ryan didn't pick up. Audrey had known he wouldn't. Ryan Mercedes always did what he said he was going to do. It was one of the things she loved about him.

Loved, as in *was fond of.* Like a friend. Or a highly respected work associate.

That she'd slept with. Once. After some wine. A twenty-four-hour sleep.

A twenty-four-hour aberration that would not—could not—be given any validity whatsoever. That meant no thinking about it. Analyzing it.

Missing it.

He phoned on Sunday. She let the answering machine pick up. She'd said she'd call him, but that was before agreeing to call last night. Which she'd done. That bit of communication had stood in the stead of the original promise. Or so she worked it out.

He apparently thought differently, judging by his message.

"Audrey. It's ten o'clock. I'm leaving for work in a few minutes. You said you'd call. I've been waiting all day. I hope you're all right. Call me."

She stood staring at the machine, listening. And she'd

have been just fine if he'd ended it there as she'd thought he was going to do.

Turning away, determination still intact, his final word reached out and hooked her.

"Please."

It was the worry in his voice that did it.

There was something compelling, addictive even, in having someone worry about you. Especially when you were as unused to the practice as she was.

She'd often thought, if only her mother had worried about her a little more, Audrey would have been so much happier doing the older woman's bidding. She'd have tried to please her mom out of love, instead of out of fear. Or emotional manipulation.

She waited until ten-forty-five—the time he'd be in the meeting that was the precursor to every work shift—then dialed his cell phone.

"Hi, it's Audrey." Her voice sounded loud in her too quiet home. "I'm fine. Have a great week. Bye."

Ryan was a smart man. Boy. That oughtta do it.

After a day filled with client meetings—which meant stopping by homes to check up on kids—and studying and writing reports in her small downtown office, Audrey went to bed shortly after the call to Ryan. She was exhausted and tomorrow was Monday. The beginning of a new week.

A new life.

She didn't sleep well that night.

"YOU LOOK TIRED. You really should do more with yourself. Exercise. Eat better. Wear that night cream I bought you."

"I walked on the treadmill for an hour last night," Audrey

told the older woman sitting across from her in the upscale seafood restaurant Thursday night. She'd put in an hour every day this week. Usually somewhere between one and four in the morning.

"What about eating? How many times have you had potatoes or pasta this week?"

I'm thirty-five years old. You don't own me anymore. "None."

"Well, that's something. I've never met anyone who loves starches as much as you do. It's not becoming in a woman."

Audrey promptly dropped the piece of French bread she'd been nibbling. You'd think, listening to her mother, that she was a porker, obese.

"I know that carbs are good for you," her mother continued, picking a cucumber from her salad with two perfectly manicured fingers. "Recent studies show that it's probably those complex carbs you eat that are keeping you slim—"

"And heart-healthy and non-diabetic," Audrey interjected, just to let her mother know that she'd listened the last umpteen times she'd heard this lecture. Or maybe just to add the occasional sound of her own voice.

"Yes, well, you still look tired. You work too much."

As if she hadn't put in eighteen-hour days when she worked in retailing for her mother, who ran a distribution business for high-end women's accessories, as well as a small, upscale boutique.

"I've got a couple of difficult cases," she said. One in particular she'd like her mother's opinion on.

If she could find a way to ask for it without actually asking. She didn't want a lecture. Just thoughts.

"I told you you weren't made out for that difficult life.

You should never have gone to law school. If you'd stayed with us, you'd have your own department by now."

Which would be great if she was enthused by jewelry and clothes.

Audrey smiled. Eyed the bread she couldn't touch.

"I stopped by last weekend. You weren't home."

"I was with clients."

Amanda set down her fork with careful precision and lifted her gaze, pointing it straight at Audrey.

"It was late. Past ten. On Friday night."

Dammit, Audrey was thirty-five, not fourteen. She lifted her chin. "I had a date."

"A date." Amanda, completely straight-faced, continued to stare. "With who?"

"A detective I met working a case a few months back." Audrey picked her words deliberately, figuring her mother would find fault with her date's career choice and that would be the end of that.

Detective jobs were too dangerous. What woman in her right mind would want to saddle herself with someone who could easily die on the job? Or bring danger home?

She'd heard her mother's voice in her head, saying just those things, during the weeks she'd been seeing Ryan.

Before she'd found out he was little more than a child.

"And?"

"And what?"

"So? How'd it go?"

The bread was tempting. So tempting. "Good. Fine."

"You going to see him again?"

"I don't think so."

Her mother picked up her fork, stabbed a wedge of

lettuce. "Typical man," she retorted. "Gets what he wants, then leaves you hanging out to dry."

Audrey almost grabbed the bread. "Why would you assume he got what he wanted?"

Amanda's brown eyes opened wide. "Didn't he?"

Audrey had walked right into that one.

"I drove by again around six in the morning." Amanda relented. "You weren't home then, either."

Exasperated on so many levels, Audrey had to resist the urge to get up and walk out.

"What were you doing out at six in the morning?" she blurted. She didn't know who the uncharacteristic response shocked more, her or her mother. "Why were you checking up on me?" Her mind stumbled over thoughts that were clamoring for release. Really, this was too much. Even for Amanda Lincoln. The audacity of the woman! "And why didn't you say anything when I spoke to you on Sunday?"

"I was waiting for you to tell me about him," Amanda said, calmly chewing her salad.

"It didn't have to be a guy," Audrey wished she had something a little stronger than the diet soda she always ordered when she was driving. "I could have been at the hospital."

"My number's in your wallet in case of emergency," Amanda reminded her.

"Anyway—" Audrey couldn't seem to shut up "—you didn't tell me why you were out."

"Don't get mouthy with me, girl."

"Answer my question, Mom."

"I couldn't sleep."

"So you drove half an hour to my place?"

"It's not a crime."

For once Amanda seemed more interested in the table-cloth than her prey. Audrey frowned.

"How often do you do that?"

With a shrug, her mother motioned a passing waiter for some more water.

"Mom?"

"I don't know. Sometimes."

"Why?"

"Why not? Driving helps. I have to go somewhere."

"You check up on me on a regular basis."

"So what if I do?" Amanda's tone, her gaze, sharpened. "I'm your mother."

"Because you don't trust me, even at thirty-five, to live my own life." Audrey reached for her bag. This was ludicrous.

"Because I care about you." Shocked at the sudden drop in her mother's voice, Audrey stilled. Watched the older woman. "I worry about you living all alone."

No other words could have worked in that moment. Audrey's heart softened. "I'm fine, Mom. I've got an alarm system. You know that."

"Yes, well." Amanda returned her attention to her salad. "How well did you do, staying with a man who dumped you afterward?"

Any other day, Audrey would have let that go. "He didn't dump me."

Amanda stared. "But you said you weren't going to see him again."

"That's right."

"You didn't like him? What was wrong with him? My God, Audrey, you're thirty-five years old. How do you think it makes me feel to have to keep telling people that my daughter isn't married yet? They're going to start thinking something's wrong with you. Besides, your clock is ticking. And so is mine."

A new line. "What does your clock have to do with anything?"

"What if I want grandkids?"

That got her attention. "Do you?"

"Not particularly. Raising you alone was hard enough."

"Then why does age matter?"

"Because I'm not getting younger." Amanda's tone changed once again, as did her focus. It was anywhere but on Audrey as she added, "I'm not going to be around forever to take care of you, you know."

With absolutely no idea what to do with that, or the sudden worry the words instilled, Audrey said, albeit gently, "So I'm supposed to hook up with someone I don't want to be with?"

Oh, God, Ryan. Forgive me. But I don't want to be with a boy almost young enough to be my son. The ramifications terrify me. She glanced again at her mother. "You chose to live your life alone."

"I had you."

As if that made all the difference? Had Amanda ever stopped to think about how focusing her entire attention on Audrey wasn't healthy? For either of them?

Their dinner arrived and Audrey tried to find enough appetite to approach the scallops she'd ordered. Avoiding the mashed potatoes that came with them wasn't even going to be an issue tonight. The sight of them almost choked her.

"So what was wrong with this guy?"

Fifteen minutes had passed.

"He's…immature."

"And?"

"That's it."

Fork in midair, Amanda studied her. "You're kidding, right? Audrey, honey, all men are immature."

No, actually, they weren't. Some were simply young. She cut a scallop in half. Got it to her lips. Inside her mouth. Started to chew.

"Anyway, what does he do that's so immature?"

Swallowing took effort. Concentration. She managed. "He...calls," she said, trying to keep her mind off the subject at hand. A feat she'd been attempting, without impressive success, all week. "Every night." Like a kid who didn't know when to quit.

"Well, honey! That means he really likes you! For a grown man to call a woman that much in this day and age...I think that's sweet." The sudden lift in Amanda's voice, the surprise, was almost insulting. "What do you talk about?"

"Nothing. I don't pick up."

"Audrey! That's rude."

She preferred to think of it as survival.

"What if he stops calling?"

The question, one she'd refused to allow voice to—even mental voice—all week, struck her heart. "I'm counting on it," she finally managed with a semblance of calm.

"Does he leave messages?"

If you wanted to call a ten-minute-long, one-sided conversation a message. "Yeah."

"Saying what? Does he want to see you again? Has he asked you out for this weekend?"

More like, he'd asked her in. He'd said they could spend the entire weekend at his place, or hers, if that would make her feel better about people not seeing her with a younger man. As if hiding away for a weekend would do anything but make the entire situation more impossible, more painful, later. An oversight that was a product of his youth.

"He asked me to call him."

"Did you?"

"No."

"But you're going to, right?"

"No."

"Audrey. Yes, you are. You must have liked him or you wouldn't have spent the night with him. Don't forget. This is me you're talking to. I know you."

Amanda had her there. And because Audrey couldn't argue with the woman, she shut up and ate her scallops. Remembering the past—the irrevocable choices.

The reasons she could never, ever love a man as black and white as Ryan Mercedes. Or as young. What would happen when time started to show on her face and she was no longer as attractive as she was, but he was? Would she resort to begging him for his love and affection? As she'd done with her mother?

She couldn't risk it.

Never again would she dare put herself in a position where she'd compromise herself because she needed to be loved.

MARCUS RYAN had been asleep for more than an hour. The little guy was only a couple of months old and still up every couple of hours for feedings. Ryan peered over the edge of the bassinet for the fourth time Thursday evening. Just checking. Just to be sure.

Then he lay back on the end of the couch closest to the

infant's portable bed—moved from the master bedroom, to home office, to living room through the course of the day— and listened to his baby brother breathe.

Only for a while. A moment out of time because Sara had needed him. And because he had a guaranteed escape—a job that required he live opposite to the rest of the world.

Odd that he'd find comfort in those innocent gushes of air. And a sense of belonging he'd never known before.

And tonight, there was more. A longing he didn't fully understand. For Audrey. For family. And for a peace too elusive for him to grasp.

Or fully believe in.

Ten o'clock, escape—from confusion, from longing, from all of them—couldn't come fast enough.

HER PHONE didn't ring at ten-fifteen Thursday night. Or at ten-thirty. He didn't call her on the way to work as he'd done all week. Or even right before he went into his preshift briefing. Not that she'd have answered.

At five after eleven, when she knew he'd be firmly ensconced in the job and not be calling her, Audrey ran a hot bubble bath. Poured herself a glass of wine. Grabbed some chocolates out of the refrigerator, an aged stash that was to be consumed only in an emergency, lit a couple of candles and settled in to enjoy herself.

To celebrate.

She'd succeeded.

She was free.

AT ELEVEN-FORTY-FIVE Thursday night, she was still in the tub. The water was only lukewarm, but she could lean forward at any moment, twist the knob and make it hot again. Her glass was empty. The candy melting. And the candles were flickering, their wicks buried in puddles of liquid wax ready to suffocate them at any second.

She didn't feel good yet. But she would.

Ryan had finally given up. Decided to leave her alone. Life would settle down now. Get easier. Just the way she wanted it.

And she wanted it desperately.

AT HALF-PAST MIDNIGHT Friday morning, lying sleepless in her bed, Audrey ignored the damp puddles on her pillow, ignored the tightness in her chest, the weight in her stomach. She ignored the taunting from the critic in her brain.

Of course more than a lifetime of loneliness and work awaited her. She was going to be fine. Better than fine. In a minute or two, a day or two. Okay, maybe a week or two, she'd be as good as new. Happy, confident.

Or at least content.

She'd be fully in control of her life and the decisions she had to live with forever. No longer in danger of giving up self for love.

And maybe she'd find some nice, mature older man to spend some time with. A man who had no interest in anything more committed than an occasional companion, a good friendship, a man who'd already had wife and family, who, perhaps, had grown children.

She was human and had been alone too long, had been starved for companionship. That was why Ryan had affected her so deeply. Her reactions to him, her supposed caring for him, had been nothing more than proximity.

Please, God, make it so, she begged silently.

Someone else, someone younger and more appropriate for him, would see Ryan's unique gifts, would appreciate his loyalty and would value the way he always did what he said he'd do. Someone else would thrill over the pleasure his body gave. Someone else would make certain that he was loved and cherished every day of his life. He would be fine.

"Stop it!"

She sat up, clutching her pillow to her chest.

"Stop this right now. You're torturing yourself."

Her voice, cracked and ragged—and loud in the quiet of her house—didn't bring her back to her senses. It hurt her more. Until she wondered if she *was* going to survive. If she did know what she was doing.

About anything.

If she knew anything.

What in the hell was she doing, crying over a man/child she'd only known a few months—and slept with once? For a weekend.

What in the hell was the matter with her?

Audrey might have come up with an answer. She hadn't been planning to lie down again anytime soon. Couldn't stand the agony she was putting herself through.

She might have come up with an answer…but the phone rang.

CHAPTER EIGHT

MAYBE IT HAD BEEN A juvenile thing to do, waiting until he'd been on shift for a couple of hours before calling her. Making her wonder if he *would* call. Hoping to force her to pick up by calling in the middle of the night.

Listening to her phone ring, unanswered, his heart pounding harder the closer he got to five rings, to speaking to the answering machine again, Ryan forced his mind to the information at hand.

A confirmation he'd just, in the past five seconds, received.

It didn't matter that she wasn't answering her phone in the middle of the night. Didn't matter that she might not be there. That she might be sharing another man's bed.

Depressing his finger on the end key, he terminated the call before her machine picked up.

It was for the best. He could get his life back under control. Be free to be alone without all the emotional rigamarole making him nuts. Making him into something he was not.

Maybe she was in the bathroom. Couldn't get to the phone. Maybe he should give her one more chance.

Hitting redial, he waited for the line to connect.

She might have shared the other guy's bed before Ryan, too. She was thirty-five years old. There had been others. Probably before Ryan had even had his first wet dream.

Audrey Lincoln's life was her own. She'd made that fact quite plain over the past five days.

And really, she'd never given him indication to believe otherwise. She'd never confessed her love for him. Or even her loyalty.

One ring and counting.

She'd had sex with him.

Didn't mean that it in any way resembled, for her, the life-changing experience it had been for him.

Hell, she was thirty-five, experienced.

Three rings.

He was acting like the kid he was, thinking that those hours in his bed had been something special. Momentous.

Four rings.

He'd lost his virginity. Nothing more.

Five rings.

It was about time. Who'd ever heard of a virgin cop?

"You've reached…" Waiting for her message to finish, Ryan closed his eyes. He could join in the locker-room talk at the station now. Not.

"Audrey, this is Ryan Mercedes. Listen, I've got some information for you regarding your father. If you're interested, give me a call. If not, forgive the intrusion."

Hanging up, Ryan still didn't regret having known the woman.

How DARE HE?

How dare he?

Fuming, pacing, the hardwood floors cold on her bare feet even in July, Audrey tried to calm herself.

Just as she'd thought, Ryan Mercedes was a kid. Didn't

know the proper boundaries between adults. What had possessed him to trespass on her private territory, her life, so intimately? He'd looked up her father?

If she'd wanted to find the man, she could have done so herself. He'd paid child support.

Someone could have traced him through that. No matter that the money came in the form of cashier's checks, with different signatures, from various states, throughout the years of her growing up.

Damn him!

If she'd wanted to deal with her father, she'd have said so. What on earth gave him the idea she'd want that?

What gave him the idea he'd had any right to jump so completely into her life?

Hadn't his mother taught him anything about respecting people's privacy?

She paced, rubbing her shoulders against the cold blowing from air conditioners set in windows in the different rooms of her little home on the hill. Her sleeveless nightgown had been fine in her bed.

Who cared about her father?

The man had deserted her long ago.

Too long ago.

Leaving her to deal with her mother's unique charms all on her own. A defenseless kid against a manipulative woman who'd ruled her world with threats, rather than love.

A woman who'd blackmailed and coerced and forced, rather than guided. Audrey hadn't had a chance.

And would pay the consequences, live with the heart-break and shame, for the rest of her life.

Damn the man who'd fathered her. He should have pulled out a couple of minutes sooner.

And damn Ryan, too.

Damn them all.

She didn't need a man. *Any* man. And she'd show them just that. She'd ignore Ryan's call. He could keep his information.

And everything else he thought he had to offer.

RYAN SWEATED IT OUT the rest of Thursday night. He worked, focusing on the bigger picture of his life, the contribution he had to make to the world that had taken him on, the world that gave him air to breathe, food to eat, songs to hear and beauty to enjoy.

What he didn't do was get in his department-issued sedan and take a run through a certain Westerville neighborhood, past a particular guardian ad litem's home. So she worked in sometimes dangerous situations, pissing off sometimes dangerous people. So she lived alone. She had an alarm.

And there were officers out there whose job it was to see that the neighborhoods were safe.

Patrol, checking up, wasn't part of his job anymore.

He didn't get to prevent crimes anymore. Only to explain. And prevent repeat offenses.

So be it.

All night long, it was.

And on the way home Friday morning, he took no detour. Whether or not she'd been out all night—even if he could tell with a drive-by—was none of his business.

Home in record time, he fed his cat, patted her on the head—something he constantly forgot she hated—climbed the stairs and fell into his unmade bed fully clothed.

Ryan Mercedes was back.

THE CHILD LOOKED ILL. Lab reports had all come back that she was healthy. There was no medical explanation for her fatigue. Psychological assessments found her to be a normal twelve-year-old. She had all the right answers. But she wasn't doing well in school. Not surprising, due to the custody battle being fought over her.

Sitting across from Carrie Woods in a booth at the ice-cream shop around the corner from the girl's father's house Friday morning, Audrey wished she could spirit the child away.

"I love my mom, Ms. Lincoln," she said, her eyebrows drawn together in an expression far too mature for her age. Her brown eyes were shadowed with unshed tears. "I love her so much."

"Of course you do, honey."

"And I love my daddy, too."

"You're supposed to."

"It hurts my mom."

Listening with more than just ears to her new client, Audrey heard something that resonated deeply. Was she looking at another young girl who had to earn her mother's love?

"How so?"

"My dad hurt her so badly and she hates him, and when I love him she thinks I'm turning traitor on her."

When, in fact, my dear sweet child, your mother is turning traitor on you. It was against the law for a woman to leave her kids locked safely at home while she went out to try to earn money for food—they called it child endangerment—but it wasn't against the law for a selfish woman to have a child and then take away its right to life by depriving it of love.

"So when she says you don't want these week-long summer visitations with your father, she's not being entirely accurate?"

"I don't want them."

Audrey heard herself telling a doctor she wanted a procedure. And felt sick.

She looked Carrie straight in the eye. "Why don't you want them?"

Silence.

"Is he mean to you?"

Eyes opening wider, Carrie shook her head, her blond hair falling in angelic curls around her slim shoulders. The girl was wearing a brown tank top that perfectly matched her eyes. And a pair of short, beige shorts. Simple. But expensive-looking. Her hair was clean. Combed.

"My dad loves me."

That was important. The fact that the child knew that even more so.

She'd known about the procedure, too. Known that the choice was wrong for her.

"What about his girlfriend?"

"She's nice, too. I like her."

"Do they ignore you, then? Leave you alone too much?"

For the first time since she'd been introduced to the child that morning, Audrey heard her chuckle. "Sometimes I wish they would!" she said. "At home I spend a lot of time in my room. I like to read and write in my journal. But here, we're always doing stuff. I haven't finished a single book all week."

So they made her do things she didn't want to do? Was that what she'd been called in to discover? Audrey didn't think so.

"What kinds of things?" she asked, anyway. She couldn't take any chances, couldn't risk superimposing her own issues on her charges.

Empathizing was good. Understanding, vital. Mistaking the facts, unforgivable.

"Oh, you know, stuff you do when you're on vacation. We went to King's Island. And we go to the pool. My dad's teaching me how to dive off the high board. And Kelly— that's his girlfriend—and I are working on a cross-stitch thing. She's teaching me how."

"Do you like it?"

Carrie's nod was more hesitant.

"Not that much?"

"Well…" The child looked down at the ice cream melting in her bowl, then up again, the shadows back in her eyes. "Actually, I do like it. Really a lot. It's just that…"

Carrie liked going to her dad's. Audrey hadn't wanted the procedure. But they both told a different story.

For the same reason.

"What?" she asked, needing Carrie to admit what Audrey already knew.

"I can't bring it home with me or anything."

"Kelly won't let you take it?"

"Yeah, she wants me to. She wants to see how good I do between now and when I come back in two weeks."

"So what's the problem?" Audrey felt the old familiar knot in her stomach, figuring Carrie would recognize it completely, figuring that a similar knot had become the young girl's constant companion.

Audrey had carried hers for most of her life.

"It would make my mom cry."

Because another woman was "mothering" her daughter. An understandable challenge to overcome. An understandable pain.

And yet, as a mother, it was Mrs. Woods's job to see that that pain didn't spill over onto her daughter's life.

"And then what?"

"She wouldn't love me."

"Of course she would," Audrey said, more because the little girl needed to hear it than because she believed it. "Let me talk to her," Audrey said. "I'm sure, once I explain how much you love her and that you can't help loving your dad, too, once she knows that you're hurting so much over this, she won't have any problem with you bringing your cross-stitching home."

Or with you coming back to see your father, either, Audrey added silently.

"You don't know my mom," Carrie said, her shoulders slumped almost to the table.

"I know that she wants what's best for you," Audrey said, understanding far too well the weight this little girl was carrying. And she knew that either the mother was going to change her method of operation or Audrey would be recommending a change in custody for her daughter.

Carrie wasn't going to someday find herself facing a doctor she didn't want to see. Or making any other life-changing choices that weren't right for her because she felt she had to, to be loved.

FRIDAY AFTERNOON, following lunch with a couple of board members from the Ohio Guardian Ad Litem Association to discuss a training event she was going to be administering,

Audrey took a detour on the way back to her office. Downtown to an old, graffiti-strewn neighborhood, not far from Ohio State University's campus.

The day care wasn't large. Or fancy. But it was clean. Had caring, licensed, dedicated personnel and enough bars on the windows to keep the toddlers inside safe.

Two-year-old Jamal was in his classroom, just as he was supposed to be.

"Dwee, Dwee!" he cried, hurrying over to her in a mixture of a plump-thighed run and hurried crawl.

"Hey, little guy!" she said, swinging him up against her for a hug before settling him on her hip. After her meeting with Carrie Woods, she'd needed a reminder of happy endings.

Needed a dose of good to bring back the believing.

"Hi, Sandy," she greeted the slim black woman who followed the toddler over.

"Ms. Lincoln! It's good to see you."

"This little man sure looks healthy," Audrey said, unable to prevent the critical gaze she ran over the child's scalp, ears, over the skin exposed by well-worn but clean shorts and T-shirt. His sandals had a broken strap that had been crudely stitched, but the knots were numerous. And tight.

"He hasn't missed a day since you brought him to us," Sandy said, raising her voice to be heard over the teacher behind her, corralling a group of six or so two-year-olds into a circle for a game of ring-around-the-rosy.

"Posy! Posy!" Jamal said, his little feet pushing against Audrey. Setting him down to join his pals, she smiled, soaking up the joy that happy little body brought.

"His mother drops him off like clockwork every day," Sandy said, her gaze following Audrey's. "And always with this look of relief when she finds out we're still here. All she needed was a chance…"

Yes, Jamal was one of Audrey's successes. A young boy who'd been neglected, left alone, locked in a one-room apartment with nothing but blankets and toys, a couple of filled bottles, while his desperate young mother went out to work to earn money for his diapers and dinner.

A young mother who so obviously loved her son. Recognizing that, taking a chance, Audrey had hooked up the young woman with a couple of social service programs, and now, not only did her son have a safe place to play while she worked, they both had a bed to sleep in, in a bigger apartment, too.

Life wasn't going to be easy for Jamal. Temptations would be numerous in that rough neighborhood, opportunities few. Even so, Audrey gave him an eighty percent chance of success.

He might not have Carrie's opportunities, or Audrey's, either, for that matter, but he had unconditional love. And that was the greatest asset of all.

BY FIVE O'CLOCK Audrey had managed to knock off most of her to-do list for the day—a feat rarely accomplished simply because she had a tendency to keep adding items way after the list was full. Today it didn't seem to matter how many times she weighed herself down, she had enough adrenaline to push back to the top.

She was going to stay one step ahead of last night's phone call if it killed her.

She should have been tired. Beat. Ready to go home, have a cool glass of tea, lie on the daybed on her back porch and fall asleep. And then, maybe, if she roused herself later, she'd put together some kind of salad for dinner and find her way into an old *Law & Order* episode. Or *Without a Trace*.

No, maybe it was a night for *Sex in the City*. Or, not that she'd ever let anyone know she watched it—ever—*Charmed*.

Driving slowly in deference to the Friday-night traffic heading out of the city, Audrey thought about that tea. And the daybed. She tried to feel good about them. To let them call out to her, pull her home.

She thought about television shows and the fiction on her bookshelf.

And in the back of her mind, she fought the same battle she'd been fighting all day. The refusal to think about Ryan Mercedes, or what she'd been doing last Friday night.

Or to allow herself to wonder about the man who'd paid her child support all those years.

She didn't want to think about men at all.

CHAPTER NINE

SWEAT DRIPPING down the middle of his back, he ran through the woods, a wolf behind him, a fugitive in front of him. Tracking them by the sounds of their footsteps in the fallen, crusty leaves covering the ground, making it slippery, Ryan gasped for air. His chest was going to burst. There was a cottage ahead, in the midst of a million acres of one-hundred-year-old leafless trees.

Could he make it inside before the wolf jumped his back? Could he convince the fugitive to join him there? Gun in hand, Ryan knew that he had no time left. One choice was going to save lives—or get him killed.

Just as he reached the side of the cottage, he heard the knocking on the door. Skidding to a halt, he pressed himself against the rough logs that were the side of the building, watching behind him, his gun pointed forward. The knocking came again. Five soft raps. Same as the first time.

It was a trap. The fugitive was there—though Ryan had no idea what he looked like. He and the wolf were partners. Ryan should have known. Should have seen…

Five soft raps. Ryan sat straight up. And blinked—saw himself fully clothed in his own bed, right arm stretched out in front of him as though pointing the gun that was on the night-stand beside him. And realized that someone was at his door.

SHE COULDN'T EXPLAIN why she was there. Ryan was a kid. Kids were full of drama and confidence, and the certainty that whatever was going on in the moment was forever. And they changed course as often as Audrey changed her underwear.

Her daybed was waiting for her. And that glass of tea. What a fool she'd been, thinking of *Bruce Almighty*. And *The Mirror Has Two Faces*. The wine Ryan had brought. His insistence they talk about why she liked that movie.

His reaction to her conversation. Pulling things out of her that no one had ever accessed before.

His even knowing they were there. Caring.

She should never have thought about those things. They were a mirage, calling her to something that didn't exist. Driving her to make turns she didn't want to make, to do things she knew were not right for her.

Just as she'd done nineteen years before. Acting against her better judgment because she needed to be loved.

Turning her back on his unanswered door, not wanting to know who this Friday night's lucky companion was, how old she was, if she'd stay tomorrow night, too, Audrey determined to throw away every single Barbra Streisand movie in her collection. And every Jim Carrey one, too.

As a matter of fact, she wasn't going to watch movies again. Who needed them?

He'd been a virgin, he'd said. Even if she believed that, most particularly if she believed that, she'd have to believe he had a woman in there. A younger woman.

She spun around and knocked one more time.

What man, after tasting the fruits, didn't gorge himself? Especially if he'd waited twenty-two years to take his first taste.

Oh, yes, he'd tasted. All of her. His tongue moving over her skin, leaving a trail of sensation that still made her tingle a week later.

Ryan hadn't loved her as though it was his first time. He'd been gentle, slow, controlled enough that he put her first.

He'd been amaz—

"Audrey? Come in. I... You should have called. I wish you had called. Or at least answered my calls."

She *should* have called. "I woke you up." The short tendrils of his hair were standing on end, his eyes sleepy-looking. Fire swirled in her belly and she wanted to take him right back upstairs to bed.

"No, really, it's okay. I... What time is it?" He glanced behind him as though Delilah were going to appear with the answer.

He'd invited Audrey in, but still stood in the doorway, blocking her way.

"Five-thirty."

Maybe he wasn't alone. Maybe he didn't know what to do with the thirty-five-year-old woman parked on his doorstep.

Her first awkward, other-woman moment.

She could have lived without it.

He raised an arm, his hand going to the back of his neck, showing her the skin beneath his unbuttoned, wrinkled white dress shirt. "Damn, is it really that late?"

Audrey stared. And nodded. That chest. She hadn't been dreaming it to be better than reality all week.

As a matter of fact, her dreams had fallen short.

Sometimes life was just plain cruel.

"I meant to sleep for a few hours is all, so I won't be up all night. Listen, I need a shower. Would you mind putting on a pot of coffee while I go try to wake up? You remember where everything is, right?"

Once again, Audrey nodded. And in spite of the fact that she hadn't said she'd come in and had had no intention of stepping foot over that threshold ever again, she wordlessly followed him inside.

It was only polite to let a man brush his teeth before you blasted him.

IF HE COULD HAVE pulled it off, Ryan would have forgone the shower. As skittish as Audrey was, she might cut out on him as soon as she heard the water running. Best guess, he figured chances were fifty-fifty.

Not good odds, but he took them. He needed to wake up. To wash away the cigarette smoke he'd encountered in the jail cell of the alleged murderer he'd visited the night before.

A bigheaded college fraternity man, a year younger than Ryan. He'd killed his own father. For drug money. Then played Russian roulette with the corpse. There'd been witnesses. Frat brothers. They'd kept score on a legal pad. And been stupid enough to leave it lying on the edge of his father's desk in the study where the man had just written him a check for five thousand dollars.

By the time Ryan got to him, though, the guy had sobered up. He'd had a visit from his mother. Had been crying. Begging.

Ryan had been given the case because they thought he could get a confession out of him.

The whole thing made him sick.

Stripping down, leaving his clothes in a pile on the floor, he stepped into the glass-enclosed shower stall, welcoming the stinging spray of water that was just a little too hot. He needed a few minutes to clean the filth of the world off his skin.

If Audrey left, so be it. He couldn't lock her to his bedpost—though the idea had some merit. He couldn't live his life worried that she was going to jump ship every second.

He couldn't even fully convince himself that he wanted her here. His heart was driving him to be completely one with her—in spite of the obvious obstacles of loving a woman thirteen years older than him.

His head knew he was a loner.

And that he wanted it that way.

So he'd leave it to fate. If she left, she left.

And if she didn't?

He'd learned a thing or two over the past five days of unanswered phone calls. Had grown up, when he'd thought himself all done with that.

He loved Audrey Lincoln. But that didn't mean life was going to be easy. All he had to do was look at Mark and Sara to know that. Now *there* were two people who'd had to face bad odds.

A rapist and his victim? Making it?

Before his mind could take him any further along that confusing path and his own connection to it, Ryan grabbed the soap, rubbing the half-used bar vigorously over his body.

It had been one hell of a long week.

THE SHOWER WAS still running by the time the four-cup pot had dripped its load. And Audrey had paced twice around Ryan's condo, avoiding the picture of the adopted parents who'd raised him. Of him with them.

Avoiding everything that was even remotely personal.

She couldn't look at the couch. That was where she'd first confided in him. Where she'd known that if he kissed her, she'd kiss him back.

The television. Well, that went without saying. Memories of that were what had gotten her into this position tonight to begin with.

She glanced upstairs. Listening. The water was still running. At least he didn't have anyone up there with him.

Tendrils of desire pooled in her pelvis—and below. What was she going to do when he came downstairs? How could she yell at him when, here, in his home, she understood why he'd tried to find her father. He was adopted. Had searched out his birth mother. Though he'd never told her how the search turned out.

Still, she had to tell him to stay out of her business. Even when he meant well. She had to stand up for herself. To make sure she was in charge of her life.

And her choices.

The shower was still on. What was he doing up there?

Tomorrow. She'd call him tomorrow. Tell him to mind his own business from now on. She'd soften the blow with a thank-you for a wonderful twenty-four hours. Tell him to call her if he ever needed anything.

No. She couldn't tell him that.

She'd just say…that she'd be seeing him around. If they ever shared a case again.

Yeah, she couldn't yell at him. They'd be working together again. Paid, attorney-guardian ad litems weren't plentiful in this city. They had to keep this civil. End as friends.

Finding herself out in the kitchen again, staring between the coffee pot and the cupboard that housed the white stoneware cups, Audrey made a decision. She opened the cupboard. Pulled down a cup. Filled it. Put in the two tablespoons of sugar Ryan took in his coffee. She'd leave this for him upstairs so he'd have it when he came out of the shower.

The friendly gesture would soften the blow of her leaving without saying goodbye.

Or even, really, hello.

Then she'd go home, lock her doors, turn off her phone and find her way back to herself.

To the woman she knew herself to be. The woman she wanted to be. The one she'd learned how to cohabitate with in a peaceful manner.

HIS EYES WERE CLOSED. Water streamed over his face and down his chest. Ryan knew he had to move. To turn off the spigot. Use the towel hanging on the hook outside his enclosure. Had to find out if she'd left him.

Again.

But what if she hadn't?

Just like that, the fire lit inside him. She could be down there, in his home, waiting for him.

And so what if she was? She wasn't there for sex. He knew that.

His penis hadn't read the memo.

He heard the click, but its source didn't have time to register before he was processing the spurt of cold air on his butt. His mind, usually on a hair trigger, was working far too slowly.

And then, as the slim arms came around him and naked breasts that were already familiar pressed up against his back, his mind quit working completely.

GOD FORGIVE ME. I know not what I do.

His skin was slick, warm, and her hands couldn't get enough. Running them along his stomach, up over his chest, around his shoulders to his back—and down—Audrey soaked up the man who still hadn't turned around, looked at her, said a word.

What in the hell am I doing?

No answer.

She had no answers at all. To any of this. She was so lonely. So god-awful lonely. She'd like to believe, as she stood naked in the young man's shower, that that was all this was. That her response to Ryan was generic, that of a woman who'd been alone too long. Nothing more.

She'd like to believe that. Tried really hard.

"I've missed you so much." The words were dragged out of her, shoved out of her, from someplace inside that she hadn't accessed all week. "I've never felt like this before. Never needed…"

Hooking her arms around him, her hands coming up over his shoulders from the front, Audrey pressed her face to Ryan's rigid back.

"This has been the hardest week of my life. I can't eat. I can't sleep. I hate being in the home that I love because you aren't there. I hardly know you and you've done something to me, to my heart, that I don't understand."

His arms squeezed against his body, trapping hers.

"It's not right. I can't be with you. I know that. I really believe that. And yet I can't get you out of my mind."

She pushed her pelvis up against his butt and almost cried at the relief of connecting to him again.

Even as she knew that, she was falling prey to her old

ways—making choices that she knew weren't right because she needed to be loved.

"I... Help me out here." He still hadn't said a word. Hadn't turned around.

But he was holding her arms. Not pushing her away.

"I don't know what to do, Ryan." She had a seemingly hopeless problem on her hands.

"Here I am, a grown woman, plenty old enough to know better," she said as much to herself as out loud. "I handle crises that would make most people's blood curdle, and manage to stay calm. It's up to me to find the solutions."

Water ran over his shoulders, splashing her face, plastering her hair against her head, and still she held on, her cheek against his skin.

"I'm thirteen years older than you. And here I am expecting you, a kid, to have some kind of solution for me."

She could feel his heart beating. Hard. Steady. A little rapid. And then she felt him move. Slowly, reaching behind himself to steady her, he turned. His green eyes were vibrant, piercing, as he looked at her through half-lowered lids—as though he were trying to mask much of what was going on inside of him.

That mask drove her further into the cauldron of emotion that was where she lived with Ryan. She didn't want him hiding from her. She needed to know what he was thinking. Feeling.

She needed to know him.

"I've got your answer." His voice was low. Husky. And assured.

"What?" She couldn't hide her tears from him. She was in the fire now. All defenses stripped away.

"Love me," he said. And while there was no mistaking the hardness of his penis against her lower body, there was also no doubt that he hadn't meant those words in a physical sense.

"Let me love you," he continued, swallowing with obvious difficulty.

Fear swarmed her, encased her in a buzzing sound that she couldn't silence. "But—"

"Just love me, Audrey," he said again. Firmly. "Let life take care of itself for a while."

God, he felt good. So good. Warm. Solid. There. Tempted to lay her head against his chest, to bury herself in the safety of his arms and forget the world existed, she looked up at him.

"I can't do that." She forced the words. "I'm not that way. I can't just let go. I see too much of what happens when people don't think ahead. When they don't make good choices. When—"

"And you think I don't?" he interrupted gently. His hands in the small of her back, he held her against him, the water falling over his shoulder to sluice its way between them. "I calculate everything, sweetie, you know that."

It was one of the characteristics that had first drawn her to him. Back when she'd thought he was her age. Or close to it.

"Then—"

"And what I know is that there are always things going on that you can't see. Things right in front of you. The way to deal with them is to acknowledge that they're there, to assess the potential damage, weigh it against the potential gain, to determine what control you have and to not waste energy and effort on things you can't control."

"I'm sure that all makes sense, but—"

"There are times when you have to rely on faith, babe. The trick is to know when. I know that this is one of those times."

"How do you know?"

"Gut feeling. It's never led me wrong before."

She wanted to believe him, but how many befores had there been for him? He was only twenty-two. And, in a biblical sense, had only been a man for a week.

"My first month on the force, as a rookie cop, I made what I thought was going to be a routine traffic stop. Something told me to call in the stop before I ever left my cruiser. And to run for the woods to the left of me. The guy was out of his car before I'd fully braked, and rather than follow him directly, I ran for the woods. Just as I was coming out of a thicket, he was running by. I don't know which of us was more surprised when I flew out of nowhere and tackled the guy. I stayed prone on top of him until help arrived. If I'd stood up, attempted to arrest him, if he'd seen me first, I would have been dead. He was lying on a pistol that was loaded and cocked. Turns out he was not only on America's most wanted, but Canada's, too."

Shivering beneath the hot water, held against the warmth of his skin, Audrey pushed the image of Ryan's body, dead and lifeless, away. So he'd been lucky. Thank God he'd been lucky. Still...

"I trusted a rapist once, too," he said now, his gaze completely serious. And a little guarded.

It was a strange statement.

"And?" she asked, tensing.

"The case was solved."

She was sinking fast. Giving in because she needed him. "This isn't a case."

"I know that."

"My head is screaming at me to go home. I'm going to get hurt. And so are you."

Ryan's gaze was intense, in spite of the water dripping over them. Had she finally convinced him? Was he about to tell her to go then? Or beg her to stay? She waited, afraid of what he'd say. Either way.

"What does your heart tell you?"

He expected an answer. She couldn't give him one. She didn't trust her heart. Hadn't since she was sixteen years old.

"Do you love me, Audrey?"

"It's not as simple as that."

His hands on her sides were gentle, supporting her. "Do you love me?"

"It's not about—"

"Do…you…love…me?"

Why had she come here? Why did life have to be so difficult? Why was she in his shower?

One answer covered all the questions.

"Yes, I love you."

CHAPTER TEN

"YOU SHOULDN'T HAVE looked up my father."

"I know that. I'm sorry."

What a strange night. A strange, out-there, disconnected moment. She'd expected to remain on his doorstep and give him a dressing-down, not to stand naked in the shower in his arms and mention his transgression.

And she'd expected him to defend himself.

"It's a problem I've got," he continued, the caring in his eyes so genuine she couldn't look away. "This tendency to charge ahead and take care of things for the people I care about, without first finding out if they want my help. I'm working on it."

What twenty-two-year-old *talked* that way? Certainly none that she'd known.

For that matter, she couldn't think of any men she'd known who were that in touch with their faults—or sincerely committed to working on them. Granted, she hadn't known a lot of men. And her choices hadn't been the best, but—

"Honey?"

"Yeah?"

"The water's gone cold."

She'd noticed. Sort of. Mostly she was outside herself,

looking down at them in the shower. As though they were a couple. As though he belonged to her.

And she to him.

When she was fifty, he'd be thirty-seven. Young. Virile. Just two years older than she was now.

It wasn't right. Couldn't be. He wasn't hers.

Any thoughts to the contrary were suicide.

"WHERE IS HE?"

A couple of hours had passed since the water turned cold. He'd made love to her—twice—and was now scrambling some eggs for their dinner. They'd talked of nothing but each other since he'd turned off the shower. But Ryan knew immediately what she was talking about.

He'd been on this journey himself. A long time ago.

With some strangely similar results. He wasn't sure how much of that he should share with her.

"Here. In Columbus."

"You're kidding." She looked about eighteen, sitting there at the kitchen table, his rumbled dress shirt hanging halfway down her thighs.

Covering the nudity that he knew was beneath those lucky tails.

Adjusting the basketball shorts he'd pulled on for the trek downstairs, Ryan tried hard to miss the tangled blond hair falling around her face, tried not to think about where that hair had been such a short time before.

He had it bad.

"I'm not kidding," he said, focusing enough to keep his answer vague. If she wanted to know, she'd ask. If not, she had a right to her ignorance.

At times, ignorance truly was bliss. Most particularly, he'd found, when it came to biological fathers.

She jumped up. Headed for the toaster. Pushed a couple of innocent pieces of bread down with a bit more force than necessary.

Ryan waited. Scrambled. Turned down the heat as he reached for the cheese.

He handed her the butter. Withheld the knife. She helped herself to another one as he got the plates.

They were halfway through the meal, sitting at his solid wood round table, before she spoke again.

"Okay." He'd never heard the one word be so definitive. But then, he'd never known anyone like Audrey Lincoln. "Where?"

"German Village."

"Nice part of town." There was no judgment, no detectable emotion at all in the response.

"Yeah."

She took a bite of toast. Pushed eggs around on her plate. "What's he do?"

Ryan was almost ready for seconds. He hadn't eaten since lunch, sometime in the middle of the previous night. "He's an engineer."

"A professional."

"Mm-hmm."

"Not some loser deadbeat."

Glancing at her over the rim of his coffee cup, he said, "No." But the word was difficult. His research had been interrupted at a critical point. There were key things he didn't know.

As slowly as he'd ever seen anyone eat, she got a bite of eggs to her mouth, and then inside.

He rose, helped himself to more eggs. Sat. Started in again.

"Is he married?"

"Yes."

"Kids?"

"Two."

She'd ripped off a piece of bread, a bite that he'd hoped would make it to her mouth. Instead, she was rolling it around between her fingers.

"How old?"

My age. He almost said. And stopped himself. Now wasn't the time for reminders.

"Twenty and twenty-three."

Audrey dropped the bread ball, her gaze dead-looking as she stared at him. "Your age."

"Yes."

"I wonder if he reads their letters."

"Don't know."

"Do they live at home?"

"One does. Or at least her address is still listed as his."

"Her."

"Mm-hmm." His plate was empty. He liked it better when he had something to do other than watch her hurt.

"I don't want to know their names."

"Okay."

Her eyes narrowed. "But you know them, don't you?"

"Yes."

"Have you seen him? Them?"

"No." But what he'd found was an omen to Ryan—a sign that he and Audrey were meant to find each other. Some things were just too in your face to be coincidental.

And everyone knew cops didn't like coincidences.

Sitting back, her arms folded across her chest, Audrey jutted out her chin. "Isn't it against code for you to access your resources for private use?"

He looked her straight in the eye. "I was following up on a tip."

"What tip?"

"Mail fraud."

"He's involved in mail fraud?"

"No. You said the letter you sent him was returned unopened. It's possible that he never saw it."

"So you looked him up to ask him."

"I looked him up so you could ask him." And he needed to be there when she did. Just in case.

Springing up, she grabbed his plate so fiercely his fork clanged to the floor, catching him on the foot. She didn't seem to notice. With her plate in hand, as well, she continued to the sink where she proceeded to scrub the paint off his china, or would have if there'd been any paint.

And if he'd had china.

Not that he cared. What he ate from didn't matter. Audrey did.

He left her alone as long as he could—about two minutes—then joined her at the sink, coming up behind her to slide his arms around her middle, holding her lightly against him.

"Forget it, Mercedes. I'm not going to see him."

"Fine." It might be for the best. And once his research was done, once he had an explanation for what he'd found, maybe he'd tell her the whole story. About her father. About his father. And the things they had in common.

"Don't *fine* me. Especially not in that tone of voice. You

don't know everything, you know." He'd received fiercer looks than the one she shot him over her shoulder, but only when he was arresting someone.

"I never claimed to know everything."

"I have no need to meet the man. Don't give a whit about him. I put that past to rest a long time ago."

"And that's why you didn't eat any of your dinner? Because you don't care? That's why my message got you here tonight, in spite of your resolve to stay away?"

That got her. She turned, her eyes still shooting bullets at him. "*You* are what brought me here tonight. Let's make that quite clear. You. Not any need to know anything about the man who was present at my conception. He's a biological, nothing more."

He had her. Not quite in the way he'd hoped his words would deliver her up. This was far better.

"*I* brought you here." He repeated her words.

She blinked. And her cheeks started to turn red.

"It's okay, honey. I'd already figured that out."

"Ryan…"

The tears were back and Ryan knew he'd pushed her enough for now. She needed to be held.

And so did he.

They had a lifetime ahead of them to sort out everything else.

"I HAVE TO GO."

Rousing himself from a state of relaxed dozing, Ryan tightened his hold on the naked woman lying against his chest. "Why?"

"I can't stay here."

"Why not?"

"Ryan—"

"Shh." He put a finger against her lips, having no trouble finding them in the darkness. Awareness of her was instinctive. Something he accepted. "It's late, babe. Go to sleep. Tomorrow's soon enough to tackle the world."

Slowly her body relaxed, growing heavier as she drifted off. Ryan dozed some, slept some, always aware, every single second during that night, of the treasure he held.

"HEY, SLEEPYHEAD." The scent of coffee wafted into Audrey's consciousness even before she heard the voice.

"Mmm," she said, squeezing her eyes shut against the world and all its challenges. She was in a cozy, warm, perfect place. A place that smelled of the man she loved.

No.

"I brought you some coffee."

Okay, yes. She loved him. Admitting the fact right out didn't change anything.

"Mmm," she said again, hoping he'd take the hint and go away. Or join her and let her drift back to the security of unconsciousness, where all could be as her mind wished it to be.

The bed dipped and she snuggled in, already on her way back to the inner sanctum.

"It's almost eight."

Time was an intrusion.

The fingers running through her hair were not. They should have been, but they weren't.

"Coffee's getting cold and I know how you like it hot."

Oh, yes. God, yes. She liked it hot. With him. Only with

him. Tendrils of desire spiraled down to her core. And she hadn't even opened her eyes yet!

What was the matter with her? Who was this woman? And who slipped a sex pill into her diet? She'd never, ever wanted sex in the morning before. Or any other time, either. Not the way she wanted it with Ryan.

His fingers moved down to her neck, around her ear and back to her collarbone. If she lay there, pretending to sleep, would he go further? Her nipples tingled in anticipation.

She'd read that the average man had a sexual thought once every three minutes and that the average woman had one three times a day. Somehow in the past couple of months she seemed to have been infected with some kind of testosterone disease.

"I know you're awake."

Not if she didn't move. He couldn't be sure.

"You make a sound when you breathe when you're asleep."

She snored?

Audrey's eyes flew open. Wide-awake, dressed in khaki shorts and a T-shirt that expanded far too nicely across his chest, Ryan sat an inch from her nose, staring down at her.

"I do not!"

"How would you know? You're asleep."

Pushing the hair out of her eyes, she sat up, taking his cup out of his hand for a hearty sip. "I don't, do I?" she asked.

"Don't what?"

"Snore."

"No, you don't snore. I never said you snored. You just make a noise in your throat. Very soft. Kind of like a purr."

If she hadn't been holding a hot cup of coffee, she'd have punched him. "I do not!"

"Yeah, as a matter of fact, you do."

He sounded serious. Peering in his eyes, Audrey waited for the smile that didn't come. "I do?"

"Mm-hmm." He took the cup back, sipped. "It's one of the many things about you that I love."

Tempted to ask what the other things were, Audrey couldn't. She had to think. To get them back on track. She was the eldest here.

"Where's my coffee?"

He held up his cup. "Right here."

"We're sharing?"

"I thought it would be kind of nice."

Nice. He was a kid. What did he know about nice? Sharing a cup of coffee? You had to be a lot older to get that that was nice.

"Who told you that?"

"Delilah." His cat, who'd been out from under the couch only long enough to eat last night. The summer heat was making her lazy.

"No, really, who?"

Frowning, Ryan turned her to face him. "Really? You're serious?"

She nodded.

"No one told me. I just thought it sounded nice. Why? Does it offend you to share a cup with me?"

All this for a coffee cup. Feeling incredibly stupid and awkward for making a mountain out of nothing, Audrey blurted the truth. "Of course not. I think it's nice, too."

Putting the cup to her lips, Ryan helped her take a sip and then, holding it arm's length away, leaned in to rub her nose with his before taking her mouth in a kiss that heated her lips far more than the coffee.

"I think it would also be nice if you met my parents today."

"No way." Even befuddled with his kiss, she got that one immediately right.

"Yes way."

"Forget it, Ryan."

"Can't. It's important."

"Why?"

"This past week has been hell. I don't want to go through another like it. The sooner I make you an official part of my life, the sooner you'll start to feel like you belong."

Audrey felt her age. And his youth. "If only it was that simple."

"Of course it's that simple."

"Ryan, just because you introduce me to your folks doesn't mean that they're going to accept me as a part of your life. And when they don't, it will make even being together like this harder."

"So you want to be together like this?"

"No!" A vision of herself, undressing in his bathroom the night before reminded her of the compelling need she'd felt to be close to him no matter what. She couldn't lie to him. "Yes. I want it. A lot. But that doesn't mean I can have it. I want to win the lottery, too."

"You don't have the winning lottery ticket at the moment. You do have this."

She loved his tenacity—when it was directed at helping kids like Scott Markovich.

"Okay, I'm one of those rare people who love cigarette smoke. But I know if I smoke it'll kill me, so I don't."

Eyes curious, a slight smile on his face, Ryan looked at her. "Did you used to?"

"Yes. Briefly. I liked it too much."

"I can't picture you with a cigarette."

"I can't, either, which is why I don't smoke." She gave him a pointed stare.

"You're saying you can't picture us together."

Smart man. Child. Boy. She was lying naked in his bed. Man. "Right."

"Which only proves my point," he said just when she thought she'd made *her* point once and for all. "You can't picture it because you can't see any way for it to work. You're putting up roadblocks that may or may not exist. Until they are really there, we can't attempt to get around them, we can't know whether or not we *can* get around them."

She wanted to argue. Intended to argue. And couldn't find an argument with him right there, being everything her heart had always wanted. "You have a strange way of looking at the world, Ryan Mercedes."

"I know."

She couldn't fight the whole world. Him. Her. Love.

And she couldn't forget the lessons life had taught her, either.

"Okay, I'll meet your folks. But I want your word that when it's as bad as I know it will be, you'll let me go."

"I can't promise that."

"Ryan…"

"I'm just being honest, sweetie," he said, his fingers brushing lightly against her cheek. "I'm not going to make promises unless I believe I can keep them. Unless I intend to keep them."

The sincerity shining from his eyes almost made her cry again. Even if she trusted her heart, there were too many obstacles. "Oh, Ry, why couldn't you have been born ten years earlier?"

"Because you needed more time to catch up with me."

He grinned and she couldn't help but laugh. She also couldn't help sliding down in the bed as he, once again, took her to a place that was everything life had to offer. Physical. Emotional. And spiritual.

She just wasn't that strong.

CHAPTER ELEVEN

"I CAN'T BELIEVE I agreed to do this."

Trying not to feed off her tension, Ryan, whose hand was interlocked with Audrey's on the console between them, gave it a squeeze. "It's going to be fine," he assured her. And tried to believe it himself.

One way or the other, it would be. Whether he was ready for it or not, understood all the ramifications or not, Audrey was a part of him. His parents were a part of him. They had to meet. There was no other option.

"I should have worn a sundress."

Why? So she could drive him crazy with desire while sitting in his parents' home? Not that the jeans and tank top toned down his desire in any way.

A burlap sack wouldn't have done that.

"You look fine."

"I'm too casual."

"They're casual people, sweetie. My dad's a mail carrier and Mom's been stay-at-home my whole life. Her strongest passion—outside of my father and me—is crocheting."

"I've always wanted to learn how to do that. My mom wasn't into crafty stuff at all."

It was going to be fine. Ryan had to believe that. "I'm sure she'd be happy to teach you."

"We'll see."

"You have to give us a chance, Audrey."

"Why do you think I'm sitting here in this truck?"

Because they loved each other. He just had to keep remembering that.

"YOU HAVE A NICE home."

Harriet Mercedes, gray-haired and dressed in baggy, knee-length shorts and a matching T-shirt, didn't look up from the salad she was tossing. "It's old and tattered."

"It's warm and filled with love."

Turning, her hands dotted with pieces of iceberg lettuce and hanging in front of her, Harriet's plump form looked more heavy with worry than extra weight. "Look, Ms. Lincoln—"

"Please call me Audrey. My mother is and always will be Ms. Lincoln to me."

"Look, Audrey—"

"It's okay, Mrs. Mercedes," Audrey said, stepping forward, wishing the floor would open up and suck her in. "I think I know what you're going to say."

When Ryan went outside with his father to help him change a turn-signal light on the older man's truck, Ryan's mother had asked her along to the kitchen to help her with last-minute touches to the lunch she'd prepared. And then refused to let her do anything.

"And I understand. I really do. I tried to tell Ryan it wasn't going to work. It's inappropriate, this difference in our ages. I know that as well as you do. But trying to convince that son of yours…"

The worried clouds in Harriet's eyes didn't dissipate as Audrey had expected.

"I make my living working with families, trying to hold them together, ferreting out problems and seeking solutions to them. I know relationship dynamics and—"

"Apparently you don't know my son as well as you think you do."

Finished with the salad, Harriet pulled out a platter of sandwiches—turkey, by the look of them. Fresh turkey. Not the store-bought packaged sandwich meat Audrey occasionally had.

"I—"

"Ryan follows his heart," Harriet said. "He always has. From the time he came to us he would not be convinced of something unless he felt the truth in it. The sense of it."

Curious to hear every single one of the stories inherent in the words, Audrey said, "That's one of the things I love most about him."

Somehow it didn't feel wrong to express feelings to Ryan's mother that she rarely came right out and said to him.

Telling him was too dangerous.

"Ryan is with you. He chose to bring you home to meet his family, because he's that certain his relationship with you is right."

Someplace deep inside Audrey, she'd known that. Hoped. But… "Ryan's twenty-two years old. If he's to be believed, I'm the first real love he's had. How can he possibly know that being with me is right for him?"

"He *is* to be believed," Harriet said, still standing with the plate of sandwiches. "That's another thing about my son. He tells the truth. No matter what."

Audrey nodded, wished she dared to take the plate, which

must be growing heavy, from the woman who, thank God, was almost as old as her own mother, over to the table.

"When Ryan was fourteen, the normal adolescent hormonal imbalances and insecurities were heightened by his frustration with his inability to understand himself. He was angry a lot of the time, and growing more and more determined to do something about the things that angered him. Which wouldn't have been so bad, except for the things that made him so mad."

Audrey didn't want to know. And was far too fascinated with the details of her young lover's life. How long did it take two men to change a light bulb? "What things?"

Harriet finally left the still-wrapped sandwiches at the table. "His father tried to get a loan at the bank. We'd gotten behind on our bills and he was trying to consolidate. It was one of those catch-22's. If you've got money, they want to loan it to you, but if you don't, you don't qualify for a loan. Ryan was so furious with what he saw as the unjust treatment of his father that he went on the Internet and God knows where else to find out everything he could about the bank manager. When he found out the man had loaned money to a certain young woman who had no job but lived in a nice condominium and drove a nice car, and who often received visits from the bank manager, he sent an anonymous letter to the president of the bank, telling him so."

"How'd he get all that information?"

"He wouldn't say."

"So what happened?"

"An investigation was done. Apparently the man had a couple of such women on the side, kept for his pleasure. He was fired."

"Was he married?"

"Until this all came out. Had a couple of kids, too. She divorced him and, according to Ryan—he contacted the woman a couple of years ago to apologize for disrupting her life so badly—she got everything, including a nice alimony settlement."

"He went back six years later?"

"Yes. That's Ryan," Harriet said, arms crossed as she watched Audrey. "His sense of right and wrong is non-negotiable and completely drives his actions."

"So did his father get the money?"

"Of course not, we didn't qualify, but according to Ryan, the manager now knew what it was like to be a have-not and perhaps he'd be a little more sympathetic the next time around."

"Wow."

"Yes, well, after that Glen and I decided that perhaps Ryan's anger was in part derived from the fact that he was adopted. We thought maybe he'd be more comfortable with the world around him if he had a better sense of self. We told him that if he wanted to find his birth mother, we'd help him."

"Did he?"

"Yes. And there again, Ryan was Ryan. We found out who she was and expected him to want to make contact, but then he dropped the whole thing. Never mentioned her again. Until last year."

Pulling out a chair at the end of the scarred table, Audrey sat, turning with her arms resting on the back of the chair. "He just met her last year?"

"It's hard to believe it's only been a couple of months over a year." Harriet's voice turned inward, as though she was speaking to herself. And then, as though with renewed purpose, she focused on Audrey again. "Unbeknownst to us, he'd looked her up on the Internet all those years ago and had been keeping track of her. After he joined the police force he had even more tracking abilities available to him. He found out that her husband was having an affair and thought it his duty to tell her so."

While it probably should have, the action didn't shock her.

"How'd that go over?"

"Sara's a delight," Harriet said surprisingly. "She was so thrilled to finally meet the son she'd given up that I think he could have told her she only had six months to live and she'd have found that good news."

Sara. The woman had a name. Had only been in Ryan's life for a year, and he'd mentioned none of this.

But it made his pursuit of her father more understandable.

"How about her husband? I'll bet he wasn't as thrilled."

"I'd guess not, though I've never met him," Harriet said. "She left him and their posh home as soon as she confronted him and he told her the truth. He'd had a long-standing thing with his assistant. Because Sara was willing to just walk away with whatever he agreed to give her, their divorce only took about six weeks."

"But I thought Ryan said his birth mother was married."

"She is. She and Mark just had a baby. Marcus Ryan."

"They named him after Ryan?"

"Why shouldn't they? They're brothers."

"Half brothers."

"No." Harriet shook her head. "Full brothers."

Frowning, Audrey was beginning to hope that changing a turn-signal light took a couple of days. "In a year's time she divorced her husband, married Ryan's dad and had another baby?"

Ryan's mother was still young enough to give birth. Of course, more and more women were having children when well into their forties.

Harriet took glasses out of the cupboard. "That's why it's hard to believe it's only been a year. So much has happened."

"So she knew him all along?"

"No. But that's a story you'll have to get from my son," Harriet said, turning with a glass in each hand. "I've already said far more than I should." She filled the glasses with ice. "Ryan's going to be really angry with me for saying this, but sometimes a mother has to do what she has to do." Her gaze bored into Audrey. "Ryan is going to pursue this relationship with you, Ms. Lincoln."

Harriet's tone had changed.

Nodding, Audrey braced herself.

"He's going to get hurt."

"You think I'm toying with him?"

"No." Ryan's mother set the filled glasses on the table. Went for the other two. "Actually, I don't. I think you really care about him," she said with her back to Audrey as she filled the other two glasses with ice.

"I do." Harriet deserved the truth. "More than I've ever cared about anyone."

Harriet sat. "It's not that I have anything against you," she said, looking Audrey straight in the eye. "I don't. You seem like a lovely woman. With a kind heart."

What did you say to that? Especially with the unspoken *but* hanging in the air between them.

"It's just that…Ryan…he won't look beyond what he believes and feels to be true. He won't care about the challenges in front of you. He's going to charge ahead, regardless of the fact that you and he are a generation apart. And, eventually, as you take him about in your circle, as people raise their eyebrows at the two of you, as he loses a promotion because his superiors doubt the wisdom of his choices, he's going to be hurt."

"I won't hold him back."

"No, I don't think you would. But don't you see, if he's committed to you, made promises to you, his sense of right and wrong will hold him there. Trapped."

Trapped. Oh, God. She could understand. Her love for a young man could stop the progression of his life before it even began. Until his youth was gone and he'd lost opportunity.

Or could it? Was today's world really that small-minded?

"Ryan said you're thirty-five." Harriet spoke again.

In that moment, she sounded ancient. "That's right."

"Sara, his birth mother, is only thirty-eight."

Practically a peer. They'd have been in high school at the same time.

"People are going to think that you're old enough to be his mother."

She'd already gotten that.

"It's off-putting."

She got that, too.

"And what about friends? You going to hang out with Ryan's high-school buddies? They're still in college, having frat parties. Their idea of a family dinner is to stop in at Mom's long enough to wolf down whatever's on the table and head out to party."

Please stop. Oh, please stop.

"Or would you expect him to associate with your crowd all the time? To talk about music and events that took place before he was born? Or when he was too young to be aware of them. What about the Gulf War? I'll bet you remember it."

"Of course I do. I volunteered at the local Red Cross—"

"Ryan doesn't remember it."

"And what about kids? If you don't get started soon, you're going to be too old to have them. Ryan's so young to be strapped with that much responsibility."

And what about when their kids went to school? Had friends over? Would an old mother and young father be an embarrassment to them? Or when they were teenagers and she'd hit fifty and was menopausal and graying and Ryan was a young, virile, thirty-seven, attractive to all the twenty-year-olds, would Ryan and the kids go off and leave her behind to rest?

The idea was only slightly ludicrous, and had a little too much truth for comfort.

"Please," Harriet said, leaning forward. "I don't mean to hurt you, but please, for Ryan's sake, save him from himself."

"You want me to tell him I can't see him anymore."

Tears brimmed Harriet's eyes as she nodded.

CHAPTER TWELVE

RYAN GOT A CALL HALFWAY through lunch. His commander, head of the Special Victims Unit in the investigative division of the Columbus Police Department, was a man Ryan greatly respected. And one he didn't argue with. He had to go to work.

"Sorry about this," he said as he was backing out of his folks' drive. Before Audrey was even buckled in.

"It's not a problem, Ry." Her voice was distant—as it had been since he'd entered the house with his father. "I understand the demands of your job."

"I'm not usually called in on my days off."

"Did the commander say what happened to Dosendall?" The forty-year-old, fifteen-year veteran was a day-shift special-victims detective whom Audrey had met a few times. He was also a man Ryan trusted.

"Only that he'd responded to a supposed domestic-violence call and ended up shot in the stomach. There's a fifteen-year-old girl involved."

"Which is why he wanted you to come in."

"Right."

Ryan seemed to have a knack for getting the truth out of young people.

"Was anyone else hurt?"

"Not that I know of. I'll be briefed as soon as I get in."

"Do they think the girl shot Dosendall?"

"That's not clear at this time." It was a standard answer. Rote. And all he could give at this point. Even to her.

When silence fell, Ryan started to get a little nervous.

"Overall, that went well back there. Mom seemed to genuinely like you. And Dad was more curious about your job than anything else." Of course, his father rarely gave an opinion the first time out on anything. Glen's way was to listen, watch and then, maybe, say something. Mostly he was there for the aftermath, either to celebrate or help pick up the pieces.

"Mm-hmm."

"Talk to me."

"I am."

Ryan reached for her hand, and when she didn't accommodate his reach, leaned farther over until he could capture it. He held it lightly, half expecting her to pull away and relaxing a tad when she didn't.

"Your mother is my age."

"My mother is fifty-four."

"Your biological mother."

Stopping at a light, Ryan stared straight ahead. Processed. Harriet was not one to speak out of turn. Or to tell others' business. But she had. Things were worse than he'd thought.

He'd misjudged. And Audrey had obviously been hurt.

Damn. Now was not the time to get lazy. Audrey wasn't a case. She was life.

"She's three years older than you are," he said slowly, carefully, until he knew how much she'd been told.

And why.

"We were in high school at the same time."

Ryan's skin grew tight. His mother had talked about Sara's high-school years?

"And?"

"It's not going to work, Ryan. I am your mother's peer, not yours."

"Funny, we were pretty good peers last week when we handled the Markovich case."

"That's different."

"How so? I can work side by side with you, sharing the same amounts of responsibility and workload, but I can't love you?"

"Ryan, please. Not again."

"No. Sorry. I can't give on this one."

"And how much am I going to matter when I'm in my fifties and you're still in your thirties, being hit on by women half my age?"

"As much as you matter right now."

"You're too young to know what you're talking about."

"I've lived long enough to have heard of a lot of men in their forties, fifties and sixties who leave wives younger than they are for women half their age. It's a measure of the man, Audrey, not the age."

At her silence, he continued, "If you're going to argue, please keep the points pertinent. My actions are pertinent. The choices I make are pertinent. The way I treat you is pertinent. The number of years I've been on this earth is not. There are people in their sixties who are less mature than I am."

He could name a couple they both knew, but they only had about ten minutes left together. He couldn't leave her this way. He might not get another chance.

"Why didn't you tell me that you just met your birth mother last year?"

"What does it matter when I met her?"

"That's a pretty big occurrence in anyone's life, Ryan. A defining moment. The fact that you don't talk about it makes me nervous. You say you're all into us, yet you don't give me key pieces of your life."

She had him there.

And he wanted her.

Taking a deep breath, trying not to think about what he was doing, only why, Ryan said, "I have…issues there."

"Obviously. So why don't you want me to know about them? Because you like being her little boy and—"

"Shut up!" Anger with Audrey was a new experience and caught him unawares. "I apologize for that."

"Apology accepted. I was lashing out."

Giving himself a couple of seconds to calm down, he finally said, "My issue isn't with Sara. As a matter of fact, I visit there at least once a week. More if I can. I was there this week, babysitting so she could get a few hours away. She just had a baby and hasn't really left him since he was born, but she agreed to leave him with me."

"Marcus Ryan. Your mother told me about him."

And had she told Audrey about Marcus Ryan's father, too? Chilling, he reminded himself how much he loved Harriet Mercedes. How good she'd been to him. He'd have a talk with her, but not until he could do so without anger.

"She said he's your brother. Your full brother. Not half."

Damn it to hell. He was a grown man. Not a boy, to be talked about by his mommy behind his back. What in the hell had his mother been thinking?

"That's correct."

"Your mother married your father. After all these years."

"That's right."

"Is that your issue, then? The fact that they got together for this baby, but couldn't make it to give you a solid home life? You have problems because they gave you up for adoption?"

What the crap? "What did my mother tell you about Mark?"

"Nothing. She said it was up to you to tell me what you wanted me to know."

Harriet's mental image grew a little clearer in the haze that had been blinding him.

"I don't blame Sara for giving me up for adoption," he said, stopping at the light around the corner from his house. "She was sixteen, a child. There was no way she could have given me a solid home life even if she'd wanted to."

"I get that."

He turned. His complex's driveway was ahead. Her car right around the corner, in guest parking.

"My issue is with Mark."

"Did he desert her? Leave her alone and pregnant?"

"He didn't even know she *was* pregnant."

He'd stopped the car. Rather than immediately jumping out, Audrey turned to him. "Well, then, how can you blame—"

"He didn't know because he was in prison."

AUDREY WAS WASTING her time. Had no need to see anyone—especially someone she'd never met. She'd rescheduled Saturday's appointments to meet Ryan's parents and now had time on her hands. Thinking to do.

And since she always thought better when she drove, she was driving.

German Village wasn't as far as she sometimes drove when she had an issue to resolve, a challenge to face. Only twenty minutes from her own little house in the northern part of the city, the quaint German neighborhood was one of those places she'd heard of, but never really visited. If she didn't have a client there, she didn't get there.

Most of Audrey's clients weren't from the affluent, renovated historic neighborhood with its cobblestone streets, big homes and upscale coffee shops and eateries.

She'd read about the village. Had always wanted to see it. Why not today? Why not stop for coffee at Cup O' Joe's? She'd never tasted the homegrown Columbus beans served there. Today they seemed like just the distraction she needed.

Perhaps they'd clear her head, wipe away the Ryan-induced fog so she could find some solutions.

Or rather, find a way to enforce the solutions. Staying away from Ryan Mercedes was the answer. That she already knew. How to ensure that she did that, how to get him to stop contacting her, was the issue at hand.

She had no other missive. Nothing else to find. The road away from Ryan was it.

Which didn't explain why, as soon as she had an iced coffee in hand, she was seeking out a phone book from the clerk. Leafing through the Ws, stopping at Wilson. Going down the alphabet until she was at the Ls. Looking for Leonard.

And jotting down the address listed there. She might not be a star detective or have state-of-the-art investigative tools at her disposal, but she could look up a name.

And after half an hour of driving in circles, find a street.

She wasn't going to stop. She'd said so before getting on

the highway downtown. But no one would know if she drove by the house. Took a peek.

Got a measure of the man who'd deserted her.

Ryan's father was an ex-con. It explained so much. And nothing at all.

With a crime scene waiting, he'd been unable to dally, even for a second when they'd reached her car. Or rather, been unable to take time, other than for the very long, thorough kiss he'd given her as he'd come around to walk her to her car and open the door for her.

She hadn't meant to kiss him back. Had been adamantly opposed to the action.

It had happened, anyway.

As had the thoughts that had continually turned to him during her drive. What had his father done? Why couldn't Ryan talk about it? How did it affect him, knowing that an ex-convict had contributed to his genetic makeup? To someone like Ryan, with his rigid sense of right and wrong, his determination to right wrong at any cost, the knowledge had to have delivered a hard blow.

Luckily she was old enough not to be affected by whatever her father had turned out to be. After all those years at the hands of her mother's emotional blackmail, her attempts at brainwashing, Audrey had a clear sense of self.

One that was impervious to a bit of biological information.

She'd prove it, too. She'd find the house. She wasn't afraid to find out that her father's was the only unkempt place in this beautiful neighborhood. The only one with shaggy grass where the others all had sprawling acreage of vivid green lawns that looked as though they'd be as soft as cotton on the bare feet of the children who ran there.

The end of the street came before she found the ram-shackle home she'd been searching for. No matter. She had time. Could turn around.

The house numbers were all in order—and clearly marked. Following them wasn't a problem. Nor did it take long to find the house that matched the address she had.

It was the one with the distinguished-looking gentleman operating an edge trimmer on one of the immaculate lawns.

She backed up. Turned. Coasted past the drive. He was in designer denim shorts and a white polo shirt.

Her foot slipped off the gas. She was staring. And couldn't make herself leave.

"Can I help you?"

The man was beside her, calling loudly enough for her to hear from inside her car.

"Are you in trouble?" He grabbed his cell phone. "I can call 9-1-1."

"No!" She hadn't meant to say that quite so loudly. Or sharply. But 9-1-1 connected, indirectly, to Ryan. She didn't want him to know anything about this foray into insanity. Ever. Rolling down her window, she said, "I'm fine, really. I was lost, but now I've figured out where I am."

In more ways than one.

"I'm Leonard Wilson," the damn man said, holding out a hand to her. "My wife's inside. Why don't you come in and have some tea? We can look up your destination on the computer, help you find your way. A young woman shouldn't be lost and alone in downtown Columbus."

Tell me about it, you jerk. "Maybe if you hadn't deserted her, left her alone with a lunatic woman all her life, she wouldn't be."

Where on earth that comment had come from, Audrey had no idea. It shocked her far more than it did the gaping man staring at her.

"What?"

She'd started it. "You heard me."

"I deserted you?"

"That's what I said."

He paled. "Audrey?"

Inexplicably, her name on his lips changed everything, drained her anger. Left her numb. "I'm sorry," she said more softly. "I have the wrong address," she stumbled over the words. She couldn't believe she'd done this.

Done any of the things that she'd done in the past two weeks. Things such as going to bed with a twenty-two-year-old kid. Falling in love with him.

She was her mother, after all. Out of her ever-loving mind.

"It's you, isn't it?" Leonard Wilson was leaning on her door. In the way of her escape. If admitting her name bought her her freedom then…

She nodded.

"My God." The wide-eyed look on his face wasn't all that complimentary, though she couldn't determine, in her addled state, if it stemmed from horror or sheer shock. "For years I prepared for this moment, but when your teens passed, and then your twenties, I assumed the day would never come."

She wasn't falling for any sob story. Any attempt at convincing her that he'd cared at all. Audrey was a pro at withstanding parental manipulation.

"Yes, well, it didn't. As I said, I'm lost—"

"On my street? In front of my house? Wouldn't you say that's a bit much to be a coincidence?"

"Len? Who is it, dear?"

Looking up, Audrey saw the fiftyish, smartly dressed woman walking toward them. Her voice sounded kind. A lot kinder than Audrey's mother's. Her expression was softer, too.

"You're never going to believe this," Leonard said, still holding the door as though he knew that if he let it go, Audrey would be gone.

Why on earth should he care?

"It's not as if I live a thousand miles away," she told the man she hated almost as much as she wanted to know him.

"It's Audrey," he said, putting an arm around the woman who came to join him.

Audrey wasn't sure he'd heard her statement. Hardly remembered it herself as she stared at the woman who'd joined them. She'd never seen her in her life, but the woman peering at her had tears in her eyes.

"Do I know you?"

"This is my wife, Becky," Leonard's words seemed to come from far away.

Audrey glanced at Leonard. "What's going on? Do I know her?"

"No, honey, you don't." Leonard shifted, taking much of his wife's weight. "But I think you should come in. We've got some things to tell you."

"I've lived in Columbus my entire life."

"And if we had contacted you, we'd have gone to jail."

CHAPTER THIRTEEN

THE GIRL HAD obviously been penetrated according to the doctor's report Ryan had just taken. Standing outside the hospital room, at the same hospital where he'd just seen the wife of one his associates waiting while her husband underwent surgery for the bullet in his gut, Ryan took a deep breath before nodding at the female police officer, Kelly Jones, that he was ready to go in.

Takeisha Baker looked more like ten than fifteen, her tiny figure seemingly swallowed up by the bars of the bed pulled up around her. The bruises weren't easily detectable on her dark skin, but the swelling around her eye was unmistakable. As were the tears that sprang to her eyes when she saw them.

Though she didn't say a word, her lips were trembling, as though there were many things she wanted to say. Or needed to say.

"Hi, Takeisha, I'm Detective Mercedes and this is Officer Jones."

"I didn't do it." The girl's voice was strong, solid, "I swear I didn't do it."

"Do what?" Ryan pulled up a chair a couple of feet from the side of the bed and sat. Much less intimidating to the girl than having someone standing over her. Especially a man.

"Shoot that cop. I didn't do it."

"We're not here to talk about that right now," he said, though he desperately needed to find out what the girl knew. Needed to avenge his brother officer—and the family that paced, fearing the worst, a couple of floors below. "We're here for you."

Takeisha frowned, her gaze dropping. She didn't look convinced. "He says it's my fault," she half muttered. "Probably it is."

"What's your fault?"

"What he did. What he's been doing."

"Who?"

"Daniel."

"Who's Daniel?"

"My old lady's man. He's been living with us awhile now."

"And what did he do?" Ryan knew. Kelly knew. There was no reason to put the child through this, except to protect her. They needed official testimony to press charges.

"He's been making me do it with him, trying to get me pregnant."

Exchanging a glance with Kelly, who was holding the tape recorder, Ryan sat forward. "Trying to make you get pregnant?" They'd get a little clearer testimony on the rest of it in a minute.

"Uh-huh. My ma can't have any more kids. Something inside her busted with the last one."

"So they want you to be a surrogate mother?"

"What?" Takeisha's eyebrows drew together.

"They want you to have their baby for them," he re-stated. Shaking her head, flipping the tiny braids covering it,

Takeisha snorted. "They don't want a baby. They want more money on the welfare check. You get so much for every kid."

It was a good thing he'd only had a few bites of lunch before he'd been called away. Ryan had seen a lot in his few years on the force, heard some horrendous things, but somehow, sitting in the presence of a fifteen-year-old child who had far too much maturity and bore the marks of gross sexual impositions, was one of the hardest things he'd ever done.

"So he made you have sex with him." Kelly's voice brought him out of his stupor and back to the job at hand.

"Yeah."

"And how long has this been going on?" It was Kelly again.

"I don't know. Four months, maybe."

"Did you tell the doctor about that?"

"Yeah. She did a pregnancy test."

Ryan wanted to kill the bastard who'd made his mark on this child—and prayed that the test came up negative. What in the hell was the matter with people? With the world?

"Can you tell us what happened today?" he asked, managing to fill his tone with the emotional calm he couldn't find inside himself.

"We were sitting there watching cartoons and Daniel said he wanted it and my ma said no. She said he'd done it enough to make me pregnant and he had to stick with her now. He got mad and said he'd have it with me whenever he wanted. He said that I was his now, too. He said he'd show her."

The girl's voice broke and her face folded as she started to cry. "He grabbed me and…he…while he was doing it, she came in with a gun. He jumped up and they started fighting and I was afraid he was gonna kill her, so I called 9-1-1."

There had been mixed stories about who'd actually made that call—the mother or the daughter.

"Then what happened?"

"He heard what I did and he slapped me." She touched her eye. "My ma hit him with the gun and he grabbed her arm that was holding it and just as that cop came in the gun went off."

"Did anyone actually point the gun at Officer Dosendall?"

"Uh-uh." Takeisha looked them straight in the eye. "They were so busy fighting they didn't even know he'd gotten there."

The shooting had been an accident. A man might die, a great cop might die, and it had been accident.

They'd still get this Daniel guy. And maybe the girl's mother, too, though he doubted that. They'd give her immunity in exchange for her testimony.

And with that testimony, they'd probably win. They'd get him for rape. And manslaughter. Give him ten to twenty years in prison.

Ryan had been hoping for first degree attempted murder. And, if it didn't mean Dosendall had to die first, the death sentence.

"I'M SORRY, I don't mean to stare, but I just can't believe I'm actually looking at you after all this time," Becky Wilson said. They were sitting in the Wilsons' living room, the older couple so close they were touching on the off-white leather couch, Audrey in a matching, oversize chair.

Sipping from the sweet tea Becky had brought, Audrey didn't respond. These people were acting as though she'd returned from another planet when, in fact, they'd lived in the same city for most of her life.

Still…

"What did you mean when you said if you contacted me, you'd go to jail?"

Leonard Wilson was perfectly fine-looking. Short-haired, slim, slightly muscular, with a distinguished air that commanded Audrey's respect even when she wanted to hurl insults at him. He had green eyes. And didn't look as though he'd ever been blond. His eyebrows were too dark. He was easily six-two.

As long as she'd waited for her legs to grow, she'd never been particularly tall.

As a matter of fact, she couldn't find even a hint of resemblance between her and the man sitting there watching her with compassion-filled eyes.

"It's hard to know where to begin," he said.

"I always find that the beginning is a good spot."

The response was more sardonic than snotty, but she'd come close to disappointing herself with a childish display.

But then, how appropriate, since she was this man's child.

How could he be so calm about all this? He should be stammering with guilt. At the very least.

"You're right, I'm sure," he said with a small grin. "I was very much in love with your mother when I married her."

Amanda did seem to attract people like magnets. Until they got to know her intimately. She had more loyal business associates than Audrey could count.

"She's a beautiful woman," Audrey offered, wiping condensation from her glass on her jeans.

"And smart and funny," he added. "When she wants to be."

"My brother said the same things about her," Becky said, her cheeks not as white and colorless as they'd been moments before.

Audrey's brow creased. "Your brother."

"He was everything your mother was not," Leonard said. "Artistic, spontaneous. He was a designer, mostly women's leather goods, but he had a line of clothes, too."

Because she suddenly needed to stall this story, Audrey asked Becky, "Is he someone I'd have heard of?" She'd worked with her mother in the stores for several years.

"No, but if he'd lived, he would have been. He'd just sold his first line to all the major houses in New York when he was killed, flying his two-seater home to Ohio. He'd taken off in bad weather…" Becky's voice fell off.

"He was hurrying home to see your mother." Leonard confirmed what Audrey had been half-expecting, half-dreading she'd hear.

"She was having an affair with him."

"Right."

She peered at Leonard. "While she was married to you."

"Yes."

"Did you know about him?"

"I'd just found out. Which was why Jeff was hurrying home to her."

Sweating, Audrey sized up the two of them, the linked hands, the love that was evident between them even after more than twenty years of marriage. And she could fill in some of the blanks.

Just not the crucial one.

She wasn't sure she wanted to know. Not now, when she'd finally brought herself here, when she'd finally acknowledged that she had to have contact with the man who'd fathered her.

"Your mother and I had been having problems. My fault,

in that I'd started to pull away from her. She always needed a lot of attention and reassurance that she was loved and I was fine with that. It was the instances of verbal and emotional cruelty and manipulation I couldn't stand. As time wore on, I started distancing myself emotionally just to survive. And the more I did that, the more abusive she became. When she told me she was pregnant, I was surprised as we'd used birth control. But I thought this was a sign that we were meant to be together and I opened my heart to her again, thinking that the child—you—would give her the emotional confidence she needed to overcome the outbursts."

So Leonard *was* her father.

As the older man paused, Becky's hand in his moved, as though she was giving his fingers a squeeze.

"I told her I wanted us to go to counseling, that with a baby on the way, I was insisting on counseling so that she wouldn't bring to you whatever problems she brought to the marriage. I wanted her happy. I wanted us all happy."

Audrey could understand that. She would have made a similar recommendation had she been called in as mediator to a home life such as Leonard described.

She wanted to hate the man—or at least resent him. Sympathizing with him, she was having a little trouble doing either.

"The request must have scared her," Leonard said, his gaze turned inward as he shook his head. "I can only guess that she was afraid someone might find something seriously wrong with her. She went off on me like she'd never gone off before. She kept telling me that if she was crazy, it was my fault. All she'd wanted was to be loved and I didn't love her."

Audrey chilled at the familiar words, only vaguely aware

that she was clutching her glass of tea the way she used to clutch her teddy bear—in front of her for protection.

"The more I tried to calm her, to assure her that I only wanted what was best for all three of us, to assure her that I would stand beside her, help her, support her no matter what was discovered, the more out of control she got," Leonard continued, his voice gaining strength as he told his story.

"And when, no matter how cruel she got, I wouldn't give in to her as I usually did, she told me that the baby wasn't mine."

"She was just lashing out," Audrey said.

"I thought so, too, except that she'd calmed as she'd said the words. There was fear in her eyes, but something else, too. Suddenly her whole demeanor changed and she told me about Jeff. About the affair they'd been having for more than six months."

"So you left." Audrey didn't blame him. She wasn't his. His wife had been unfaithful.

"I wanted to leave. I told her I was leaving. And then Jeff was killed and she was alone and pregnant and falling apart."

"She said you were divorced before I was a year old."

"She wouldn't let me touch her. Said that would be unfaithful to Jeff. As the months wore on, she wouldn't let me near her at all. I'd met Becky at Jeff's funeral—yes, I went with your mother to her lover's funeral because I was afraid she'd fall apart and there would be no one there to help her—and Becky had asked to be kept apprised of the pregnancy and your particulars. You were her only sibling's child and she so desperately wanted to know you."

"I would think my mom would have welcomed Jeff's sister into the fold."

"She caught us talking one time and wouldn't let Becky anywhere near. I'm sure she was afraid that Becky and I had something going, or would have. She was afraid that I'd leave her."

"Even though she so obviously didn't want you." Knowing her mother, the picture was becoming so crystal clear.

"Eventually it got so bad that she changed the locks on the doors. She was convinced that Becky and I were having an affair—which, at that point, we were not. I came home to find that I couldn't get in my own house."

Audrey would like to have been surprised.

"A week later she filed for divorce."

"Before I was born."

"Yes."

"But she still named you on the birth certificate."

"I suspect that was to punish me. To make me pay child support. I'd just started my own engineering firm and she knew that I was scraping every penny to get by."

Audrey suspected he was right.

"You could have fought that."

"I know."

The things Leonard left unsaid, as he and Becky watched her with expressions full of love, hurt even as they promised miracles to come.

She had a family.

"She robbed us of a lifetime."

She heard her words speaking about her mother, and felt sick to her stomach as she saw herself, as well. Had she been so busy trying to control her world, to prevent further pain, to keep others from hurting her, that she was robbing herself of a lifetime?

RYAN CALLED Audrey on his way from the hospital to his office. He'd stopped by to check up on Dosendall's wife again. There was still no word about the officer's condition.

And there was no word from Audrey, either. No voice-mails. No text messages, not that she'd ever sent him any. And she didn't pick up her phone.

With lead in his gut, afraid that his mother had scared her off again, that another long week of unanswered calls was going to follow, he dialed his parents' home.

"I love her, Ma," was the first thing out of his mouth when his mother picked up.

"I know you do, Ry."

"I want you to stay out of it."

"You're going to get hurt."

"Since when have you thought you could prevent that?" Silence followed his remark.

"You hurt her," he said.

"I didn't mean to, son, but I've told your father about our conversation and have been worried about how she left here feeling. I've never in my life let someone leave my home feeling unwelcome."

"You didn't pick a great time to start." The intake of breath on the other line, along with the words still ringing in his own ears, showed him his cruelty. "I'm sorry. That was uncalled for."

"I'll call her, Ry."

"No! Please. Just leave her alone. I'll take care of it. I only need to know what you told her."

His heart didn't feel any lighter when, five minutes later, he hung up the phone.

"I CAME HERE thinking I'd find a deadbeat father and, instead, I find out that my father has been dead since before I was born," Audrey said, trying to assimilate the cacophony of emotions assailing her as she stared at the couple across from her.

Their home was cool in the middle of a hot summer. Yet warm, too.

"But you found an aunt who's desperately wanted to be a part of your life since before you were born," Leonard said softly.

Audrey's heart started to pound as she glanced at the other woman, read the anticipation and barely concealed emotion in her eyes, in the trembling of her lips.

"I—I didn't get that far in my thinking yet," she allowed. "I mean, my father is more than a name now. The fact that he has family never even occurred to me."

And something else dawned.

"What about your mom and dad? Are they alive?" Did she have grandparents somewhere?

"No. They passed away when I was seventeen. In a car accident. Jeff was only twenty-three at the time, but he'd already graduated with a degree in design and was apprenticing with a house in New York. I finished high school there with him, then came back to Ohio State to attend college with my best friend. When he'd established himself enough to be making a living from his own designs, he moved back to town, too."

A photo on the mantel caught Audrey's attention. A photo she'd purposely avoided upon entering the room. "I have cousins."

"Yes, Carla and Kaylee, and they know all about you," Leonard said. "From the time they were little they heard about cousin Audrey. We'd so hoped you'd get in touch with us, and had them prepared for the eventuality."

Her heart plummeted. For a few minutes there, caught up in the wonder—and shock—of it all, she'd forgotten thirty-five years of abandonment. And a letter that was never even read.

"I did get in touch." Audrey forced the words into the loving atmosphere. She was here to face the truth, not to be wrapped in loving-family dreams. "When I was in high school, I wrote you a letter. My mom even gave me your address. I mailed the letter myself. The letter came back, canceled, unopened with 'return to sender' scrawled across the front of it."

Becky's jaw dropped open. "We never received a letter."

Audrey looked at Leonard.

"We absolutely never received a letter," he said. "We'd have been all over it, I can assure you. Every single Thanksgiving since Becky and I were married, there's been a prayer offered at the dinner table that you'd find us."

"It was sent to a Dayton address."

"We've never lived outside of Columbus city limits."

"What about the support checks? They came from all over the country."

"There were no checks," Leonard said. "I paid child services, and they paid your mother."

"Surely she…" Audrey wasn't sure why she was surprised. Amanda's need for control was so complete, so total, she'd go to any lengths to preserve it. Except, maybe, breaking the law. Maybe.

"My guess is she told someone at work a sob story about protecting you and gave you their address. Thinking they were helping, he or she wrote return to sender on your letter and put it back in the mail."

It sounded sickeningly like something Amanda Lincoln could do.

Still…

"I was right here in town. You could have contacted me."

Leonard leaned forward. "After I left your mother she swore she'd make Becky and me pay for the rest of our lives for hurting her. She called the police on me when I stopped by the house to pick up some of my things. She called and reported my car as stolen. Her name was on the title. Mine was on the title of the car she'd said she wanted and was driving. I was arrested that time, but the charges were dropped. Then she really started to play dirty."

Leonard looked away, out the window, before meeting Audrey's gaze again. Becky rubbed his back. "When I was first in love with your mother, when I thought I'd found my life's mate, I poured out my soul to her. Because I wanted her to know me completely, I told her all my dark secrets and indiscretions. With the blindness and confidence of young love, I trusted her to keep them sacred. Systematically, throughout the years, she used them all against me. Except one."

Elbows on his knees, Leonard said, "When I was eighteen I had sexual relations with my girlfriend. We'd been going together for a couple of years, but she was only sixteen at the time. Her father pressed charges and I was found guilty of statutory rape."

"You went to prison?" Considering the quiet dignity, the

soft speech of the man sitting with her in his well-to-do living room, the thought of him housed with hard-core sexual offenders was difficult to imagine.

"I went to jail for the few months it took to have a trial and sentencing. Because I was only eighteen and the sex was consensual, the judge was able to give me a suspended sentence and a monetary fine."

Audrey had no reason to feel relieved. This man was nothing to her except her mother's ex-husband.

"Your mother ran into one of our friends at the grocery store shortly after the car incident and happened to bring the conversation around to rape—mine in particular. This friend was also a business associate of mine."

"And you couldn't get her for slander because she spoke the truth."

"Right. I went to her, begging her to let it go, reminding her that she hadn't been happy with me, appealing to her on Becky's behalf, for Jeff's sake. That got to her. Sort of. She said that we'd have complete peace from her if we signed a contract agreeing that we would not contact you, ever, either directly or indirectly, by any means. She said that was the only way she'd feel assured that I would not be popping in and out of her life. She wanted to never see Becky or me again." He shook his head.

"At first he point-blank refused." Becky took over the story. "I insisted we get a lawyer and that's when we found we had no rights whatsoever where you were concerned. Your mother could prove that Len wasn't your biological father. At that time we didn't know she was planning to name him on the birth certificate or come after him for child support. In those days extended families, an aunt, had even fewer rights than they do now. So we weren't going to see you, anyway."

"I hated to leave you alone with her," her uncle inserted. "But we didn't have enough grounds to have her proved unfit. She had a respectable job, employees who would vouch for her. You weren't even born yet and the courts almost always placed children with their mothers in those days, anyway."

"We talked," Becky nodded toward Leonard, sliding her hand along his leg. "And we figured that you had the best shot of her being a good mother to you if we bowed out. But at our lawyer's suggestion, we did get your mother to add a caveat to the contract. If you ever contacted us, we could see you."

"So she made sure I didn't contact you," Audrey said now, the whole thing making sense. Horrific sense, but sense. "She was afraid she'd have had to share me with your family—a family she couldn't be a part of."

"Probably." Leonard's smile was sad.

"Regardless," Becky said, her lips trembling again, "we signed the contract, but have prayed every year since that you would come to us."

So much pain. Heartbreak. Loneliness. For all of them. All because one woman feared them. Amanda Lincoln, in trying to control what couldn't be controlled—the heart—had brought emotional agony to everyone who had loved her. Including herself.

Somehow, the cycle had to stop.

CHAPTER FOURTEEN

SHE DIDN'T ANSWER her phone. Or return his calls. Ryan thought about the advisability of giving her a day to recover from the meeting with his mother, wondered if it was the mature thing to do.

And as soon as he was finished at work, he presented himself outside Audrey's front door, knocking with the confidence of one driven by instinct, not head trips. He was who he was—a man who did what he felt to be right. If that made him young, so be it. He guessed, if that was the case, he'd still be as young at eighty-two as he was at twenty-two.

A new youth serum. He could market it. Make a million.

And didn't believe for a second that Audrey Lincoln would be any more swayed by him as a millionaire than she was with him as an underpaid detective.

It wasn't his job that bothered her. And she wasn't the kind of woman who could be bought.

By the third knock he was shifting his weight from foot to foot, stewing. He couldn't harass her. That was against the law. He couldn't break in. That was against the law.

Unless he had a search warrant.

Which he did not.

Dialing her cell again as he stood there on her front porch, he counted the rings. It was almost eight o'clock. Where in the hell was she?

He could get a search warrant easily enough. All he had to do was claim that she was a woman living alone—a woman who dealt with some pretty rough characters in her line of work. He could...

Was she really just going to refuse to see him? To give them a chance?

He could write a letter. Leave it in her door.

And write more. And leave them again and again for as long as it took to get her to talk to him.

Thoughts of how it would look for a detective to have a civil stalking order against him were just surfacing when he saw Audrey's car come up her street. Half expecting her to drive right on past when she recognized his car at the curb, he had to concentrate to quiet the pounding of his heart when she pulled into the drive.

"Hi." She wasn't frowning as she approached him, still in the jeans and tank top she'd had on that morning, her purse slung casually over her shoulder.

"Hi."

"Would you like to come in?"

Hell, yes, he would. Of course he would. There was nothing he'd like better. "Okay."

Ryan had never actually been inside Audrey's home. Inside her body, but not her home. Feeling kind of awkward, he stepped into the Victorian-style cottage, with its real hardwood floors, coordinated yellow and green walls, matching furniture and a flat, big-screen television set.

The place, compared to his bachelor apartment, made him feel about twelve.

"It's nice." He looked around—at the wall decor that ranged from what appeared to be real art to shadow boxes and filigree shelf things filled with expensive-looking collections.

"I like it."

"How long have you been here?"

"Five years."

"All through law school?" He wanted to be impressed, not depressed.

"Yeah. I got a thirty-year, fixed-rate mortgage when the rates were low. The payment was less than the rent I was paying on my apartment."

He chose not to share the fact that he hadn't been old enough to qualify for a loan on his own when the rates had been at an all-time low four years before.

She offered him a drink. He wanted lemonade and asked for a beer. With her glass of lemonade in hand, she led him through the fully equipped and immaculate kitchen to an enclosed porch with a rounded back wall of screened windows and tightly woven wicker furniture. A couch, a love seat, rockers, end and coffee tables. There was no new discount-store patio furniture here.

"Where were you?" Cringing at the abruptness in his tone, Ryan dropped onto one end of the wicker couch. He felt awkward as hell and hated it. He sipped his beer, uncharacteristically aware of his youth. Then she sat beside him and his gaze was captured by those brown eyes, which gave him glimpses of some deep, nonverbal communication that he instinctively knew was a once-in-a-lifetime experience.

"Out driving."

There was more. But he didn't ask.

"I went to German Village."

She'd pursued his lead. He'd had a hunch that Audrey had ancient history to settle before she could trust a man with her heart. Any man.

So maybe Ryan had a chance. He leaned his shoulder against hers.

"How'd it go?" He forced calm professionalism when, in fact, he'd have given his right arm to have been there with her.

"He's not my father."

Ryan's eyes narrowed as he watched her, looked for signs of prevarication or hiding. Of residual turmoil.

She seemed strangely at peace.

Nothing at all like he'd felt after meeting his biological mother the year before.

"Did he tell you that?"

Audrey's lips tilted into a soft, half smile that was filled as much with sadness as joy. "He did. And his wife, my aunt, did, too."

Loving the sound of her voice, the look in her eyes, Ryan listened as she told him the story she'd heard that afternoon. And wanted to meet the man who hadn't fathered the woman he loved, but who'd financially supported her, anyway—the man who'd told her the whole truth, sparing himself nothing.

"How'd you feel about him then?" He stopped her when she got to the part about Leonard having been convicted of raping a minor.

"She was his girlfriend," Audrey said. "It was completely consensual. They made love. Her father found out and went berserk."

"So that's why his sentence was so lenient." Ryan had wondered. But then, his biological father had received only five years for a nonconsensual-rape conviction more than twenty years later.

"You knew about his record," Audrey said, as though only now realizing that.

"Yeah."

"And you didn't tell me."

"It wasn't my story to tell."

"Most people would have done so, anyway."

"I'm not most people."

"You didn't want to prejudice me against him."

With his beer held between both hands in front of him, Ryan stared at the floor. "The conviction was almost forty years ago, the sentence indicative of mitigating factors, and he's been clean as a whistle ever since. I knew you weren't in danger." There was more he owed her. Or maybe he owed her nothing.

Maybe he was meant to struggle alone with finding a way to accept Mark Dalton. To forgive him.

Maybe Ryan was alone in his belief that some things were meant to be sacred, and no matter if a man had been drugged or not, there should be something inside him that stopped him from participating in a three-men-to-one-girl foursome.

"Do you think Leonard was wrong to have sex with his girlfriend?"

Ryan had no idea why he was pushing this. He lived within rigid boundaries, but that was because they were right for him. They spoke truth to him. He didn't expect others to live by his conscience. Did he?

"I think it was understandable," she said, not helping him out at all. Would she understand Mark's situation, too?

"They'd been going together for a couple of years,"

Audrey continued, defending a man who'd been irresponsible with his penis, leaving Ryan feeling more foreign than ever. "They had normal, healthy needs."

"So you don't think he should have been punished."

"I do. But I think she should have been, too. From what I heard, she wanted to make love as badly as he did. Maybe more so. He was leaving for college and she wanted to have something to hold him to her. She was afraid of losing him to some college coed."

Ryan was surprised to hear her, a woman, blame the girl.

"But he was older. The man. It was up to him to stop things." The view was old-fashioned. But still true.

Frowning, Audrey cocked her head as she looked at him. "Why?"

"Because." *Real mature, Mercedes.* "A penis is a wonderful thing, but responsibility goes side by side with the incredible pleasure it provides. Women definitely affect its responses. They can cause it to get hard. But that doesn't give a man the right to stick it where it doesn't belong."

"Even if she gives him the right?"

"If you tell me I can use your state ID to get into the courthouse without security screening, and I do so, am I blameless?"

"Of course not."

"If I got caught, I'd be charged and convicted and sentenced."

"Yeah."

Her eyes glistened as she stared at him, as though assessing if he was for real.

"Yeah," he repeated.

Some things were still black and white.

CHAPTER FIFTEEN

NESTLED IN RYAN'S ARMS on the wicker couch in her
sunroom Saturday evening, Audrey sighed. She belonged
here. She didn't. The war inside her raged, battle after battle,
with no clear victor.

"What was that for?" His fingers were rubbing up and
down her arm. She didn't want him to stop touching her. Ever.

"I'm confused."

"Okay, let's talk about it."

Listening to the deep tenor of his voice, to the words he
said, she could close her eyes and believe that Ryan
Mercedes was a member of her own generation.

"I feel so safe here."

"In your house? That's natural," he said softly. "This is
your home. You've been here a long time."

She almost left it at that. Except that she wasn't going to
be a coward anymore. Today, finally facing the truth about
herself, finally having the courage to face her life, had netted
her a family.

And fear of the unknown had robbed her of that very
same family for many years that she would never get back.

"I meant here." She tapped his chest. "Against you. In
your arms."

His silence allowed the sea of doubt to wash back up to the shores of her mind. And heart.

He was only twenty-two. Far too young to take on the responsibility of a thirty-five-year-old woman's emotional baggage.

"Does that scare you?" she asked.

"Hell, no!" Ryan moved only enough to meet her gaze, his hold on her body changing, but not loosening at all. Then, still holding her gaze, he added, "And yes."

Trying to pull away, Audrey fought back more tears. For a woman who rarely cried, she was doing far too much of it these days.

"Hold it," he said, holding her head to his chest with a gentle hand. "Let me explain."

Audrey lay still. She could have escaped if she'd wanted to. They both knew that.

"I love you so much it hurts," he started to say, his voice clear, though not quite steady. There was no mistaking his sincerity. "I want nothing more than to have you need me as much as I need you. And yet, is it fair to ask that of you? I'm rigid, I get that. I see what I see. I'm not sure I'm good for anyone on a fully committed basis. I expect too much. And then there's the other side of it. The obstacles our age difference presents. I know I can handle them, but what if you can't? The thought of having you, then losing you scares the hell out of me. Does that make sense?"

It did. So much. Too much.

"I can't make any promises, Ryan." But, God, how she wanted to.

"I'm beginning to realize that."

"Meeting my aunt and uncle today, hearing their story,

seeing what fear did to my mother all tell me that I have to listen to my heart, just like you're always preaching."

His arms tightened. "Well, then…"

"But I'm just as certain that we're meant to learn by our life's experiences."

"I agree with that."

"I saw my mother in myself today, Ry. I see her in me when I look back on some of the choices I've made. I'm too much like her. But instead of trying to hold on to love with manipulation and control, I do it by compromising myself."

"That's something we can change, sweetie. Something we can work on together. You just have to see that you'll be loved whether you do what I want or not."

"But don't you see, Ryan?" She sat up, looked at him. "I'm already doing it. Simply by being with you right now."

When he didn't say anything, she knew she was finally getting through to him.

"Maybe you want me because you can't have me. It's human nature."

"That's not my nature. But as you say, neither is this my nature." He sighed and she'd never seen him look so defeated. "I don't know what to say anymore," he continued. "I love you. I don't want to leave here. But I can't fight against both of us and the age thing, too."

Cold, hard tendrils of fear spiraled through her.

"You're leaving?" He had to eventually. She knew that. But…

"Of course not," Ryan said. His voice had lost its luster. "I just don't see a future for us right now. Can we let it all go for tonight? Just be together and to hell with the future?"

It was the dumbest suggestion he'd ever made.

"Yes," she said, forgetting to act her age.

AN HOUR LATER, in Audrey's bed for the first time, Ryan roused himself to ask, "Have you talked to your mother about Leonard yet?"

He felt Audrey shake her head against his shoulder, the movement brushing the sheets against his skin. Her sheets were a lot softer than his.

Thread count, she'd told him. He was off to the store again in the near future.

Right after he got out of her queen-size bed in the light-gold room filled with rose everything. Which wouldn't be that evening, if he had his way.

"I'm not sure what to say to her," she answered at last, her voice groggy, whether from sleepiness or spent passion, he wasn't sure. It turned him on, though. For now that was all he wanted to think about.

And who was he kidding? Audrey washing dishes turned him on. Or driving a car. Sitting on the corner of his desk at work. Talking to a client on the phone.

Answering her door.

Standing outside his…

"I wanted to talk to you first, see what you thought."

The words had him fully alert, all thoughts of sex fleeing. Couples ran life's decisions by each other. Real couples.

The thought thrilled him—and urged him to run as fast and as far as he could.

And yet his legs wouldn't move. Wouldn't disentangle themselves from the limbs wrapped around him.

This was time out of time, he reminded himself. An hour, or a day, just to exist.

So where was the harm in acting like a real couple? What was wrong with trying on the concept for size? his inner voice asked. How would they ever know if there was any real compatibility if they didn't explore a little bit?

And that reminded him…

"My mother sends her apologies." Seemed like a year ago since he'd told his parent he'd pass on her message. A year since he'd introduced Audrey to Harriet and Glen. "She feels awful for making you uncomfortable and would like you to come back. She promises to welcome you."

Her hand on his chest clenched, but she didn't move her head from his shoulder.

"She was being a good mother. Looking out for your best interests."

Ryan studied the art on the opposite wall—a series of children engaged in different activities and wearing different attire, from formal dress to swimsuits. "She was overstepping and she knows it."

"She loves you."

"And she's wrong about this one." One young boy on the opposite wall held up sparkling clean hands while the smile stretching his face from ear to ear was covered with smudges of what looked like chocolate. "Whether we make it or not, it won't be because of our age difference."

"Her concerns were valid."

"She didn't factor in the positives…the fact that I am in love with you."

"You don't know that."

"Yeah. I do."

"For now."

"Forever."

His focus was solely on Audrey as she twisted to meet his gaze. He wished he could read her mind. "I love you, too, Ry, and it scares me to death."

Knowing it was impossible, Ryan set about kissing away her fears. They were going to be there in the cold light of day. But he continued to apply his antidote regardless. He just plain didn't know what else to do.

AUDREY WATCHED the clock. Time was ticking. The evening was ending, turning into night. And then day would follow. She should rest. Sleep in Ryan's arms while she could.

She didn't want to miss a second of the time left with him.

"So your dad was a designer."

Apparently he wasn't ready to sleep, either. "Yeah." The idea seemed so foreign. "I don't think I've really digested the fact that Jeff was my dad. Leonard seemed like my dad to me." Turning her head on the pillow she was sharing with Ryan—the pillow she'd been sleeping on alone since she'd bought it a couple of years before—she looked for his reaction.

"Did you see pictures of him?"

"A whole album of them." She'd felt no kinship, but then, she'd been working under the assumption that her father had been alive all these years. Identifying with a man who, in his oldest pictures was still younger than she was now, seemed too far a stretch. "He was smiling in almost every one of them," she told Ryan, remembering the impressions she *had* had. "Aunt Becky says that he was a charmer—that he had a way of always making people feel good. She also said he had an uncanny ability to take things in stride."

"Like his parents' unexpected deaths and having a seventeen-year-old sister to raise?"

"And finding himself head over heels in love with another man's wife."

"You sound like you don't approve."

"I like Leonard. He deserved better than that."

"But you said he admitted of his own accord that things between him and your mother weren't good. And it sounds as though he found the woman he was really meant to share his life with. Through Jeff, as a matter of fact."

She hadn't thought of it like that. "I just don't feel…I don't know…any kind of attachment to him, you know? I finally see pictures of the father I've been curious about my whole life and I feel nothing at all. I could have been looking at pictures of anyone."

"You spent your whole life angry with someone for deserting you—and wondering what was wrong with you that made him desert you—only to find that you weren't deserted at all."

His lips were a little swollen. And it was no wonder, considering how many hours they'd been in her bed. Still, she was ready to make love again, always. The appetite she had for this man apparently couldn't be assuaged.

Was something wrong with her? Something that led her, a mature woman, to the bed of a young man? Or was this really that great emotion she'd been seeking her entire life but never found. Was it that once in a lifetime true love?

"I spent my whole life wanting to give him a piece of my mind." Wanting to meet the man who, with her mother, had created her. The man whose genes had made her who she was. "I'd like to have met him at least."

"I'm sorry, sweetie." Ryan moved in, kissing her softly on the mouth. "I'd hoped, when I nosed my way into this, that you'd find your father, be able to meet him, make peace with his desertion. Instead, you find that you'll never be able to meet him."

"True." And there was some disappointment in that. Probably a lot once the residual shock wore off. But… "At the same time, I found out that I wasn't deserted at all."

"YOU SAID ONCE that your mother blackmailed you the whole time you were growing up." They were in Audrey's kitchen, preparing a snack to take back upstairs.

"She did blackmail me," his gorgeous companion said. "Emotionally, at least." Dressed in a short white terry robe that barely covered her butt, Audrey had never looked cuter to him.

Or more vulnerable.

Adjusting the towel he'd hooked around his waist, Ryan bent to grab some vegetables from the fridge. "But from what your aunt and uncle said, it sounds as though she loved you. A lot."

"As much as she can love anyone."

Glancing over his shoulder, he noticed the lack of expression on Audrey's makeup-free face. There appeared to be no bitterness attached to the words. Just acceptance.

"You honestly don't think she's capable of loving deeply?"

"I don't know," she said, putting some dip into a little glass dish. He'd have stuck the container on the tray. "Maybe she could if she could get rid of whatever fear drives her. Maybe not. I figured out a long time ago that my mom needs me. I provide her with emotional security, and I guess that's a kind of love."

"That's you loving her. How does she love you back?"

"She cares about me," Audrey said, leaning back against the counter with her arms crossed. "But with her it seems more like the way people care about the walls that keep them warm, or the car that drives them safely or the money that provides life's necessities."

"She cares about you for what you do for her, not for what she can do for you."

"I guess."

"Does she ever do things for you?"

"Sure she does. She's always wanting to know what I'm dealing with, wanting to offer advice…"

"The well-meaning, painful kind?"

"Not always. My mom's a smart woman. In a lot of ways she's very savvy. She deals with people every single day and often has good insights."

Not at all the picture Ryan had painted in his mind.

"It's just that she has this tendency to follow up on whatever advice she gives to make sure you took it."

Ah. "She wants to control you."

"Yeah, but it's more than that. It's like a personal victory to her every time she gives advice that I follow and she turns out to be right. Like she somehow becomes more valuable to me. I swear, she has advice-accepted-and-I-was-right notches on her bedpost. Counting them every night is what gives her the security to go to sleep."

Ryan might not have been an adult for fifteen years, but he'd been around enough to know that nothing in life was simple.

In her mother's world, everything had conditions. Everything.

"It's more about being right than being loved."

"Exactly. She's right in the name of love."

"Because to her, love is a tally."

"Yes."

"Sounds like a pretty painful way of life she's chosen,"

he said. "She's negating the ability and right to be loved just because you exist."

Audrey's hand on his back sent chills of awareness throughout his body. Awareness of her. Of loving her.

"You have this uncanny ability to put into words things that are usually too nebulous to fully understand."

"I cut to the chase, you mean."

"Maybe." Coming around, she leaned against the counter next to him, facing him, her hip touching his. With her fingers she softly explored the side of his face. He could easily stand here forever.

"I tend to think that you have the gift of real insight," she said, admiration shining from her eyes.

"More like I spend too much time in my head, analyzing everything to death." It was a fault he'd long ago recognized. "In any case, the bottom line here is that to your mother, love is conditional."

"With my mother, everything is conditional."

"So when we go see her tomorrow, you need to lead into telling her about having met your aunt and uncle by letting her know how valuable her opinions, her side of the story, is to you, too." Ryan talked fast, knowing how much was resting on the next few minutes. He was pushing. He knew that, too. He just didn't know another way. "She's going to be feeling insecure if she thinks that you don't need her anymore, or if you judge her and find her wanting. If you blame her…"

"Wait a minute."

"What?" Busted.

"What was that you said?" Her hands were planted on her hips as she watched him.

"About your mother's insecurities?"

"Ryan Glen Mercedes, don't play stupid with me. *We* are *not* going to meet my mother tomorrow."

"You said earlier that you had a lunch date with her tomorrow."

"I do."

"You said you wanted my opinion where she's concerned. I think I need to be there to give it."

"You going to go to my gynecologist with me, too?"

"If you needed me, I'd be there in a heartbeat."

"Ryan, stop this." Her voice cracked.

He turned, taking hold of her elbows as he bent to meet her at eye level.

"What's it going to hurt if I meet her?" he asked, instinctively using the tone he'd used with Takeisha Baker earlier that day. "Look at us tonight. We can't go to sleep, can't let each other out of our sight, can't lose a second of this time together. How's it going to hurt any less to see where this takes us and then break up, or break up now? Because I have to tell you, if I walk out of here tomorrow and we're done, there's nothing that's going to hurt more than that."

He was talking too much. And he couldn't seem to stop. Conviction drove him. Desperation drove him.

For the first time in his life he didn't have the answers.

"What are you suggesting?"

"That we give us a try that lasts longer than a moment. That way we know for sure."

"Are you forgetting all the things we talked about earlier? Your aversion to being part of a couple? My inability to maintain autonomy when I love? The agony my mother caused when she loved? Not to mention the fact that I am old enough to be your mother?"

"No." He had to be honest with her. "And I'm not sure we're going to make it," he told her. "But at the same time, I'm remembering about the wasted thirty-five years between you and Leonard and Becky. And I know how it feels right now, tonight, here with you. I ask myself, what do we listen to? Our heads or our hearts?"

"I don't feel good about us going forward."

"I know."

"But you want to go, anyway."

"I don't know what else to do."

"Walk away."

"*You* walk away."

"I am not taking you to meet my mother."

"So I'll drive."

"Ryan."

"Sweetie…"

She stared at him for so long he started to sweat. She was going to refuse to give them this outside chance.

"Fine." Ryan was so relieved to hear the word, he didn't mind the anger in the voice that delivered it. "But when this backfires and we're forced to see how impossible it is for us to even think about being together, you'll have only yourself to blame."

Fair enough. Blame wasn't what he was scared of.

RYAN MOVED, adjusting his legs—and the one of hers that was thrown over his waist. His breathing had quieted.

"You awake?" It was the middle of the night.

"Yeah." Ryan's arms tightened around her and Audrey

snuggled her face up to his chest. Nothing had ever felt so right.

She'd been lying awake for the past hour, her thoughts battling each other, worrying about lunch the next day, and life every day after that.

Audrey trailed a finger over the mostly hairless chest and around one of his nipples. Raw hunger for a man's body was new to her. Her passions had always been contained, soft nudges. Without real fire.

He shifted again, pushing her leg a little lower. It now rested across his groin—and a penis that was already half-engorged.

She moved her leg ever so slightly, back and forth, unable to ignore that vital part of him.

His hips lifted slightly.

And Audrey was filling up with desire for him. Her body ached, her belly trembled, and the liquid fire between her legs was back.

His penis, hard and hot, pressed against her inner thigh, again and again, establishing a rhythm that was already familiar to her.

She shifted again, moving over enough to find the tip of him with her wet opening, and slid down on him, accepting him as part of her, welcoming him home, while her head still rested against his shoulder, her torso plastered to his.

Her hips moved only slightly, back and forth across his groin, caressing him inside her warmth.

Ryan's hands were at her hips, holding them over him, as his body surged upward. Still without a word.

She held her hips firm, refusing to join him in the dance. Wanting to savor him inside her as though he'd always been there. And always would be. Filling her up with him. A part of her.

His hips dipped, as though he were going to pull out of her enough to surge back in. And she couldn't let him.

Audrey sat up, keeping his body still. "Are you sure this isn't all we're about? Some pheromone reaction we've fallen prey to?"

His hips stilled as his eyes narrowed on her in the darkness. "Is that what you think?"

Audrey froze, past and present mingling together in a confusing mass of emotion-induced panic. "I don't know what to think."

Sliding backward, she intended to release Ryan's body from hers, but he was there, his hands on her backside, holding her to him.

"What just changed?" he asked, his voice soft.

"Nothing."

"Don't lie to me, Audrey."

"I'm not…" Her hands on his chest, she stared at him in the shadows cast by the nightlight she always left glowing. "Yes, I am."

"Thank you."

"For what."

"Being honest."

He wasn't moving at all. And suddenly, sitting on him, accepting his intimacy, was far more than she could bear. And she knew that their little idyllic fantasy had ended.

The past had caught up with her. Landed.

CHAPTER SIXTEEN

"WHEN I WAS SIXTEEN I had a crush on my band instructor," Audrey said, sitting next to Ryan, in the robe she'd pulled on, her arms wrapped around her legs as she spoke of something that had been locked up and buried for nineteen years. And, she'd thought, forever.

That feeling of doing something dirty with her body. Using her body to feel loved.

"You played in a band?" He'd pulled the covers up past his hips. His gaze was intensely focused on her.

He knew there was something more. And, she suspected, was taking time to prepare himself. She considered dropping the key to her past right back into the dark abyss she'd created for it all those years ago.

"Until I was sixteen."

He didn't move, other than to cross his arms over his chest. "What instrument did you play?"

"Flute."

"I can picture that. Do you still have it?"

"No."

"What did he look like?"

"Medium height. Dark hair, a little longer than what was completely respectable."

"That's what you liked? His long hair?"

"No." Going back was far more difficult than she'd anticipated—and she'd known it wasn't going to be easy. "He had this way of looking at you that made you feel as though you were the only person alive. He was a musician. Intense. Kind of earthy and rugged and…"

Stopping, Audrey started to sweat. She'd been such a twit. Paid such a huge price.

And no matter how many years passed, she couldn't change the past. Couldn't make it go away.

She turned her head toward him, and he said, "So what happened?" His eyes had narrowed.

"You don't want to know."

"Probably not, but I have a feeling I need to know."

She opened her mouth, but couldn't find the words to express what she felt—either then or now. Couldn't find a way to tell this young man what a fool she'd been.

"Tell me."

"Can't you guess?"

"Probably," he said again. "But I think it's important that you tell me."

"The summer before my junior year, we were at band camp."

"And?"

"One night after the campfire, he came on to me."

"Came on to you, how?"

"He'd asked me to help him carry some stuff up to the main house. Said he'd walk me back to the cabin I was sharing with five other girls."

She paused, waiting for Ryan to let her off the hook. He simply continued to hold her gaze with eyes that were encouraging, loving and relentless at the same time.

"I was shivering on the way back and he put his arm around me to warm me up."

"How old was this guy?"

"Twenty-four."

Older than Ryan was now. The irony wasn't lost on her.

"He told me I was different from all the other girls. More mature. He said he'd never met anyone like me."

Ryan didn't move. Not a muscle. Anywhere.

"This is too difficult."

"What doesn't kill you makes you stronger."

He had an answer for everything.

Audrey took a deep breath. "He said he'd been fighting his feelings for me all year."

"Go on."

"He said that when I turned eighteen, graduated, he wanted to marry me."

She couldn't tell that Ryan was breathing, he was so still. Silent.

"By the end of camp, I'd slept with him. And by the end of the summer he'd introduced me to his twenty-three-year-old fiancée."

Even in the shadows she could see the tightening of his jaw. But Ryan said nothing. For a very long minute.

"Was he prosecuted?"

"No."

"Why not?"

There were some things that just stay buried. Even in moments that were time out of time.

"I couldn't bear the idea of the scandal. My shame was hard enough to live with. The thought of others knowing what I'd done, how immoral I'd been, how stupid—"

"You were a victim."

"I was stupid."

"You were a young girl trusting a man who was in a position of authority over you. You were supposed to be able to trust him."

"I knew sleeping with him was against school rules."

"Did you also know it was statutory rape?"

"Not then, I didn't." Nor did she know that, when he'd denied the whole thing, saying she'd made it up because she'd had a crush on him, come on to him, and he'd gently told her no, there'd been a way for her to prove differently.

"Did your mother know?"

"Only that I'd slept with a boy and he'd dumped me."

And only because, in the end, she'd had to tell her.

"I'm only guessing here, but based on what you've said about her, it would stand to reason that she used that mistake as proof of your poor judgment with an end goal of convincing you to trust her judgment, instead of your own."

He was good. Far too good.

"Change *used to* to *still uses* and you're pretty much on the mark."

"And the bastard? Whatever happened to him?"

"I have no idea. I was…sick a good part of my senior year and only ran into him once in the hall. I pretended I didn't know him, and he acted like he didn't see me."

With his hand in her hair, lightly caressing her, Ryan kissed her forehead. "I'm so sorry, babe. So sorry you were hurt. That you had to go through it alone."

He had no idea. Nor was he going to.

"It's okay," she said, her heart braced, as always. "It was a long time ago. I learned a hard lesson, though. And if this is some kind of adult repeat, a pretense to get sex, then let's just get the sex and be done with it."

"Is that how you feel about it?"

She didn't know how she felt. Scared. Unsure. Stupid. And weak.

"I didn't feel that way about it back then." It was a cop-out. And also the truth.

"What are you telling me?" He had that intent look again.

This was her chance. The chance to tell him that this relationship wasn't going to work. She could still salvage part of her heart.

"I'm not telling you anything," she finally admitted.

"You're not getting ready to tell me you don't want to see me anymore?"

He'd never sounded more like a kid than he did in that moment. It should have been enough to push her forward.

"No, Ryan, I'm not getting ready to tell you that."

"So then what does it matter what you call it? Sex, making love—the important thing is that we're going to continue together until we find out what it is."

Ryan sounded so calm. So confident. Audrey pretended to believe him.

CHAPTER SEVENTEEN

RYAN DIDN'T KNOW what he'd been expecting at lunch the next day, but the petite, well-dressed woman who stood at the table as they approached, then gave Audrey a hug and a kiss on the cheek, wasn't it.

"Mom, this is Ryan."

Amanda Lincoln's glance was shrewd as she looked him over, taking in the sandals he wore without socks, and probably every single hair on his legs as well, Ryan thought.

"This better be your detective, Audrey Lynn."

Glancing at Audrey, Ryan caught the embarrassment on her face before she could turn her face away from him.

"I hope I am, too, ma'am," he said, taking the seat opposite Audrey's mother. Audrey had her nose. And cheekbones. But there the resemblance ended. The older woman's eyes, while brown, had no depth. No sparkle.

"I told you to call him, and I was right, wasn't I?" Amanda said, leaning in to her daughter. "If you're bringing him to me, he must be important."

Audrey had told her mother about him? She couldn't have given him a nicer gift.

She looked over at him, putting a hand on his leg under the table. A trembling hand.

"Yes, he is," she said.

Ryan covered her hand with his.

"So, Ryan, how long have you been a detective?"

Audrey's stomach clenched around the little bit of salad she'd nibbled at.

"A year."

"Oh." Amanda's eyebrows rose with the "I see" tone in her voice. Audrey knew disaster was about to strike.

They'd almost made it through lunch, too.

"You were a police officer for a long while before that?" her mother asked, dotting her mouth with her napkin in spite of the fact that not a single spec of anything would dare leave itself sitting on her person.

"A couple of years."

Amanda put down her napkin. "That's it? You made detective in record time, then. Did you have previous investigative experience?"

Ryan's look in Audrey's direction was a warning—and perhaps an apology—and she knew she should never have brought him to lunch.

"I have no formal, professional investigative experience, Ms. Lincoln," he said, using the same tone he'd used while charming her mother with answers to her many questions about his favorite television shows, what kind of wine he drank and what he thought of the current presidential delegates. Audrey had yet to tell her mother about meeting Leonard and Becky Wilson. "I have no former professional experience at all. I am, in fact, a somewhat recent high-school graduate. Class of 2004."

Amanda's jaw dropped. As did the glass of tea she was holding.

And while Audrey tried to stay out of her mother's direct line of fire, Ryan, the consummate gentleman, calmly helped clean her mother up.

"THAT COULD HAVE BEEN worse." They were two streets away from the restaurant before Ryan broke the silence in the car.

"Just wait, it will be," Audrey said, staring straight ahead. "My cell phone should be ringing any second now. Please take me home and let's get on with our lives. Alone."

Ryan wasn't prone to hot bursts of anger. His ire was usually of the slow-burning variety. Which was maybe why he didn't contain the shot of pique that rent through him.

"You're a fraud, Audrey Lincoln, you know that?" There was no teasing in his tone. No kindness. Only weeks' worth of frustration. And a fear that he was finding harder and harder to contain.

"What?"

He didn't blame her for looking so shocked. He'd only once come close to talking to her that way and he'd stopped, calmed, after one word.

He didn't much talk to anyone that way.

"Look at you. You say you can't stay away from me, but the truth is you're looking for excuses to get away."

He executed a turn, then another. Watching his speed, but only barely. He could get away with nine miles over. Four, once he got to Audrey's neighborhood.

"How do you figure?" Her expression, when he took a quick glance at her, was not encouraging. He couldn't tell if she was pissed, or retreating to that place she'd been hiding all her life. He only knew she wasn't open to him.

Fine. Apparently he was going to have to wise his twenty-two-year-old baby-ass up and be done with this whole thing. It took two to have a relationship, and even he could figure out that one plus zero didn't equal two.

"Yeah, I admit that our age difference is going to present some challenges along the way," he said, not trying to filter at all. "But they aren't our biggest problem. My rigidness isn't, either. *You* are."

"Okay, we've established that you can point fingers, Ryan. Now how about backing up that childish act with something substantial? Or don't you have anything? Things didn't work out like you'd planned, my mother didn't take your age in stride as you'd apparently hoped, and now you're throwing a tantrum—"

"Audrey," he interrupted.

"What?"

"Shut up."

"Another juvenile respon—"

"Talk about pointing fingers, this one's coming right back at you, my dear," he said, holding his temper in check with effort. What in the hell was the matter with him? He'd mastered self-control years ago.

Unless he was around this woman.

And that meant being with her took away his control, Ryan realized with a sickening in his gut. Shit.

"How is it coming back at me?"

"You're the one acting like a child, Audrey. All scared and hiding and trying to keep yourself safe. You just spent the past hour with some important news to share and, instead, sat back and listened to idle chitchat. Your mother still doesn't know you met your aunt and uncle. My God, you were even afraid to tell her how old I was. You were going to go all the way through lunch and leave without ever letting her know that, either."

"Just because I don't happen to think it's wise to make an announcement doesn't mean I'm a child."

"The mature way to handle a problem is head-on." As quickly as his anger had come, it disappeared. He couldn't be mad at Audrey. She wasn't perfect, but no one tried harder than she did.

Her silence was Ryan's first indication that she was ready to really listen to what he had to say.

"I am completely certain that when we believe something, we make it happen," he said quietly, and even then his voice sounded too loud. He turned up the air conditioner. Maybe a little cooling off would help both of them.

"I've heard that before." He couldn't tell if she believed it or not.

"Every time you say you know it's not going to work strikes a chord of fear in my heart," he said. "You're manifesting our failure."

Signaling their exit, Ryan changed lanes. Turned off the freeway. Past one neighborhood. And another.

"I'm scared." He almost missed her words.

"I know," he said, wishing he could hold her hand, even while he needed his distance. "Me, too."

"I do love you, Ryan." Her eyes were glistening as she looked at him.

"And I love you."

But he was beginning to realize that love wasn't going to be enough.

"WELL, BIG BOY," Audrey approached the man sitting in her living-room chair, with somewhat false determination. "What do you want to do with the rest of our Sunday afternoon?" He wasn't leaving. She wasn't telling him to go.

But she had no idea what to do with him.

"Besides celebrate the fact that we came through our first fight with minimal damage, you mean?"

He was so Ryan. Putting everything right there on the table in front of them. Making them face life in all its glories. Good and bad.

"Yeah, that's what I mean." She'd been more apt to go back to pretending that they were one moment in time with no outside—or inside—forces working against them.

"I usually stop by to see Marcus, but his parents took him to Cleveland to see his aunt and cousin this weekend."

"We could try to catch up on some of the sleep you've lost." What in the hell was the matter with her? She wasn't the type to use sex as a means of escape. Abhorred the idea, actually.

"Are you coming on to me, woman?" Ryan's expression was stern. The hand between her legs told a different story.

And she was going to let it. Regardless of the breakup she knew they both knew was coming, she wanted him. Needed him.

"Depends." She licked his lips.

"On what?" He nipped her tongue.

"On whether or not I'd be successful if I were." She tried to laugh and almost cried. They weren't meant to be but, God, she wished they were.

"Aha. Afraid to commit, even now, huh?" he asked, pinning her with a stare that she'd seen intimidate more than one person on the other end of his handcuffs. "You have to be sure you'll be okay before you try? Do you have any idea how much of life you miss by letting fear hold you back?"

God, yes, she knew. She'd lost an entire family. But this

wasn't about fear. It was about learning from life's lessons. It was about facing reality.

And, maybe for one more moment, it could be about forgetting all that.

Standing, Audrey stepped out of her sandals and reached for the hem of her dress. Pulling it up slowly, in spite of the fact that, in this broad daylight, he'd see every dimple on her thighs, every imperfection on her body, she showed her teacher what a good pupil she could be.

Ryan said he loved her. *Her*. Not some ideal of what he wanted her to be. So she'd give him her. All of her.

And show him that she'd never be enough.

RYAN'S ENTIRE BEING responded to the woman stripping before him. Her skin glistened in the sun's rays, making her more angelic than human.

If he'd ever doubted that joys existed beyond his ability to imagine, he no longer did. He wanted every inch of her.

Standing, he undid shorts that had grown uncomfortably tight, pulling them and the underwear beneath them down only enough to release the evidence of his reaction to Audrey's stunt. The dress came over her head and her eyes widened, focused completely on his groin, then raised to meet his gaze.

"You, uh, got a problem there?"

"I don't think so. Unless you expect me to get these pants back on anytime soon."

"You really should do something about that. There might be an...emergency...or...something." She was staring again.

Tempted to take a hold of himself, just to call her bluff, Ryan resisted. "I'm not sure how to do that," he said, instead.

"Can I help?"

He met her gaze again, feeling the pressure build inside him as she drew closer. If he didn't think of something else, like having to clean Delilah's litter box, he was going to humiliate himself all over her living-room floor. "I don't know," he said, embarrassed by the strangled note in his voice. "What do you think?"

"I think—" Her cell phone rang. Audrey stopped. Glanced toward the couch where she'd dropped her purse—then back.

"I think..." The phone continued to ring. She glanced over again.

Ryan waited. Remained standing there in all his glory.

And then she was before him, staring into his eyes with promises that were probably going to haunt him for the rest of his life.

"I think I can." There was fear mixed with the desire in her gaze.

And Ryan was done playing. Pulling her against him, he kissed the breath of his life into her. And prayed it would somehow be enough.

A COUPLE OF HOURS later, Ryan was completely dressed again, ready to go home and feed Delilah and let Audrey get some preparation done for the breakfast meeting she had the next morning. He stood at the door, watching as she hung up from her voicemail.

"What did she say?"

"There were six messages. One a confirmation of my

meeting in the morning, and four from kids who needed to talk." Suddenly she felt like shit. A selfish shit.

"You don't owe your life twenty-four/seven to the work, babe." His face froze as he stared at her, his words hanging between them.

"I can't believe I just heard Detective Ryan Mercedes say that."

"To be honest, I'm not sure where it came from, either," he said, his voice without vigor, and she knew it was only a matter of time.

Ryan was Ryan. By his very nature, he wasn't going to be able to accept the changes being with her brought to his life. And he was beginning to see that.

He reached for the door. And though every instinct in her body screamed at her to go to him, to give him a goodbye kiss that would bring him back to her, she didn't move.

He was leaving. She didn't know when she was going to see him again. He went back to work the next night, which meant they'd be living in different worlds again.

"What did your mother say?"

He'd moved away from the door. Was standing right in front of her.

"She said that while she finds it embarrassing that her thirty-five-year-old daughter has chosen to have a boy-toy, she would advise, if I really care for you, as opposed to engaging in a sexual fantasy, that I give this relationship every chance to succeed."

"Engaging in a sexual fantasy?"

She'd known people weren't going to understand.

"She's leaving on an extended buying trip but wants to have lunch with us when she gets back." She couldn't look at him. A month seemed like an eternity right then. What were the chances that she and Ryan would even be friends a month from now?

"She wants to have lunch with *us.*"

"Yes." Audrey tried not to hope. Or to build anything substantial out of her mother's pseudo-approval. She was thirty-five. Didn't need her mother's acceptance. She wasn't going to do anything just because her mother wanted her to do it. Not again. Not ever again.

"Did she suggest a date?"

"A month from Wednesday."

With a finger under her chin, Ryan lifted her face. "Nothing like planning ahead. Does she expect an answer right now?" he asked.

They both knew they couldn't give one.

"This is my mother, Ryan. She doesn't ask, she gives edicts. I'm sure she assumes we'll be there."

"If we're together, we will be."

And that, pretty much, was that.

"I'm going," he said, turning to the door. "I'll be back in a couple of hours."

"You're coming back?" It didn't occur to her to be upset that he was telling, not asking. There was too much else to care about at the moment.

"I'd like to sleep with you tonight. Is that okay with you?"

His gaze demanded honesty. "Yes. But…"

"Don't worry, Audrey, I'm not putting the condo up for sale. Or bringing Delilah with me."

"I like Delilah."

"Yeah, well, she's not really fond of traveling and I never

had her declawed. It's best for my skin if she stays right where she is." Turning, he reached for the door handle.

"What's going on here, Ryan?" she blurted to his back. She couldn't let him walk out on her with a promise to be back—but only for a night. "We keep playing with these moments out of time. When do they become back in time?"

He didn't turn around. "I think maybe right now."

"What does that mean?"

Silently he stood there. Let go of the door handle. And slowly turned. "I expect you're going to think this is crazy and come up with all kinds of reasons why it's a bad idea, but I think we should try living together for a couple of weeks."

She started to speak but Ryan held up a hand. "I know, I'm hearing all of the reasons why it's a bad idea from my own inner critics. But I just don't see any other way," he continued. "Think about it, Audrey. We're having sex. We say we care about each other. We keep finding ourselves together, yet we both know that it's not going to work. So why drag it out with months of weekends in bed and stolen meals through the week while we both dread the inevitable? Let's just face this thing. Let it take its course and end up on the other side, whatever that turns out to be, wiser people."

She wanted to argue. Knew she should argue. She opened her mouth to argue. They could as easily face it by ending their relationship right now. But she couldn't find the words to say so. Neither one of them was ready to end it. He was right, of course, that the agony would only be prolonged if they were weekend lovers.

"As soon as I make one choice that I know is not right,

just to please you, you're out of here," she said. "As soon as I start to feel like I have to beg for your love, you leave."

"Fine."

"And as soon as you start to feel cramped, you go."

"Agreed."

"Okay, then."

"Okay."

Without another word Ryan turned back to the door, pulled it open and left.

He was going to be moving in with her.

And she'd never felt more distant from him.

CHAPTER EIGHTEEN

THERE WERE PROBLEMS WITH living together. Other than the obvious difficulty of having to leave for work while his lover was snuggled under the covers going to sleep.

Ryan had no time to live his private life privately.

"Hi, Ry, it's just us. We haven't heard from you in several weeks and wanted to make sure you're okay. Give us a call. I love you."

Ryan listened to the end of his birth mother's message on his way home from work almost a month after he'd taken Audrey to meet his parents. Listened and felt guilty as hell. Sara was still so vulnerable where he was concerned—still that young girl who'd been forced to give up the baby she both loved and feared. The son.

And a grown woman, a mother in spite of the years she hadn't mothered.

He should have called her.

Just as he should have gone back to see his adoptive parents.

Instead, for the past weeks, he'd been living in no man's land with the woman he still couldn't get enough of. And Delilah.

He'd brought the cat over after the first couple of days of running home to feed her. The damn creature had her nose out of joint for the first couple of weeks, refusing to come out from under the living-room couch except to eat—and then only when the house was vacant. Or Ryan was asleep.

Turning onto Audrey's street, his gaze went immediately to the bedroom window, looking for the light that would signify that the love of his life was awake. Seeing it, he glanced farther down, to the tiny bathroom window. It was illuminated, as well.

She was in the shower.

If he hurried, he might be able to join her.

RYAN HAD DINNER cooking—spaghetti with sauce from a jar, frozen garlic bread and fresh broccoli—by the time Audrey's car pulled into the garage that night.

He'd made a decision and had to talk to her about it.

"Hey, babe," he greeted her, opening the door from the garage into the kitchen for her and taking her briefcase. They'd perfected the pretense of happily ever after in their day-to-day living—but only because they'd isolated themselves from the real world.

Instead of ending their time out of time and moving back into real time as they'd intended, they'd managed to stretch a moment into a month.

"Hi." She didn't quite smile as she leaned over for his kiss. He figured that she knew as well as he did that they were living on borrowed time.

"You're awfully quiet this evening," she said as they finished a mostly silent dinner.

Resisting the urge to jump up and tend to the dishes, which, in his other life, he'd have been more apt to leave for a day or two, Ryan remained in his seat. Tried to find the right words. Delilah jumped up onto the table and, willing to take the distraction, he shooed her away, giving her long, sleek back a stroke just because it was there.

Audrey was still waiting.

"We need to talk." He finally got the words out.

"Okay." Her lips tight, Audrey looked as though she was bracing herself. "Are you missing your place? Your independence?"

"It's not that." But in all fairness, he had to ask. "Are you?"

Her smile was more poignant than happy. "No, Ryan, you've been the perfect housemate."

Yeah, and perfection was an illusion. At some point one of them was going to have to quit trying so hard to make this work and just relax and be real.

They'd had a call from her mother, confirming their lunch on Wednesday. Audrey was planning to tell Amanda about Leonard and Becky then.

She'd seen the older couple several times over the past weeks, always while Ryan was home sleeping—deliberately, he was sure, but, true to current form, he hadn't called her on it.

He hadn't wanted to start a fight that would be the beginning of the end.

But he couldn't go on like this. He took her hand.

"I think it's time for you to meet Sara."

"Your biological mother."

"Yeah."

"Does she know about me?"

"Not yet. I haven't called her since I moved in here."

"I thought you were in touch every week."

"I was."

The reason for his neglect obvious, and now in the open, Ryan added, "But she's going to know about you within the hour. I need to stop and see them tonight. It's been too long. Marcus Ryan will probably be sitting up by now. Or talking or something. Anyway, I think you should come with me."

Audrey pulled her hand away, started stacking their plates and silverware.

"You go ahead this time, Ryan. Tell her about me and then we'll see." She stood and walked into the kitchen to put the dishes in the sink.

Ryan followed her, wrapping his arms around her from behind. "Please. We have to start facing things. And Sara's easy. She won't judge."

"Mm-hmm."

"I mean it."

She stood there, not turning on the water. "Just like you meant it with your mother?"

"That was different. Mom had a momentary blip in her emotional radar. She relapsed back about fifteen years in her role in my life and she apologized. Sara wasn't even known to me fifteen years ago, nor is our relationship such that she'd judge what I do or try to give me advice. We just have this need to spend time together on a somewhat regular basis."

Turning, Audrey studied him. "Then why do you have to push yourself to introduce me to her?"

She'd put him on one of the spots he'd been avoiding.

With his own hands firmly at his back, Ryan withstood her scrutiny. And opened his mouth.

"It's not just her. You meet her, you meet her husband."

And that was a bit too close to Ryan for comfort. Opening himself up that far wasn't wise.

But then, neither was this fragile, inauthentic existence.

"Mark? I thought you hardly knew him."

As always, Ryan's heart shuttered as he considered the man who'd fathered him. "I know him enough."

"So what's the problem?"

"Mark is." There, he'd admitted it. And was still standing.

"He's not going to approve of me?"

"I don't approve of *him*." Ryan almost bit out the words. "They will both welcome you with open arms. They'd welcome an alien if I brought one to their house. It's not them meeting you I worry about. It's you meeting him."

Stepping away, Audrey rested her hands on the counter.

"Why? Because he's my age? Is that what this is about? You're afraid I'm going to relate to your parents more than I do to you? But wait, you said Mark is all that worries you, right, not Sara? So is this guy some kind of womanizer? A charmer that no one can resist? Don't you trust me any better than that?" She stopped the tirade only long enough to shake her head. "I can't believe this!"

To Ryan, her outburst was merely confirmation of what he'd already known. Their avoidance of anything that was a problem between them was building inner tensions that were escalating to explosive proportions.

"Audrey." Ryan took her elbows, held on. "Stop." He waited for her to look at him. "You're completely misunderstanding."

With doubt-clouded eyes, she waited. And Ryan knew his time was up. One way or the other. Either he gave more of himself to her. Or he had to leave.

He took a deep breath. Pictured himself walking out her

front door to the safety and freedom that awaited him at the
condo he'd slept in that afternoon.

"I don't want you to meet Mark because I don't want you
to associate me with him." Pouring out the depths of his heart
was not what he'd intended. "I don't want to be colored by
his genes in my blood. Period."

Her brow furrowed as she continued to stare up at him.
"Why? You said once that he spent time in prison. Is that it?
I meet up with a lot of ex-cons in my line of work. I care
about their spouses and kids." Her soft voice almost broke
his heart in that moment. Or the truth he had to tell did. "I
certainly don't ever see those spouses and kids as a reflection of their husbands and fathers."

"Mark is a rapist." In the end, there was no other way to
say it. "I am the result of a gang rape when my mother was
sixteen years old."

Audrey had to sit down. "I…don't know what to say." Or
what to think. How to help him. How did you assist with
understanding when you didn't understand yourself? She,
whose everyday life was filled with troubled kids, had never
come up against something like this.

"Your biological mother married her rapist?"

Ryan nodded.

"Tell me about it."

Seemed like the only place to start.

"They were at a frat party at a lake in Maricopa, a small
community outside Dayton. Sara, posing as a twenty-one-
year-old, was there as a rebellion against her far-too-strict
sheriff father. Everyone was drinking. No one remembers
much after that. Sara woke up the next morning with her
father's coat wrapped around her naked body as he carried

her away from the lake. Her clothes were strewn around on the ground where he'd found her, passed out."

Ryan paced around the table.

"A medical exam showed that Sara had been pretty brutally penetrated."

He made it around the table one more time. Audrey wanted to grab his hand as he passed.

"Later that afternoon a kid came forward, said he knew who'd done it. He named three freshmen. Later tests proved that all three of them had been with her that night."

"Oh, my God." She'd been hoping, in spite of Ryan's agitation, to hear that it had all been a mistake. That Sara and Mark had been secretly in love.

Or at least that the sex had been consensual.

As though just realizing she was there, Ryan gave her a hard look. And then sat. His elbows on his knees, he stared at his hands.

"All three were convicted and sent to prison. Only Mark is still alive."

Alive and married to his victim? How in the hell had that happened?

"But not necessarily your father."

Ryan glanced up at her, his lips twisting. "Oh, yes. He's my biological father. I submitted to DNA testing last year."

"You sound as though you wish you hadn't." She knew how to do this, how to help young people through times of emotional familial crisis. How to determine what they needed and how best to get it for them.

She didn't know how to sit in her home where she'd made love with a young person and do her job at the same time. Or how to ignore the fact that Ryan's struggles went a lot deeper than she'd thought.

"I don't know that it matters," Ryan said now. "Fact is, whether it was Mark or one of the other two bastards, I'm still what I am. The son of a rapist." His eyes were shadowed when he looked up at her. "How does anyone know what compels a man—or allows a man—to take a natural, God-given instinct and twist it into something devilish and sinful? Who knows if it's a temperament characteristic, the result of his environment or some kind of genetic malfunction that can be passed down?"

"Surely you don't think that." But ideas were occurring to her. Was Ryan so rigid, not out of an inordinately strong sense of right and wrong, but out of fear? Of himself? Of the darker capabilities possibly lurking inside of every human being?

Was his fear of his parentage why he'd been a virgin at twenty-two?

"I don't know what I think," Ryan finally answered, drawing out the sentence as though, if he withheld the words long enough, he'd be able to figure everything out.

"How long have you known that you were a product of the rape?"

"I found out for sure last summer, but I'd suspected since I was fourteen."

Suspected. And feared?

"You know the four general rapist profiles, Ryan. Most often, the act has nothing to do with sex, but with a need for power and or control. That need is bred in someone. Not born to them."

He nodded. Swallowed. Continued to watch her.

She wanted to take him into her arms. "What profile does Mark fit into?"

Running his fingers over his hair, Ryan sighed. "None."

The admission seemed to come with difficulty.

"I investigated him last year," Ryan continued, his statement not surprising her. "The guy had a sizable savings and an A+ credit rating. He owned his classic-car-restoration business free and clear. His probation officer reported regularly that the state was wasting money by paying him to meet with Mark, but he enjoyed their visits tremendously. Mark's got a law degree. And I couldn't find a single person who had a beef with the guy."

"How long was he in prison?"

"Five years."

"And when he got out he never repeated the act or exhibited any other violent behavior?"

"No."

"But he was violent that night with Sara?"

"Not necessarily." He rubbed the back of his neck. "Someone was, and Mark was there, a part of it all. He had sex with her during the same incident involving two other men also coming inside her. But other than what can be told from the solid evidence, no one really knows what happened. No one remembered a thing the next day."

"That's odd in and of itself."

"We found out last year that their drinks had been laced with PCP." Ryan went on to tell her the rest of the fantastic story—the murder he'd suspected after years of teenaged research, the pushing he'd done, Sara's seeking out Mark and his agreement to help. The final discovery that Ryan was right—his grandfather had missed key evidence and the rape had been used as a cover-up to murder.

Audrey nodded. "It was a popular date-rape drug in the seventies, wasn't it?"

"Yeah."

"And none of them knew about it?"

"No."

"So if Mark was drugged, he wasn't really guilty at all."

"He had gang sex with a sixteen-year-old."

"PCP enhances sexual drive."

"But it doesn't obliterate all morality. Besides, Sara was a virgin. He should have been able to tell that. To stop himself."

"Unless he wasn't first."

"And then we're right back to the gang-sex part. He did it to her after other guys had already done so."

"Sara has obviously come to terms with Mark's part in the incident since she married him. And just had his baby."

"Sara's too steeped in guilt over her own part in the whole fiasco to point fingers. She wasn't supposed to be there at all. Had never had anything to drink before and went there purposely to get drunk. She pretended to be older than she was. Those guys had no way of knowing, even if they'd been sober, that they were engaging in statutory rape. And all three of them went to prison.

"Besides, she's the forgiving type. And she's too trusting."

Sara Dalton sounded like someone Audrey would have gravitated to if circumstances were different. Someone who might have been a friend—if not for the fact that Audrey was sleeping with the woman's twenty-two-year-old son.

Watching the expressions chase themselves across

Ryan's face—the disgust, distaste, fear—as his words rang in the quiet room, Audrey searched for a way to reach him.

"This is a gray area, Ry," she said softly. "There's nothing black and white about a man being drugged without his knowledge. Nothing black and white about actions resulting from hallucinogenic substances. How can he be held accountable for something he doesn't remember? Something he did because he was being controlled by an illegal foreign substance?"

"He couldn't help the PCP. But no one tied him up and stuck his penis inside a sixteen-year-old girl."

Ryan wasn't bending. Even a little bit.

Audrey tried another route. "How does he feel about what happened?"

"I don't know."

"You don't know?"

"I don't talk to Mark much."

"Do you talk to him at all?"

"Not really."

"Don't you think you should?"

"I don't know what to think. And when I don't know, I wait to act until I do know."

She couldn't argue that point.

IN THE END, Audrey went with Ryan to visit the Daltons. He was right—it was time for them to quit kidding themselves and face the fact that they had separate lives. They had to get back to living their lives.

They had to start seeing each other as they really were. Not as the fantasy they'd created.

As they were driving over, silent in his truck, Audrey

didn't miss the irony of realizing that her mother had been right again.

She'd been living in a sexual fantasy.

Glancing at Ryan in the fading light of day, she saw a different man than she'd seen before. His rigidity was suddenly not the completely positive trait she'd previously considered it. Standing up for what you believed was one thing.

Judging and condemning, something else entirely. Acceptance—forgiveness—was sometimes more important than right and wrong. If Ryan didn't bend a bit, life would eventually break him.

No one was perfect.

Sara Dalton, a strikingly beautiful woman with long, dark hair and warm, green eyes, stood with baby Marcus cradled against her chest an hour later. She'd asked Audrey to come see the nursery.

Remembering her time alone with Ryan's adoptive mother several weeks before, Audrey had been reluctant to be alone with the woman.

But with Sara, Marcus and Audrey out of the way, Ryan would be alone with his biological father. A man Audrey liked tremendously, a man she trusted even after only a couple of hours of acquaintance. Maybe some good would come out of the next minutes. For all of them.

Maybe Ryan's time with her, their time together, wouldn't be a total waste.

"I'm glad Ryan brought you over," Sara said. "I wanted to meet you." She'd said she had to change the baby before his nine-o'clock feeding, but she'd yet to put the baby down.

"I wanted to meet you, too," Audrey said, wondering if she dared enlist this woman's aid in helping Ryan to accept the past and the father who, while a strong, self-contained man, obviously needed Ryan's forgiveness. And approval.

Probably as much as Ryan needed to be able to give it.

"You did? Why?" Sara asked.

"Because you mean so much to Ryan."

Sara laughed self-consciously—the first time Audrey had seen a lack of confidence in the woman all night. "I'm not so sure about that. He's only known me a year."

"I'm sure. He gets a protective look on his face every time he mentions you. Your opinion matters to him."

Audrey felt so awkward standing there with a woman who was much more her peer than her son could ever be. The fear of losing Ryan grew stronger by the second.

"You think that's why he waited so long to bring you here?" Sara asked.

"I think that's part of it." Audrey was certain it was. Ryan didn't want to face the truth about them, about their age difference, about their issues, and Sara's existence pretty much put it right in their faces.

"I'm married to a man who raped me," Sara said softly, "which hardly leaves me in a position to judge others. Or to think that choices should be made based on what others think. Ryan is a smart man. A responsible adult more mature than many men twice his age. The fact that he's chosen to love you is not for me to question."

Narrowing her eyes, Audrey watched the other woman. The speech was too rehearsed-sounding to have come in the shock of the moment.

"You knew about me before Ryan called tonight," she guessed.

Sara didn't look away as she nodded. "Harriet called a couple of weeks ago."

After her conversation with Ryan. So much for Ryan's belief that the older woman would no longer meddle in his life—or his decision to love a woman thirteen years his senior.

"And?" Audrey asked. She was too old for game playing. Too weary of fighting the fears, the inevitability of her breakup with Ryan, to pretend.

"I don't agree with Harriet," Sara started to say, and Audrey was almost surprised, until the other woman continued, "But I am worried about Ryan."

"Because when I'm sixty and sporting cellulite and wrinkles he'll be forty-seven and catching the eyes of thirty-somethings?" And she'd be home begging him to still love her—feeling needy and alone, sixteen again, instead of sixty.

"No." Sara frowned. "Ryan's not that shallow. It goes deeper than that."

She needed to be home where her heart was safe. Where she could soak in a hot tub all alone, crawl under her covers and go to sleep.

"They say that boys go for women like their mothers," Sara said slowly, hugging her baby up to her shoulder, rocking him back and forth, as she looked Audrey straight in the eye.

"Right."

"Usually that refers to character traits."

Sara wasn't telling her anything new.

"Did you know that Ryan has been watching me, following my life, since he was fourteen?"

"Yes." But only because Harriet had told her.

"He said he needed to know me, to be close to me, but

that he couldn't hurt his mother's feelings by actually having me in his life."

That last part sounded like Ryan. And any number of other adopted kids.

"He's been investigating me since he first found out who I was."

"He had a natural need to know his mother," Audrey said, thinking of the lifelong hole in her existence where her father was concerned.

"Right. And while he could garner facts, he didn't know me, or my character traits, until this year. And now suddenly he's taken up with a woman who's practically my age…"

The blood drained from Audrey's face. She was cold in spite of the warmth in the nursery. The warmth outside.

The warmth in Sara Dalton's eyes. A woman who was more her peer than…

"You think he's with me because of my age. Because I remind him of you. You think he's trying to recapture some of the security he lost when you gave him away."

"I don't think it," Sara clarified. "I don't know it. I'm just afraid of it."

And just like that, Audrey was afraid of it, too.

CHAPTER NINETEEN

"THAT WASN'T SO BAD."

As she spoke, Ryan glanced over at Audrey, having difficulty reading her expression beneath the unnatural red glow from the stoplight above them. Something was different about her.

"What did Sara say to you back there?" He didn't have time to gently persuade Audrey to talk. He was due at the precinct in twenty minutes and was still five minutes from her house.

"Nothing, really. We chatted about the baby mostly."

"Yeah, I got that. And about the wallpaper and the fact that she still works for her father's foundation, but is able to do so from home…"

"So what did you and Mark talk about?" she asked, her voice conversationally sweet—and not personal enough. "It seems to have put you in a bad mood."

"Your prevarication is frustrating me," he countered. "Just tell me what she said and let's deal with it together."

"Ryan, I told you—"

"You aren't going to convince me that Sara had you alone and didn't mention you and me. Together." They were only two streets away from home.

"Actually, I mentioned us."

Now they were getting somewhere. He turned into their neighborhood.

"And?"

"She said, married to Mark, she's hardly in a place to judge and that she believes in everyone's right to make their own choices."

Not exactly an avowal of support, but it could have been worse.

"She also said that you're more mature than a lot of men twice your age."

He made a mental note to thank Sara. "So why are you being so distant?"

"I'm not. Really."

"You always say *really* when you're hiding something."

"And you're far too observant." She made a noise that sounded like an attempted chuckle, but it didn't work. "I'm just tired, Ry," she continued, reaching for her seat belt as he pulled into their drive. "And I'm worried about you. About you and Mark."

He had to go. Had work to do. Had to shut her up. And still, tonight, as with every night, he hated to leave her.

"My feelings for my biological father have nothing to do with us."

"What if someone drugged me, Ry? What if, not realizing that, I got in my car and drove and killed someone? Would you hate me, too?"

Rape was different.

And she had a point. He just wasn't ready to contemplate it.

"You're sure that's what's bothering you?" he asked,

instead, tending to what he had time for. "My aversion to my father?"

"Yes." There was conviction in the word. But she didn't look him straight in the eye.

He was going to be late.

"You have nothing to worry about there," he said far more quickly than he'd have liked. "No matter what you might do, I know you. And because of that, I believe in you. We'll talk more about this tomorrow, okay?"

"Okay." Audrey smiled, and there was no sparkle in her eyes.

"Everything's going to be fine. I promise."

She nodded.

But there was something vital missing from her good-night kiss.

RYAN TOOK the long way home Tuesday morning, replaying, as he had many times during the night, last evening's events, not sure what to make of any of it. Not sure what to do.

Once again he'd managed to avoid the man whose body had fathered him.

"I'm going to check on Jerry," were the only words he'd spoken to the older man the night before.

Jerry, the fourteen-pound cockapoo rescue dog he'd given to Sara the previous summer when he'd thought she was going to be living alone, had been banned to the backyard when he'd jumped up on Audrey.

Ryan had stayed with Jerry until he'd seen the light in the nursery go out. He'd barely made it back to the living room ahead of the two women.

So he'd had an out the night before. He wasn't always

going to be that lucky. Which meant he was going to have to resolve his feelings for his father one way or another, he saw that now—even if that meant staying out of the man's home. He owed it to Audrey. To Sara and Marcus. And to himself. Sometimes life just plain sucked.

Audrey didn't mention anything about the night before when he joined her in the shower a few minutes later. Nor did she speak of the desperation he felt in her kiss during the extra fifteen minutes they took in the bed afterward. She didn't mention Mark or Sara or the tension lining their lives when she kissed him goodbye.

But he knew it was there. Knew, too, that it was time to get on with his life. No matter what that meant.

Thinking he'd go back to his condo to sleep, as he'd done once or twice during the past week, finding peace and solace in his aloneness there, Ryan picked up the phone first and dialed.

"Mark Dalton's office."

He didn't know what he'd expected, but a receptionist wasn't it.

"Is Mark in?" He couldn't bring himself to call the man Mr. as though he respected him. Or as though Mark deserved the respect.

"May I ask who's calling?"

No, you may not. Hand on his hip, Ryan almost hung up. Then he saw the wet towel Audrey had left on the end of the bed. A bed he needed to fall into and sleep life's problems away.

They were ganging up on him.

"Ryan Mercedes."

The click came almost immediately.

"Ryan? What can I do for you?" Mark sounded more hopeful than curious.

Ryan had hoped the woman had hung up on him.

"You doing anything for lunch?" He couldn't find the wherewithal to fake a nicety. Like hello.

"Nothing I can't reschedule."

"I need to grab a couple of hours of sleep. Can you meet me at Hathaway's at twelve-thirty?"

"Absolutely."

That was it. No questions asked.

Ryan really wanted to hate the man.

TAKEISHA BAKER mangled the tissue Audrey had given her.

"I need your help, Ms. Lincoln. I just can't do like they want. I get that my ma needs money. Especially now that Daniel's in jail. But I just can't do it. It isn't fair. It isn't right. Not to me or any kid."

"Terminating a pregnancy is a huge decision, sweetie." Audrey chose her words carefully. She'd been with the girl, from a doctor's appointment to a counselor and now here, for most of Tuesday morning. Her mother's boyfriend was in jail. Detective Dosendall was fully recovered. And it still wasn't over for the girl. "This is a decision that you will live with for the rest of your life."

"If I got a life." The girl's statement wasn't dramatic. Or threatening. It just was.

"If I have this baby, I've got no hope left, Ms. Lincoln. Even though it's Daniel's, I'd love it and be tied to it. And it wouldn't matter if I wasn't, my ma would take it and then it would always be there, waiting for me to love it. I'm only fifteen. I've got two years left in high school.

How long you think I'm gonna be able to keep going there if I've got a kid at home? I'll tell you what I'm going to have to do, Ms. Lincoln. Get a job, that's what."

Audrey listened with what she prayed to God was an unbiased ear. Her job was to try to give the young woman other options—which she'd already done—then to determine if Takeisha was mature enough to know what she was doing. To make certain that she had considered all of the ramifications of her choices.

Audrey's job was not to feel anything personal whatsoever.

"You've talked to the doctor," she said. "You know the risks. We've talked about your other options, about adoption and planned parenthood. About the halfway house."

It was a facility that Audrey had helped establish. One where she regularly gave free legal advice. One that she believed in with all her heart.

For the right girls. And women. In the right circumstances.

"Yes, ma'am," Takeisha said. "If I did this to me, if I was with a boy and made a baby, then I'd think I owed it to me and the baby and to God to see this thing through. But I didn't do this, Ms. Lincoln. I have a life, too. And I'm little and the doctor says I might have a tough time of it, being so young and all. I could end up like my ma, not being able to have kids someday. When I'm ready."

It was the girl's clear gaze that told Audrey they'd talked enough.

"Okay, sweetie. If you're sure this is what you want to do, you call me tomorrow and I'll advocate for you. And once the judge signs the papers, I'll go with you to have the procedure and to see that you get home okay afterward."

Fresh tears sprang to Takeisha's eyes. "Thank you,

Ms. Lincoln. I can't remember ever having someone be so nice to me…"

Audrey saw the girl out of the conference room in the city building that housed her little office, certain she'd made the right choice.

And then, back at her desk, with the door firmly closed, she sat down and cried.

"THE WHITE CHILI'S pretty good," Mark Dalton said, not even looking at his menu as he sat across the window booth from Ryan. As if on cue, their waitress, stopped by their table.

"You guys ready?"

White chicken chili was a Hathaway's special and one of his favorites. "I'll have a buffalo burger," Ryan said. "Coleslaw, instead of fries."

Buffalo had half the fat of beef, fewer calories, less cholesterol. And a nation of Indians who'd survived on buffalo meat had escaped even one case of cancer among them.

Ryan had just read so on the menu.

Slouched back comfortably in the booth, he busied himself with a slow stir of cream and sugar he didn't want in his coffee.

He'd dressed up for the occasion. Instead of his usual jacket and tie, he'd gone all out with an old faded T-shirt, cutoff shorts and flip-flops.

"I liked Audrey," Mark said after the waitress left. "You've made a good choice."

Ryan wanted to tell the man to wipe his lover's name from his lips and never say it again. "Thank you."

"How are things at work?"

Ryan looked at the other man—his biological father—

trying not to see the resemblances. "This isn't a social lunch," he said.

"I didn't think it was. You can barely be civil to me."

"So why make small talk?"

"Because I've learned that life is a lot more valuable when lived with kindness."

Valuable. A word Ryan might have chosen. He valued life. Which was why desecrating it was unforgivable. This man had ruined the life of a sixteen-year-old girl.

"I can't stand that you're my father."

"I know."

"I need resolution."

"Okay."

"I've never hated anyone before in my life. But I really think I hate you."

Mark didn't flinch. "I understand."

"What's with you?" Leaning forward, Ryan kept his voice low, but he couldn't hold back the venom. "You sit there so calmly taking personal insult as though you don't have a care in the world. Do you have any idea what you've done? How many lives you affected? Do you care about anything?"

Ashamed of himself, of his uncharacteristic lack of compassion, Ryan slumped back. Was it any surprise Mark Dalton brought out the worst in him? The man had given him dirty genes.

No, that wasn't right.

But what was?

Staring into his coffee, disliking the light-brown color because it signified weakness, he waited. Wondered how to extricate himself from the pointless meeting.

Mark wasn't going to say anything. Even now, he just sat and took. Did the man have no backbone at all?

The waitress brought their lunch, asked if they wanted anything else and didn't seem to notice that neither of them were talking. To her. Or to each other.

"Like you, Ryan Mercedes, I care about justice." Mark didn't touch the food in front of him. "I care about people. I care about right and wrong. I care deeply about my family. What I don't much care about is how others see me. I was branded a long time ago in a way that I will never be able to change. I had a choice back then. I could believe the branding, live it and become something I was not—a two-bit criminal who would spend his days on the dark side of life, driven by evil and revenge and a bitter spirit. Or I could live from the inside out, listening to my conscience, to my inner voice, and become the man I was meant to be."

Ryan's gaze had become locked on the other man. As though spellbound, he couldn't break away.

And he couldn't stand being there.

"You raped an innocent young girl." He pushed his burger away. The smell was nauseating him.

"You're a detective, Ryan. You, more than most, know that, in order to gain understanding, it's best to stick to the facts. The fact is, I had sex with a minor who I thought was older than I was. Whether that sex was consensual or not, no one knows."

Yeah, but…

"She was bruised where a woman should never be bruised."

"And I pray to God every single night that I was not responsible for a single one of those bruises. I am not that type of man. I cannot believe that of myself."

Eyes narrowed, Ryan said, "But the fact is, you don't know that you didn't do it."

"And that is a fact I will live with for the rest of my life."

And now Ryan had the man where he needed him, "Another fact for you—you participated in gang sex."

Mark's lips pursed—the only sign that Ryan had hit a mark. But the man never broke eye contact. "And that, Ryan, is the one fact I can neither escape nor live with. It will keep me from ever truly knowing real peace in this lifetime. I was celibate for twenty-one years because of it. But that's the funny thing about love. It's stronger than sin. Stronger than any mistake. It is the be-all and end-all. I know this. I believe this. And still, I have moments, days, when I feel unworthy of Sara's love. Of Marcus's love."

The sincerity in Mark's tone reached something inside Ryan. Touched him where he didn't want to be touched. Not by this man.

"But you feel worthy of my hatred." He was beginning to get a picture that scared the hell out of him.

"I understand your hatred," Mark qualified. "I've found in the past year of observing you while you're in my home, with my family, that you and I are a lot alike. In ways I wouldn't have thought were genetic. Were I you, I would hate me, too."

Ryan was not like this man. He just wasn't. He wouldn't allow such a thing. "So you just accept that."

"What choice do I have?" Mark sat back, still watching him. "I've done what I've done, Ryan. I can't change that. Nor can I change how you view what I've done. But along with that, I am who I am. Now there is something I *can* affect. Living true to the man inside me is where my power lies. Where my peace lies. And that is something I think you relate to completely."

Ryan rejected the comment. He couldn't share anything so intimate, so all consuming, with this…this…this…man.

"I don't expect you, of all people, to forgive me my past," Mark said. "Your very existence is marked by that night. That mistake. It works the other way, too. You are a constant reminder to me of a sin I will never escape. But I am alive for a reason, son. I have time on this earth to bring some small bit of good to this world. Time to learn how to forgive."

Ryan couldn't afford softness. His world was at stake. "Who've you got to forgive?" He sounded like a belligerent kid. But certainly Mark wasn't referring to Sara, a naive girl who'd lied about her age. Or a sheriff who'd been hell-bent on avenging his only child and missed a key piece of evidence. Neither of those things compared to what he'd done.

Mark's answer, when it came, touched Ryan again. "Myself." Mark stood, threw a twenty on the table. "You will never be as hard on me as I am on myself," he said. "So do what you have to do. Bring it on. I will stand beside you and take it for as long as I am alive. And if you ever need anything—*anything*—for any reason, you call me and I will be there. No questions asked."

Ryan sat there, staring after the tall, blond, muscular man, suspecting, for a wild second, that he'd just met his match.

Until he picked up the bill and, leaving all the food on the table untouched and the twenty as a tip, went to the cash register.

Mark Dalton knew all the right words. He wanted to suck

Ryan into the little family he'd created. Probably because he needed Ryan's approval for Sara's sake. And Marcus's.

He wanted Ryan to believe they were alike in ways that mattered most. He wanted Ryan to believe in his unconditional love.

Ryan wasn't convinced.

CHAPTER TWENTY

RYAN WASN'T in any better mood, or any less confused, when he got a call from the prosecutor that afternoon. Dennis Hall was working on the Takeisha Baker case. Defense for Daniel Wood was moving to suppress Takeisha's testimony in the hospital, as she was a minor who'd been questioned without parental supervision.

They were grasping at straws and Ryan was quick to assure Dennis that they'd taken all proper measures in securing the girl's testimony. He agreed to testify at the pretrial hearing scheduled later in the week.

And then Dennis passed on another piece of information.

"The poor kid's pregnant."

Ryan's heart sank. "She got a boyfriend that quickly?"

"The kid's Wood's."

"But they did all the medical procedures…"

"He'd been with her before."

Ryan swore. Sometimes life's timing was ironic. He'd spent a good majority of the day fretting over an ancient teenage pregnancy, and now this.

"It's what her mother wanted," Ryan said, more thinking aloud than anything. "The kid's in trouble. She has her whole life hanging in the balance, and she won't get any help from the one person whose job it is to be there for her."

"Don't fret that one," Dennis said. "She's got help. They assigned Audrey Lincoln to her case."

Audrey. Thank God. Some good news in an otherwise bad day.

"Rumor has it you and she are pretty good friends these days."

"Rumor is rumor because the truth is no one's business," Ryan countered easily.

"Got it. Well, for what it's worth, she could do worse."

"So could I."

Dennis's chuckle sounded tired. "Yeah, you could. That woman is a steamroller when it comes to looking out for those kids. She's already approached the judge, advocating on Takeisha's behalf for an abortion without parental approval or permission. It's on the docket for tomorrow morning…"

Ryan was sure Dennis finished his sentence. Said goodbye. But he couldn't testify to it. He hadn't heard a word past the roaring in his head.

And his heart.

THE HOUSE was dark. Hungry, having grown used to having dinner almost ready by the time she got home from work, Audrey couldn't help a stab of disappointment. That was quickly followed by fear.

Something had happened to Ryan. Otherwise, if he'd had to go out, wasn't going to be home for dinner, he'd have called.

Unless, she told herself as she pulled into the garage and saw his truck parked in the spot next to hers, he'd slept through his alarm. It would be the first time since he'd been there, but he'd told stories of having done it before.

And he'd been existing on little more than four hours or

so a day of rest for most of the past month. If he kept up that way for much longer, he was going to have serious sleep-deprivation issues.

Comforting herself with the knowledge that at least he hadn't left her yet, as she let herself quietly inside, she thought about the state of their freezer and canned-goods cupboards. They'd shopped together on Sunday—as they had every Sunday since Ryan had started staying with her. She could make chili. With onions and cheese. She'd fill a tray. With crackers and the sweet tea Ryan liked so much. And then she'd wake him with dinner in bed.

But first, she'd take a peek in at him. Just to make sure he was there. He slept naked most of the time, the covers curled around his hips, his long legs exposed, and Audrey felt a pang that took away her appetite as she faced the fact that she could be losing the right to the sight very soon.

Drawing close to the bedroom door, she walked on tiptoe. She didn't want to wake him. Which was why she'd turned on no lights in the windowless hallway. And prayed that she didn't trip over Delilah. The cat was underfoot a lot these days, now that she was growing more comfortable in Audrey's home. Not that Audrey was complaining. Having constant company was nice.

Better than nice.

When Ryan eventually left, she'd have to get a cat. Or maybe a dog. Or a bird.

In contrast to the hall, the bedroom was suffused with light. Which made it very easy to notice the empty, made-up bed, and beyond, the bathroom with towels hung and dry. There was no residual steam from a recent shower. If Ryan had gone to bed that day, he'd been up a while.

Backtracking through the house, her stomach in knots, Audrey thought back to that morning, to anything she might have said or Ryan might have said to explain this change in routine. The only thing out of the ordinary was that he hadn't called.

He called most every day when he got up.

She'd been so busy she hadn't thought much of the missed communication. Besides, there'd been a few days when he'd missed.

There was no sign of him in the den. No note on the hall table. Or the kitchen table. And in the living room...

There was Ryan. Sitting on the couch.

"Hi." She looked over every inch of him as she approached. And knew, when her searching reached his face, his eyes, that something was horribly wrong.

He was leaving. She'd known the time would come. In truth, she'd known it was coming soon. The life they'd been living wasn't natural, isolated as it was.

Because it was what they always did, every single time they came together, she leaned down for a kiss—as though the act could somehow fix all the problems between them.

He didn't move away. But didn't really return the kiss, either.

"Why didn't you say something when I came in?"

"I've been sitting here trying to make sense of the turns life has taken."

Her stomach recoiled as fear engulfed her. Panic. This was really it.

"What turns?" she asked when she thought she was braced to handle whatever came next.

Ryan shrugged, his eyes reflecting more emptiness than

hurt. She'd never before seen the old shorts and T-shirt that he was wearing. And wondered what the change signified.

Sitting down on the couch, a full foot between them, she thought about all that Ryan had taught her. About facing challenges. About not hiding.

"When are you going?"

"What?" He stared at her.

"I assume you've decided to move out." She pushed further. Getting through.

She could fall apart when he was gone. When he wouldn't see that she hadn't changed all that much, after all. Had grown hardly at all.

"Why would you assume that?"

Well... "Because it's obvious things aren't working out."

"We need to talk, Audrey." His voice didn't hold even a hint of the softness she'd grown used to. And begun to crave. "You're right, we can't go on like this."

"Okay." His bags weren't packed. She had a couple of hours, at least. "So talk."

"I had lunch with Mark today."

Apparently it hadn't gone well. "Tell me about it."

His eyes were still dark, dead, when he looked at her. "There's not much to tell. Just made me think about forgiveness. About right and wrong and what happens when the lines are so blurred there *are* no rights and wrongs."

"I'm not sure where this is going."

"Dennis Hall called today."

"What did he want?" And what did the prosecutor have to do with their private lives?

"He said that you're advocating for Takeisha Baker's abortion."

"That's right." Again, where was the connection between professional lives and their private one? Unless... She grew hot as realization dawned. Dennis must know about them.

He must have said something to Ryan that embarrassed him.

"It's clearly understood that no one in the courts, including judges, have to take on those issues. You can recuse yourself on the basis of personal morality."

"I know that."

Ryan nodded. Looked at her as though he didn't know her. "I would have bet my life that you'd take that out."

"Why? The child is fifteen years old. She was raped. This is her body we're talking about. Her life. I've talked with her extensively. Took her through all the necessary and recommended appointments. She knows what she's doing and I want to help her."

"Why? Abortion is killing an innocent child. Why would you want to be involved with that?"

"Ryan! You can't be serious. We're talking about a fetus that may or may not develop properly, in a body that is not ready for childbirth. Takeisha could die. What right is there in that?"

"My mother was raped, Audrey. If she'd had someone like you around back then, I wouldn't be here. I wouldn't even exist." His voice was almost hard and she knew that this wasn't really about abortion. The abortion was only the catalyst, the surface issue that was allowing him to play out what was really going on inside him. It was his excuse to get away from her and back to the self he was comfortable with. The self he knew and wanted to be.

He was right. They had a real problem. One Audrey knew was going to get much bigger as soon as she opened her mouth. She and Ryan might share some miraculous emotional connection, but they were clearly not meant for each other.

He was going to leave her. But not sometime in the future for another, younger woman. He was going to leave her because of the woman she was.

"I had an abortion, Ryan." Her darkest secret. One only her mother knew. And she told it in a monotone, as though it was no more momentous than a stock-market report. "That band director who denied ever having slept with me left me pregnant. My mother figured it out even before I did, and while I was still reeling from the bastard's betrayal, still coming to terms with the fact that I'd given myself to a man who couldn't have cared less, who'd used me, she had me at a clinic and was signing papers." Audrey didn't look back often, but the visions, the feelings, were as clear as though she was speaking of yesterday. "She told me that I had no choice, that I couldn't survive without her and she would absolutely not take care of me if I didn't do as she said. She reminded me that my father had abandoned me. And her. She threatened to take my car. My college fund. Mostly, she threatened to disown me—to take away the only love I'd ever known. And she said she was doing it all because she loved me so much. She was the adult, the one with experience. It was her job to look out for the two of us. She knew best. She pointed out instance after instance where she and I had differed and she'd been right…"

Audrey wasn't really talking to Ryan anymore. Wasn't even sure he could hear her. Or that it mattered.

At some point she fell silent. At some point Ryan looked at her. "Do you regret it?"

"Of course I do! How could I not?"

Turning, he seemed to come back to life. "Then do something about it, Audrey. Help this girl. Save her from a lifetime of the same regret before it's too late to take back…"

Hope died within Audrey as she listened to him. If only life were as black and white as Ryan saw it. Or as he pretended to see it.

As he needed to see it so that he had his out—his sure way to maintain permanent independence.

Maybe life really could be black and white. For someone like him.

But not for her. Most definitely not for her. Or the Mark Daltons of the world.

"I can't, Ryan."

"Of course you can."

"No." She shook her head. "I can't. For two reasons. One, while I greatly regret the abortion, I also know that I would have regretted having the child. I would either have had to kiss any kind of career and security goodbye, or I would have had to kiss my own baby goodbye. Ask Sara how that feels, how that affects the rest of your life, your beliefs in and about yourself."

"And the second reason?" He was looking at the blank television screen.

"I think, in Takeisha's case, this is the best decision."

"You mean that."

"I do."

He stood. "Then I guess there's nothing more for us to say. I'll go gather my stuff."

Jumping up, panicking in spite of the fact that she'd known this was coming, Audrey planted herself in front of him, her hands on his chest. "Just like that, Ry? You're going to walk out on me just like that?"

His eyes were sad, with no spark at all, for the minute he studied her. "We aren't the people I thought we were."

Tears choked her. "I'm not the person you thought I was, you mean."

"I…" Running his hand over his head, Ryan looked sick. Mentally and physically ill. Exhausted. "When you start compromising on right and wrong, where do you stop?" he asked. "You don't. You end up justifying and accepting until there are no standards at all and life is nothing but a free-for-all where the strongest and most powerful bully wins. I can't be a part of that, Audrey. There are some things I can't compromise on."

She held back her tears. Looked him straight in the eye. "I understand."

And she did. With a calm that was complete. She couldn't keep pretending, either. Couldn't keep watching every move, every word.

Not looking back at him, she stepped away, grabbed her keys and purse and left the house. Audrey drove for hours. Out to Alum Creek. Up toward Cleveland. On sideroads and byways. And by the time she returned home just after nine that night, her house was all hers again.

Ryan's key had been left on the kitchen table.

There was no note.

RYAN LAY IN BED Friday morning, tossing and turning. No matter how tired his body felt, no matter how exhausted his mind, his soul's struggle prevented rest. He'd done little more than work and doze since leaving Audrey's house earlier in the week.

Even after knowing her for only a matter of months, her

voice was in his head, one of his own inner beings, coaching him. Berating him. Reminding him. Critiquing him. Until he didn't know what was her and what was him. Was that his own inner critic? Or hers?

And in those rare moments when the two of them weren't ganging up on him, oddly enough, his biological father showed up. Mentally that was.

Mark hadn't preached. To the contrary, he'd left Ryan with the impression that Mark thought Ryan was on the right track. One of the few lucky ones. That his strong sense of right and wrong, his ability to live true to that sense, was a precious gift.

Except that he was alone. And Mark was not. Mark had it all. A wife he adored and who adored him. The real bone-deep kind of love that surpassed everything—including the darkest of pasts. He had a job he loved. A son. A baby son, that was. He had friends and a nephew who thought he walked on water. A sister who idolized him. A mother who had never stopped believing in him.

Punching his pillow—hard—Ryan turned over. Mark was a criminal. A rapist. Rapists were bad.

But Mark Dalton was not a bad man.

Ryan would have to be stupid and blind to think that he was. And while he'd done a pretty good rendition of being both over the past year, in truth, he was neither stupid nor blind.

And now was the time for truth.

Mark Dalton was a good man who'd made a bad choice.

And he'd paid for that choice—would continue to pay for it until the day he died. And beyond that was anyone's guess.

Certainly it was out of Ryan's field of knowing or responsibility.

Mark was what he was. A man. With a heart. With a conscience. With regrets and accomplishments. A man with a history.

But as he lay there, eyes half-glazed with weariness, Ryan had a hard time making that history black. Or white. There were definite dark smudges. And there were twenty years of service and goodness. Compassion and striving. Twenty years of near perfection.

More than he could say for himself.

At best, he'd give himself…

Zero.

He was a bigoted, unrelenting, judgmental ass.

So…there. He'd arrived. He knew who he was. And with the knowing came a measure of peace. Ryan's muscles settled, falling into the softness of his mattress, letting it cradle him. Hold him.

And…

The knocking started on his head. If he didn't get some sleep, the headache that had been plaguing him for days was going to drive him to the point of insanity. As it was, it knocked incessantly. Preventing sleep. Here he was, in a cloud of cotton, being tended to all around by little white beings, and still the knocking continued, like some black vapor, pounding at him, preventing nirvana.

It hurt.

And grew louder.

Swearing, sitting up, ready to take on the vapor, to show it he was still boss, Ryan woke up with a start.

And realized that his head didn't hurt at all. A quick glance at the clock told him he'd been out almost twenty-four hours.

And the knocking—it was at his front door. Pulling on a

pair of shorts as he hopped for the stairs, Ryan made himself decent and ran the rest of the way to the door.

Too disoriented to figure out who he was expecting, he had a quick apology on his tongue, a planned request for a shower, as he pulled open the door.

"Do you always sleep this late?"

He had an appointment with Amanda Lincoln? Didn't seem like that was something he'd forget.

"I work nights," he said.

"Thursday night was your last shift. This is Saturday."

Right. "I'm sorry." The woman seemed to command the response. He was sorry. A sorry-assed fool.

"Well, you weren't expecting me so I can hardly expect a welcome. But I'd like a few minutes of your time, just the same."

"Of course." It didn't even occur to Ryan to argue. Or to wonder why, in light of the fact that he and Audrey were over, her mother would have any business with him. "Give me fifteen minutes to shower and—"

"I've been knocking for five." Amanda glanced at her watch. "I can give you a couple of minutes to put on some clothes. The shower isn't necessary. I'm not anyone you need to impress."

He'd been thinking of waking up, feeling human, but Ryan didn't see any good to come from pointing that out. He nodded, left the door open for her to make her own way in and took the stairs two at a time.

"HE HASN'T CALLED, Delilah girl. Guess you were an oversight, too. Another one he pretended to care about who he can cut off at the quick without a second glance. We're better off without him."

Delilah purred. Snuggled up to Audrey's chin and went back to sleep. They'd been that way most of the week. On the couch, with the television on, but muted, taking solace from each other.

She'd gone to work. And to lunch with her mother. And she'd come home to Delilah.

"You saved my life, you know," she said to the sleeping cat. "If you hadn't come walking out that first night and kissed me, I don't know what I'd have done."

Tears filled her eyes, as they'd been doing all week.

"How long does this grief process take?" she asked the all-knowing feline. And wished, for the hundredth time, Delilah could actually impart her wisdom. "We've got to get up. Get out. Get busy."

Doing what she didn't know. But doing something.

"It's Saturday morning. The sun is shining. What do you say we take a walk?"

Delilah didn't like walks. She didn't like to leave the house.

Which was fine with Audrey. She didn't feel like leaving, either.

"YOU DON'T MAKE bad coffee."

"Thank you."

"I didn't come to discuss your coffee. Or even to have any."

Dressed in a skirt and light, short-sleeved blazer, with tasteful gold jewelry and enough makeup to enhance her natural beauty, Amanda Lincoln looked ready for a designer showroom.

"Why are you here?" he asked, comfortable with her tactics. Up front and in your face. It was about all Ryan was capable of first thing in the morning. Without a shower.

Or any other time, these days.

"I have something to tell you. I've known there would be a day when I would have to tell my secret. I just didn't know when. After seeing my daughter yesterday for the lunch we were all three supposed to have together, I was impressed with the notion that the time had come. I gave it overnight and woke with the same conviction this morning."

She was talking conviction. A concept he could understand.

With a sip of strong coffee, he motioned her to continue.

"Leonard Wilson is Audrey's father."

Ryan choked. Spilled hot coffee on his thigh. And more on the carpet when he jumped up. Dropping the cup in the kitchen sink with one hand, while turning on the cold water with the other, he accepted the towel being handed to him without question.

Third-degree burns were painful. And he was in enough pain.

SHE'D MADE IT to the shower. Had dried her hair. Sprayed it. Managed foundation. And it was only noon. At this rate, she'd have mascara on by five. Time enough to begin reversing the process in preparation for bed.

Audrey needed her rest. Tomorrow she was going to return Delilah to her owner. With a request that he sign over adoption papers.

In the process, she was going to give Ryan Mercedes a piece of her mind. Assuming she had any left. It was disappearing by the hour.

But at least she wasn't crying. She'd gone two hours with no moisture other than the shower. Decided improvement. Worth celebration. She'd skip lipstick as a reward.

Her cell phone rang and she glanced toward the bedroom, but didn't move.

And maybe ignore the phone, too.

It rang again.

Or maybe not. It could be one of her kids.

"Hello?" She was out of breath, hadn't had time to check caller ID on the screen before her voicemail was due to pick up.

"Hi."

It was him. She'd waited for days. Too many days. That made her mad.

"What do you want?"

"Just to let you know I'm in the kitchen. I put a pot of coffee on."

"What, why?"

"Because I haven't had any. I spilled mine all over myself, had to take a shower to clean it off and didn't want to wait to make another pot."

What on earth was he babbling about?

"Why are you in my kitchen?"

"I told you. I needed coffee."

Audrey exhaled, lifting her bangs off her forehead. Exasperating her at this point wasn't wise. She was apt to start bawling.

Stopping could take most of the afternoon.

"How'd you get in my house?"

"Your mother gave me her key."

Weird was getting surreal. "My mother."

"Yes."

"When did you see my mother?"

"This morning."

She tried the harder question again. "Why?"

"Because she came over. Woke me up, actually. I'd been out for almost twenty-four hours."

That pissed her off, too. Here she'd been, too broken up to sleep for more than an hour at a time, and then it had been sleep fraught with nightmares—and he'd been blissfully unconscious for a whole day.

Ready to give him a real piece of her mind, to send him to hell and take her life back, Audrey said, "I'm coming out."

"I was hoping you'd say that."

"Don't mess with me, Ryan. You aren't on my good side."

"Point taken. There's a cup of coffee waiting for you."

Hanging up, Audrey gave Delilah one last stroke. "I'm just going out there to secure your future," she whispered. "I'll be back before you know it and you'll never have to go back to that…that…"

Unable to come up with a word that properly described what she and Delilah thought of Ryan Mercedes, Audrey left it to the higher being of the two of them and walked slowly out to her kitchen.

SHE LOOKED exhausted. Dark shadows under her eyes, hair straight and hanging around her as if its weight was too heavy to bear. An old pair of shorts and a tank top. No shoes.

Ryan had to physically hold himself back from pulling her into his arms and keeping her there forever.

"I'm sorry," he said before she was even fully in her seat. He'd taken a seat on the side of the table. She'd chosen the end next to him. He wasn't sure what that meant. If anything. Just noticed, anyway.

"Apology accepted." She was sipping coffee as though

she hadn't a care in the world, and Ryan might have panicked if not for the fact that she was avoiding his gaze.

She wouldn't be doing that if he didn't still have some effect on her.

"I was wrong."

"Yes."

"I'd like your forgiveness." His honesty wasn't getting through to her. "Let me rephrase that. I need your forgiveness."

"You have it." Her glare pinned him. "Now is that all?"

"No, I—"

"If you think you're going to walk back in here, with or without my mother's support, you're dumber than I thought, Mercedes. You, with all your promises. Your avowals of unconditional love and talk about the bigger picture, about eternity and forever and a bond that surpasses this surface human life. You're full of shit. Now get out and leave me alone."

He deserved her anger. "I made the biggest mistake of all," he said aloud, thinking of Amanda. And Mark. Of Takeisha. Of Audrey. "I felt the love. I knew it was there. And I walked away from it."

The realization stunned him. Floored him. Staring at Audrey as the lifeline she was in that moment, his one attachment to reality, he felt the flood of shame, of regret. Of knowing he'd screwed up and there was absolutely nothing he could do to take back his actions.

"When my critical moment came, I chose to live by my head, not my heart."

She didn't relent. Didn't give him anything at all. And he didn't blame her.

"I can't believe it."

Standing, Ryan pushed in his chair with precise care. Grabbed his keys. Dropped hers on the table and walked to the door.

"Wait just a damned minute, buster."

He stopped as the venom hit him in the back of the head.

"If you think you're going to casually walk away from me a second time, you'd better reconsider. I'm not having it."

Turning, Ryan stared at the tornado coming at him. Her face was red. Her arms were flailing. Her fists clenched. He had only enough time to raise his arms to deflect her blows. They came at him one after another. Not hard blows. Not bruising or damaging blows.

Not even blows he couldn't prevent. He could have grabbed her wrists at any time. He didn't.

Those fists striking him were symbolic. He deserved this.

And if fate had kept a tally, they could be at this a long, long time.

HER ANGER had long since been depleted, and still Audrey pounded at Ryan's chest. How long was he going to stand there and take it? How long could she keep it up?

Where did they go from here?

Out of the corner of her eye she saw Delilah walk in. And suddenly the words came to her.

"Take me in your arms, idiot." Had she really said that?

Before she could follow the thought any further, Ryan's arms were around her and all thought fled. He clutched her so hard it hurt. His heart pounded against her until she couldn't tell what was his life beat and what was hers. And without warning, before she could even try to stop herself, she started to sob.

THEIR LOVEMAKING was hot. Desperate. Wet with tears. And completely silent. Ryan entered Audrey without gentleness, just as she rose to meet him with a force she'd never shown before. He kissed her, mating their tongues, their mouths, their breath. He touched her breasts. Her nipples. Touching her everywhere that was intimate. That was his.

Pumping in and out of her, he started to cry—something he couldn't remember ever doing before. Tears filled his eyes, dripped down his cheeks, and still he thrust forward, withdrew and thrust again.

She was his. He was hers. Period.

There was no other option.

"THANK YOU."

Not bothering to lift her head from his chest, Audrey asked, "For what?" It was early yet. Ryan had only been there half an hour or so, but a lifetime had passed.

A life of aloneness.

"For this."

This? As in sex? Lying naked on the living-room floor together? Or the deeper this? The one that rewrote her definitions of herself.

"It took you long enough."

"What does that mean?"

Maybe if she wasn't so tired this would be easier.

"To get back here."

Ryan's hand running lightly across her shoulder blade froze. "You knew I'd be back."

"In my rational moments. You left Delilah."

His hand started to move again. And Audrey knew she had to be completely honest.

"I know you, Ryan. One of the key characteristics that makes you you, that makes you so special to me, is that you *do* live by your heart. I didn't. At all. Until you, I let fear of repeated hurts, of not measuring up, control my life. I made all my decisions consciously, logically. I didn't trust my heart."

She was out of breath, her lungs squeezed with emotions set free from the unnatural chains that had bound them all these years. "You changed all of that," she told him. "You, my soul mate, recognized me on that deeper level you talk about. And I, in spite of myself, recognized you. The other day, you were me. Scared to death. Acting from your head as a means to try to prevent the emotions from overwhelming you. Trying to control what can't be controlled. And when I saw myself in you, when I saw how wrong you were, how much you were hurting yourself, I saw me. A lifetime of me. A me I don't want to be."

She waited. Expected some argument. She had it on the best authority—her own experience—this stuff was hard to take.

"You're right."

"That's it?"

"That's it. You are one hundred percent completely right and I feel like a first-class fool. I let you down. I let me down."

In spite of the seriousness of their conversation, Audrey couldn't help but smile. This was so Ryan.

"Welcome back, my friend," she said.

Shaking his head, Ryan lined her lips with his finger. "I am so sorry, Audrey. Here I thought I was all grown-up and a match for you or any man any age, and I was acting like a little kid."

"Hey, big boy." Lifting herself up on one elbow, she tweaked his chin. "Don't be so hard on yourself. You're human just like the rest of us. Welcome to the imperfect world of human existence."

RYAN COULDN'T GET enough of her. Of love. Of living. He made love to Audrey again because there was no other way to accept and communicate the depth of passion raging through him. Gently this time. In the bed. And in the shower, he washed her, every inch of her, discovering the eternal gift she was. Vowing to himself, to the gods, to whatever powers there were, that he was going to be faithful to the life he'd been given.

"We're still going to have tough issues to face," he said, watching as the water ran over her breasts. "You're thirteen years older than I am and people are bound to make remarks."

"I know."

"And you're going to have moments when you think that you aren't pretty enough for me anymore."

"I know."

She was too calm. Too accepting. Ryan watched her. "You're sure you're okay with that?"

He couldn't pretend anymore. Couldn't live with the fear of losing her.

"What I'm sure of is that no matter how hard it is living with you, it's harder living without you. I found that out firsthand."

Ryan hadn't thought she'd find words to reassure him; he'd expected it to take time, lots of it. And here he was, feeling the chains of fear break away, leaving him light and young and strong and ready.

"I'm going to make mistakes," he reminded her just to be sure, as he turned the hand sprayer toward her shoulders.

"Of course you are. I am, too. And you're going to have to deal with that."

"I'm going to be thankful for your mistakes for the rest of my life," he said, not sure he'd ever again be able to truly see anything Audrey did as wrong. She'd have a reason. And he'd love her enough to see it.

"Why is that?"

"Because they allow me mine."

Maybe it was a twisted way of thinking, but it worked for him. And apparently for her, too, judging by the way she was inching her mouth up toward his.

THEY WERE IN the kitchen, midafternoon, making peanut-butter-and-jelly sandwiches before Audrey remembered something.

"You came over here for a specific purpose this morning," she said, licking jelly off her knife. "With my mother's key," she added. "What was that about?"

Her heart stopped a moment, all joy on hold, as Ryan's hands stilled above the slice of bread.

"Let's sit down." Taking her hand, he left the half-made sandwiches on the counter and led her to the table.

"What?"

Was her mother dying? Had he come out of pity?

"Your mother came to tell me something that she should be telling you herself, but in her strange way, she's turning you over to me. Giving up her control, she says. She knew the time would come when she would have to let you go and that when that time came, there was something you had to know."

This sounded ominous. Audrey wasn't ready for anything else.

Ryan took her hand. She concentrated on the strength that existed from their togetherness.

"Sweetie, your mother has been lying to you, to everyone, for your entire life."

"How?"

"Leonard *is* your father."

Shocked, Audrey stared at him. Words of denial sprang to mind, but quickly faded. To be replaced by a sense of knowing that brought a peculiar calm to her heart.

She jumped up, knocking her chair over. "How could she do that? How could she keep him from me? Keep me from him? Why?"

"The answer's simple really." Ryan's voice brought sanity to an insane moment, reality into desperation. "She *was* in love with Jeff. She wanted to marry him. But they hadn't slept together. When your father started talking about those psychological examinations, she panicked. What if it was found out that she really was whacked?" Ryan grabbed Audrey's hand, pulled her down to his lap. "Her word, not mine," he said. "She got it into her head that they were going to lock her up, institutionalize her or put her on meds that would make her into a zombie. So she told your father about Jeff, taking away any right he had to look out for your best interests. And then Jeff died, and she saw the writing on the wall where your father and Becky were concerned, and somehow worked it out in her mind that it was all for the best. Your father and Becky could have their own family. And she'd have you."

"But what about *me?*" Embarrassed when she heard the

little-girl plea in her voice, Audrey continued, "I mean, what about my right to have a father?"

"Your mother's father was abusive, she says."

"That's right."

"She grew up without the love of a father and didn't think the loss of a father's love was as bad for you as being split between two families would have been."

"Do Leonard and Becky know this?"

"No, she said she'd wait to hear from you on how you want to handle telling him. She said to tell you she's willing to meet with them if you'd prefer it happen that way."

"I want to tell them, I think. But only if you'll be there."

"Of course I will be."

"He's my dad," she said, resting her head against Ryan's chest, a little girl and a grown woman both at once. The two of them coming together inside her, completing her. "I have a dad. And he's a good man. And he wants me."

"That's right, sweetie." Ryan's voice above her was soft and filled with compassion.

"We have to go there," she said. "But not yet. Not today."

She needed today—a day to be with the love of her life, to solidify all that they were to each other, to focus on Ryan and the woman she was, the life she had, before she went back to the beginning.

"You name the time," he said. "I just have one stipulation."

Pulling back, looking up at him, Audrey asked, "What?"

"We don't go anywhere to meet anyone until we get a diamond for that finger."

"Which finger?"

"The one that's going to wear my wedding ring just as soon as we can get a license."

"Oh, that finger." Laughter bubbled inside her. Mixed with the purest joy. And total exhaustion. "Is that a proposal, Mercedes?"

"Yes."

"You're going to have to work on that. An older man would have had more finesse. He'd have gotten down on his knees and—"

His lips cut off her words right when she was really getting going. And they kept her occupied for the next hour, in the next room on the couch she'd shared with Delilah all week, crying for Ryan.

And when they were spent, when they'd made love, spoken of love and promised a lifetime of love, she laid her head on Ryan's shoulder, took a deep breath, and finally, after a lifetime of fighting demons in the dark, fell peacefully to sleep.

* * * * *

THE BACHELOR'S STAND-IN WIFE

BY
SUSAN CROSBY

Susan Crosby believes in the value of setting goals, but also in the magic of making wishes, which often do come true – as long as she works hard enough. Along life's journey she's done a lot of the usual things – married, had children, attended college a little later than the average co-ed and earned a BA in English. Then she dived off the deep end into a full-time writing career, a wish come true.

Susan enjoys writing about people who take a chance on love, sometimes against all odds. She loves warm, strong heroes and good-hearted, self-reliant heroines, and will always believe in happily ever after.

More can be learned about her at www.susancrosby. com.

To Gail Chasan with gratitude, for the long-time support and enthusiasm, then and now.
Thank you for the wonderful opportunities.

And to Sandra Dark, my wordy friend, who proves the statement, "Writers write." You do it well.

Chapter One

David Falcon dragged his hands down his face as a woman took a seat across the desk from him.

"Well?" she asked.

"What's to think about? I just interviewed my twelfth candidate in two days, and I finally realized I'm delusional to hope I can find someone who fits my needs." He tipped his chair back to look at Denise Watson, the efficient, thirty-something director of At Your Service, a prestigious domestic-and-clerical-help agency nicknamed by many clients as "Wives for Hire." They were seated in her interview room.

"If you have to compromise on something, what would it be?" Denise asked.

He'd been doing a lot of compromising lately—for three years, in fact. He wasn't interested in more of the same. "I'm not giving up on the ideal yet. You've got other candidates, right?"

"One."

"That's all?"

"From my own staffing pool. As you pointed out, you have specific and complex needs. I'd be happy to advertise and screen them for you."

"What are your thoughts about the one remaining?"

She set a folder on the desk in front of him and smiled. "I've learned not to second-guess the client."

He half smiled in return. "Send her in, please." He skimmed the woman's résumé. Ten years' experience as a domestic, seven in clerical jobs. He speculated on her age—midthirties to forty, maybe? There were too many questions he wasn't allowed to ask legally, tying his hands, leaving him only intuition and guesswork about her age. He was twenty-nine. It was critical that she be older than him.

"Hello. I'm Valerie Sinclair," came a quiet but level voice.

He looked up. The woman was either extraordinarily well preserved or had lied about her work experience. She didn't look a day over twenty-five. She wore a dress and jacket that was way too formal and warm for a hot August day in Sacramento, as if trying to look older. And her hair, a rich, shiny color, like chestnuts, was bundled up in some kind of bun or whatever that style was called, but couldn't take away from her young age. Her eyes were hazel and direct. No rings on her slender fingers; her nails were short, clean and unpolished.

"I'm David Falcon. Please, have a seat," he said, wondering how she'd passed At Your Service's background check. She had to have lied—

To hell with the law, he decided. If she could lie about her work experience, he could ask the questions he wanted to. "How old are you, Ms. Sinclair?"

She stiffened. "I'm twenty-six."

"How is it you have seventeen years of work experience? You started working when you were nine?"

"Eight, actually. Not legally, of course, but my mother has

been housekeeper for a family in Palm Springs since I was five. I was put to work early."

"Doing what?"

"In the beginning, dusting and sweeping. New responsibilities were added as I could handle them."

"Your mother allowed you to be used like that?"

"Used?" She smiled slightly. "Didn't you do chores as a child? The family wasn't in residence full-time. We lived on-site. It was my home."

David didn't know what to think. On the one hand it seemed that child labor laws were violated. On the other, her point was well taken—*to* a point. "Did you receive a salary?"

"An allowance from my mother, which increased as my responsibilities did. I don't think it's worth a lot of discussion, Mr. Falcon. My understanding is that you're looking for someone to run your household and also be your administrative assistant. I listed the domestic work so that you would know I had a lot of experience in that field."

David studied her. She was…soothing, he decided. Her feathers didn't ruffle easily.

"May I ask the nature of your business?" she asked.

"My brother and I own Falcon Motorcars."

"I've never heard of that make."

"They're custom-made. Our clients aren't the average car buyers, so we don't need to advertise. Most buyers are European, which is why I've been out of the country more than I've been home the past few years. Which is also why I'm looking for someone to take charge of things here, personally and professionally."

"Denise said you want a live-in."

A wife without the sex was what he wanted. Someone experienced, efficient and of a certain age. "That's a requirement. Is that a problem?"

"Not at all."

"Given the time difference between California and the continent, you might be awakened during the night to take care of business for me, or work until midnight, or get up at four."

"I can do that."

"How are your computer skills?"

"Denise tested me on five different programs. I assume the results are in my folder."

He found the report and read it, letting her wait, testing her patience. She didn't fidget. "Why did you leave your last job?"

"Sexual harassment." She said it as easily as she might have said she'd gone to the grocery store.

He flattened his hands on top of the folder. "Did you file suit?"

Again that slight smile touched her lips. "*I* was accused of sexual harassment."

David looked her over once more. Was that the reason for the buttoned-up outfit she wore? Beneath it was a slender, attractive body, he could tell. And maybe with her hair down and some makeup on, she would look sexy. She didn't want to look sexy? "Were you guilty?"

"Quite the opposite."

He let that information sink in. "He was harassing you?"

She nodded once, sharply, the only outward indication of how much the situation bothered her.

"Why didn't you report him?"

"I did. That's when he turned it around to me instead. Look, it's dead and buried for me."

"Is it? I would imagine it's followed you and made it difficult to find a job," he said, knowing how such things worked.

She hesitated, then gave a taut smile.

Pride. He understood it all too well. "Let me share my recent experiences," he said. "My last housekeeper stole from me. My last four administrative assistants left because of pregnancy or child-care-related issues, each of them at just about the time they were fully trained. Frankly, I'd pretty much decided this time around to hire a woman beyond child-bearing age. You don't fit that qualification."

Her stark disappointment flashed, but he couldn't let that interfere with his decision-making process. "As much as I'd like to hire you—"

His cell phone rang. He would've ignored it, except it was his brother Noah, the only caller David couldn't ignore. "Excuse me a moment," he said, then left the room.

Valerie waited for David Falcon to shut the door before she closed her eyes. *As much as I'd like to hire you.* His mind was apparently made up. Her hands shook; her mouth went dry. She was at the end of her already short rope. If she didn't get this job she didn't know what she was going to do. She'd used every penny of her meager savings. Her credit card was maxed out. How could she convince him to hire her?

She was *this* close to being homeless, although a homeless shelter might be better than the apartment complex where she lived, in a part of town where drive-by shootings weren't uncommon. This job would mean a steady income and a safe place to live. For her and—

"Sorry about that," David said, returning. "As I started to say, as much as I'd like to hire you, given your job skills, I'm hesitant. I would need your assurance that you won't be taking off to get married anytime soon. I need to know you're not pregnant or intending to get pregnant anytime soon. I would be hiring you to take care of *me*—my house and my business—not a baby."

Valerie clenched her hands. She still had a chance. *Say the right thing. Say the right thing.* "I'm not even dating anyone, so the issue of marriage is nonexistent. Which would also, therefore, mean no pregnancy or babies in sight. However, I do have a daughter, Hannah. She's eight." Valerie saw his eyes dull with disappointment. "She's a quiet, obedient child, I promise you."

She waited for lightning to strike her for the fib, then continued to plead her case. "My daughter doesn't require the care that a baby does. You won't even know she's there."

Valerie had her own reasons for not letting Hannah get close to him, anyway. "Just give me a chance to prove myself," she said, trying not to beg.

He leaned back in his chair, his gaze never leaving hers. She didn't look away, either. *Please hire me. Please.*

"Let's try it for a month," he said at last.

Emotions tumbled through the desert of what her life had become. She couldn't even speak.

"I'll pay your rent for where you're living now so that you have a place to go back to if it doesn't work out."

She wouldn't move back to that hellhole under any circumstances. She swallowed against the still roiling emotions. "It's not necessary. I was going to look for a new place anyway."

"All right. You'll be living in a cottage behind the main house, and it's fully furnished, including all the kitchen things. I'll arrange for some movers and a storage unit for your belongings."

A cottage? Their own space? "My apartment came furnished. I have very little to transport." She and Hannah had moved so many times, they had the routine down pat.

"You're making this very easy, Ms. Sinclair."

"Valerie. It's my job to make your life easy."

"If you can pull that off, you're a miracle worker."

He stood; she did, as well. Apparently when he made up his mind, that was that.

"How soon can you start?" he asked.

"Where is your house?"

"In Chance City, close to Grass Valley and Nevada City. Are you familiar with the area?"

"Not much. I know it's a Mother Lode location from the gold rush era."

"Right. It's beautiful country, but the house itself is a little isolated."

"Isolation doesn't bother me." They would be about an hour north of Sacramento. Clean air, and stars at night. Trees. *Their own cottage.* "I can be there tonight."

"I'll send someone to help."

"I can manage, thanks." She smiled, hopefully diverting him from becoming insistent on helping her. She really didn't want anyone associated with him to see where she lived.

The tiredness in his face smoothed out—his very handsome face, she finally realized, admiring his tall, athletic body.

"Whatever expenses you incur in moving out, I'll pay. Just let me know how much."

"Thank you."

"And if everything works out, I'll buy out your contract from At Your Service. Falcon Motorcars would become your employer, so you'd have benefits."

Benefits. Valerie wished he would leave so that she could sit down. An internal earthquake had her trembling. She was surprised he couldn't see it.

She'd been without health insurance for the year that she hadn't been able to find permanent work. "Feel free to start putting through the new-employee paperwork," she said.

"You're very sure that things are going to work out."

"Three things you'll learn about me, Mr. Falcon. I'm competent, I'm reliable and I'm loyal. I also know I have to prove myself."

"You can call me David." He pulled a large envelope from his briefcase and handed it to her. "You'll find a map to the house inside this envelope, and some general instructions. A few forms you need to fill out. A key to the cottage, in case I'm not there when you arrive." He gestured toward the door. "I'll walk you out."

"I think we both probably have to talk to Denise."

"Right. I'll go first." He shook her hand. "See you later."

"Thank you for the opportunity," she said. *Now go away.*

He walked out the door.

She sank into the chair, her knees giving out. He stuck his head back around the corner. "You like dogs?"

"Yes." She tried to stand.

"Don't get up," he said, eyeing her intently. "Are you okay?"

"I'm fine. My foot got caught in the chair leg."

He waited a couple of beats. "Is your daughter good with dogs?"

"She loves them, but she's never had one of her own."

"I have a great old-lady dog. I've had to foster her with my brother and his four kids because I've been gone so much. She looks at me with accusing eyes every time I leave their house without her. I'd like to bring her home."

"By all means."

He slapped the doorjamb and nodded. "Thanks."

"You're welcome."

He disappeared, but she held herself together, in case he surprised her by returning—

"One more thing," he said, again appearing in the doorway. "Can your daughter swim?"

"Yes."

"Good. I have a pool. I don't want to have to worry about her."

"She'll abide by the rules."

"Okay." Then he was off again.

She stared into space. He had no idea what having this job meant to her. None. She didn't care if she had to work 24/7. Didn't care if she lost sleep or weight or her mind. Well, maybe she would care if she lost her mind.

It was a good job, out of the city, working for a man Denise assured her was decent and successful. He'd have to sign a contract, the same as Valerie would, spelling out the details of the business arrangement, including that there would be no sexual contact between employer and employee. She could live with that.

All she wanted was to provide for her daughter.

Finally she could do that.

Chapter Two

"Over there, Mom." Hannah pointed straight ahead. "See the mailbox? That's the address. But where's the house?"

Valerie braked, slowing, then came to a stop next to the mailbox. Ahead she spotted a break in the abundance of trees and shrubs and assumed it was a driveway. She nosed the car down the gravel road, past a small forest of wild oaks, fragrant pines and stately cedars. Then she came upon a wide firebreak clearing and an amazing house, all glass and logs and rocks, reaching toward the sky, the stark edges softened by clouds, the windows reflecting treetops.

"Awesome," Hannah said reverently. "We're gonna live *here?*"

Valerie was no less awed. She'd expected a nice house, but not one that should be profiled in *Architectural Digest*. "Remember we won't be living in the house but in a cottage on the property."

No one came out of the house to greet or question them,

so Valerie continued on, following a gently curving path around the house, discovering several buildings—a four-car garage, what looked to be a stable and the building referred to as the cottage.

The word *cottage* had conjured up visions in Valerie's mind of rosebushes and wood shingles. Instead the structure was a smaller version of the main house, except with cedar-plank siding instead of logs, but with the same large windows, and more space than she and Hannah had ever lived in.

"There's the pool!" Hannah exclaimed, scrambling to unbuckle her seat belt and flinging the car door open. "And a hot tub. Mom, it's got a hot tub. We get to use it, too, right?"

She was out of the car and running toward a free-form pool that seemed carved out of the landscape, with a small, rock waterfall at one end that spilled into both the pool and hot tub.

Gravel crunched under Valerie's feet as she followed Hannah, reaching a flagstone path that branched into others heading toward the cottage, the main house, and through a wild, obviously untended garden to the pool. Lack of interest in gardening, she wondered, or his intent? He must be able to afford a gardener.

Valerie reached her daughter, who'd crouched beside the pool, dipped her hand into it then flicked a few refreshing drops at Valerie. "Can we go swimming, Mom? I'm sooo hot."

They'd spent the afternoon packing their belongings and cleaning their apartment in the 101-degree Sacramento weather, squeezing everything into their small car. They both needed a cool swim before unpacking and settling in. And the man of the house didn't appear to be home.

"Pleeease," Hannah begged, tugging on Valerie's hand.

"How fast can you find your bathing suit?"

"I put it in the last grocery bag we loaded." She grinned, obviously pleased at her planning ahead. "Yours, too. I swiped it from your suitcase as soon as you said there was a pool."

"Have I told you lately how smart you are?" Valerie hooked an arm around her daughter as they returned to the car.

"Just every day."

They grabbed the bag from the car then headed to the cottage to change. A note was taped to the front door: "Welcome. I expect to be home by 7:30. I'll bring dinner. We'll meet later to discuss your specific duties. DF"

It was only six o'clock, so they had plenty of time, provided she could drag Hannah out of the pool at some point.

"Way cool!" Hannah declared as they stepped inside the cottage.

Valerie wondered why David called it a cottage when it was really more of a guesthouse. A large great room, dining area and kitchen comprised the visible living space, while in the back were two bedrooms with a shared bath between. The modern furnishings looked brand-new and perfectly suited to the structure, not exactly "cabin" decor but dark greens, reds and browns, with some wrought-iron pieces and trim, and a stone fireplace.

She'd never lived in anything like it.

"Which bedroom do you want?" she asked her daughter, her words trailing off as Hannah raced into one of the rooms and slammed the door shut.

"Hurry, Mom," she shouted through the wood.

Valerie took a moment to enjoy the bedroom that would now be hers. The pine furnishings included a rustic four-poster, queen-size bed and an armoire that housed a television, drop-leaf desk and six-drawer dresser. The comforter was red-and-green striped. Overall, it was a streamlined, masculine look, but that didn't really surprise her. David Falcon was all male.

"I'm ready!"

"Almost done," Valerie called out as she peeled off her sweaty, sticky clothes and tugged on her bathing suit, a black one-piece as old as Hannah. Valerie found a linen closet inside the bathroom and grabbed two pool towels. On her way out she caught sight of herself in the mirror. Her suit sagged a little, as much from old elastic as the fact she'd lost weight in the past year, leaving her, according to her mother, skin and bones. She didn't think she looked *that* bad, but maybe the new situation—especially the lack of worrying about life in general—would bring back her lost curves, or at least what there'd been of them to begin with.

She would be happy here. She could feel it. She and Hannah would have a place they could call home. They wouldn't have to triple-lock their door. They could sleep with windows open.

"Mo-om!"

Valerie hurried out of the bathroom, grabbed Hannah's hand and ran to the pool, jumping straight in. They touched bottom then shoved themselves up through the bubbles, still holding hands, laughing as they broke the surface.

This is what freedom feels like—cool and clean....

She ignored the hot tears pressing at her eyes. She wouldn't do anything to mess up this incredible situation, would make sure that Hannah understood what her boundaries were. Valerie would make herself completely indispensable to Mr. David Falcon. He would find no fault with her work or behavior. She would be a consummate professional, do nothing remotely improper....

For the next half hour she and Hannah played and romped and floated. They turned on the jets in the hot tub and climbed in, just because they could, letting the heat seep into their bodies, then getting out and doing cannonballs into the cooler pool. Valerie planted her hands on the pool edge to push herself out as Hannah grabbed her ankles, trying to tug her back in. They were laughing and taunting each other.

The stretched-out straps of Valerie's bathing suit slipped a little. She pulled free of her daughter's grip. Breathless, she shoved herself up and almost out of the pool...and came face-to-face with a huge golden retriever—and her boss standing right behind.

* * *

So. The buttoned-up Valerie Sinclair did have a body—a very nice body—beneath all that fabric, David thought, studiously avoiding watching her directly as she jammed her straps back into place and hurried over to a chair to grab a towel, covering herself, apologizing the whole time.

"Hi, I'm David Falcon," he said to the worried-looking little girl clinging to the side of the pool.

"I'm Hannah. What's your dog's name?"

"This is Belle." Belle looked up at him at hearing her name, her tongue hanging out the side of her mouth in a goofy dog smile. She'd become like a puppy again since he'd loaded her in his car. "She'll swim with you, if you want."

"Really?"

"She won't go in on her own, but if you slap the water and call her name, she'll dive right in. Don't call her near you, because she's strong and her claws can hurt. Just let her swim around on her own. She'll climb up the stairs when she's done."

"Cool!" Hannah patted the water. "C'mere, Belle. Come on, girl."

With one last happy look at David she jumped in, thus apparently forgiving him for her years of exile at Noah's. She was too old to be having to put up with all those children, even Noah's sedate children. But having one child around, this eight-year-old Hannah, would be good for her, especially when David was out of town. Belle needed company, and someone to care about, follow around and curl up with.

"I'm sorry," Valerie said again, coming up beside David, watching the dog and the girl swim in circles.

"For what?"

"Not being ready for work when you arrived. I thought we had more time."

"I didn't expect you to work tonight." He finally eyed her directly, all wrapped up in a towel that matched her hazel eyes, her wet hair dripping down her back. He'd been right about her looking younger with her hair down. "Your daughter is a miniature of you."

"I can't tell you how excited she is to be here. The cottage is beautiful."

Belle followed a giggling Hannah across the pool, then headed for the stairs. The dog didn't climb out but stood, resting.

"Are you all settled in?"

"We haven't even unloaded the car yet."

He considered taking a swim himself, but decided to wait until later. He figured Valerie would keep a strict employer/employee relationship with him, which would include making sure her daughter didn't get in his way.

Which was fine with him. David had nothing against kids, he just didn't know how to relate to them, even his nieces and nephews. He particularly didn't want to get attached to an employee's child. She had to be separate from the working relationship as much as possible.

"I picked up a pizza," he said to Valerie. "Come up to the house when you're ready and we'll reheat it. We'll talk business afterward."

"Both of us?"

"Your daughter needs to eat, too, right?"

"I can take her a plate."

"We'll make an exception for tonight."

Valerie nodded. He walked away, sensing her relief. He knew, given her background of false accusations of sexual harassment, that she would be more wary than most, more aware of potential impropriety. He respected that. He wanted a long-term, employer/employee relationship with her. He would be just as careful as she.

He got partway down the path when he heard the thunder of Belle's paws pounding the flagstone behind him, getting closer. He turned. She bounded to a halt and shook the pool water from her fur, head to tail, drenching him.

Hannah shrieked with laughter then clamped a hand over

her mouth. Valerie stood frozen, awaiting his response. He hunkered down and wrapped his arms around his great old dog, getting himself wetter in the process, glad to have her home.

So much for impeccable behavior, Valerie thought with a sigh as she and Hannah walked to the cottage a few minutes later. He'd caught her in her bathing suit, totally goofing off, acting like a kid. How embarrassing. Not an auspicious start to their business relationship at all.

"Belle's a neat dog," Hannah said. "I never knew dogs liked to swim. I mean, I know they can, because there's even a name for it, right? The dog paddle? But I didn't know they would just jump in and swim around."

"Just don't get too attached. She's his dog, not yours."

"But he's gone a lot. You said so. She'll be staying with us, won't she? She can't stay in that big ol' house by herself. She'd be sooo lonely."

Hannah's eyes pleaded with Valerie, who tried not to laugh. Right. *Belle* would be lonely.

Valerie and Hannah unloaded the car, then showered and dressed for their first dinner with the boss. The evening temperature was perfect as they took the path to the house and climbed the back stairs. Through a window Valerie saw a kitchen and was glad she would be working in a space with such a spectacular view, not only of the pool but the tree-studded hills.

She knocked on the kitchen door. After a minute she knocked again. Finally she turned the handle and leaned inside. "Hello?"

"Be right there. Make yourself at home," David called, the words muffled by distance.

"Wow. Our old apartment would fit in here," Hannah said, looking around at the kitchen and breakfast nook.

The stainless steel appliances made it contemporary, but there was a rustic feel, too, in the pine cabinets and autumn-toned granite countertops. Not a curtain in sight, either, nor any plants. Nothing to soften the streamlined feel of the place, the home of someone who didn't really live there, but used it as a base camp.

David breezed into the room. He'd changed from slacks and a dress shirt to jeans and a T-shirt, and was barefoot. Belle trailed him. Valerie wondered how old David was. Thirty?

"Settled in?" he asked.

"Almost. We haven't put everything away, but it's all in the house," Valerie answered, keeping a hand on Hannah's shoulder so that she wouldn't run to Belle, who wagged her tail in greeting.

"The stove's preheated," David said. "Shouldn't take too long. I hope you like pepperoni." He slid a large pizza into the oven. "How about a tour while it heats."

"That would be great."

The inside of the house was as stunning as the outside. It was a man's home, but a classy one, the environment clearly of someone who liked art and color, who had style. Maybe a decorator should get credit, but David would have had to approve everything purchased, so he must've had a hand in the final result in some way.

On the first floor was a living room with a stone fireplace, a family room holding a woodstove that piped heat into the rest of the house, a large dining room with a table and chairs for twelve, an office and a powder room. Upstairs were four bedrooms, two baths and the master suite, with its enormous bed and spectacular view, the same as in the kitchen, of the pool and mountains, even the cottage. Heavy green drapes framed the windows. She wondered how often he shut them.

She wondered, too, how often he had company. Female company. He was an attractive and successful man. Did he have a regular girlfriend?

"It's an incredible home," she said to him, having given

up on keeping Hannah by her side. She and Belle had teamed up, following at their own pace. "Although a lot of house for one person."

"I spend much of my life in airplanes and hotel rooms. I need a place to spread out."

"How long have you lived here?"

"Had it built five years ago."

They headed out the bedroom door and downstairs. Valerie motioned to Hannah, who played on the landing with Belle, tossing the dog's rag doll, then throwing it again after Belle brought it back.

"How much are you gone?" she asked.

"At least half the month. My oldest brother, Noah, and I have owned the business for eleven years. We used to share the overseas work, but Noah's wife died three years ago, and now he has their four children to take care of." They reached the bottom of the staircase, which faced a wall of family photos. He pointed to a photo of a man and woman with four children. "He's needed to be with them, I understand that, so I've been doing all the traveling. But someday I hope we can split the work again. I'm also trying to figure out ways to do less overseas and more here in the States."

Valerie heard frustration in his voice. Or maybe weariness. "How old are the children?"

"He has two sets of twins, as you can see. Ashley and Zoe are twelve. Adam and Zachary are nine. They're...very well behaved."

Valerie wondered why he said that as if it was a bad thing. "You said he was your oldest brother. You have others?"

"One, Gideon." He tapped a photo. "He's the middle child."

"Your parents like biblical names," she said with a smile.

"Our father did."

The man in the picture he pointed to resembled Noah most of all, but she could see David in him, too.

"We have different mothers. This one's mine," he went on

to say, moving to the photo of a young woman, the picture probably taken twenty years ago, given her hairstyle.

"Do you want to eat in the kitchen or on the deck?" he asked in a quick change of subject.

"The deck," Hannah said, focused on the photographs, apparently fascinated. Then she caught Valerie's pointed look. "Please," she added.

"You got it. I'll cut the pizza into slices. There's a salad in the refrigerator. Paper plates and napkins are in the cupboard next to the sink," he said.

They settled around a table on the deck overlooking the backyard. Belle curled up at their feet.

"If you had the house built," Valerie said, "then you also had the stables put in. Do you plan to get a horse?"

"It's a dream. I'm not here enough."

"Do you know how to ride?"

He grinned. "Nope."

"Then why…?"

"Wide-open spaces."

Valerie was beginning to understand him. He needed space but felt hemmed in by his work. He must feel handcuffed or something. And resentful? she wondered.

"What grade are you in?" David asked Hannah.

"Third."

"Do you like school?"

"It's okay."

Valerie sympathized with her daughter. She'd attended three different schools in her short life. It was another reason for making sure she kept her job—she wanted Hannah to have the luxury of staying at one school and making long-term friends. Living a normal childhood, if Valerie could make that happen.

She wondered about David's childhood, if, having different mothers, he and his brothers were raised together. Maybe they weren't close in age. As an only child, Valerie had desperately wanted siblings, but her father had divorced her mother when Valerie was a toddler and had rarely contacted Valerie since. As far as she knew, he hadn't fathered more children.

When they were done eating, Valerie stacked the paper plates and started to stand.

"I'll take care of that later," David said, then pointed toward the floor under the table. Hannah had joined Belle and was now asleep against the dog, who looked at David but didn't make a move to get up.

"We might as well go over your duties," he said. "I've written them up for you. Be right back."

"What a good dog you are," Valerie said to Belle, petting her. Belle closed her eyes, making a happy sound.

David returned, taking the seat next to instead of across from her. He set a piece of paper on the table between them so they both could read it. She was aware of him, of his arm almost touching hers. He hadn't stepped over any line at any time, either with comments or looks, in fact had gone out of his way not to look at her at the pool until she'd wrapped the towel around her, covering her bathing suit. Not interested? She knew it was better that way, but—

"You're probably worried about working at the house during the night, and leaving Hannah on her own at the cottage," he said. "There's an intercom system between the houses. You'll be able to hear everything that happens in the cottage—or vice versa, if necessary. You just have to set the buttons. There's also an alarm. I've never had problems here, but I know it'll probably make a city girl like you feel more comfortable."

"Okay, good."

He went down his itemized list, explaining each of her duties. He would make his own breakfast but preferred she prepare his dinner. He was rarely home at lunchtime, so they would play that by ear on the occasions he stayed home. Valerie and Hannah could use the pool and patio anytime except when he was entertaining, and then he expected privacy, unless he asked for something.

Privacy for women friends? Valerie wondered. Probably.

"I know how to serve a household," she said. "And Hannah will know to stay in the cottage."

"She's not to work in my house," he said decisively. "I know your mother allowed it, but I think children should enjoy childhood. She's welcome to have friends over when I'm not here, including to use the pool, as long as they're supervised every second."

Valerie's throat closed. She blessed whatever fates had sent her to the At Your Service agency, which had led her here. "That's very generous."

"My childhood was one crisis after another. I don't wish that on any child." He cocked his head. "What about her father?"

"Not in the picture."

A long pause followed. She figured he was waiting for her to expand on her answer, but she had no intention of doing so.

"Okay," he said finally. "I've never had live-in help before, so we'll both be feeling our way through the situation. You should speak up if you think something should be handled differently."

"I will. You'll do the same, right?"

"Of course. I'm sure we'll spend a lot of time communicating, in person and by phone. There's no purpose in holding back. The relationship depends on honesty and openness."

"Like a marriage," she said. Without sex, she reminded herself. Without any physical contact whatsoever. Without innuendo. They couldn't even joke about it.

"I'll take your word on that," he said, flashing a quick grin. "Like a *good* marriage, maybe. But since I've never taken part in that institution, I wouldn't know."

"Neither would I." She let that bit of information set in for a minute without explanation.

He glanced at Belle and Hannah. "And, as you know, I never expected a child to be part of the deal, so we're especially going to have to feel our way through that, figure out what works for all of us."

"Your needs and demands come first. You have to tell me if Hannah is bothering you. She's obviously already made herself at home."

He nodded. "We'll talk more in the morning. You'll have to come to the house for breakfast, since I know you haven't had time to shop for groceries yet. I'll be heading to the office for the day."

He stood, so she did, as well. "Where is that?"

"In Roseville, just north of Sacramento."

"What time do you want breakfast?"

"Eight."

"Okay." Valerie looked out over his property. Garden lights illuminated the pool and pathways, creating a beautiful picture. "Is the yard my responsibility?"

"I have a gardener."

"You do?" She put a hand to her mouth, surprised that she'd blurted that out.

He grinned.

"You like the untamed look, I guess," she said.

"I've pretty much just left it in his hands." He walked to the railing, leaned on his elbows there and looked around. "I guess it's not as nice as it could be."

"It could be a showpiece, if that's what you want."

"Are you saying you want to add gardening to your many duties?"

"Maybe your gardener and I could work together on a new look. Would that be okay?"

"Sure, why not. I'll give him a call and tell him you're the boss."

She'd never been the boss of anyone, unless she counted Hannah. "That would be great, thanks." She knelt down to wake up her daughter, who made sleepy sounds of resistance as she snuggled against Belle. "Bedtime, sweetie."

Hannah finally got her to her feet, although she leaned heavily against Valerie. It had been a long, tiring day for both of them. "Say good-night to Mr. Falcon."

"'Night," she said softly.

"Thank you for everything," Valerie added, still unable to believe her luck.

"It's a month, Valerie," he said.

The grace period. She'd already forgotten about that, she was so sure of her ability to please him.

She nodded. "Good night."

"I hope you both sleep well. Belle, stay," he ordered quietly as the dog started to follow.

Valerie was aware of him watching as she made her way down the stairs and through the yard, holding Hannah's hand and stepping carefully. She didn't look back until they were entering the cottage. She could just make out his silhouette. He hadn't moved.

Her heart swelled at the protectiveness of his actions. She was accustomed to looking out for herself and Hannah, without help from anyone. And although David was her employer, she felt he was also looking out for them.

It was a very nice feeling.

Chapter Three

Valerie had learned to cook at a young age and had begun teaching Hannah when she was a toddler. She wasn't a picky eater. They often read recipes and talked about them—how a dish might taste, what could be served with it. Valerie looked forward to cooking for David, starting this morning.

Hannah was still asleep when Valerie was ready to head to the house. She went into her daughter's room and sat on her bed.

"Good morning," she sing-songed, brushing Hannah's long hair away from her face.

"Mmpff."

"Are you awake? I need to tell you something."

Hannah flopped onto her back and opened her eyes halfway. "I'm awake."

"I'm going up to fix Mr. Falcon's breakfast. As soon as he leaves, we'll eat. In the meantime, you can watch television."

Hannah's eyes opened fully. "I never get to watch TV in the morning."

"Some things are going to be different for us here. We'll have to figure out new rules." She stood. "There's an intercom by the front door. If you need me, push the talk button and shout, okay?" She guessed that's how it worked, anyway. She wasn't worried, since she could see the front door of the cottage from the kitchen window at the big house.

"Okay."

"After breakfast we'll go grocery shopping and stop by the school district office to get you registered, so put on some nice clothes. I put everything away before I went to bed last night. Check your dresser and your closet."

Hannah sat up. "I'm kinda hungry."

"There's a box of cereal and a couple of granola bars in the kitchen cupboard but no milk. I'll probably be gone about half an hour, however long it takes to make breakfast and put it on the table. Unless he has more to tell me or some job to do."

"Mom, I'm eight. I'll be *fine*."

Yes, her grown-up girl. She'd had to mature fast, like so many children of single parents.

When Hannah was settled on the living room sofa, granola bar in hand and the TV turned to cartoons, Valerie opened the door and was greeted by Belle. She got up, wagging her tail.

"Good morning, Miss Belle. I assume you're looking for Hannah."

Belle barked. Hannah jumped off the couch and ran over, falling to her knees and wrapping her arms around the dog. "Belle! Mom, look. Belle came to see me. Can she stay?"

"For now. I'll find out when I get up to the house. Don't let her on the sofa with you, though."

"Okay. C'mon, Belle." They sat on the floor in front of the couch.

Valerie headed out and up the pathway. The morning was exquisite—a crystal-clear sky, the crisp scent of pine in the air, a mild midsixties or so, although probably another hot day ahead.

At the house, the kitchen door was unlocked, and since

Belle was out, Valerie knew David must be up. She'd checked the contents of his refrigerator when she'd gotten the salad out last night, seeing very little beyond condiments, although he did have eggs.

"Good morning," he said, coming into the kitchen. "How'd you sleep?"

"Exceptionally well." He also looked exceptionally good in his khakis and light green polo shirt, a shade lighter than his eyes. His dark hair was still damp. He smelled good, too, fresh from the shower, kind of soap scented or a light, pleasant aftershave. "Could I fix you an omelet?"

"I'll just have cereal, thanks."

"Are you sure? You've got eggs and cheese and—"

"Okay, you talked me into it." He poured himself a cup of coffee from a carafe on the counter. "I made a full pot, if you're interested. Didn't know whether or not you drink it."

It was something she'd given up because she couldn't afford it. "Yes, thanks. Do you have likes and dislikes, foodwise?"

"I like meat and potatoes. And most vegetables. Not a big dessert eater, except apple pie and chocolate-chip cookies. And ice cream." David leaned against the counter, sipping from his cup, watching her whisk eggs and grate cheese. "When you have time today, I'd like you to read through the files I left on my office desk and familiarize yourself with them. We'll talk about them tonight. Tomorrow I'll stay home longer in the morning and show you how to access files on my computer."

"When will you leave town again?"

"Sunday."

This was Wednesday. He figured she should be up to speed by the time he left. They would spend a lot of time together, just the two of them....

She poured the eggs into the pan, moving gracefully and efficiently from task to task, then he saw her realize he was watching her, and her cheeks turned pink. He shoved away from the counter and went to the window, surveying the morning.

"It's so quiet here," she said hesitantly, as if needing to fill the silence. "I feel like I'm on vacation."

"I know what you mean. Some days I can't wait to get home. And now that Belle's home, too, it'll be even better."

"Oh, I forgot! Belle is with Hannah in the cottage. I hope that's okay."

"It's fine. I saw her wander down there this morning and sit in front of your door."

"You'll need to tell me what to feed her, and when."

"Her bowls are in the laundry room, and an extra water bowl on the deck. One scoop of dog food, twice a day."

"When you're gone, should she stay in the cottage with us?"

"If you don't mind."

"I think my daughter would raise quite a ruckus if Belle couldn't be there."

"I figured that." He took another sip of his cooling coffee. He rarely had someone to talk to in the morning, and now he couldn't decide if he liked it or not, accustomed to silence as he was.

"Is this enough food for you or do you prefer a bigger breakfast?" she asked.

"I eat what's put in front of me." Maybe he shouldn't have told her he'd fix his own breakfast most of the time, after all. Maybe it would be nice having her there in the morning, fixing something hot and filling.

"You look like you work out...." Her words drifted.

He turned in time to see her swallow, obviously uncomfortable.

"I mean, you don't look like you overeat." She stopped, closed her eyes. "I mean— Shoot."

He decided to rescue her. "I could say the same about you."

"Good genes," she said in a tone indicating that conversation was over. She tipped the omelet onto the plate next to the toast she'd just buttered.

He came forward, taking the plate from her, not wanting

things to get any more personal—for both their sakes. Maybe he should have let Hannah hang around more, to keep things professional.

"I'll eat in front of the computer while I answer some e-mail, then I'll take off," he said. "See you around six o'clock."

"When would you like dinner?"

"Plan on seven." He went out the kitchen door then retraced his steps. "Don't try to do too much today except get settled and acclimated. I know the house needs cleaning, but it can wait one more day."

"All right."

He didn't believe her. Based on what she'd told him, he guessed she had a stronger work ethic than most. "I hope this works out, Valerie."

"Me, too."

He went to his office and shut the door. His computer was on, but he stood at the window instead, eating, the view of the yard the same as from the kitchen and his bedroom. After a minute he saw Valerie make her way to the cottage, carrying a carton of milk. She didn't seem to be in a hurry, taking a little time to stop and look around, maybe visualizing what she wanted to do with the yard.

He should've probably held off letting her start on any major project until their trial month was up, but what damage could she do in the yard? The worst that could happen was that it got tamed some, thinned out.

Except he didn't want a bunch of flowers planted. He should tell her that before she got started. He liked the natural look, which was why his pool seemed to be carved from the rocks. Women always had different ideas about things like gardens, however. His mother had loved to garden....

An hour later David pulled into the company parking lot in an industrial area of Roseville. The large metal building housed several bays in which cars in various states of completion were being hand built. At the far right of the building were his and Noah's offices. David had been a partner in Falcon Motorcars since he was eighteen, the year his father died, leaving his three sons the business in equal shares. For the first eight years it had been fun, each day a challenge, each job different. But since Noah's wife's death, it had become exhausting.

David tried to hide his resentment from Noah, who was still grieving and had enough on his plate with four children, but the resentment was becoming increasingly difficult to conceal, especially as it was compounded by Noah's inability to see the pressure cooker David lived in daily. If only Gideon hadn't left the company, then the responsibilities would have continued to be more equitable. But Gideon marched to a different drummer, always had, always would. Nothing would lure him back into the family business.

"Morning, Mae," David said to the woman who'd been office manager of the business for thirty years, and Noah's administrative assistant.

"The conquering hero returns." She looked at him over the top of her glasses while continuing to type. She hadn't changed her supershort hairstyle since he'd known her, the color as bright red as it had always been.

"Hero?" he repeated.

"You brought home gold, I hear. Literally."

"Oh, yeah. That."

She smiled. "Nice job."

He'd sold twenty cars to the sultan of Tumari, each personalized, and each vehicle netting a tidy profit for Falcon Motorcars, their biggest single order in their thirty-year history. The sultan required so many gold accessories that they might have to open a mine somewhere. The order would keep them busy for two years, would require hiring and training a few new craftsmen.

"Welcome home," Noah said, coming into his doorway.

He was taller by several inches and heavier by twenty pounds of rock-solid muscle. "I heard you arranged a prison break for Belle."

David grinned. "She's finally speaking to me again." He trailed Noah into his office, both taking a seat on the leather sofa.

"So, you found someone to live in," Noah said.

"Yep. Which is why I took Belle home. Valerie started yesterday."

"If she's good, maybe she'll come work for me when she gets sick of you."

"Don't tell me you're losing another nanny."

"She hasn't quit yet, but she's been there for two months. Shouldn't be too much longer."

Get a clue, David wanted to yell at his brother. His nannies quit for good reasons. "Keep your overly generous job offers away from Valerie," he said instead. "I think she's the one."

Noah raised his brows. "The one?"

"Not *that* kind of one. The perfect employee. The only hitch is that she has an eight-year-old daughter. We're doing a one-month test run." He didn't want to jinx the relationship by talking about it more than that.

"You do seem mellowed out."

"I do?" The idea took him by surprise.

"You're not pacing. Or jingling your keys in your pocket. Like Dad."

David couldn't give credit to Valerie for that, not after less than a day. Maybe the *idea* of how his life could settle down and run more smoothly had relaxed him some, but he couldn't have changed in twelve hours.

"I'd forgotten that about Dad," David said, glancing at the photo of him—with Noah, Gideon and himself—on the wall. "Never could sit still."

The brothers stared at the picture for a few seconds. Dad. Another topic David didn't really want to get into.

Mae leaned into the office. "The third secretary to the sultan is on line one."

David hopped up.

"Third secretary, hmm?" Noah said. "Guess you didn't make as much of an impression as we all thought."

"The sultan's got fifteen secretaries. Having number three call ranks me high," he said over his shoulder as he hurried out the door and into his own office. Fifteen minutes later he slid a note into Noah's line of vision as he talked on the phone: "They added four more to the order."

Noah gave a thumbs-up.

David wandered into the shop. The sound of pneumatic tools created an odd soundtrack to work by, and the journeymen craftsmen stayed focused on the work except to give David a wave or nod.

The bays were filled with four cars in various stages of assembly. At the company's European operation in Hamburg, Germany, eight bays were filled at all times. They had orders for fourteen more cars, plus the twenty-four for the sultan. Most took about two thousand hours to build. The company created three basic models: a two-seater convertible sports car, a larger four-seater luxury passenger car and limos, each custom-fit to the customer's specs, including bulletproofing.

The brothers had increased twenty-fold the business their father had founded. With the new order for the sultan, they'd sealed their financial stability for years to come. David could finally relax a little.…

If Noah let him. In that sense Noah was like their father—he could never slow down, never miss out on any potential business. He hadn't taken a vacation in years. But maybe that was because he couldn't handle that much concentrated time with his children.

Which made David wonder about Valerie, and why Hannah's father wasn't in the picture. Had he ever been? Had he abandoned them?

David headed back to his office, channeling his focus elsewhere, not wanting to be reminded of parental abandonment.
It was something he couldn't afford to think about.

Chapter Four

At six-thirty, through the open kitchen windows, Valerie heard a car make its way up the driveway, the tires-on-gravel sound distinctive. Earlier in the day she'd peeked through the garage window and spied two cars: a large mocha-colored pickup and a shiny black SUV. She'd wondered what he'd driven to work, and assumed it was a Falcon car because his other two were American-made brands she knew.

Sure enough, a sleek silver convertible sports car came into view, the sun reflecting off a soaring-falcon hood ornament. One of the garage doors opened and David drove straight in. When he emerged a few seconds later, her pulse thumped in anticipation. Would he approve of everything she'd done? Would he even notice? She'd worked hard all day, never stopping to rest except to sit by the pool for a half hour while Hannah swam, but even then reading the files he'd left on his desk for her.

Her mind reeled with the details of a business completely

foreign to her. Her body ached from scrubbing and vacuuming. But she'd caught herself humming several times during the day. Work had never been so much fun.

Much of her happiness came from the general situation— she and Hannah had a safe, beautiful place to live. She worked for a decent man. And in a month she would have health insurance and a sense of security. All of that would spill over to Hannah, too, who had tuned in to Valerie's stress, especially this past year, even though she'd tried to hide it from her daughter. Worry about ever-increasing debt had robbed Valerie of sleep many nights.

The kitchen door swung open, and David breezed into the room, his hair windblown from driving with the top down. The messy look made him seem younger—or maybe just carefree. At the agency yesterday, his jaw had been as hard as granite, his brows drawn together, forming deep lines that had aged him. By evening, he'd relaxed considerably.

"How was your day?" she asked, locking her hands together.

"Productive." He set his briefcase on the nearest counter, next to the stack of mail she'd brought in earlier. "Yours?"

"The same."

"You get your daughter registered in school?"

"All taken care of. She starts a week from Monday. The bus will pick her up right out front."

He picked up the mail and thumbed through it. "Good."

Valerie stood by silently, wondering what to do. Apparently, she'd been wrong—he'd only seemed looser. He was taut with tension.

"Would you like a drink?" she asked.

"Yeah. I'll get it, though," he said vaguely, perusing the contents of a large envelope. After a minute he looked up at her. "Don't let me keep you."

She smiled. "I'm here to serve."

Everything about him seemed to relax then. He put aside the mail and focused on her. "Something smells great."

"Ribs. They're precooking now, then I'll put them on the grill to finish them up. There's also potato salad, corn on the cob and apple pie."

"Where have you been all my life?"

Looking for you. The wayward thought caught Valerie by surprise. No way was she letting herself wish for something she couldn't have. A smart woman learned from her mistakes.

"I've been out there in the world," she said lightly, "getting enough experience to be a great employee for you."

"I'd ask if you got a chance to look over the files I left for you, but I'm sure you did."

"Yes."

"And went grocery shopping. And made dinner from scratch. And cleaned the house, right?"

"I'm kind of an overachiever."

"No kidding." He smiled. "Where's my dog?"

"Oh! I'm sorry. She's at the cottage with Hannah." She should've thought about that. She should've realized that he would want to see Belle when he got home from work. "I'll go get her."

He put his hand on her arm as she started to pass by him but quickly released her. "Belle can stay put for now, although I'm surprised she didn't hear my car and come running."

Her heart pitter-pattered at the brief contact. She didn't need this. She didn't need this at all. "Belle's probably shut inside. I could use the intercom...."

"Are you nervous about something, Valerie?"

"I gave you my word that you wouldn't know Hannah was here, and the first thing she did was latch on to your dog."

"I believe it was mutual latching. It's fine. Don't worry about it."

Regardless of what he said, she would deal with it as soon as she could. "Do you still want to eat at seven?"

"I think I'll take a swim and kick back for a while. Would an hour ruin dinner?"

"Not at all."

He nodded and walked away, grabbing a bottle of beer from the refrigerator on his way out. She turned down the oven, then headed to the cottage. Hannah was watching a movie, with Belle curled up next to her on the sofa.

"Oops," Hannah said as the dog climbed off the couch without being ordered. They both looked guilty.

"Mr. Falcon is home. Didn't you hear his car pull in?"

"I heard it."

"You need to make sure that Belle is let out so she can greet him. He hasn't seen her much the past few years. He's really missed her."

She looked about to argue but said, "Okay."

"Belle, David's home." Valerie held the door open and hoped the dog understood. Her tail wagged slowly as she passed by, as if apologizing. "You're a good girl," Valerie said. Belle gave a little bark then hurried off, heading straight for the house and her dog door.

"Am I in trouble?" Hannah asked.

"No. You didn't know. Now you do, however." Valerie sat beside her. "I know it's hard on you, not having any friends yet. And I've been so busy all day and ignoring you most of the time."

"It's okay, Mom."

Valerie brushed her daughter's hair away from her face. It wasn't okay. Kids needed friends, and it seemed like every time Hannah made a new friend, she and Valerie moved again and Hannah had to start over. *Please let this work out,* Valerie prayed silently.

She refused to look ahead at the negative possibilities— that David wouldn't be happy with her work or his business shut down or something.

That he might meet someone, get married and not need her anymore.

If that happened, she vowed there and then not to move out of the area. She would find another job and stay put, let

Hannah have a stable life. They'd both earned that. Valerie needed to find some friends herself. She missed having a girl-friend to hang out with.

"When's dinner, Mom?"

"At seven-thirty. Can you make it that long?"

"Can I go swimming until then?"

"No. Mr. Falcon's in the pool."

"Aw, man. I'm *tired* of watching television."

Valerie patted her cheek then stood. "Read a book."

"I'm not *that* tired." She grinned.

"He'll be out of town for a while starting on Sunday. You'll have plenty of time to swim." She moved to the door. "I'll bring our plates here when everything is done."

"We're not eating at the house?"

"Hannah, employees don't eat meals with employers."

"We did last night."

"We hadn't settled in yet, so he invited us. It's different now." Valerie closed the door behind her and headed to the house. She glanced at the pool, saw David swimming laps, methodically, rhythmically, his tempo never altering. She looked away as she rushed by, giving him the privacy he'd given her the day before.

In the kitchen Valerie put on a big pot of water for the corn, then went out to the deck to fire up the gas grill. She set the patio table for one, then realized she couldn't hear him swimming. She looked at the pool in time to see him push himself up and out of the water.

Valerie went still. Water drops glistened off his chest. His swimmer's body was long and lean and perfectly muscled. There was strength there, enough to pick a woman up and carry her, to hold her close....

Belle trotted up to him, waited to be petted. He crouched down and scratched behind her ears, and she wagged her tail, rubbing happily against him. Valerie heard him talk to the dog, but couldn't hear the words.

He stood, toweling his hair, then saw her. She should've returned to the kitchen, pretended she wasn't watching, but she couldn't make her legs work. He was one beautiful male specimen....

He looked away first, then knotted his towel at his hips and headed toward the stairs leading to the kitchen. Her face burned. What would he think? That the sexual harassment claimed by the jerk she used to work for was true? That she'd lied? If they didn't have trust, they had nothing. She was living on his property, would have full access to his home, his computer, the details of his business.

She picked up a grill brush and scrubbed hard at the already clean racks until she knew he'd made his way through the kitchen and she could comfortably return.

Would he say anything? Had she already ruined her future with him?

Her hand shook as she lifted the pot lid to check on the water. And so the wait for answers began.

David stood under the shower spray, letting the ultramassage setting work magic on his tight shoulders, trying to pound out the image of Valerie watching him. If she weren't his employee, he would be flattered. She was an attractive woman, both soothing and sexy, a rare combination.

But she worked for him, so now what? Just ignore it? Discuss it so they could deal with the situation before it escalated into something uncomfortable, or even impossible?

Man, he needed a date. If all it took was for Valerie to stare at him for a few seconds—

But maybe he was wrong. Maybe she hadn't been looking at him. She'd been a good twenty-five feet away, after all. He could've read something into it that wasn't there. Perhaps his ego had gone into overdrive. His body certainly had, which was why he'd wrapped the towel around himself and headed for his bedroom so fast, before she saw how affected he'd been.

He stepped out of the shower, the question still foremost on his mind. *What should he do?*

The phone rang as he zipped his jeans.

"David? It's Denise Watson. Just checking in to see how Valerie is working out."

Hearing the voice of the director of At Your Service made David's decision for him. He didn't want to interview any more candidates. He wanted his life settled. And maybe he was wrong, anyway.

"She's fitting in very well," he told Denise, grabbing a T-shirt from his dresser drawer. "She's a very hard worker."

"And her daughter?"

"So far, so good." He hoped it continued after Hannah felt comfortable in her new surroundings. You never knew with kids.

"I'm so glad to hear that. You'll let me know if anything comes up, right?"

David almost choked. Like something hadn't already come up when Valerie had stared at him so intently, so directly? "I'll do that."

Belle followed him downstairs a minute later. He could smell the ribs on the barbecue—or the barbecue sauce, anyway. He walked into the kitchen. Valerie didn't acknowledge his presence.

"Smells good," he said.

"Everything's ready." Still she didn't look at him but moved around the room, putting corn and potato salad on three plates then taking an empty platter to the barbecue, returning with a stack of ribs. She piled a mound on one dinner plate. "I set the table on the deck for you," she said, adding ribs to the other two plates. "If you'd rather eat inside, I can move your place setting."

He was a little intrigued now at how she wouldn't look at him. He'd been right. It hadn't been his ego. "Outside is fine, thanks." He took the plate from her. "You don't need to wait hand and foot, Valerie."

"Okay." She slid her hands down her apron.

He wondered where she'd gotten it. He also wondered when the last time was that he'd seen a woman wear an apron at home. It seemed so old-fashioned. Or maybe she thought it put a division between them, a reminder of their employer/employee status.

"I'll be back in a half hour to clean up the kitchen, if that's okay," she said, picking up the two remaining dinner plates and walking away.

"That's fine." What else could he say?

She apparently hadn't thought about the fact she had a plate in each hand, however, because she stopped at the door, looking bewildered.

"Hang on. I'll get it," he said. He grabbed the handle, then waited for her to look at him. Her cheeks took on a pink tinge. "The food looks great. The house is cleaner than it's been in months. I'm not going to make your day longer by discussing the files tonight. I don't need to go into the office tomorrow, so plan on a full morning with me tomorrow."

"Okay."

He opened the door. She slipped past him, the scent of hickory trailing her. He shut the door then grabbed his beer and took his plate outside, Belle following and settling under the table, just as Valerie reached the cottage. She didn't turn around and look back at him.

David turned his attention to the panoramic view, something he never tired of. The sun hadn't quite set but had dipped behind the hill, creating an aura that backlit the scene. Peace washed over him.

After a minute he picked up a rib, the meat so tender it almost fell off the bone. He was used to eating alone at home, although not a meal as good as this one, and he certainly never set the table, place mat, cloth napkin and all. It made him seem even more alone.

He picked up his plate and moved to the railing, leaning a

hip against the wood as he dug into the potato salad. From the cottage came laughter, first Hannah's then Valerie's. Even Belle lifted her head, her ears pricking. Were they reacting to something on television or just making each other laugh? They did that a lot.

He hadn't grown up in a household where laughter was a constant. His mother had left when he was eleven. Before that, his parents had fought all the time, one of the reasons why David refused to fight with anyone. Noah had left for college the same week David's mother left, and Gideon was fourteen and entering high school, so Gideon hadn't had a lot of time for a kid brother. Their father hadn't been an easy man to please.

Hannah laughed again. Did she miss having a father, as he had missed his mother? Hannah seemed well-adjusted enough.

Belle got to her feet and wagged her tail as she looked up at him with soulful eyes.

David sighed. "Okay. You can go see Hannah."

The dog hustled off. Hell, even Belle wouldn't keep him company....

That settled it. Time to take back his life. He would start by accepting invitations, even when he was too jet-lagged. His world had become too routine, too closed in. Too all work and no play.

Time to liven things up.

Chapter Five

"So, your home base in Europe is Hamburg, Germany, but you're rarely there?" Valerie asked the next morning after spending a few hours with David in his office.

He was searching for a particular file on his computer, his focus on the screen. "I go where the potential business is, which means I'm taking a train or plane constantly, following leads. I go to Hamburg only to keep a personal hand in the business, because that's where the cars are built. It's good for the crew to see a boss now and then."

"And you've been the one solely responsible for wrapping up the deals for the past three years?"

He nodded.

No wonder he seemed so tired. It made her want to rub his back....

Valerie picked up her notepad and ran her pen down the notes she'd taken. "When you leave on Sunday, where will you go?"

"London first, then Rome."

She'd never traveled outside of California. It all sounded exotic to her, while to him it was probably just routine, maybe even mundane. "Do you have a favorite place?"

"Yes, a newly discovered one. Tumari."

"Where's that?"

"In Malaysia. It's a sultanate, an extremely rich little country with lots of oil. And it's beautiful. Completely different from the places I usually go." He double-clicked on a folder. "Usually it doesn't matter much to me where I go, since I rarely do anything but work—wining and dining being part of that."

"So you have no interest in vacationing anywhere you've been?"

"Coming home is my vacation. This house is my ultimate five-star resort." His gaze flickered to her. "You have dreams of traveling?"

"I've always wanted to go to Hawaii."

He smiled. "A small dream."

"Not to me."

"I didn't mean you were dreaming small, but that accomplishing it is relatively easy."

She couldn't contradict him without telling him how close she'd been to being homeless two days ago. How long it was going to take her to be debt free. He'd never been poor. "I'm saving my pennies. Maybe for Hannah's high school graduation."

He seemed about to say something, then looked at his monitor instead. "Here's the breakdown of clients, real and potential. How are you with spreadsheets?"

"Classroom taught, but no work experience."

"The data is here in various forms. What I need is for you to extract the data and import it into separate spreadsheets." He opened a blank spreadsheet and showed her how to transfer the numbers, as she took notes.

"What's your goal?" she asked.

"I want to know if there's business potentially big enough anywhere in particular to justify hiring a local rep permanently for the area. I know where we've sold well. I want to know where we've made inroads but no sales success—and, therefore, why. Which models have customers been interested in, then didn't buy? Which engine displacement is being considered? All these things have merit." He met her gaze. "All the information is here, but I need it separated and sorted."

"Okay." Maybe not as hard as it seemed, she hoped. She would need an atlas, though, since she didn't know where a lot of the European cities were in relation to each other. The Internet would help. "Do you want me to work on this now?"

He looked at his watch. "It's almost lunchtime. Why don't you take an hour off and spend it with your daughter. My guess is she's anxious for a swim."

She didn't like that he had to take Hannah into consideration, but she was glad he did. "Can I make a sandwich for you?" she asked.

He stretched. "I'm going for a drive. I'll eat while I'm out. I may take a couple hours."

"Okay."

"Good work today, Valerie. You're a quick learner."

"You're a patient teacher."

"Am I?" he asked.

She nodded. Why did that surprise him?

"I've never been known for patience." He jangled his keys in his pocket for a moment, then pulled them out. "I'll see you later."

"Okay."

He disappeared around the corner then came back into the doorway a moment later. "We never discussed your hours."

"In what way?"

"Obviously you're supposed to have days off. *Need* to have days off. Everyone does. And this job may be sixty hours one week and twenty hours the next."

"Let's not worry about it at this point. I'll keep track for

now and see how it averages. At some point I'll probably want
a weekend to go visit my mom in Palm Springs."

"Works for me." He left again. This time he stayed gone.

Days off? She smiled as she stood, laying her notepad on
the streamlined black and teak desk, aligning the items on his
desktop. Her salary was generous already, plus it included
room and board. She could work eighty hours a week and it
would still be a good deal for her.

Valerie put the computer to sleep, slid David's chair under
the desk, then moved hers back into position against a wall.
She closed the blinds a little, blocking the sun. After a final
glance around the room, she turned off the light and headed
for the cottage, but before she reached it, a truck pulled in, a
trailer full of gardening tools hitched behind it.

She changed direction and headed for the truck.

A man climbed out of the vehicle, thirtyish, not overly tall,
brawny. His dark hair was pulled back into a ponytail and tied
with a leather thong. His T-shirt hugged his torso, his jeans
were torn in interesting places, his boots well worn. He looked
like the kind of bad boy that teenage girls go for before they
learn that good men make better partners.

Bad boys—the kind of man Valerie had gone for. Gotten
pregnant by. Although he'd been less rough around the edges
than this guy.

"You Valerie?" Bad Boy asked, his fingers splayed low on
his hips, a knee cocked, challenge in the stance.

She kept her voice pleasant. "Yes."

He angled his head toward the big house. "David says I
take my orders from you now."

"What's your name?"

"Joseph McCoy."

She offered her hand. "I'm looking forward to working
with you."

His belligerent pose eased a little, but he wore sunglasses,
hiding much of his expression. He shook her hand.

"I'll get my notes," she said. "Be right back." She didn't wait for him to respond but headed for the cottage.

"You want to swim?" she asked her daughter as Belle slunk off the couch.

"Yes!"

"Go change. I'll be outside talking to the gardener." She grabbed a notepad from the kitchen counter and left.

Joseph was leaning against his truck, arms crossed. He didn't acknowledge her, even though he couldn't have missed hearing her footsteps. She tapped his arm with her notepad.

"Yeah, boss?" he asked.

Not a promising start. "This is my vision," she said, holding out the notepad for him to take, ignoring his hostility.

He gave her design a cursory look but didn't take the pad from her. "No flowers."

"Why not? Won't they survive the weather here?"

"Most things survive with proper tending. But in this case David specifically said no flowers."

"He didn't tell me that."

"He told *me*."

"I think the garden needs more color variation."

"You can do that with plants. There's lots to choose from. All shades of green. Yellow. Red."

"Why haven't you used them?" She mimicked his hostile pose now, tired of his attitude.

"He never said to."

"*You're* the expert."

"Look, lady, David and I have been friends since second grade. He would've said something if he didn't like what I was doing."

"Mom! Can I get in the pool?"

"Just a second." As Valerie turned back, Belle came running, but straight to Joseph.

"Hey, girl. You're home." He crouched and gave the dog a

good rub. Belle pushed herself against him, knocking him down, making him laugh.

"We need to continue our conversation by the pool so that I can watch my daughter," she said, heading that way, expecting him to follow.

"Yes, ma'am."

She stopped, turned around and looked down at him, speaking quietly so that Hannah couldn't hear her. "Look, I don't know what bee got in your bonnet but don't take it out on me. I'm your partner in this project, not your enemy. I think the place could look spectacular. It's a good basic design. It just needs…refinement."

He seemed to be glaring at her, but how could she tell with his sunglasses in place? Belle looked back and forth between them. He said nothing.

She threw up her hands. "Fine. I'll be your boss, then. Follow me. I'll give you your orders." She climbed the path, gestured to Hannah, who was dancing pirouettes around the pool, that she could dive in, then sat on a lounge chair and waited for Joseph to join her.

He took the chair next to hers. "Bee in my bonnet?" he repeated.

She couldn't gauge if he was making fun of her. "It's just an expression."

"One that grandmothers use." Before she could say anything, he held up his hands. "Truce."

"Why should I agree?"

"I was taking out my bad mood on you. I apologize."

She eyed him for a few seconds, then shrugged. "Okay."

"Thanks."

"Don't do it again or I'll fire you." She grinned.

He gave her a slight salute and reached for her notes and preliminary drawing.

"Were you mad because David put me in charge or because I was critical of how the property looked?" she asked.

"Wow. You're direct."

"Saves time and energy."

Hannah called Belle into the water. Her daughter's laughter was contagious.

"Dixie—my girlfriend—walked out on me this morning."

Valerie angled her head toward him. She wasn't surprised he confided in her, as many people did. She didn't know what it was about her, but even strangers, like this Joseph, poured out their hearts to her.

"Then two of my employees didn't show up for work. Then David called and said I needed to fix the yard, and I should do whatever you said."

Valerie chose the issue that probably bothered him the most. "I'm sorry about your girlfriend."

"She'll be back. It's a pattern. Except she was a little more ticked off than usual this morning."

She wanted to direct the conversation away from his problems. "As for doing whatever I say, that's not true, Joseph. I have a vision, but I don't even know if it's doable. We need to work together."

"I got it, okay? *Teamwork.*" Then he pulled a pencil from his back pocket and redesigned her entire plan.

David chose to drive the Falcon so he could feel the wind in his hair. He'd been shut in the office with Valerie too long for comfort.

She'd smelled good, but not flowery. Not like perfume, but soap. Fruity soap.

And woman.

He downshifted hard as he headed into a turn, an image of her burned into his memory. She'd worn a proper outfit of cotton slacks and a blouse, buttoned to the neck, her hair twisted into some kind of knot, a plastic clip holding it in place. Which left her neck exposed, long, slender, that fruity scent drifting... Peaches, maybe?

He took another curve, testing the limits of his car and his skill, jettisoning Valerie from his thoughts. When he pulled into a parking lot a few minutes later, he didn't even question why he'd come. The only question was, how would he be received?

David shoved his fingers through his hair then headed for an office on the first floor of the professional building. Laura Bannister, Attorney at Law, the sign said in gold leaf on the window. Laura, a Miss Universe contestant five years ago, had hung her shingle in her hometown three years ago, and now had this office and one in Sacramento, near the capitol building.

She was beautiful, sexy and smart. She'd been perfect for him because her biological clock hadn't begun to tick. Career first, she'd said for the year they'd dated—or tried to date, given how much he was gone. Three months ago she'd sent him a Dear John e-mail, ending the relationship.

He didn't know what he expected of her today, except that he needed to do something about his personal life. He was already too focused on Valerie, the last person in the world he should be attracted to. He needed a diversion of some kind.

David opened the front door and went inside.

"Hey, stranger!" said Laura's assistant, who also happened to be her mother. She got out of her chair and came to give him a hug. Mothers usually liked him.

"How are you, Dolly?" he asked.

"Overpaid and underworked."

He laughed. "You always were the exception to the rule."

"I try. Her assistant in Sacramento's the overworked one." She took her seat again. "I'm assuming you came to see my daughter, not me. She's on the phone. Shouldn't be too much longer, though. How's tricks?"

"Tricky." He sat on the edge of her desk. "Business is good. Better than good, even."

"David."

Laura stood framed in her office doorway, looking every bit the beauty queen, even in her understated skirt and blouse, and with her long blond hair pulled back into a twist. She might think she looked more professional dressed as she was, but in truth it made her look hot. All that fire beneath the prim surface. Fantasy come to life.

She also didn't look happy to see him, as evidenced by the way she folded her arms and didn't come forward to greet him.

"Got a minute?" he asked.

"Not really."

"Oh, give him a break," Dolly said, pulling her purse out of her desk drawer. "I'll go get us some lunch. Talk to the man." She winked at David and left the office, the resulting silence deafening.

Laura sighed. "Come in," she said.

He followed her into her office. On the walls were photos of her reigns as the winner of several pageants, starting at age eight. A glass case held several trophies. Her display at home showcased the flashier crowns and sashes.

He hadn't realized until now how much she'd surrounded herself with her memorabilia, as if everyone needed to be reminded of her success. Or *she* did.

The photo of her in her Miss Universe–supplied bikini caught his eye. He hadn't forgotten what an incredible body she had. But…a vision popped into his head of Valerie in her stretched-out black one-piece, her slender body nicely curved, but her suit as sedate as her personality.

"What do you want, David?"

He eyed her client chair but didn't sit. Revelations were coming at him full force—even the reason for why he'd come to see her. "I didn't like the way things ended between us. I should've at least answered your e-mail."

"Yes, you should have. But it doesn't change anything."

"I know." He didn't want it to, except to get it off his conscience. "I wanted to say thanks for putting up with me for as long as you did. I don't want us to run into each other around town and have it be uncomfortable."

"You waited three months to tell me that?"

"Yeah. Sorry." He saw her relax. The frown left her face. "Thanks."

He nodded, then headed for the door. "See you around." Chapter closed.

"Is this some kind of game, David?"

He faced her as she walked up to him. The woman moved like a cat. He'd forgotten that. She put a hand to his chest lightly, just her fingertips, really. Her perfume saturated his pores.

"Interested in a final farewell get-together?" she asked, her tone and expression leaving no room for doubt about her meaning. "We really didn't get to end things well."

"Do relationships end well?"

"Good point. So?"

He was tempted, more than a little. He covered her hand with his. "I don't think that would be the wisest move."

"Maybe not. But it might scratch a couple of itches. Or are you getting scratched elsewhere?"

He'd forgotten how forward she was, something that had appealed to him in the beginning. But now? Now, subtlety—and the scent of peaches instead of perfume—affected him more.

He kissed her cheek. "Goodbye, Laura."

As he pulled out of the parking lot a minute later he felt a huge load lift from him. *Making amends.* He hadn't known how good that would feel. He'd been juvenile to have ignored her e-mail all those months ago.

Now. How many other items did he have on his regret slate that he could wipe free?

Valerie huddled at David's computer, sorting and resorting information to run different reports from the same data. Hannah had begged to help Joseph in the garden, which gave Valerie worry-free time to work. Valerie found David's project fascinating and time-consuming.

The phone rang, his office line. He'd instructed her to

answer his home phone, but they'd never discussed his work number, so she let it go to the answering machine.

"Hi," a female voice said, low and kind of sexy. "I know you can't be home yet, since you just left. But I wanted to tell you how much your visit meant. It was exactly what I needed. And my invitation stands, David. Anytime. Bye."

Valerie sat frozen, staring at the machine.

Well, really, she thought, what did you expect? That he didn't have a girlfriend? Or two? Or three? A handsome, healthy, wealthy guy like that? She'd fallen victim to his charm herself, without his even trying. Imagine what would happen if he turned on that charm full force?

Valerie shoved herself out of the chair and went to the kitchen. She looked out the window, spotted Hannah tugging on a small bush—where had she gotten those gardening gloves?—until she lost her grip and fell on her bottom, hard. Joseph trudged over, said something, to which Hannah nodded, then he grabbed the bush and yanked it out.

Hannah scrambled to her feet. Joseph flexed an arm, showing off well-defined muscle. Hannah flexed hers, showing none. What their conversation was after that was anyone's guess, but they seemed to be joking around with each other, then Hannah got busy tugging on another plant as Joseph broke up the dirt around its base.

Valerie poured herself a glass of water and stared blindly at the cupboards. She should've poured herself coffee instead, she thought, since she'd just been given her wake-up call. She'd tried to see David only as her boss, but she'd ended up seeing him as her knight in shining armor, rescuing her and Hannah from almost certain peril.

Yes, she'd needed to hear that call from…that woman. To know he had someone in his life to take care of his *needs*. He only needed Valerie to take care of his house and office, nothing more. A wife without sex. A stand-in. She'd known that going in.

She heard David's car and wandered back to the window as he pulled in and stopped beside Joseph's truck. The men shook hands, then stood talking. Hannah waved at them and took off for the cottage, knowing her place.

Valerie would take her cue from Hannah and remember her place now, too.

Chapter Six

"Satisfied?"

Valerie looked out at the garden from the deck above it. Joseph waited for a response to her question.

"Very," she said. "You did an amazing job in, what, nine days? The question is, are *you* satisfied?"

"Yeah."

"And are you willing to say I was right?"

"I don't know that I'd go that far." He grinned when she raised her brows at him. "Yeah, okay. You were right. Not that David will notice any difference when he gets back. When *does* he get back?"

"Tomorrow. How're things with Dixie? Has she come home?"

"She's playing hard to get. But it's Saturday. I know where she'll be tonight."

"Where's that?"

"The Stompin' Grounds. We go every Saturday night to

dance. Except last Saturday. But she wouldn't miss two in a row." He leaned his elbows on the railing, surveying the scene.

Valerie had come to like him a lot as they'd redone the garden. He worked hard, which she admired, and was more creative than she'd given him credit for. He may have been taking the easy route before, not doing more than general upkeep, but now he seemed fully invested in the project.

She wondered how he was going to react when he saw the purple sage she was going to plant as soon as he left.

And then the daffodil bulbs she would put in for spring blooming. Just a small patch, but chock-full for a brilliant, eye-catching area of color. And the herb garden she intended to start in pots on the deck, keeping them handy for cooking. And that arc of lavender below the waterfall.

She wouldn't do much, just add splashes of color here and there, mixing up the look of the garden a little, as the seasons changed. She knew she had to choose deer- and drought-resistant plants, had already talked to the garden expert at the nursery.

Joseph turned his head toward her. "Hey, why don't you come tonight, too?"

"To the Stompin' Grounds? Is it a bar?"

"More than that. It's a place to kick up your heels. You'd like it. You *need* it."

The implication being that she was too dull, she supposed. People often misunderstood her calm exterior for a lack of adventurousness. It was only true because she had a daughter to support and raise. Or so she liked to believe.

"I don't have a babysitter, but thanks."

He slipped his cell phone from his pocket and dialed. "Ma? You busy tonight? Remember Valerie and her little girl? Wanna babysit?"

Faced with the real possibility of having to go out with Joseph, she shook her head at him.

"I'll come get you at eight. Thanks." He turned off the phone and grinned at Valerie.

"Joseph, I can't go with you."

"Can't or don't want to?"

"Both." Yet as she said it, she wondered if it was true. She wanted to get out. Do something. And his mother, Aggie, had been over twice during the week, bringing lunch, then staying on to watch Hannah swim so that Joseph and Valerie could keep working on the garden. Valerie gathered that Aggie had practically raised David through his teen years. But go to a bar? Valerie wasn't sure—

A light went on. "You want to make Dixie jealous," she stated.

"Maybe."

"Aha. Well, my fingernails aren't long enough."

He laughed. "No cat fights. I promise."

"You can't promise that. Your Dixie sounds too unpredictable. I'm a pacifist."

"Pretty please? I guarantee you'll be safe from harm."

Why was she even considering it? It wasn't the kind of thing she did....

He bumped shoulders with her. "You know you want to. There's a wild Valerie inside you that's dying to be let out."

Maybe not a wild Valerie, but a curious one. And one who knew she had to keep her thoughts off David, who would be home tomorrow. She should take advantage of his being gone, shouldn't she?

"Okay," she said finally. "But you can't paw me to get Dixie's attention. I'm not playing that game."

"Deal."

"I assume the dress code is jeans."

"Dress code?" His eyes sparkled.

"Don't make fun of me. I don't have to help you out tonight."

"Does David realize just how cute you are?" he asked with a wink.

Hannah came flying out of the cottage then, wearing her bathing suit, Belle at her heels. "I'm ready!"

"I have to get down to the pool," Valerie said, walking away.

He followed, until they reached the path that split into different directions. "See you about eight-fifteen. Bye, Hannah," he called out, waving.

She waved back. Valerie joined her daughter—and stewed about what was to come.

Joseph's mother, Aggie, reminded Valerie of Mrs. Claus, except her hair was bottle black. She gave Hannah a big hug, tucking her against her in a way that Valerie's mother never had. Hannah not only tolerated it but hugged her back, smiling and shrugging at Valerie at the same time.

"Got me eight children and sixteen grandbabies," Aggie said, shooing Valerie and Joseph out the door. "I know how to have fun with kids. Get along now."

"I left a note on the counter," Valerie began as she was pushed from behind. "There're cookies in—"

"Your girl's eight years old. She can tell me what she's allowed to have and do, and I know Joseph's cell number. Scram."

"I'm dazed," Valerie said to Joseph as he drove away from the house.

"She's competent."

Valerie laughed. "I can tell." She felt relaxed all of a sudden. How long had it been since she'd been out without Hannah? More than a year. Since she was forced to leave her job and the co-workers she'd become friends with.

"Where'd you get those boots?" he asked. "I would've sworn you didn't own any, city slicker."

"I didn't until this afternoon." She'd bought boots, new jeans and a white Western-style shirt. She thought she looked pretty darn good.

Valerie hoped she fit in. The outfit had been a huge splurge. She figured she needed to save every possible penny until she knew that David would keep her beyond the month, but it felt so nice to have something new to wear.

The interior of the Stompin' Grounds didn't surprise her, from the dark decor to the twang of the song playing from the jukebox. If the volume dropped some—well, a lot—when people realized Joseph had brought a new woman, that wasn't a surprise, either. He said they came every Saturday night, like probably most of the crowd. Loyalties would be tested.

Valerie saw heads turn toward a corner table in the back and figured Dixie had to be sitting there, but there were four women at the table, all about the same age.

"Bar okay with you?" Joseph asked over the din, which hadn't returned to its former volume yet.

"Sure." She took a seat.

"What's your pleasure?"

Somehow she didn't think asking for a strawberry margarita was a smart move, not if she wanted to fit in. "Beer, I guess."

Joseph held up two fingers to the bartender, then turned around to face the room, resting his elbows on the bar behind him.

"Which one of the four women in the corner is throwing daggers at me?" she asked.

"Probably all of 'em. But Dixie's wearing the red shirt."

Valerie smiled at the bartender, who set her drink in front her. She reached for it, positioning herself in a way she could sneak a look at Dixie. Valerie swallowed hard. The woman didn't look dainty or helpless, for all that her hair was a mass of blond curls. "I think this was a bad idea," she said to Joseph.

"Why's that?"

"You know that saying about if looks could kill? I'm already a dead woman." She decided not to drink much so that she wouldn't have to use the restroom, wouldn't let herself get into a situation where Dixie and her friends could trap her.

"Just ignore her." He took a long sip, then grabbed her hand. "Let's dance."

After a minute the conversation volume spiked again,

although she noticed that people's interest didn't really fade. Heads turned like at a tennis match, watching the two players. One dance led to another, with barely a break to take a cooling sip. A few people called out to him, but mostly he was left alone. Somehow, she didn't think that was normal. It looked like most people sided with Dixie. Valerie wondered what had caused their rift.

"Are we entered in a marathon that I don't know about?" she asked him, trying to catch her breath. "Last one standing wins, if we don't die first?"

"You gettin' tired, city slicker?"

Valerie stopped in her tracks. She spun away from him, walked over to the bar and sat down.

"Sorry," he said, sitting beside her, lifting his beer. "I'm hurtin'. Guess I hadn't admitted that."

It seemed to be a signal to others that it was safe to take the dance floor, like maybe no shootout at the OK Corral was going to happen. Soon it was crowded, too crowded to see the corner where Dixie sat. "I'd like to go home," Valerie said, leaning close to be heard over the noise. "You can come back here after and beg her to give you another chance. But I want out of your drama."

"But it's early—"

"And who might this be?"

Valerie pulled back fast. She'd never heard Dixie speak, but knew it had to be her.

Valerie stuck out her hand before Joseph could say anything. "Hi, I'm Valerie. I'm just a friend."

Dixie's gaze flickered to Valerie, giving her an icy once-over, then dismissing her by turning back to Joseph, who didn't look the least cowed. For a man who wanted his woman back, he sure didn't have a clue how to go about it.

"Is that right, Joey? She's a *friend?* Like that other friend a couple of years back?"

"We were on a break. You even said—"

"Hey, baby. Sorry I'm late," interrupted a low voice as an arm slid around Valerie's waist, making her jump. Stunned by the sudden appearance of her boss, who wasn't due to come home until the next day, she sat speechless, staring at him.

He stuck out his free hand at Joseph. "Thanks for taking care of my girl. I owe you one."

Joseph shook his hand, pumping it hard.

"Have you two met?" David asked, looking from Valerie to Dixie.

Dixie looked suspicious. "Since when did you starting trusting Joey with a girlfriend of yours, David?"

"Joe's my oldest friend. We have an unwritten code."

"A code?" Dixie drawled.

"And Valerie only has eyes for me, don't you, baby?" David's tone of voice was matter-of-fact and almost adoring, which was at odds with his expression, although only Valerie could see that as he faced her directly.

Well, two could play that game, she decided, fascinated at the lengths David would go to protect his buddy. She put her hands on his face, bringing him a little closer. "Welcome home, *baby.*"

He went very still. "Sorry I'm late."

"You're here now. That's all that matters."

"Well, kiss her, you idiot," Dixie said from behind, shoving him almost on top of Valerie. "A girl doesn't like to be kept waiting."

He looked at her mouth—

"But a girl also likes anticipation," Valerie said, dropping her hands to his chest—his very nice chest—and keeping him at bay. "And privacy."

He smiled, slow and sexy. "Then I think we should get ourselves home."

Valerie leaned around him and put out a hand. "As I said, I'm Valerie."

"Dixie."

"So I heard. Joseph's been moping about you all week."

"How would you know that?" Dixie may have been speaking to Valerie, but she was looking at Joseph, her expression melding anger and hurt.

"He's been redesigning David's yard. Even my daughter noticed how sad he was, and she's only eight."

Dixie's gaze collided with David's then. "You're involved with a woman with a kid?"

"Shall we go?" he said to Valerie, who was more than a little curious about what Dixie meant, why she seemed so surprised.

"I'm sorry," Dixie said to Valerie. "Geez. Me and my big mouth."

"It's okay." It wasn't, of course, but at least David would have a good reason to tell people why they'd broken up—*She had a kid, you know*. But if he hated kids, she hadn't picked up on that. He was certainly keeping Hannah at a distance because of the professional relationship—Valerie did the same—but the moments David and Hannah had been in each other's company had been fine. He'd seemed at ease.

Dixie put a hand on each of their shoulders. "Dance with your girl first, David. It's great foreplay." She smiled at Valerie as if apologizing again.

The music was loud and fast. "You game?" he asked.

"Sure. But just one."

"I know." He grinned. "I'm anxious, too."

She just barely stopped herself from rolling her eyes, then swallowed hard as he took her hand and moved onto the dance floor, greeting people, introducing her. Then just as they started to dance, the music changed to something slow.

"I think we're stuck," he said, taking her into his arms.

She tried to hold herself away a little.

"Everyone thinks we're lovers," he said, wrapping his arms around her, drawing her against him.

It was a moment out of time, never to be repeated. Why not just enjoy it, she thought? It was only a dance, after all.

Because you're already getting in too deep, and you, of all people, should know better. Fool me once, shame on you. Fool me twice, shame on me.

She let the cautionary words in her head override her body's response to David's nearness. "Baby?" she said.

He laughed, low. "It just popped out."

"Well, you were a good friend to rescue Joseph like that."

"Joseph? Hell. I was rescuing you, Ms. Sinclair. Joe can fend for himself. Dixie's a force to be reckoned with."

"And you didn't think I could handle her?"

He put his head back and laughed. The feel of his chest moving against hers made her forget her need for caution, especially when their abdomens touched, and then their hips.

"Look over there," he whispered in her ear, making her shiver.

She followed his gaze and saw Joseph and Dixie kissing passionately, a reunion apparently under way.

"No, you wouldn't have been able to handle Dixie. Not if she was in full siege mode," he said, as the song continued. "She wrestled in high school. She lifts weights. They both do. It's something they do together. She could take you with her pinky finger."

"I'm scrappy."

His gaze touched her gently. "I'll bet you are."

"What's the deal with them, anyway?"

"They've been together since they were fourteen. Every once in a while she walks away because he hasn't asked her to marry him. And one day she probably won't come back. Joe's crazy to let her slip through his fingers. There's no other woman for him."

"Do you believe that? That people have soul mates? That there's a special person meant just for each of us?"

"I believe that applies to *them.*"

Valerie considered his words. So, he believes for other people, but not for himself? It made her wonder. "Why are you home so early?"

"I was done. Was able to grab an earlier flight. Even got a sleeper seat on the flight, so I'm not as worn-out as usual."

"What are you doing *here?*"

"I saw Joe's truck in the parking lot on my way home. When I got to the house, your lights were out. I assumed you were in bed. Your car was in the garage. I decided to hang with Joe for a while."

"He picked me up. His mom is babysitting."

"I figured that out when I got here and checked out the action, seeing the two of you together at the bar. Same as I figured out why he brought you here. I'm surprised you agreed, though. Doesn't seem like something you would do, make another woman jealous like that."

"I told him he couldn't paw me. I told him I wouldn't play that game. I felt sorry for him. I knew she'd left before, but I didn't realize it was such a regular thing with them or I wouldn't have bothered. Except, it was nice to get out, too. And that's probably what drove me to say yes more than anything."

"You've been lonely?"

It wasn't the words so much as the way he said them that almost brought tears to her eyes. "A little."

"I warned you the place was isolated."

"You don't have to get defensive, David. I wasn't complaining. I love living here. It was more about the opportunity to get out without Hannah, for once. Even good moms need breaks."

The song ended. He seemed reluctant to let her go, so she stepped away, breaking the contact, which, indeed, had been great foreplay. Her body hummed.

David called out to Joseph that he would take Aggie home. They headed to the door, bidding farewell as they went, then they were outside. Few stars were visible in the dark sky because of a full moon. Music drifted. She welcomed the cool night air against her skin.

They made their way to his SUV. He opened the passenger door and she climbed in.

"You look nice, by the way," he said.

"Thanks."

"Seriously. The cowgirl look? It suits you."

"Okay." She finally noticed that he was wearing a similar outfit, except his shirt was dark.

They pulled out onto the highway, not speaking again until they stopped in front of his garage. "Thanks for all your hard work this week," he said. "You've already made a big difference."

She didn't tell him how many extra hours she had spent on the projects he'd given her by phone. She wanted him to believe in her competence while she was feeling her way through a lot of it, especially since his kind of business was nothing she'd encountered before, even working as a temp in various places.

"You're an easy boss," she said, grabbing the door handle. Being confined with him wasn't a good idea, not after the way they'd held each other, and he'd whispered in her ear as they pretended a relationship for Dixie.

"You're the first person to say so."

"Really?"

"Yeah. I think we've got some sort of vibe going. You seem to know what I want before I want it."

"I don't have any other distractions, David. No other employees in the office, no drama. It makes it easy to focus and anticipate. And it's worked out okay, too, that you've needed me late at night while Hannah's asleep." She let go of the door handle and faced him, deciding he wanted to talk, and therefore she should listen. It was only part of being a good employee....

"Are you getting enough sleep?" he asked.

"I'm fine. Are you?"

"My body's permanently confused about day and night."

"Let me know if you'd like me to fix your breakfast." She opened the door then, too wound up to stay with him any longer. Too much about him appealed to her. "I'll send Aggie out. What about Belle?"

"Send her, too. I'll take her along for the ride."

"Okay." She hopped out then after a moment turned back to him. "Thanks for the rescue."

"Glad I came along at the right time."

She didn't want to start thinking he would always be around when she needed him, but the coincidence of his coming home early, combined with the timing of his hiring her when she was desperate, didn't escape her.

"Aggie adores you," she said instead.

"Same here. She became Mom for me after mine left."

They hadn't talked about that before. She didn't know the circumstances, only that his father raised him. "My dad left me, too."

He was quiet for several seconds. "And Hannah's father?"

"A long story."

He nodded, but she didn't know what he meant by it and didn't want to get into it now. "See you in the morning."

"Good night, Valerie."

She gave him a small wave, then headed to the cottage. Aggie refused to take any money but did accept an invitation to dinner as payment.

Valerie changed into her nightgown and went to bed, reliving the evening in her head. She heard David's car return and climbed out of bed, catching a glimpse of him and Belle taking the stairs to the back door. The kitchen light came on then went off soon after. After a few seconds his bedroom light came on. He appeared in the window, a silhouette of stillness until he took off his shirt and tossed it aside. He bent over, she assumed to remove his boots, then he pulled his belt free.

He stepped away from the window then. It wouldn't have mattered, as the dim light only backlit him, not allowing for details from where she stood.

She was just about to go back to bed when she saw him come down the back stairs, a towel wrapped around him. His back to her, he stood beside the pool, tossed aside the towel and dove in. He was naked. And gorgeous. Sculpted. She'd seen a photograph of a statue in Greece of the god Hermes, and David's body matched it—muscular, sleek and tempting.

Her conscience niggled at her, whispering that she should give him privacy and step away from the window. Yet she stayed, waiting, telling herself that no one should swim alone, and someone should be watching, just in case.

But she was waiting for him to climb out, and she wouldn't lie to herself about her attraction, even if she couldn't do anything about it. Didn't dare do anything about it.

After fifteen or twenty minutes of swimming lap after lap, he got out. He stood on the side of the pool, lit by the moon, sluicing off water with his hands. She'd like to do that for him.…

He reached for the towel. Her mouth watered. Suddenly he seemed to look right at her. She was pretty sure he couldn't see her watching him, but her heart pounded at the possibility, both from fear of being caught and from hope that he might like the fact she was watching, something so out of character for her, trespassing on his privacy as she was.

He held the towel around his hips and headed back to the house, taking one last look at the cottage when he reached the door.

She slipped into bed and pulled the covers over her head, willing the visions of him away.

Because the last thing she could afford was another obsession that would go nowhere.

Chapter Seven

David wandered onto the deck the next morning and admired his garden. The change was remarkable. Valerie was right. He'd let it become too wild, too overrun. Somehow she'd managed to tame it *and* keep it natural. Obviously she had more vision than he did.

He watched her come out of the cottage and head up the path, the view completely unobstructed now with the foliage trimmed. She wore a sundress—turquoise, sleeveless, the skirt soft and flowing, ending at midcalf. She'd left her hair down, held away from her face with a band the same color as her dress.

In the car the night before he'd been tempted to finger her hair. As they'd danced, he'd inhaled her scent, not peaches like before, but something else. Strawberries?

Danced. For all his determination to keep his distance, he'd not only ended up spending social time with her, but dancing, as well. She'd fit in his arms—and against his body—perfectly. He'd wanted her to lean her head against his shoulder. Crazy idea. Stupid idea. It was a good thing she'd forced some distance between them.

He heard the kitchen door open and shut. A few seconds later she stepped through the open sliding door. He realized he'd felt a little on edge as he'd waited for her.

"Good morning," she said, her hands folded, her expression serene. "How can I help you?"

Loaded question, one he put from his mind. She wouldn't like the answers.

"You rang?" she said into his continued silence.

He'd used the intercom, asked her to come up as soon as she comfortably could. "You didn't have to rush."

"I was up and ready. Do you want breakfast?"

"I already ate." Cold cereal. He didn't know why he didn't just let her fix him something every day, but he hadn't been able to, not since the first morning. "I've decided to throw a party."

She lit up. "Oh, how fun!"

"I haven't given one in a long time. And the yard looks impressive, thanks to you, and should be shown off."

"I can't take all the credit. Or even half of it. Joseph reconfigured my design and did most of the labor. Joint effort, but mostly his."

"It wouldn't have gotten done otherwise, so thank you." He'd brought out a pen and paper for her and left it on the table. "Labor Day, I'm thinking, which means you would only have a week to get ready. If you want to use a caterer, I'd be fine with that."

"Oh, no. I'd like to do it all." She sat, pulled the pad close. "What kind of theme?"

"I have to have a theme? Well, a pool party. And barbecue."

"Adults only? Kids?"

"Both." He took a seat. He liked looking at her. He hadn't seen her really excited about anything, as she generally kept a warm but understated demeanor. "My brother Noah and his children. My brother Gideon and a guest. I don't know who he's dating at the moment. Joe and Dixie. Aggie. Mae, from my office, and her husband."

"Is that it?" Valerie asked when he hesitated.

"No. A few of Joe's brothers and sisters. I may add more when I've had time to think about it."

"Will you bring a date?"

Her tone was casual but pitched a little higher than usual. He recalled the voice mail from Laura, letting him know she was willing to see him again. If he wanted to have a date at his side that day, she would probably say yes.

Then he realized he couldn't do that, even if he wanted to. "That could be tricky, since several people now think you're my girlfriend."

She sat back. "I hadn't considered that. That's…awkward. We should come clean with your friends before rumors start."

He tipped his chair back against the railing and contemplated her. "You don't know much about small towns, do you?"

"Meaning?"

"Meaning, by now everyone who knows me, and some who don't, already have us locked as a couple."

"But it isn't true."

"It appeared to be."

She looked at the table, her expression hidden. When she finally looked up, she appeared more serious than he'd seen before. "You have to fix it."

"How?"

"With the truth. Tell people we're not a couple. That I was putting on a show for Dixie, trying to help them reconcile. I can't have anyone thinking there's more between us, David, *especially* my daughter. In fact, I think you should bring a date yourself. *Need* to bring a date, or else no one's going to believe us."

He knew she was right. "I'll make some calls."

"Thank you." She picked up the pen again and got back to

business so suddenly it caught him off guard. "Do you want to do the barbecuing yourself?"

What had just happened? "Yeah, although Gideon will probably take over. He's the chef in the family. But let's keep it simple. Hot dogs and hamburgers. You can go crazy with the rest, if you want."

"What kind of budget will I have?"

"I don't know. Is a grand okay?"

She coughed. "I think I can pull it together for less than that."

"Whatever. And I was hoping you could organize something for all the kids later in the evening, maybe in the cottage so the adults could enjoy some time without them."

"Sure. Do you know a teenage girl who would like to help out? It'd be hard for me to work both places."

"Give Aggie a call. She probably has some names."

"You didn't mention Noah bringing a date."

"He's not going out yet." He'd been widowed for three years, but to David's knowledge, Noah had never taken a woman out, not even for coffee.

"Will you be calling and inviting people or do you want invitations mailed?"

"I'll call. That way I can get RSVPs at the same time."

She hugged the pad to her chest. "This will be so much fun."

"I'm glad you think so." He let his chair settle on four legs again. "I want you to take today off."

She frowned. "Why?"

"Hannah starts school tomorrow. You two should spend the day together. Feel free to use the pool as much as you want."

"Okay, thanks." She stood. "And you'll take care of telling people?"

"I will."

He looked at his watch instead of her as she walked away.

He would talk to Joe and Dixie in person, even if it meant waking up the sleeping tigress.

"The whole day?" Hannah screeched happily. "Just me and you?"

"Yep," Valerie said, smiling.

"And we can do whatever we want?"

"Within reason. And budget. What would you like to do? Do you want to go to the movies?"

"Mom, I've watched sooo many movies. I'm sick of them."

Understandable. "So, what appeals to you?"

"I saw a miniature-golf place when we were out once."

"Okay. Anything else?"

"Can we afford anything else?"

Valerie took her daughter into her arms, resting her chin on Hannah's head. "I'm sorry we had such a bad year, honey. I'm sorry you haven't had any treats in so long. Yes, we can afford lunch before we golf, and an ice cream after."

"But we bought new clothes for school."

Valerie kissed her daughter's head, then held her at arm's length. "You can officially stop worrying about money, okay?" Valerie hoped, anyway. Even making it past the thirty-day trial period didn't mean the job was secure forever. But this time she would have more in savings, just in case—as soon as she paid off her debts. And since she didn't think she could lose her job because of incompetence, she would have a good recommendation to take with her, therefore a better shot at getting a new job faster than the last time.

As long as there were no more evenings like the previous one. She had to stick to a professional relationship with him. Period. He was far too tempting.

"Okay, Mom. No worries."

They headed to Chance City and found the Take a Lode Off Diner, where they ate lunch. Their round of miniature golf after was lively as they goaded each other, challenged each other and shared a carefree afternoon.

At an ice cream parlor, Hannah begged, "Please, Mom? A double scoop. Pretty please? It's a special occasion. Just this once."

Valerie slipped an arm around Hannah's shoulders. "Yes, it is. Two double scoops of bubblegum on sugar cones," Valerie said to the teenage clerk, then to Hannah she added, "We'll have a bubble-blowing contest. Winner... Winner gets what?"

"Um. Winner—"

"Hey, hi," said a woman coming up to them. "Sorry to interrupt. I don't remember your name from last night." She laughed. "You probably don't remember mine, either. How're you doing? I'm Sheryl."

Valerie recognized her as one of Dixie's friends, all of whom must be weightlifters. The four Amazons of Nevada County. Had this one gotten the word yet that Valerie wasn't David's girlfriend? "I'm Valerie. This is my daughter, Hannah."

"Hi. Nice to meet you. That's great that Joseph and Dixie are back together, huh?"

"Yeah, great."

"And everyone was surprised to hear about David and you. We didn't have any idea he was involved with someone."

Hannah looked up at Valerie, who tried to laugh it off. "Oh, that. I don't know why anyone assumed that. I work for him, that's all."

Sheryl frowned. "But Dixie said—"

"Honey, our cones are ready." She put a ten-dollar bill in Hannah's hand and prodded her toward the counter, then turned back to Sheryl. "Truly. He's my boss."

"Sure didn't look like it."

"David was just having some fun with all of you."

"Does Dixie know that?"

"I'm sure she does." Valerie made herself smile. "I hope she forgives him. Boys will be boys."

"Don't I know it! Well, I'm glad that's squared away, but I must say I'm surprised. You two seemed so…close."

Hannah came back and handed Valerie her cone and the change. "Thanks, honey." She swirled her tongue over the cold, creamy dessert. "I'm glad you introduced yourself," she said to Sheryl. "We need to get going, though."

She urged Hannah forward and out the door. "Let's walk up the street and window shop as we eat."

"What did that lady mean, Mom? You and Mr. Falcon didn't go out last night. You went with Joseph."

Valerie hedged only a little. "Joseph and I went as friends. He and his girlfriend had a little argument, and he wanted to—" Make her jealous. How could she tell Hannah that? "He wanted to try to make up with her, and he knew she would be there. Then David saw Joseph's car in the parking lot and stopped in to say hi. We danced one dance together, and people just assumed we were dating."

"That's silly." She scooped out a gumball with her tongue. "He's the boss," she mumbled.

"Exactly. And that's how rumors get started. So, if anyone says anything to you at the party next week, you can tell them that."

"Okay. This gumball is too frozen to bite!"

And just like that the conversation changed, which was a big relief to Valerie. Hannah declared herself the winner of the bubble-blowing contest later and claimed, as the winner, the right to having Valerie make her bed for a month. Valerie negotiated it down to a week.

When they got home, Hannah took off toward the cottage to change into her bathing suit as Valerie followed more slowly.

David called out from the deck. "Did you have fun?"

"I beat her!" Hannah shouted. "At golf and blowing bubbles."

"Good for you."

"We're going swimming now."

"Okay."

"Oh, and Mom told that lady that you weren't on a date with her."

He straightened. "Um. Good."

She rushed into the cottage. The door slammed behind her.

"That lady?" he asked Valerie.

"Sheryl. We ran into her at the ice cream parlor. I hope you were able to clear things up, because I gave her the scoop."

"Was that a pun?" He grinned. "Hold on a sec. I'll come down rather than yell."

Valerie didn't know what to do with her hands. If she crossed her arms, she would look defensive, so instead she picked dead leaves off the nearest bush until he came up beside her. She didn't look at him, just kept scrounging for leaves. "So, everything is squared away?" she asked as Belle bumped her nose against Valerie's leg, looking to be petted.

"I don't know that everyone has heard yet, but the grape-vine has been activated."

She scratched Belle behind her ears, Belle's tail wagging slowly. "What happened with Dixie?"

"She actually found it endearing that Joe tried to make her jealous. Apparently he hasn't done that before."

Valerie closed her eyes, relieved. "We got lucky."

"I didn't say that. She's forgiven *him*. I don't know about us. You in particular."

So much for her first foray into the new town. "And you'll invite a date for the party next week, so there's no doubt in anyone's mind that you and I aren't…a couple?"

"I already did."

So fast? Valerie wasn't prepared for her reaction, as if someone had punched her. "Great." She straightened. Belle wandered off toward the cottage. Standing so close to David reminded Valerie of how it felt to be in his arms, safe and excited at the same time.

He's not your knight, she reminded herself. He's your boss. And you need to keep it that way.

She gestured toward the cottage. "I'd better go change. Hannah will be waiting."

"Have a nice swim." He turned around.

"Did you have a good day?"

"I drove all over town, clearing up misperceptions and extending invitations. I haven't talked to Joe's brothers yet, but everyone else said yes."

"So, your brothers live nearby?"

"They're both in Chance City, but we've got a few miles separating us. You have any siblings?"

"No. I wish I did."

"Yeah. Most of the time they're great. I see Hannah's waiting for you. I'll let you go."

"Mo-om. Why aren't you ready?"

"Give me three minutes." Valerie hurried off. She'd gotten a new bathing suit, still a modest one-piece, but one that fit her well.

He has a date. She pulled off her clothes, stepped into the light blue suit and shimmied it up her body. The woman who'd left a message for him? Probably.

Or maybe not. He could be dating five different women, for all she knew.

Because, really, when it came down to it, she didn't know him at all. She just knew it was getting harder day by day to think of him only as her boss.

Chapter Eight

Valerie scanned the Labor Day party crowd as she set a tray of chips, salsa and guacamole on a table near the pool. No one new had arrived in the past fifteen minutes, while she'd been in the kitchen.

David's date was fashionably late, as were his brother Gideon, and Joseph and Dixie. Valerie counted heads in the pool—nine—eight children, plus one of Joseph's brothers. Two teenagers, Mindy and Jessica, were lifeguarding, then would entertain the kids later in the cottage.

During Hannah's first week in school, she'd made a friend, Gabby, who'd been invited to join the fun. The two eight-year-olds huddled in one corner of the pool, whispering and giggling. Most of the noise came from Joseph's sister's two children, who propelled themselves like seals out of the pool onto the deck, then did cannonballs back into it, screaming, until Mindy and Jessica managed to quiet them a little, probably by bribery. Valerie understood now what David meant—by comparison to the other children in the pool, Noah's kids were well behaved and quiet. Too quiet for nine- and twelve-year-olds.

Valerie headed back toward the house thinking how quickly she'd become used to the peacefulness of David's property, because, in contrast, the party noise seemed as loud as a rock concert, even though the music coming from the outdoor speakers wasn't booming. Conversation was steady and normal, except for Aggie's contagious laugh. Even David's brother Noah was laughing.

An interesting man, Valerie thought, assessing him. He was taller and broader than his youngest brother, and although he didn't pace, she sensed a high level of energy and impatience. He watched his children most of the time, frowning, although whether from concern or disappointment or something else altogether, Valerie didn't know.

She looked for David as she climbed the stairs to the kitchen but didn't see him. Was he worried about his date's late arrival? Annoyed? Angry? Perhaps she had called David on his cell to say she would be late—or not coming, after all.

"The party can start now!" bellowed Joseph as he and Dixie strolled up the driveway, having parked out front.

Valerie was glad to see them holding hands. She'd worried all week about facing Dixie again. Would she turn her back on Valerie for her part in the game last weekend? Valerie wanted to make friends, especially girlfriends, to make a real community for herself, as Hannah was already doing.

But her daughter could also use a strong male role model, something that Valerie had been denied after her father left her and her mom....

And maybe it was the reason for some of her own problems, she was finally coming to realize, perhaps even why she'd ended up in trouble at her last job, not to mention getting pregnant out of wedlock.

Since David couldn't be that role model for Hannah, it was up to Valerie to find someone who could. Having girlfriends could lead to finding a boyfriend. It would force her to get out and mingle, the first step in expanding her social life.

"Coming up or going down?" David asked, startling her, obviously on his way down the stairs, his arms loaded with cartons of soda to add to the depleted supply by the pool.

"Up. To the kitchen. Joseph and Dixie just arrived."

"Couldn't miss hearing that," he said. "It's going well."

"Everyone knows each other, though, right? Makes it easy."

"Easier, anyway. Small towns make for interesting histories."

"Like what?"

"Like Noah and Joe's brother, Jake. He's in the pool with his nephews. Big rivals in high school, not just in sports, but academics and campus politics."

"And girls?"

"That I don't remember. Noah is seven years older than me. We didn't really become close until our dad died and we ended up sharing the business. By then Noah was married and had Ashley and Zoe. I only remember his and Jake's rivalry in high school because I was friends with Joe, so I heard the trash talk at both houses."

"It looks like there's still a feud going on. Jake's playing with all the kids rather than standing and talking to Noah, as his other brother is." She slanted a look at David. "So, if you knew about the rivalry, why'd you invite Jake?"

He hesitated then finally said, "I'm hoping."

"Hoping what? For a fight?"

"Honestly? Yeah. Not a fight, but something to shake Noah up some."

"Look what the cat dragged in!" Dixie announced as a man and woman came up the driveway. "Good grief, Laura. Couldn't you do better than that?"

Dixie was grinning, so Valerie gathered that she and the man knew each other well enough to make a jibe like that. She recognized Gideon from the photographs on David's wall. And "Laura" would be Laura Bannister, David's date.

She was stunning, with her long blond hair, shorts and body-hugging T-shirt. And what a body her clothes hugged.

Valerie felt a swoosh of air as David went past her and down the stairs to greet the new arrivals. Would he kiss her hello?

No. A brief hug, then a handshake with Gideon, who had come without a date.

Valerie hurried on up to the kitchen, from there not once glancing out the window as she finished putting food on platters. She started the gas grill to preheat it, keeping to the timetable she and David had decided on.

After a minute she gave up avoiding looking at him and his date and searched them out. They stood with several people, Laura putting her hand on his arm now and then, smiling at him, her body language announcing how comfortable they were with each other physically.

The pain that stabbed Valerie in her chest didn't catch her completely off guard. During the past week, she'd spent a great deal of time with David as they worked together on projects. With Hannah in school most of the day, the house seemed way too intimate. No one needed her attention. No one dropped by. Valerie and David had almost lived in his office. She made sure they never touched, not even innocently. She'd petted Belle a lot.

But he complimented Valerie on her abilities and teased her a little when she got too serious, and she'd enjoyed being with him.

Which made it hard to see him with that woman, Laura, who looked like every man's fantasy.

The kitchen door opened and Dixie breezed in. A headband kept her tight blond curls away from her face, taming them slightly. But nothing about her well-defined muscles seemed tame.

She crossed her arms and tapped her foot. "Well, if it isn't David's...girl? Isn't that what he called you? His *girl?*"

"He explained the situation to you, right?" Valerie asked, almost holding her breath. She didn't like conflict, and this could easily become one.

"I don't like liars," Dixie stated.

"Neither do I." Valerie stood up straighter. "I did your boyfriend a favor so that you two could make up. Am I sorry I did it? Yes. I didn't understand how small towns operate. I wanted to make friends here, and now everyone thinks I'm not a good person. If I had it to do over, I wouldn't agree to go to the Stompin' Grounds."

"Is that an apology?" Dixie asked after giving Valerie a piercing look.

"Yes." *Please don't make me get on my knees.* She'd promised herself after she got pregnant with Hannah and all that followed that she wouldn't ever beg anyone again.

"Yeah, okay," Dixie said finally. "I actually thought it was kinda cute of Joseph to plan something like that. Anything I can do to help?"

Situation defused, just like that. "No, but thanks."

"Do you want me to round David up for you?"

"I hate to take him away from his date." She wished she had something left to do, to keep her mind off the woman.

"Boy, that's a shocker, isn't it? I mean, I thought they'd split up months ago." Dixie grabbed a carrot stick and took a bite. "I had no idea they'd started up again."

It was her own fault, Valerie thought. She'd made him bring a date so that everyone would know there was nothing between David and her except an employer/employee relationship.

"Well, I have no problem telling David you're ready for him." She opened the door, then stopped. "Would you like to get together for lunch or something sometime?"

"I'd love to, thanks."

"We'll figure out a time and place before the party's over."

"Great."

"You want me to invite Miss Universe so you can get to know her better?"

Valerie smiled at the nickname, which suited Laura Bannister to a T. "Do you call her that to her face?"

"Well, no, since it would remind her she was only first runner-up. I'm not *that* catty." She grinned and left.

Valerie stared at the platters of food. Laura was the first runner-up to Miss Universe? Seriously? Which meant she'd been Miss USA. Miss California. Miss…whatever else.

How was she supposed to compete with—

Valerie squeezed her eyes shut. She wasn't competing, couldn't compete. Which made this the best news possible, because now she knew he wouldn't be tempted by her, either, not with Miss Universe in the picture.

She should be relieved.…

"So? You and Laura again?" Gideon asked, seated on a lounge next to David, both of them watching the woman in question play pool volleyball, her bikini-clad body a sight to behold, perfection in motion.

David glanced at his middle brother and shrugged. "I'm not sure yet."

"She seems to be into it, if I'm any judge of such things. But you seem to be holding her at bay."

One of Gideon's strengths was his above-average understanding of human nature. It had made him a good pitchman for Falcon Motorcars, for gauging the right kind of sales pitch for the individual. Unfortunately, his business sense wasn't always as accurate as his people sense. "I don't want to make the same mistake as before," David said.

"Of?"

"Of starting a relationship that requires too much patience and understanding of a woman."

"Very wise."

"Yeah." David swigged his beer. "Not personally satisfying, however."

Gideon flashed a grin. "Not getting any, huh?"

"Nope." Although Laura's offer had been made and was waiting to be accepted.

"That new housekeeper of yours is a looker," Gideon commented.

"No trespassing, bro. She's the best thing that's happened to me in years."

Gideon raised his hands in surrender. "I won't poach."

"Damn straight you won't." He followed Valerie with his gaze as she cleared tables. She hadn't mingled much, although he had encouraged her to. She and Dixie and Joseph had talked a little, and Aggie was never to be ignored, but otherwise, Valerie had worked, quietly, efficiently, occasionally giving Hannah a hug, whispering in her ear, getting a nod or giggle in return.

David caught Valerie eyeing Laura, who'd scored a point in the pool and was whooping about it. Competitive, sexy Laura. David wondered what Valerie thought of her. As far as he could tell, they hadn't exchanged words.

Noah joined his brothers. It was rare for all three of them to hang out together anymore, given David's overseas schedule, the demands of Noah's home life and Gideon's ongoing projects, which took him far afield at times. Belle wandered over and curled up at David's feet.

"She's ignored me all day," Noah said, angling his head toward the dog.

"You're a bad dream she's trying to forget." David grinned.

"She had it pretty easy. Lots at my house to keep her active." He grabbed a slice of watermelon from the tray beside him and took a bite. "So, what've you got your hands in these days, Gid?"

"A project near Tahoe. In fact, I've been meaning to talk to you both. See if you want in on the ground floor."

David exchanged a look with Noah. Gideon had sold his share of the business to them years ago, not wanting any part of the family business. Since then nothing had turned to gold for him. Although he'd managed to keep out of bankruptcy, just barely, he'd lost his wife because of the risks he'd taken. She'd walked out two years ago.

"We came to an agreement about you asking for money," Noah said quietly. "You want our input on your business plan, we're there for you. But our money's tied up in Falcon and needs to stay there, where it's safe."

"I hear business is booming. Something about a sultan and a whole lot of orders."

"Which means more in expenses, too. Employees, manufacturing, work space. You know that."

"Don't say I didn't give you a chance," he said lightly, but David sensed a bit of desperation.

"Do you need a loan?" he asked. "For yourself, personally, I mean?"

Gideon's jaw hardened. "I'm fine."

"You could come back to Falcon." David didn't look at Noah when he made the offer, but he felt the breeze die and the air heat up from Noah's direction.

"Not interested, thanks."

"Remember, he doesn't look back," Noah said, sarcasm heavy in his tone. "Forward. Only forward."

"What's wrong with that?" Gideon asked. "Wallowing in the past may feel good, but it doesn't get you anywhere."

Noah straightened. "I don't wallow."

"The hell you don't. You wear your grief like a suit of armor. That's what keeps you upright, instead of standing on your own two feet."

"What do you know about grief?"

"Nothing about having a wife die, I admit, but I do know David's wiped out. Look at him, Noah. Just look at him. He's aged ten years in three."

Noah fired a look at David, who didn't know what to say. He hadn't talked to Gideon about the situation, but he couldn't deny Gid's words. He hoped Noah understood his silence was agreement.

"David knows what's important. He does what needs to be done. He's a company man. I've got enough leads to keep David in Europe for a month. And he'll go do the job without complaint. If you cared enough about him, you'd come back and help out for a while. It'd give you money in your pocket, anyway."

"Been there, done that, don't wear the T-shirt anymore."

Noah stood. "I don't need this crap." He walked away, his stride long and heavy.

"Why don't you speak up for yourself?" Gideon asked David.

David was trying to absorb the bombshell that he would be expected to stay overseas for a month. "He has four kids who need him. He can't go running off to Europe every month the way he used to."

"Martyr."

"He's not—"

"You, bro. You. You lost Laura over it once. Probably will again."

"If the relationship had been right, it would've stuck." His gaze found Laura's. She smiled, more than a little flirtatiously. Why was she doing that? Why was she interested? Nothing had changed. Nothing *could* change, except to get worse.

"You'll never get married with that attitude," Gideon said.

"Why would I want to do that? As far as I'm concerned, the only reason to get married is to have children. I have no interest in being a father. Like you, Gid, I've witnessed too much marital misery to fall into that trap."

"The difference is, I still believe in it."

"Even though Jeanne left you?"

"Should I serve dessert now?" Valerie asked from behind him.

Her calm voice washed over him. He was grateful for the interruption, would figure out the mess with Noah later. It was party time now. "Why don't you just sit down for a few minutes and get to know my brother, Valerie. Everyone is fine for now."

She hesitated. He knew that she felt her place today was as his party giver, not partygoer. He hadn't seen her sit all day, not even to eat.

Laura climbed out of the pool, pushing herself up and over the edge instead of climbing up the stairs, giving him an eyeful of cleavage. Even Gideon stared, his beer a couple of inches from his mouth.

Laura flicked her dripping fingers at David. "Why don't you come in for a while. It's heavenly." She came up to him, her slick, taut body so close he could've licked the water drops off her.

But he didn't want to, he realized. Well, that wasn't entirely true. What he didn't want was the complication that would follow. He'd been wrong to invite her today, had invited her only to protect Valerie's reputation, and now he was paying for it.

He looked to where Valerie had been standing, saw she was gone. The woman moved as quietly as a butterfly.

He spied her talking with Aggie, who leaned close and said something that made Valerie laugh so much she bent over, her hand pressed to her chest.

He'd very much like to know what made her laugh like that.

Aggie and Dixie made a grand entrance into the kitchen at the end of the evening as Valerie was packaging leftovers. They didn't ask if she wanted help but just pitched in, the conversation light and fun. Dishes were washed and put away, and the kitchen tidied in what seemed like five minutes.

Valerie would never have asked for help, and even found it hard to graciously accept it, but she did, relaxing then enjoying their company. Both women hugged her before they left.

David was huddled with his brother Gideon in chairs by the pool as she passed by, headed to the cottage. She tossed a wave in their direction.

"It was a great party," David called out. "Thanks."

"My pleasure."

Hannah was already in bed. Valerie tiptoed in and found her sound asleep. She brushed her daughter's hair away from her face, kissed her cheek, then headed to the shower.

As she stood under the spray she thought about the day, how much fun it had been to plan the party and fix the food. She'd enjoyed being part of the group, but was also glad to have her job to do, giving her reasons to disappear for a while and regroup. Not that people hadn't welcomed her or had made her uncomfortable in some way, but seeing David with Laura had bothered her more than she'd expected it would. Not only because Laura was beautiful and sexy, but because she *was*. She existed.

Hannah had seen them talking by the side of the house, then hugging goodbye a little while ago. She was a big part of David's life.

"Which is good," she said aloud. "Necessary." She was sure it would help keep her attraction in check. Well, mostly sure. It was hard to control what didn't want to be controlled.

Valerie got out of the shower and dried off. She moved into her dark bedroom and stood at the window. David was alone. He'd settled in a lounge chair, tucked his hands behind his head, looking toward the sky. Or maybe his eyes were closed. She couldn't tell from where she stood.

She dropped her towel and reached for her nightgown, then left it sitting on her bed as she stood, silent and still, watching the man who was fast becoming way too important to her. And way too exciting. Her body felt heavy and achy. Needy.

Finally he stood, walked to where the light switches were, then turned off the lights, leaving only what light a partial moon provided. She could barely make out him peeling his shirt overhead and tossing it on the lounge, then his shorts. He scratched his belly, stretched, then dove into the pool.

She wished she could join him, wished she could see him

up close, admire the perfect details of his body. In the short time she'd been with him, she'd put on a few welcomed pounds, and she felt much more womanly, more desirable. She wanted him to notice; she didn't want him to notice.

She was one mixed-up woman, she decided, forcing herself to put on her nightgown and get into bed before he climbed out of the pool.

Who would have ever thought she would turn into a voyeur?

Chapter Nine

Valerie grabbed the hose and began to wash down the pool deck the next morning after Hannah boarded the school bus. She loved this time of day, was grateful she didn't have a normal nine-to-five routine. Maybe she worked more hours than the average office worker, but she had no commute, no office wardrobe to purchase, no time clock to punch. The trade-off worked for her.

She turned the hose nozzle to jet and attacked some stubborn debris trapped in a corner. David was leaving again today. This time he didn't have a return date.

The image of him with Laura yesterday still clung tenaciously to Valerie's memory. Every man had watched her climb out of the pool, her bikini leaving plenty of skin and curves to admire. Then there was the hug Valerie had seen between Laura and David at the end of the evening.

Valerie had avoided Laura all day. Aside from a greeting at their introduction and a good-night later, they'd said nothing to each other, Valerie staying out of her range.

Then there was the moment when Valerie had accidentally overheard David and his brother Gideon talking. David had called marriage a trap, one he wasn't going to fall into. Where did that leave Laura? Did she know how he felt? Why was he so opposed to marriage?

Something touched her shoulder. She jerked around, hose in hand, avoiding spraying David only because he grabbed the nozzle, diverting the stream.

"Oh, I'm so sorry," she said, turning it off, stopping the flow.

"That's my line. I didn't mean to scare you."

What scared her was how much she wanted to put her arms around him and kiss him. She didn't want him to leave… but she needed him to.

"Guess you were off in another dimension," he said.

"I was just thinking how much I love my job. How diverse it is, and how flexible."

"Speaking of which, I just got off the phone with Denise Watson. I asked her to send me a statement to buy out your contract from At Your Service. Mae Carruthers—you met her yesterday, the company linchpin?"

She nodded, words escaping her. He wanted her. Before the thirty-day test run was done…

"Mae will send you the new-hire paperwork to fill out and return. It can't be finalized until I get back from this trip, whenever that is, but as far as I'm concerned, you're hired permanently."

"Thank you," she managed to say.

"Valerie, I have never worked with anyone like you. You seem to know what I want before *I* know what I want. Everything you touch turns to gold."

"Don't put me on a pedestal, David. I'm not perfect."

"Well, you're perfect for me. I take it you're in agreement?"

She was perfect for him—as his employee. "Agreement?"

"On the job? You want to stay on, right?"

Only more than breathing. "Yes."

For a second it looked as if he was going to hug her. She made eye contact. Waited.

Then he took a step back abruptly, firmly. "I'll call you when I get to Hamburg."

Just her imagination, then. He seemed fine. Normal. "Okay," she said. "Have a good flight."

"I don't know one from another anymore." He left.

She watched him grab his suitcase and briefcase from the bottom step and head to the garage. She went toward to the building, too, not wanting him to go. Crazy. You're crazy, she admonished herself. There were too many reasons why she couldn't let herself feel that way about him.

He backed the car out, saw her and stopped. The passenger window lowered. She walked over to it, leaned down.

"Did you need something?" he asked.

Before she could answer she saw his gaze dip down to where her blouse was gaping, giving him an eyeful. Stand up, she ordered herself. Maintain your professional relationship. But she didn't move. He didn't let his gaze linger, but lifted it to reconnect with hers.

His hand clenched the steering wheel. "You want something?" His voice was tight.

"I was just going to wave goodbye."

He lifted a hand, then backed up, made a quick turn and he was off. Gone.

She wandered back to the deck and picked up the hose. Was he…attracted? Or was it just her imagination—or wishful thinking? No, not wishful thinking. She couldn't wish that way at all.

She opened the hose nozzle full force. A few seconds later a car pulled in. She didn't recognize the bright red Miata, but she headed to the driveway. Laura Bannister climbed out of the car.

A chunk of hot lead landed in Valerie's stomach. How could she have forgotten about the woman? David's girlfriend.

"Hi," Laura said breezily, shoving her sunglasses up. She

looked chic and graceful in her silk blouse, short blue skirt and three-inch heels "Valerie, right?"

"Yes, Ms. Bannister. I'm sorry. You just missed David. He's on his way to the airport."

"Actually, I came to see you."

Valerie kept her expression impassive, but curiosity ran a marathon inside her. "How may I help you?"

"I was hoping you would share your recipe for the potato salad yesterday. I heard you did all the food yourself." She smiled engagingly.

Valerie could see why she'd won beauty contests. Valerie needed to try to like the woman, since they would probably see each other frequently. It wasn't wise to alienate the boss's girlfriend. "I'd be happy to share the recipe. Come on up."

Valerie let Laura lead the way, grateful the kitchen was spotless after last night. It was what she did well. Even if Dixie and Aggie hadn't helped, Valerie would've had it cleaned up before she'd gone to bed.

Most of her cookbooks were in the cottage, but the recipes she'd used for the party she'd left in a drawer. She grabbed the one Laura wanted.

"Um. I'll make a copy for you." She headed toward David's office.

"You're a life saver," Laura said. "I can stop by the market during my lunch hour."

Valerie stopped. "You're making this for tonight?"

"Yes. Is there something wrong with that?"

"It's just that it takes a while. You have to cook the potatoes and cool them. Chop up everything. Mix it with the dressing. Let it sit so that the flavors marry."

"Oh. Well, maybe I'll just buy some this time. But I'd still like to have the recipe."

What was going on? Valerie wondered as she made a photocopy. She didn't know Laura well, but she seemed nervous, and Valerie had figured she was usually well controlled. A woman didn't win beauty pageants without a lot of poise. Lawyers weren't slackers in that department, either. Something else was happening. Laura Bannister was here for a different purpose altogether. Her arriving just a few minutes after David left seemed odd, too.

"Here you go," she said, handing the recipe to Laura. "I've got some salad left over, though, and I'd be happy to share. How many people are you serving?"

"Oh, you're a doll! Thank you so much. Is there enough for four?"

"I think so." She grabbed a plastic container from a cupboard and got out the salad, then decided to just give Laura the whole thing. It wasn't Hannah's favorite food, anyway. She wouldn't miss it.

After more thanks, Laura headed to the door then stopped there. "I forget how long David is supposed to be gone this time."

Really? If it were *her* boyfriend, Valerie would have all the details of his itinerary. "He didn't know for sure."

"Oh, that's right. He told me that. Well, thanks again."

She went out the door in a hurry, almost slamming it. Valerie followed more slowly. She finished hosing down the deck, all the while trying to sort out what Laura had been up to. A fishing expedition for information, at least, she decided. But why? And she doubted very much that Laura cooked a lot, or she would have known that potato salad wasn't a quick dish to make, at least not the traditional kind that Valerie had made.

So, it was personal.

Her cell phone rang. She saw it was her mother. Taking a steadying breath, she sat in a lounge chair. "Hi, Mom."

"Hey, stranger."

Guilt. Just what she needed. She loved her mom, but... "I know. I'm sorry. I've been settling into a new job and home, and I didn't want to jinx things by telling you too soon."

"Keeping your mother informed is jinxing?"

Valerie refrained from noting that her mother hadn't called

her, either. "I've got a great job, Mom. The best I've ever had. But it was a trial run first, and now I've been hired full-time." She told her mom about David and the job.

"You always were able to land on your feet."

Valerie took the blow in silence, and rethought her idea about going down for a visit. Except that she wanted Hannah to know her grandmother.

"I've worked hard, Mom."

"Wagner Rawling is dead."

Valerie sat up straight. She squeezed the phone. "When? What happened?"

"Yesterday. A boating accident off the Amalfi coast."

"I don't know what to say. I don't even know how I feel about it, except that now Hannah never has a chance to know her grandfather. That's so incredibly sad, Mom."

"Not Wagner, Sr. Junior."

Blood rushed to Valerie's feet. She grabbed the chair cushion and held on. "Her father. Hannah will never know her father."

"He made his bed."

Valerie pressed her fingers against her closed eyes. "One that Hannah and I had to lie in. His choice, and his loss, not knowing his daughter, what a beautiful little girl she is." She opened her eyes and looked around, seeing little. "You don't expect me to come for the funeral, do you?"

"I doubt you would be welcome, since you would have to be explained. And don't think you can get something from his estate. You gave up your rights."

Valerie clenched her teeth. "I know what I did and didn't do, Mom. I don't expect anything. He had more than eight years to make contact, and he didn't. I have no intention of stirring things up."

"Okay. Well, I only told you because you might see it on the news or something, and I didn't want you to be surprised."

"I appreciate that. Is the funeral in Palm Springs or L.A.?"

"L.A. Then Mr. and Mrs. Rawling are coming here for a couple of weeks. They'll probably bring along the young widow."

Valerie forced herself not to react to the reminder that Wagner had married someone else, even before Hannah was born. "You'll be busy."

"That's what I'm paid for."

"Of course."

"Aren't you glad I taught you how to take care of a family? Sounds like you wouldn't have had your cushy new job otherwise."

"Yes, thank you." Yet again. Her mother always reminded her of how much she'd sacrificed for her daughter, and how much wisdom she'd imparted. But Valerie hadn't learned her parenting skills from her. In fact, Valerie had decided to be a very different kind of parent, a more loving one, strict but not unbending, openly affectionate, too. She hadn't gotten many hugs through the years.

Which had also been part of the problem, and a reason why she'd craved Wagner's attention when he offered it. She'd loved being in his arms.

She'd also believed everything he'd told her. Big mistake. Big, big mistake. One she'd paid a heavy price for.

"Well, I've got lots to do here," her mother said. "I'll be talking to you."

Valerie ended the call, then sat back, clutching the phone to her chest. The father-and-child-reunion fantasy was dead. What could she say to Hannah?

She hadn't asked about him in a while, but she would again, at some point. He wasn't real to her, since she'd never met him, but children spun fantasies about such things. How would this affect her?

Valerie tucked the phone back in her pocket. Because David was traveling all day today, she'd agreed to meet Dixie in town for lunch, knowing David wouldn't call with work to do. She drove to the Take a Lode Off Diner.

Dixie hadn't arrived, so Valerie found a table near the window and waited. After a minute she spotted her new friend making her way up the sidewalk, her curls bouncing, looking dressed for comfort in a tank top, jeans and boots, her working wardrobe for her job at a local hardware store owned by her family. The contrast between her outfit and Laura's dress-for-success outfit this morning was huge.

Valerie caught a glimpse of herself reflected in the window, seeing her own dark brown hair pulled back into a ponytail at her nape, knowing the rest of the package included sedate, light blue crop pants, blouse and sandals. She had no curves to speak of, certainly no bustline that brought stares like Dixie's—or Laura's.

Dixie waved after she came through the door and headed to the table, calling out greetings to the other customers and staff. It was what Valerie wished for Hannah, a life in one town, where people knew and looked out for each other. Not that Chance City was tiny, but it was small enough.

"You throw a great party," Dixie said, plucking a menu from the holder beside the mini jukebox.

"Thank you. I like doing that kind of thing."

"I would say it showed, but you never sat down and just enjoyed yourself. You're a worker bee, aren't you?" She raised a hand toward the woman behind the counter. "Honey, can we get a couple of iced teas?"

"Sure thing, Dix."

"Iced tea's okay with you, I hope?"

Valerie nodded.

"You're awful quiet."

Valerie wanted to confide about Wagner dying, but knowing the way gossip got around here, it wouldn't be a secret for long, and she needed it to be a secret, for Hannah's sake. Her daughter needed to fit in.

"I'm sorry," she said as Dixie waited patiently. "A little tired, I guess."

Two glasses of tea were delivered. Dixie sugared hers. "What'd you think of everyone?"

"Very nice people."

Dixie grinned. "You can do better than that. I saw you taking it all in. You quiet types are like that—big thinkers. Mull things around a lot. Don't act without thinking things through."

"That pretty much describes me."

"So, what'd you think of Noah and his brood?"

"Attractive man. Intense. Worries a whole lot about his children but doesn't have a clue about how to parent effectively." Valerie clamped her mouth shut. She shouldn't be talking about her boss's family that way. She looked over the menu, decided on a Cobb salad. Dixie shouted their orders at the counter person.

"We're all worried about Noah," Dixie said. "He loved his wife so much, and he can't seem to get his life back together. I can't tell you how many nannies and housekeepers he's had. Those poor kids." She swirled her straw in her tea. "And Gideon?"

"Didn't get a chance to talk to him." Just overheard some interesting tidbits.

"And Miss Universe?"

Valerie smiled, because she knew it was expected of her. "She's a beautiful woman. She and David complement each other very well."

The bell over the door jangled. "Speak of the devil."

Valerie had her back to the door. "Laura?"

"She's headed our way," Dixie whispered, then leaned over to sip from her straw.

"This is a nice surprise," Laura said, stopping at their table. "I called in a lunch order. May I join you while I wait for it?"

Dixie raised her brows at Valerie, who shrugged slightly.

"Pull up a chair," Dixie said. "I thought you worked in Sacramento on Tuesdays."

"Schedule's always a little off during a holiday week How's the rest of your morning gone?" she asked Valerie.

"The rest?" Dixie repeated. "You talked today?"

"She dropped by the house this morning."

"Really?" Dixie focused on Laura.

"I wanted her potato salad recipe."

Valerie noted the surprise on Dixie's face. Before Dixie could say anything, Laura added, "She was kind enough to give me the recipe but also her leftovers. Saves me a whole lot of time cooking tonight."

The look Laura gave Dixie intrigued Valerie, something resembling a challenge. Dixie sat back and sipped her iced tea. Valerie figured it was rare that Dixie didn't speak her mind so it made Valerie even more curious.

Small talk followed. Valerie asked about fun things to do especially for Hannah, but also as a single woman. Aside from the Stompin' Grounds, there didn't seem to be a whole lot of places to socialize. She could also go to Nevada City or drive down to Sacramento.

She hadn't expected a miracle. She just wanted her life to be interesting and fulfilling…and fun. Yes, she'd missed out on the fun part for too long.

"Laura, your order's up."

She stood. "I've got a client in ten minutes or I'd stay and eat with you," she said, but looked reluctant to leave the two women alone. "Maybe we can do this again sometime."

"O-kay," Dixie said, dragging out the word. Valerie just nodded.

The moment the diner door shut, Dixie leaned toward Valerie. "You were holding out on me. So, Miss Universe paid a call on you this morning, and she wanted your potato salad recipe?"

"Is something wrong with that?"

Dixie started to laugh, then couldn't stop. Finally she sat back, grinning. "The woman can't boil water. She couldn't follow a recipe to save her soul."

Since Valerie had already figured out Laura didn't cook much, that didn't come as much of a surprise.

"Well, I don't think that recipe was what she was after, do you?" Dixie asked.

"No. But I don't have a clue otherwise. Do you?"

"I think she was checkin' out the competition."

"What competition?"

"You."

"But…David told everyone it was just an act he and I had been putting on to help Joseph win you back."

"Heck, Val, I believed it. You fit, you know? And the way you and David ignored each other most of the day yesterday made everyone wonder, too."

"Are you serious?" She felt her face heat. "My job yesterday was to run the party. Why would I socialize with my boss?"

"I'm telling you that we all watched you two dancing together the other night. I don't care what kind of act you think you were puttin' on, there's something there."

"There's nothing there. Nothing. There can't be." Panic set in. She'd just got hired. She couldn't lose the job now, not over gossip. She'd lost her other job over maliciousness. "Dixie, I need you to help me make sure people don't think that about me."

"If I protest too much, it will make everyone even more curious, you know. You don't want to give them more ammunition for gossip."

It was disastrous to Valerie. "So, what do I do now?" On top of the news of Wagner's death, it was almost more than Valerie could handle. Not to mention the fact she *was* attracted to David. She didn't want to leave him— The job. She didn't want to leave the job. And Hannah deserved to live in a nice place and feel safe.

Tears sprang to her eyes.

"Oh, no!" Dixie looked horrified. "I made you cry. I was just having some fun with you. People don't think you and David are having a fling or anything."

"You were joking?"

"I swear I was. Don't be upset."

Dixie didn't know her history, didn't know that the sexual harassment claim still haunted her, still influenced her behavior every day and in every way. But Valerie couldn't share that, either.

She looked down at her empty glass of tea. She wished she had a best girl friend, wished there was someone she could confide in. She was so tired of holding everything in. But until she knew the information wouldn't spread across the gossip network instantly she would keep her secrets.

Even though it had been keeping secrets that had caused so much harm to her life in the past.

"I need to get back to the house," she said, pulling out her wallet. "Hannah will be home before too long."

"You forgive me?" Dixie asked.

Valerie forced a smile. "Of course."

"Good. We can try this again without Laura sometime."

Valerie laughed. "I gathered from your expression that you two aren't friends."

"We're not enemies, but she's living on a different stratosphere from us now. Ex-beauty queen. Lawyer. Rubs elbows with lots of important people these days. When she and David were dating before, we never saw him. She doesn't hang out at the Stompin' Grounds."

Valerie frowned. "You said they broke up months ago. Why was she there yesterday as his date?"

"The million-dollar question. We were all whispering about it at the party."

Valerie couldn't discuss David's love life, so she changed the conversation, then said goodbye and headed home. When the school bus pulled up, she was waiting for her daughter, as usual. Hannah waved to someone before she hopped down the stairs to the ground with a thud.

"Hi!" She grinned ear to ear.

Valerie gave her a hug. They walked up the driveway. "You had a good day?"

"The best. I like it here, Mom. I don't ever want to move."

"I can't guarantee that, but I'll do my best." She slipped an arm around Hannah's shoulders as they stepped inside the cottage. "I have something to tell you."

"What?"

"Let's sit down."

They took a seat on the couch. Valerie held Hannah's hands. "It's been a long time since you asked about your father."

"I know. It always made you sad, so I stopped."

"Well, I heard today that he died."

Hannah's face paled.

"I'm really sorry you never got to meet him."

"Why? He wasn't a nice person, was he? He didn't even want to know me."

"It was more complicated than that, but, yes, he made the decision not to know you. That was his loss, not knowing how beautiful you are, how bright and smart you are. But I know it's a loss for you, too. A loss that can never be made right now. I had hoped that he would change his mind. But, Hannah, you also need to remember that it wasn't about you as a person. His decision not to see you wasn't about you, but about his own inadequacies."

"What does that mean?"

"He didn't have it in him to be a father. It wasn't about you. He would've been the same with any child. If he had known you, I think he couldn't have resisted you."

"Is it okay to be sad? I feel so sad." Her eyes brightened. "And I want to be mad at him."

She took Hannah into her arms and held her. "I know. Yes, you can feel sad or mad or whatever." Someday they would find a special man to love them both.

"I know lots of kids who get new dads. Maybe we can find one, Mom. It would be fun to have a baby brother."

Valerie kissed the top of Hannah's head and smiled. She wouldn't mind that herself.

Except this time she wanted to have a husband holding her hand while she gave birth.

Chapter Ten

Home. The refuge David had created for himself beckoned as he pulled into his driveway. He'd been gone three and a half long, exhausting weeks. In his briefcase were orders for twelve more cars. Four were for repeat customers, who'd required only a little wining and dining before signing on the dotted lines. The others were new, a couple of the men playing David against a competitor to try to drive down the price or add expensive options free. But David believed that if he cheapened the business by cutting the price, he cheapened himself. He'd nailed the deals by emphasizing quality and customer service, as he always did.

Valerie's car was in its place in the garage. He felt his tension ease further. This was what he needed—to be home, where life was peaceful. It was Saturday, so he would have the rest of the weekend to relax and had told Noah he was taking a couple more days off. He wanted to lie around the pool, visit friends, hang out with the guys.

He wanted to let Valerie take care of the details of his life for a little while.

She wasn't to be found, however, not in the kitchen or the living room, at least. He set his luggage on the bottom step of the staircase, then headed to his office to leave his briefcase. He could hear singing as he neared the room.

He reached the doorway. Hannah was there, a duster in her hand, singing and dancing around the room, flicking surfaces. She stopped cold when she saw him. Belle barked a greeting and hurried up to him.

"What are you doing?" he asked, scratching the dog's ears. He'd specifically told Valerie that Hannah could not work in his house. He'd expected her to honor his wishes.

"Don't tell my mom, please," Hannah begged. "Pleeease."

"She doesn't know you're here?"

"She knows I'm in the big house, but I'm supposed to be doing homework in the dining room. The cable's out on the television, so she's with the man in the cottage while he works on it."

David had noticed the van in front of the house but hadn't given it a second thought.

Hannah inched closer. Belle moved to stand beside her, as if protecting her. "I know I'm not supposed to be here. I won't do it again, I promise. Just don't tell Mom."

He wasn't knowledgeable about the inner workings of kids' minds, except for having been a kid himself. "You know she doesn't want you working, Hannah, so why did you do it?"

"I wasn't working. I was dusting. I love to dust. It's fun."

"What's fun about it?"

"Oh, you know. Making swirls. Writing your name. Except Mom doesn't usually let enough dust pile up to do much. But I like it. I get to dust the cottage."

"And you like to dance, apparently."

Her eyes lit up. "It's the best."

"Do you take lessons?"

"Someday. Mom promised."

"Well, your mom probably heard my car arrive, so you'd better get to where you're supposed to be before she catches you herself."

"Are you going to tell her?"

"Don't you think *you* should?"

"Only if I do it again." Her smile was beguiling.

"Go on," he said, not giving her an answer, but grinning as she raced out of the room, Belle on her heels. Such drama over a small disobeying of the rules. He guessed little girls were like that, though.

He decided to head to the cottage and check out the cable situation himself. He passed the dining room, countered Hannah's bright smile with a stern look and a gesture to get back to her homework, then walked to the cottage.

The front door was open. He could hear Valerie laughing inside. David stopped before he came into view, listening. Was she flirting? Yeah, definitely a flirtatious lilt to her voice.

He frowned. He wasn't paying her to flirt on the job. How—

He stopped the thought. She was entitled to a social life, although she never mentioned having one, and they'd talked every day. She was always home when he called.

Before David could make his presence known, someone came out the door, the cable guy. He was big, burly, bearded and over sixty. And David had known him all his life. He'd been the baseball coach for his Little League teams for years.

"Heya, Dave."

"Rodney." They shook hands. "You working Saturdays now?"

"We alternate. Emergencies only. Got you all fixed up."

Valerie came up beside him and smiled at David, her eyes…glowing. He'd never felt so welcomed. He took a step toward her then stopped. He'd almost hugged her.

"You're home," she said, looking pleased.

His last bit of lingering tension melted away. "Yeah. So, what was wrong with the cable?"

"Water and rust," Rodney said. "Old lines."

"Only five years."

"Old by today's standards. Job security." Rodney winked. He passed a clipboard to Valerie and pointed to where she needed to sign for the work done. "I'm off. Got a few more stops to make."

"Good seeing you, Rod," David said.

"Thank you!" Valerie called to his back, getting an over-the-shoulder wave in return as he trudged off. She clasped her hands in front of her. David realized she did that whenever she wanted to keep things professional between them. Her "employee" pose. "How was your trip home?" she asked.

"No different from any other. The yard looks good. I think I see a few flowers in bloom that weren't there before."

She looked a little guilty. "Just some purple sage."

He noticed she didn't apologize or justify. "I didn't know their name."

She glanced around. "Joseph has begrudgingly let me tend much of the garden. He does all the heavy and tedious stuff."

"Do you ever rest?"

She blinked in surprise. "Gardening relaxes me."

"If you say so. Does Hannah help?"

She put a hand to her mouth. "Hannah. She's in your dining room doing homework. I'll go get her."

She started past him. He put a hand on her arm to stop her, then didn't let go. Her skin was warm and soft.

"She can stay until she's done. Interrupting her might not be the best thing," he said, releasing her because he felt her arm tense up.

"If you're sure." Her voice was tight, pitched a little higher than usual. "Normally she's not allowed in the house at all, except the kitchen. I want you to know I don't let her violate the privacy of your space."

Little do you know. "I trust you." Although he wasn't too sure about her daughter.

She cocked her head. "You must be exhausted."

"Understatement."

"Are you hungry? Could I fix you lunch?"

She's paid to take care of you. Let her. "Yes, thanks."

They walked back to the house in silence, yet he was completely aware of her. Absence makes the heart—

"I'm going to take a swim," he said, knowing he had to distance himself right away.

"Should I bring your lunch down to the pool?"

"Yeah, thanks." He strode through the kitchen, grabbed his luggage from the bottom step and took the stairs to his bedroom, two at a time. He tossed his luggage on his bed. Valerie would take care of it later.

It didn't take him long to change into a swimsuit and T-shirt. He grabbed a towel, then the phone rang.

"You're home."

He sat in an overstuffed chair, dragged a hand down his face and tucked the phone closer. "Hi, Laura."

Valerie glanced at the Caller ID on the kitchen phone when it rang. Laura Bannister. She hadn't wasted any time. Or maybe he'd called her from the road. Maybe she would zip into the driveway in that fancy red Miata, haul her bikini-clad perfect body out of it and loll by the pool with David all afternoon.

Valerie sniffed. If David told her to stay away from the house, that he wanted privacy…

He has every right. The booming voice in her head irritated her because it spoke the truth. He did have every right. It was just that she'd begun to feel proprietary—about the house and the yard and even about him. The time they spent on the phone every day had taken on an importance she shouldn't have allowed. But once the business was discussed and handled, the conversation usually turned personal, if only for a little while. Most of the time he called after he was in his hotel room for the night and almost ready for bed, an hour when Hannah was in school.

Day by day Valerie had heard the increasing weariness in his voice, making her wish she'd been free to travel with him, to help with the load somehow.

Liar. The honest voice in her head took her to task. She just liked being with him. The time apart hadn't been easy, but she'd done her best to expand her social circle. She'd gone to the Stompin' Grounds twice with Dixie and Joseph, had danced a lot, but no one asked her out. She had a sinking feeling that people still didn't believe she and David had been putting on a show that night, that she didn't belong to him. The men were friendly, but kept her at a respectful distance.

Not that she'd wanted to date any of them. But still, it would be nice to be asked.

She grabbed some deli roast beef from the refrigerator and threw together a sandwich for David, adding macaroni salad, sliced cantaloupe and a chocolate-chip cookie to the plate.

The phone-line light went out. Ended. Not a long conversation. Because she was on the way over?

"I'm done," Hannah said, coming in and pulling a cookie from the jar, her homework tucked in her arms. "Can I swim now?"

"Mr. Falcon is going to use the pool. Maybe later. You need to get on down to the cottage and clean up your bedroom before Gabby gets here." It was going to be Hannah's first sleepover.

Valerie heard David pad down the staircase. She and Hannah both turned toward the kitchen doorway as he came through. His gaze connected with Hannah's. She looked down and shuffled her feet. He seemed to be challenging her with his eyes.

Valerie frowned. What was going on? "Is there…something I should know about, Hannah?" she asked.

"No." The answer came too fast and strong.

Yes, there was. Valerie knew when her daughter was lying, but she would ask her again in private, wouldn't confront David about it until she knew what she was dealing with and there was definitely something. "Get going now, Hannah."

She scurried out, snatching another cookie on her way and grinning at her mother. They'd had a difficult few weeks since learning her father had died, with Hannah alternating between sad and mad, so to see her smile now was a relief. Still…that didn't mean she would be allowed to keep secrets. Secrets hurt too much when they were revealed.

David picked up the lunch plate, grabbed a beer from the refrigerator and started to leave without comment.

"Will you be home for dinner?" she asked.

He stopped at the door. "No, don't plan anything for me."

When the door shut behind him, she stared at the counter-top. A date with Laura? Would he be gone all night?

She didn't like the feelings that swamped her at the thought of them together. She'd seen Laura twice more while he was gone. Once she'd stopped by to bring Valerie some wonderful bakery cookies as a thank-you for the potato salad, and the other with Dixie at the diner again, the timing coincidental—or so Valerie thought. Both times Laura was friendly but curious, asking an occasional question about David, ones she should've known the answer to already. Small talk, Valerie had thought.

She gave David enough time to eat, then went down to the patio to pick up his dishes to put away before she headed to the cottage for Gabby's arrival. He hadn't gotten in the pool, but had eaten then fallen asleep on a chaise lounge wearing just his swimsuit, looking like every woman's dream—except for the lines of exhaustion on his face, even in sleep. She stood watching him, wondering how she could make his life easier.

He opened his eyes. Not asleep, after all. Caught staring at him, she did nothing, not risking letting him see how flustered she was at being caught. He stared back for several seconds, his gaze intense.

"You're blocking my sun," he said finally.

She picked up his plate and the empty bottle. "Can I bring you another?"

"No, thanks."

"I'll be in the cottage if you need me. Hannah's friend Gabby is spending the night."

"Okay."

She started to turn around.

"Valerie?"

"Yes?" She waited and waited but he said nothing, keeping her in suspense. "If that's all, then?"

"I wanted to thank you for your great work. You made my job a whole lot easier."

Music to her ears. "I'm so glad. Thank you for saying so. You're the best boss I've ever had." She hurried off before he saw how affected she was by his words. She'd spent a whole year without being praised, without being recognized for her job skills and work ethic. Even her mother hadn't offered encouragement but constantly made Valerie aware of her failings.

A few minutes later she walked into Hannah's room as she struggled to make her bed. "What's going on?" she asked her daughter, going to the other side of the bed to help.

"Nothing."

"You're keeping a secret."

"No, I'm not." She tugged hard at the blanket, pulling it out of the foot of the bed.

Valerie eyed her. She trusted David, had no reason not to, but she knew her daughter. "Is Mr. Falcon…treating you okay?"

"What do you mean?" She kept working at the bedding instead of looking at Valerie.

"You know what I mean. We've talked about it before. If an adult does something—"

"No! Mom, no. He's cool." Hannah finally looked her in the eye, which made Valerie believe her.

"Just remember you can tell me anything, okay? Anything."

"I *knooow*."

"Okay."

Later in the evening she heard his car pull out of the garage. The girls were immersed in a DVD but doing more talking than listening. "How about a swim?" she asked. The late-September evenings cooled quickly. They wouldn't be able to swim for much longer.

"Yay!" They'd been wearing their bathing suits for a couple of hours, waiting for their opportunity, and headed out the door instantly, tangling arms, legs and bodies in their hurry, giggling.

Valerie brought her glass of iced tea and sat on a lounge, watching them. Evenings were hardest on her. It was the hour when all across the country families were sitting down to dinner together. Okay, so maybe that was a bit of a stretch. Times had changed. Life wasn't like those old sitcoms anymore, where families gathered to talk and laugh over their evening meal. Everyone was busy with soccer and baseball and gymnastics, moms and dads chauffeuring constantly, grabbing meals on the run, getting home in time for homework, baths and bedtime.

But Valerie longed for that fantasy. It'd been only her and her mother for eighteen years. Now her and Hannah. They did eat their meals together, at least so far. But Valerie wanted the whole package, an entire family around the dinner table. Including a husband.

The longing for that ideal had begun to invade her dreams, waking her up at night, a steady thumping in the hollows of her heart, aching. It had probably intensified lately because of Wagner's death. Even though they never would have married, he'd always been the placeholder in her dreams, the possibility, as Hannah's father. Now there were no possibilities.

Except…David had materialized now instead, hazy but undeniably there, waking her from a sound sleep, tempting her.

And she'd promised him if he hired her that she wouldn't run off and get married or have a baby anytime soon. She wouldn't go back on her word, even though she wanted that dream of home and family.

When she saw Hannah's and Gabby's lips turning blue, she made them get out of the pool and into the hot tub, then served them spaghetti and meatballs in the cottage and popcorn later as they finished their movie. They stayed up for hours in Hannah's bedroom, giggling and whispering.

Valerie didn't order them to sleep but let them wear themselves out, the clock striking midnight when they finally gave in. She wandered out into the yard and let the cold air wash over her. Ever since David had gotten home, she'd been agitated. And frustrated. Excited. Tense.

Happy.

She heard his car ease up the driveway, got caught in the beam of his headlights before he disappeared into the garage.

The night seemed extraordinarily dark and quiet as he approached.

"You okay?" he asked.

"The girls finally fell asleep. I was unwinding before bed." The domestic moment relaxed her. "Did you have a good evening?"

"It was okay." He slid his hands into his pockets. "Just trying to stay awake long enough to adjust to California time again. Another Saturday night at the Stompin' Grounds. I'm taking Monday and Tuesday off, too. I don't think I told you."

"No, but that's no problem. I adjust to whatever you need."

"I won't be working. Not sure what I'm going to do, but Falcon Motorcars can function without me for a couple of days." He lifted a hand toward her, lightly touching her forearm. "You're cold."

She'd been rubbing her arms without thinking about it. "Nippy nights."

"You should get inside."

"In a minute." It was easier to talk to him in the dark. "I know something happened between Hannah and you."

A beat passed. "What did she say?"

"She didn't, except to say it wasn't something I should worry about."

"It isn't, but I told her she should tell you, not me. Why don't we wait and see what happens. It's not a big deal, Valerie. Truly, it is not a big deal at all."

"I promised you she wouldn't interfere in your life."

"She didn't. Don't worry about it."

She couldn't help but worry, especially since she didn't know what *it* was.

"If it gets to be an issue and she doesn't tell you," he said, "I will."

"Good."

An awkward silence ensued. "I'll see you in the morning," he said. "I'll get my own breakfast. Joe and I are going to do a little power biking early."

"Do you want me to pack a lunch?"

"We'll stop somewhere. Good night."

"Good night. I'm glad you're home." She walked away, even though she would rather have sat by the pool for a while. She figured he needed to know she was safely in the cottage before he went to bed himself.

I'm glad you're home. Simple words, David thought as he lay in bed a while later. Home. He'd missed it more than ever. It was the longest he'd been away in years. Noah must figure that since Valerie was there to take care of things, David could be gone even longer. But living out of a suitcase, always being "on" for clients, had lost its appeal. It wasn't fun anymore.

He needed to have it out with Noah. Gideon was right,

pointing out what Noah, and even David himself, hadn't seen. He'd hit breaking point. He was almost thirty years old. He needed a life beyond work. With all the new orders, the company could afford to hire a Europe-based sales rep, although that would alter David's place in the company, as well. He'd have to give it all some thought, see how he could shift company priorities somehow so that he remained challenged by the job but not worn-out.

He tucked his hands behind his head. Noah was so much like their father—in charge, in control, his views about everything almost unchangeable. *Almost.* That was the key word. David just had to have a plan. One that would keep him at home more but also not require Noah to be gone, either. Something win-win. But would Noah trust an outsider to drum up business at the European end? Their father had started the business. They'd never had someone outside the family take on a major role.

His thoughts swirling, unable to sleep, David grabbed the remote and turned on the television, flipping through channels until he came across a show about the history of the American Le Mans series.

The TV was still on when he woke up, and a note-filled pad on the floor beside him. It had been a long, busy night.

Chapter Eleven

"Go to a dinner party? With *you?*" Valerie made herself sit, instead of plop, in a chair in front of David's desk the next afternoon after he'd issued the invitation—or perhaps *edict* was a better word. He'd pretty much told her she would accompany him, not asked.

"You don't have to look so horrified," he said, leaning back.

She schooled her features. "I'm just surprised."

"Right. As I said, it's a business dinner."

What about Laura? She didn't say the words aloud. His personal life was just that. "Why me?" she said instead.

"I want a second opinion of these men. You'd be neutral. Plus you'll probably pick up on things I wouldn't."

"How dressy will it be?"

"I've heard most women have the little black dress. Something like that."

She didn't have one, but didn't want to admit it. And she'd splurged enough lately on Hannah and even herself that she didn't want to charge anything else, if at all possible. Her savings account was just starting to grow again.

"If you don't have anything," David said, "I'll assume the expense. It's for the job, after all."

She lifted her chin. "That won't be necessary."

"Okay. So, tomorrow night. We should leave here by five-thirty for Sacramento. You'll need a babysitter."

"I'll take care of it." She had to go shopping. Would she find something appropriate in Chance City or have to go elsewhere? How much could she charge before her credit card would deny it? Were the right stores open on Sunday?

"So, you don't get to take a little vacation, after all," she said, because he was examining her too closely.

"I'm still not going into the office." He steepled his fingers in front of his face. "You look upset, Valerie."

Not much escaped him. "I'm just surprised. I didn't figure this kind of thing would be part of my job description." *Why aren't you taking Laura?*

"I'll make sure to add it officially." He smiled slightly. "It hadn't occurred to me, either. You're okay with it, though, right?"

Like she had a choice? "Yes, of course. Is that all?"

"You sure you want to do it?"

"I'm fine with it." She left his office and headed to the cottage. Hannah was at Gabby's house. Valerie was supposed to pick her up after dinner, which meant she had about two hours to shop. She called Dixie and asked where she might find a little black dress.

"A friend of mine runs a consignment shop. Why don't I give her a call? See what she's got on hand," Dixie said.

"That would be great, thanks."

"Have a hot date, do you?"

"A business meeting to attend with David, that's all." She hung up still wondering why he wanted her along. Laura was impressive, in looks and brains. Valerie was just…ordinary.

Then the realization struck her. Laura might be a distraction to the business at hand. She was too beautiful and too naturally sexy. David would need to keep the focus on himself and the business. No one would look twice at Valerie. She was *safe*.

Now that she'd figured out her role, she relaxed.

Dixie called back. "Surie says she's got a couple of things that might work for you. Want me to meet you there? Give my objective opinion?"

"Oh, yes, thanks. I need to pick up Hannah at six o'clock, though."

"Store'll be closed by then, anyway." She gave Valerie directions. "See you there."

Later, when Valerie got home and hung up her purchase in anticipation of the dinner the next night, she sat on her bed and stared at the dress. Had she made a mistake? Should she have gone for something high-necked and long-sleeved instead of the sleeveless, scooped-but-not-too-much-cleavage-revealing neckline? Of course, she didn't have a whole lot of cleavage to expose, anyway, so it was hardly an issue.

She sighed. If it wasn't right, she would know it by the look on his face the next night, and she'd picked another more sedate dress to have as a backup, figuring she could return one or the other.

Hannah came into the room, dressed in her pajamas, all warm and sweet from a shower. She sat next to Valerie on the bed and looked at the dress hanging in plain sight.

"That's pretty, Mom."

"Thanks. I like it, too." She slipped an arm around her daughter and held her close, kissing her damp hair.

"Where are you going?"

"To a dinner meeting with Mr. Falcon tomorrow night, and it's kind of formal. Aggie's going to come watch you."

"Cool."

She was quiet long enough that Valerie wondered if she was working up the nerve to talk about whatever the issue was with David, but she said nothing.

"Did you have fun this weekend with Gabby?"

"Yeah."

The way Hannah said the word made Valerie wonder. "But?" she prompted.

Hannah moved away a little. "Her dad's really funny."

"Isn't that a good thing?"

"I wish I had a dad like that."

The yearning in her voice made Valerie ache. "I know you do, honey. Maybe someday. We have to meet the right man."

"You need to be going on dates, Mom. You can't find the right man unless you go where guys go."

Valerie smiled at her grown-up little girl. "I'll put more effort into it."

"Gabby's got a real family. Her little brother and sister are kind of bratty, but they're kind of fun, too."

Well, pile on the guilt, why don't you, dear daughter? She pulled Hannah to her feet and headed to her bedroom to tuck her in. Valerie had missed having a traditional family, too, growing up. She understood the longing to be like other families, even if "real families" were all different kinds of mixes these days. She certainly considered her and Hannah a real family, just not the old stereotypical fifties-sitcom kind.

Valerie pulled out her finances folder and a calculator, then sat at the kitchen counter to examine the documents. She had two more car payments, then that debt would be gone. Then she'd tackle the big bill, her credit card. She calculated how soon she could pay it off. Even keeping her expenses to the bare necessities, it would take a year.

She'd been putting money into savings, even though she should add on to her payments, but she needed the security of cash in the bank, too. She would never let herself get into that tenuous financial position again.

Which meant she had to work a little harder at keeping David at a distance, physically. And emotionally, which was even more dangerous, especially when they were going on a—

Not a date. They weren't going on a date tomorrow.

She needed to keep remembering that.

As they drove home from Sacramento the next night, Valerie sat quietly, thinking about the evening, starting from the moment he'd shown up at her door with Aggie.

"You look nice," she'd said before she could censor herself. "I've never seen you in a suit before."

"So do you."

"Thanks." She'd figured he was just being polite, returning a compliment, and yet his gaze lingered on her, looking surprised, then appreciative, if she was reading him right. She'd hurried past him to the garage, wanting to reestablish their professional relationship, unable to stop herself from sneaking glances at him now and then as they made the trip, admiring the way he handled the Falcon. How his wrist rested on the steering wheel, how capably he drove, how relaxed he was.

He'd briefed her on the two men and their wives they would be having dinner with, as well as on the idea he had, one he wouldn't share with his brother until it was a done deal except for signing on the dotted line. David was trusting her to keep his plan secret until then.

But the evening had been mostly social, a getting-to-know-you occasion. David would have a sit-down with both men before the week was up.

Social, indeed, Valerie thought. David had even been social with *her*.

She looked out the passenger window and rubbed her arms, remembering the times he'd touched her during the evening—his fingers pressing the small of her back as they walked through the restaurant, brushing her arm during dinner, even tucking her hair back when the Delta breezes had swirled while they waited outdoors for the car to be brought around. She'd gone on alert, getting more confused about her role with every gesture. He'd made it seem to the other people as if they were lovers.

"I'd appreciate your thoughts," he said to her now, giving her a quick glance as they moved along the freeway toward home.

She pulled herself together. "Mr. Peterson seems straight-forward. And he adores his wife. He has character. Mr. Koning? I can't say the same. And they're business partners? It's hard to believe."

"Peterson's the money man. Koning would be responsible for the details of the project. This wouldn't be his first time. Proven track record."

She frowned. "He seems rigid to me. He also keeps his wife on a short leash."

"Meaning what? I noticed she drank a lot."

"The Petersons noticed, too, and didn't approve. So, does Mr. Koning have her on a leash because she drinks a lot? Or is it vice versa? I know you said he's had a lot of success with this kind of project, but I'd hesitate to involve someone I didn't fully trust."

"Thanks. I appreciate the input."

She caught him eyeing her low neckline for just a moment. Heat zapped her, head to toe, as it had many times during the evening. How little it took to arouse her…

"You were a great asset tonight, Valerie."

"I was nervous."

"It didn't show."

Her confusion increased at the tone of his voice, soft, almost seductive. "I need to ask you a question," she said.

"Shoot."

"Why didn't you introduce me as your assistant? Everyone assumed I was your girlfriend."

"It was a social meeting. At least on the surface. I don't want them to know the specifics of the project until I decide they're the people I want for the job."

"So, why didn't you take Laura?"

He frowned. "Why would I?"

"Well, she's your girlfriend. And she's definitely an asset."

"What makes you think she's my girlfriend?"

Valerie clamped her mouth shut. Had she heard him correctly? "Isn't she? You brought her to your Labor Day party."

"As a decoy. You told me I had to bring a date so that people wouldn't think you and I were an item."

"Hold on. I'm really confused. You date her, right?"

"I used to. She ended it."

"Then…I don't understand. And I know it's none of my business, either."

He took the freeway exit and headed toward home. "She agreed to come as a favor, that's all."

But she talks as if you're together. "That wasn't her only reason for doing it." She closed her eyes. She had no right saying that to him, trying to force a confidence.

He blew out a breath. "Yeah, you're right. She wanted to pick things up again. I had to end it."

He ended it? She really wasn't his girlfriend? "When did that happen?"

"Right before she headed home after the party." He turned into the driveway, then stopped in front of the garage, since he still had to take Aggie home. He turned off the engine and angled toward her. "I haven't mentioned her to you since, have I? Why did you think the relationship was continuing?"

The dark night enveloped them. Knowing they may never speak so personally again, Valerie wanted to continue the conversation, to learn the truth. She couldn't tell him about Laura trying to get information out of her, though. She didn't want any scenes because of it. But Valerie remembered seeing them hug after the party, too. So, it was a goodbye hug? "I just assumed, I guess. She's certainly your type."

"What would that be?"

"Beautiful. Smart." Probably great in bed. Valerie didn't have enough experience to know whether the same could be said of herself.

"You're more my type." He touched her shoulder, a feathery whisper of fingertips against her skin, then pulled away abruptly, grabbing the steering wheel and looking straight ahead. "I apologize. That was way out of line."

Out of line, maybe, but it felt nice. A little sinful. Forbidden. "It fit the evening, I guess, which has been unpredictable for me."

"It wasn't…appropriate behavior."

His irritation at himself calmed her. She was glad he was struggling with the attraction, too. Was it just proximity? The fact he didn't currently have a girlfriend? Or was it specifically her?

It was crazy to even be thinking about him in that way. Crazy. She'd promised herself she wouldn't do anything to mess up the best job she'd ever had. And even just admitting there were feelings could mess it up. Giving in to them definitely *would* mess it up.

She felt his gaze on her, and anticipation in the air, hot and palpable. They'd been playing at the whole boyfriend/girlfriend thing all evening. If she'd been aroused by it, he could be, too. In fact, seemed to be, if she could judge by his unsteady breathing. She wanted to touch him. He'd touched her but she hadn't done so in return, confused by his attention and not knowing exactly what role she was supposed to be playing.

Now she wanted—needed—to touch him, if just for a moment. He'd taken off his jacket and rolled up his shirt-sleeves before they'd driven away from the restaurant. His forearms looked strong and sinewy. Tempting. She rested her fingers on his arm.

He turned to her in an instant, slid a hand behind her neck and pulled her to meet him. He stopped, his mouth an inch from hers.

"This is a stupid idea," he said.

"Yes." Her heart thundered.

He didn't move. "You look beautiful tonight. And very sexy."

Her pulse went supersonic. "I'm glad you think so."

"I had a hard time keeping my eyes off you."

She waited, letting him dictate what would happen. She

should be saying no, loudly, adamantly. The word stayed stuck in her throat.

"This is really stupid," he repeated, but he didn't wait for her response this time, settling his mouth on hers, taking the kiss deep right away, his tongue searching, arousing. She groaned, giving back with everything she had, giving in to the feelings that had been building since she'd met him, her knight, her rescuer. She tried not to think of him in those terms, but it was useless. He was all that to her. He'd changed her life in every possible way.

And now she could taste him, put her hands on him and feel him, hold him...

He stopped, moved back slightly, his hand still cupping her neck. "Damn."

Valerie panicked at the word. It had started already, the regret. They'd ruined—

"I've been wanting to do that for a long time," he said, soft and gruff.

"You have?"

"Yeah."

"I don't want to complicate our relationship, our business relationship, David."

"I know." He brushed his thumb along her jaw.

"Please don't fire me."

He dropped his hand. "I have no intention of firing you."

"You can't sleep with me, either. We can't go there at all. We can't kiss again. I can't lose this job, David. I can't."

His gaze held steady. "Can you forget this happened?"

"I have to, okay?" She was so wrong to have given in to her feelings, her needs. "I have to. So do you." She grabbed the door handle. "I'll send Aggie out."

He didn't stop her, either with words or action. She hurried to the cottage, then paused outside the door long enough to calm herself. She put her hand on the doorknob, twisted it open, stepped inside.

Aggie looked up from the television, then shoved herself up off the sofa.

"Did you have a good time?" she asked.

Valerie nodded. "How was Hannah?"

"An angel, as always." Aggie started to walk past then stopped and scrutinized Valerie's face. After a moment she nodded. "G'night."

Valerie shivered at the straightforward, soul-searching look Aggie gave her. When the door shut, Valerie pulled out her cell phone. She'd gotten a voice message earlier in the evening that she'd ignored because it hadn't identified the caller.

She punched the buttons to retrieve the voice mail.

"Valerie, this is Wagner Rawling, Sr."

Valerie reached blindly for the sofa and dropped into it, gripping the phone.

"I need to talk to you. I don't care how late it is." He left his number, then ended the call.

The last time she'd heard from him was when she'd graduated from business school, more than six years ago. He'd come to make sure she'd completed the courses he'd paid for. Since then, silence.

She set down the phone as if it were on fire. Wagner Rawling, Sr., he said. Maybe he thought she didn't know his son had died. He sounded as arrogant as she remembered.

Yes, arrogant—except for when his son had slept with the housekeeper's daughter and gotten her pregnant. Then Senior, as the family called him, had gone from merely superior to despot.

Valerie couldn't stand up to him then. She'd been eighteen and scared to death. But now? Now she was older and wiser and not so easily pushed around.

She closed her eyes. Her mother had to be involved in whatever he wanted, since she was the only one who knew her phone number.

Valerie put her phone on the charger, turned off the lights

and went to bed, knowing she wouldn't sleep, but determined not to let him think she would jump when he snapped his fingers. Not now. Not ever again. She was not returning his call tonight. Maybe not ever.

As she lay in bed ignoring Senior, her thoughts turned to David, which didn't ease her mind, either. She'd messed up, big-time. Even though he said he wouldn't fire her, the kiss would change their relationship forever.

And probably not for good.

Just when everything was going so well…

Chapter Twelve

David settled in a deck chair the next morning, coffee mug in hand, newspaper on the table, the rubber band still in place. He waved back to Hannah as she danced—there was no other word for it—up the driveway to wait for the school bus. Valerie followed a few seconds later, not looking in his direction.

Not a good sign.

He probably should regret that he'd kissed her, but he rarely regretted any life experience. Experience was just that—something to try out, declare a failure or success, then file in your memory.

Yet regret over kissing her niggled at him. Not the actual kissing, since that was damn good, but her reaction afterward, and the sure-to-follow tension in their relationship.

He'd spent a lot of time watching her at dinner, enjoying the way she seemed so interested in everyone and their conversations, appreciating an occasional brush of their arms for the surprising little jolt of reaction. Hearing her laugh, a fairly rare occurrence, although she smiled a lot, more with her eyes than her mouth.

Unlike Laura, who exuded sex appeal all the time, Valerie was more girl-next-door and yet even sexier to him, even with the unrevealing clothing she usually wore. Which had made last night's exception so interesting. She'd definitely shown more skin than she ever had before.

In only six weeks she'd somehow become important in every aspect of his life.

Which was a big complication.

He heard the kitchen door open and shut, then she opened the slider to the deck.

"Good morning," she said, her hands folded in front of her.

"Hey."

"Have you eaten breakfast?"

"No. Have you?" He couldn't read her. She seemed calm, until he looked at her eyes. And then he noticed her fidgeting a little, rare for her.

"Yes. Would you like an omelet?"

He wanted to keep her nearby, maybe get a chance to clear the air. "Sure. Thanks." She made great omelets now that she was doing the shopping and had actual ingredients on hand, not just what was left over in his refrigerator from his own occasional shopping trip.

She shut the door, turning away. He opened the newspaper and scanned the headlines. After a minute she came out onto the porch, a portable phone in her hand. She wore her apron, which still had the power to turn him on.

"Noah wants to talk to you."

"Tell him I'm on vacation for one more day."

She relayed the message, then listened. "He says it's urgent."

"Everything is urgent to Noah." He went back to reading his paper.

"Is there blood involved?" Valerie said into the phone.

"No one's in the hospital?… In jail?… Then he's not available, Noah."

David raised his brows and smiled. She smiled back.

"Thanks," he said when she pushed the off button.

"He said he sent you an e-mail."

"Well, damn. My e-mail is going to be down all day."

She smiled a little wider. "What *are* you going to do with your day off?"

"I'm thinking about going to a movie."

"Really?"

She didn't add, "Alone?" but he heard the word, anyway. "Yeah." He grabbed the entertainment section. "Wanna go with me? We'll go to an early matinee and be home in time for Hannah's bus."

"That would be a date, David. You know we can't do that."

"What if I make it a job responsibility for the day?" Well, that was pathetic. Order her to go with him. Cool.

"Then I would go. I'd take my steno pad and my PDA and await orders."

She said it in a light tone, but he heard her frustration.

"I enjoy your company, Valerie."

"I'm your employee."

He stood.

She took a step back. "I need to finish fixing your breakfast." She shut the door in his face.

Skittish. He wondered if he'd ever used that word before. Not out loud, for sure, but even in his mind? It described her perfectly, but it wouldn't have been part of his definition of her until now. And he'd caused it.

Well, hell, she'd kissed him back. Gave it her all, it felt like.

Edgy, he moved to lean against the railing, surveying his yard. Soon she opened the door and said his breakfast was ready.

He didn't turn around. "I see yellow flowers."

"Do you?" came the innocent-sounding response.

"I remember specifically saying no flowers. Now I've got purple and yellow ones."

"The garden looks nice, doesn't it? The color gives your eyes someplace to linger. Your breakfast is getting cold."

He turned to look at her and saw worry in her expression. Because of the flower business? Because she really was worried about losing her job?

Her cell phone rang. Her face paled.

"Aren't you going to answer that?" he asked.

"I'll check it later." Tension coated her words, making her voice tight.

"What if it's about Hannah?"

She slipped the phone out of her pocket and looked at the screen. "It isn't." She tucked the phone away. "I'll be back in a little while to clean up."

He got inside the kitchen in time to see the back door close behind her. After weeks of predictable behavior, she was all of a sudden...not behaving predictably. She'd shown more varied emotion this one morning than the rest of the time put together.

What was happening? She looked worried. No, beyond worried—scared.

It couldn't all have to do with the kiss, so what else was happening?

And how could he find out?

"Why is Mr. Rawling calling me, Mom?" Valerie had tucked her feet up in a chair, making herself small, as she called her mother after Senior phoned a second time, and Valerie had ignored his call a second time.

"I don't know."

"He had to have gotten my number from you."

"Yes. He asked for it and I gave it. But I don't know what he wants. He's my boss, Valerie. I don't ask questions."

"You should've called me and let me be the one doing the calling. I don't like him having my number."

"A man like him can get any number he wants."

She was probably right about that. Valerie rubbed her forehead.

"Please call him back," her mother begged. "He's already upset with me because you haven't."

"Why should he be upset with *you?* I'm an adult. You have no control over me."

"In his world, the parent always has control, you know? I have to go now," she whispered in a rush. "I hear the missus coming."

Valerie pushed the off button but didn't move. She didn't want her mother to be in trouble, but she also didn't want to talk to the man. It couldn't be good news.

She pressed her hands to her face. Her life had just settled into a good rhythm. She didn't want anything disrupting it. Especially now that Hannah had stopped talking about her father.

But Valerie knew Senior would find a way to get to her, probably even track her down here at David's house. She couldn't have that.

She blew out a shaky breath and dialed his number. Her stomach roiled.

"Hello, Valerie," he said amiably.

"Mr. Rawling."

"Long time."

Not long enough. "Yes, sir."

"Your mother told you about my son?"

"Yes, sir. I'm very sorry for your loss." Tears suddenly burned her eyes and throat. She hadn't given in to grief until this moment, the grief of a mother for her child who would never know her father. The grief of an eighteen-year-old girl for her first love, who'd never loved her back but had given her a child she cherished, one she couldn't imagine life without. For that she had always been grateful to fate for sending Wagner her way.

"I hadn't wanted to involve your mother in this," Senior said, "but I had someone track you down at your last known residence, and learned you'd moved without a forwarding address."

"I see." She closed her eyes, trying to prepare herself for whatever came next.

"I've seen your credit report. I know how deeply in debt you are. And I saw photos of the apartment building, Valerie. I can't believe you were living there."

Horrified at the intrusion into her privacy, she almost couldn't answer. "We don't live there anymore. We're in a very nice place. I have a great job, with benefits. I was just down on my luck for a little while."

"Over a year. And you got fired for sexual harassment. Apparently you haven't changed. Still going after what you can't have."

Ice flowed through Valerie's veins. "What do you want?"

"To see you."

"Why?"

"I'll explain it, but in person."

"Well, I have no interest in that. At all. Goodbye." Anger like she'd rarely known surged through her. She hung up, then ignored the immediate call back. She knew what he wanted. Now that Wagner was dead, Senior wanted to make sure that Valerie wouldn't sue the estate, wouldn't make public—or even to threaten it—how Wagner has messed up and had a child out of wedlock. Well, Valerie had promised long ago. No further action required. How dare he question her integrity like that?

Or maybe he wanted to offer her some cash to continue to keep quiet. That wasn't acceptable, either—or even desired.

Valerie shoved herself out of the chair, tossing the phone into the cushions, furious that he was intruding in her life again. He'd actually seen where she lived. He'd gotten a copy of her credit report. Nausea rose again at the thought. She shouldn't have forgotten his pull and power.

"Valerie?" David's voice came from the intercom, startling her.

She forced herself to move across the room and press the button to answer him. "Yes?"

A pause, then, "Are you okay?"

She swallowed, trying to settle her nerves. "I'm fine."

Another pause. "Okay. I need you here, please."

She didn't want him to see her yet. She needed a few minutes to calm down. "Will ten minutes be all right?"

His pauses seemed to have great significance, but she wasn't sure why. "Sure," he finally answered.

"Thanks." She knew she sounded too cheerful, too upbeat, but it was all she could manage. After a moment she sank into the sofa, fighting tears, but mostly fighting panic. Wagner Rawling, Sr., was a powerful man. He could make a lot of trouble for her.

She sprang off the sofa and headed for her locked documents box to dig out the contract she'd signed years ago but hadn't looked at since. A knock on her door stopped her in her tracks.

"Valerie?" David called out.

She swallowed a groan of frustration. "What?"

"Open up."

"I said I'd be there in ten minutes. You can't wait that long?"

"Open the door, Valerie."

She didn't have to obey his order, but she figured he might break it down, so she forced a smile and pulled the door open.

"What's wrong?" He came inside, took her by the arms.

"I— Nothing."

"Something. It's clear as a bell in your voice. Not to mention the look on your face when your cell rang earlier." His hands tightened. "How can I help?"

Her knight in shining armor. She almost gave in to his offer. It had been so long since she'd let anyone help her. She knew it was a fault of hers, but it was better to admit and accept it than to start allowing herself to feel complacent, to think that someone would always come to her aid. She knew how things worked in real life, especially with the class differences between her and David. She'd grown up with it.

Paid for it.

Just hold me. The need overwhelmed her but instead she said, "You can't," careful not to deny there was a problem, since he'd already recognized the existence of one.

"You're more than just my employee," he said quietly. "Let me help."

She stared at him, debating, tempted. "I'll be fine. It won't affect my work."

His jaw hardened. So. She'd made him angry, after all. She couldn't do anything differently, couldn't appease him.

"I'll come to the house in a few minutes," she said.

He moved his hands to her face. She watched him lower his head toward her. She could have stopped him with little effort, but she let him continue, let him kiss her. Then kissed him back.

His mouth was warm, his lips sure. His arms slid down around her, pulling her closer. She let herself enjoy him, ignoring her logical mind screaming at her to stop. No. She wouldn't stop. Couldn't. She needed him, if just for the moment.

He groaned into her mouth, spurring her to grab him and hold tighter. He molded his hands over her rear, tugging her against him. She gasped, tipped back her head. He dragged his mouth down her neck, leaving a damp trail with his tongue, setting her on fire, a wild, uncontained, uncontrollable fire.

She felt herself being moved backward—toward her bedroom. Reality came back into focus with a hard click of the lens—her conscience sharpening the view again, knocking down the fantasy.

"I can't," she whispered, frantic. "Please. I can't."

"And you won't let me help you?"

"There's nothing—"

Her cell phone rang. She moved away from him, grabbed it, looked at the screen, flipped it open. "Hey, Dixie," she said with relief, turning her back on David.

A few seconds later she heard the front door shut.

* * *

David headed straight for the garage. He took the Falcon and drove north, not knowing where he was going until the got there. By the time he'd parked and gotten out of the car, Gideon had come onto his deck to greet him.

"You alone?" David asked as he climbed the stairs, his muscles taut so that he moved stiffly.

"Yep. Want some coffee?"

His stomach rebelled at the thought. "No, thanks."

"Whiskey?"

David laughed a little. "I guess I look like I need it."

Gid nodded. "Woman trouble or Noah?"

"Both."

"Pull up a chair."

The last-day-of-September weather was perfect for sitting on a tree-shaded deck and talking. David hardly knew where to start.

"Things tense with your new assistant?" Gideon asked, getting to the heart of the matter, as he usually did.

"How'd you know this wasn't about Laura?"

"No sparks anymore. On her side, yes, in a desperate kind of way. But not yours. You only had eyes for the subtly sexy Valerie."

Since David hadn't even known how attracted he was to Valerie a month ago, he didn't see how Gid could've seen it, but he had a knack for noticing such things and seeing the truth.

"Complicates things, having her working for you."

David looked up, following the adventures of two squir-rels chasing each other. "Yeah."

"If it's any consolation, she feels the same about you."

"Against her will."

Gideon's silence brought David's head down, leveling his gaze on his older brother. "Nothing to say?"

"Are you looking for advice?"

"Usually I don't have to ask."

"Okay." Gideon rested his elbows on his thighs, leaning

forward. "Sounds like she's being a lot smarter than you are. She overheard our conversation at the party, you know, when we were talking about you never getting married. She's a home-and-hearth woman. Anyone can see that."

"How do you know she heard me?"

"I had a different vantage point from you. You also said she's the best employee you've had. Why are you messing with that?"

David picked up a fallen pinecone and tossed it over the railing. "Because she turns me on."

"Plenty of women have done that. Plenty more will."

"She's keeping a secret, one that has her scared."

Gid's brows raised. "Any idea what?"

"No. Her past catching up in some way, I think. But she hasn't shared anything about Hannah's father or why he isn't in the picture. There's a story there."

"Sounds like a good reason for you to back off."

"Yeah." His shoulders dropped. "I'm tired."

"That's why you're here. To figure out how to change that." Gideon stood. "I'm getting another cup of coffee. Sure you don't want something?"

David shook his head. Gideon left, then all David could hear were birds, the squirrels and a whisper of wind in the trees. Gid's house was even more isolated than David's, and much smaller. He'd chosen a different path in life. Maybe he'd been the smart one, after all, to get out of the family business.

"So," Gid said, returning. "What do you plan to do about it?"

"About Valerie?"

He cocked his head. "No. I think not having a plan about her is the best way to go. Let things happen. What do you plan to do about the job and The Enforcer?"

David grinned at the old nickname they had for Noah. "Stand up to him."

Gideon nodded. "How can I help you do that?"

"Well, I've been working on an idea I'd like to run by you.…"

Chapter Thirteen

Valerie kept waiting for a shoe to drop. Two shoes, actually—David's and Senior's. She decided they were taking lessons from each other, keeping her in suspense, in limbo. On edge.

Senior's call a week ago hadn't yet yielded any surprises, unwelcome or otherwise. She assumed he hadn't tracked down her address—yet, anyway—and he'd stopped calling.

And David had been professional and amiable, but hadn't attempted to kiss her again. He was leaving town this morning, but this time to go to Los Angeles for preliminary discussions for his new project, still excluding Noah from the plans. Having learned how controlling Noah was, Valerie wondered if it was a good idea to keep him in the dark.

But that was David's decision to make.

"Did you find that folder?" David asked as she stood in his bedroom watching him pack a change of clothes in case he stayed overnight.

"I put it in your briefcase. I also updated the information on your laptop and stuck that in, too."

"Thanks." He zipped up the bag and set it on the floor, then looked at her.

It had been all she could do to keep her hands off him all week, yet he hadn't seemed to have the same problem. Which should make her happy...

"What did you tell Noah about the trip?" she asked. "In case he says something to me."

"That I had a solid lead for some stateside business."

"What kinds of objections do you think he would raise?"

"Noah isn't a visionary. He needs all the details in place when a project is presented to him. He also likes status quo. Routine. He's never been good with change."

"Must be hard, then, since he has four children. That's the definition of constant change."

"One would think." He grabbed his suitcase and headed for the door. "I'll call you when I get to L. A."

She didn't want him to go. He'd been home for eleven days. While he'd gone to the office frequently, he'd been home a lot, too. They'd done a complete overhaul of his computers, PDA and offices, both at the house and at work. She'd spent time with him in the Roseville office and had come to really like Mae, who ran the place.

David stopped in the doorway. "Thanks for all the extra effort you put in the past week. I haven't been this organized in...well, ever. The new filing system is great."

"You're welcome. I hope your trip is successful." She wanted to kiss him goodbye. How dumb would that be?

"Me, too." He hesitated a moment longer. "I'll stay in touch."

She could follow him downstairs and say goodbye at the kitchen door or even outside as he drove off, but she stayed put, afraid she might do something to let him know how she felt.

How she felt. She'd tried her best to avoid acknowledging her feelings for him, but they filled up her mind, night and day.

He's not the marrying kind, she reminded herself constantly. He doesn't want children. There could only be pain ahead for her if she let the relationship go any further, get any more personal. She would fall in love; he wouldn't. Then at some point another woman would take her place. How could she live with that? She wouldn't be able to revert to being only his employee again, so she would be out of a job.

No matter how many times that refrain rang in her head, it didn't stop her from feeling. Caring. Being aroused by being near him.

Valerie stepped onto his bedroom balcony and waved goodbye as he drove off. She returned to his unmade bed, reached for the pillows, then stretched out instead.

The doorbell rang. She hopped off the bed. No one rang the front doorbell. Everyone came to the kitchen door and knocked.

She hurried down the stairs, could see the top of someone's head through the square glass panes at the top of the door. Gray hair. A man's style.

Valerie slowed as the bell chimed again. *Senior.* He'd found her.

"I know you're in there, Valerie," he announced. "And I know you're alone. You don't have to be afraid of me. Please open the door."

You can do this. He holds no power anymore. You do.

The thought calmed her. She opened the door.

He looked old. Not just older. Old. And he wasn't sixty yet.

He smiled, trying to look benign, but all she could see was his overbearing dominance when he'd learned she was pregnant with his son's child.

"May I come in?"

She hesitated. She should take him to the cottage, but she didn't want him in her private space. So she stepped back, inviting him inside silently, then leading him to the living room.

"Beautiful home," he commented, setting his briefcase on the floor at his feet, then taking a seat.

She had no intention of signing whatever documents he'd brought along.

"David Falcon has a good reputation," he went on as she stayed silent. "Good head for business. Stays out of trouble."

She took a seat so that she put herself even with him, not the help waiting for orders. "Please get to your point."

"I understand that you don't want to see me. What I did years ago... I regret it more than I can tell you."

Too little, too late.

"Valerie, I want to get to know my grandchild."

Shock zapped her. In her wildest dreams she hadn't imagined that. Reputation was everything to him and his wife. How could they acknowledge a bastard child?

"No way," she finally said.

"Think about your daughter. She's entitled to know her grandparents, too."

"I do think about her. I put her first, always. And I've grown up a whole lot since you last badgered me into doing things your way. You don't wield that power anymore."

"I can see you have. And I hope you can see a man in pain, a man in mourning for his only child. You're a parent. Surely you understand what I'm going through. What Wagner's mother is going through."

Oh, he was good. Play the grieving parent card. "The last I knew, she wasn't aware of Hannah's existence," Valerie said.

"She still isn't. Not until you and I settle things. I don't want to get her hopes up."

Valerie sat up a little straighter. "How do you think she'll feel being grandmother to the same child as her housekeeper?"

He smiled slightly—or was it a grimace? "I know it's an odd situation, but I think her joy would outweigh the...unconventionality of the circumstances."

"In the beginning, perhaps. But you wouldn't be a good influence, and that's why I'm saying no. You spoiled Wagner, gave him everything, and expected nothing of him.

Then you bailed him out of a jam he should have faced himself—the fact he was going to have a child. You raised a shirker."

A long pause ensued, then, "He never knew."

She couldn't have heard him right. "What?"

"That letter he sent you, telling you he didn't love you, telling you he'd gotten engaged the year before? He didn't write it. I did. Or rather, I paid someone to forge his handwriting."

Valerie dug her fingers into the chair arms. "Get out," she said, the words scraping painfully along her throat. Wagner had never known about his own daughter? What would've happened had he known? How would their lives have been different?

"I'm willing to take whatever you throw at me, Valerie, to do whatever you want in order to make it up to you. But I want a relationship with my grandchild."

"You're delusional. Get...out." She pushed herself upright.

He stood, as well, reaching into his briefcase and pulling out a large envelope. "Just look this over, please. Give me that much. For Hannah's sake."

When she didn't take it, he left it on the chair then walked to the front door. She followed several feet behind, her legs unsteady, her vision blurred.

"I'm staying at the Red Rover Inn. I'm not leaving town until I hear from you."

She tried to picture the private-plane-flying, five-star-only hotel guest at the Red Rover Inn. "Don't hold your breath."

"You may change your mind when you see what's in the envelope." He opened the door.

"I can't be bought."

"Everyone has a price."

"Not me."

"Even you, Valerie. Because it isn't always about money."

The door closed with a click that echoed like a cannon blast in the entryway. Valerie didn't move for a long time. From where she stood she could see the envelope on the chair.

There would be money in it for sure, but what else? A new contract, replacing the old one—the one that she'd been coerced to sign when Senior told her Wagner was married. She should've sought legal help before she'd signed it, but she'd been too hurt and too angry, and without financial resources or even life experience to know what to do next. She'd signed it because she hadn't wanted Wagner to have rights to Hannah *ever*. He'd denied paternity. She didn't want him changing his mind later.

But the truth was that everything was based on a lie. Wagner had never known about Hannah.

Valerie had harbored such anger at Wagner all these years. But her anger should have been aimed at Senior and his lies.

She wouldn't make any more mistakes. This time she would know her rights and stand up to Senior.

First she had to see what he had in mind.

She grabbed the envelope and sat down, peeling it open, her hands shaking.

Valerie read a four-page legal document, then a one-page personal letter from Senior. Finally she stuffed everything back into the envelope and went out the back door and down the stairs to the cottage. Keep your head straight, she reminded herself. No emotions this time.

She got out a legal pad and started writing down her concerns and rebuttal points.

Then after staring at the phone for several long seconds, she picked it up.

"Thank you so much for seeing me so quickly," Valerie said to Laura Bannister as she took a seat opposite the attorney.

"You sounded pressed for time."

An understatement. Laura was probably being kind, because Valerie knew she sounded frantic. "The man I need to discuss is here in town. I don't want him hanging around longer than necessary, and he's not going away until I give him an answer—the answer he wants. If I don't do that, he may camp out here. Or make my life hell some other way."

Valerie launched into the details of her past and the predicament of her present and future, then shared the contents of Senior's envelope. Laura wrote notes and asked questions, then read the documents.

Valerie hadn't seen her since David said he'd broken things off with her. Going to a different lawyer would've been a wiser move for Valerie, if there'd been time. There hadn't been.

"The man writes a convincing, heartfelt letter," Laura said, putting aside the final piece of paper, a personal plea to Valerie from a father devastated by the loss of his son to the woman who'd loved that son once.

Valerie had fought tears while she read that letter. Senior's open emotion had swayed her in a different direction from the legal and financial document she'd first read.

"What are you wanting to hear, Valerie?" Laura asked, setting down her pen.

"Legally, can he force grandparent visitation, as the first document insists?"

"Probably so. The law is still broadening on the grandparents' rights issue, but unless you knew he would mistreat your daughter, it's doubtful he would be denied his right to know his granddaughter. You could drag it out in court for a while, but probably with the same results."

Valerie looked at her hands locked in her lap for a moment, letting Laura's words settle. "I figured that. I guess it comes down to the fact that I don't really want to deny Hannah the right to know her grandparents, not the other way around."

"I understand that. It's also very generous of you, considering what Mr. Rawling did to you. How he lied."

"I know he was horrified at the thought of his son marrying the housekeeper's daughter. I'm not excusing his behavior, but I understand it, especially now that I'm older and wiser and a parent myself. But I don't want any legal documents binding us. It should be a choice, one that Hannah is included in making."

"Very wise."

"Am I required to sign his documents?"

"No. If you fought him, he could pursue the issue in the courts and then you might have to sign agreements to appease a judge, but if you're willing to go along with what he wants, then there's no reason for documentation. Or the expense of a hearing."

"I'm not willing to do everything his way. He wants an official, carved-in-stone visitation schedule. I want to be flexible. And for a while, I want them to come here, until I know Hannah is comfortable being around them."

"That's reasonable."

Valerie looked around the office, gathering her thoughts, noticing the trophies and other beauty-pageant paraphernalia in a large glass case. "I don't want his money, at least not the check he included in the paperwork that covers my debts and then some. I incurred them, and I'm paying them off. The trust he wants to provide for Hannah's college education is okay, even a relief, frankly. I wouldn't turn it down. Her father would have provided that, if he'd known, I'm sure."

"Also wise. I know it's tempting to just turn down all offers, but you're being sensible to look at the future for your child."

"Well, I have to admit I like the idea of Hannah having a man in her life, someone she can count on," Valerie said. "My father left my mother and me when I was a baby. I know what it's like not to have male influence." It had driven her into Wagner's arms, desperate for love and attention. She'd known nothing about men then. Still didn't know much, to be honest. But she'd done some studying on the subject, since she was raising her daughter without a strong male role model, too, and she'd come to learn that not having one impacted a child for life. If she could get Senior to agree to her stipulations—

"Would you like to call Mr. Rawling and have him come

to my office?" Laura asked into the silence. "We could talk everything over together."

"Could I? Yes, thank you so much. That would be great. If only explaining it all to Hannah could be handled so easily."

"Does David know any of this?"

"No. It hasn't had any impact on my work."

Laura's brows raised. "I wasn't thinking professionally, but personally."

"He's my boss."

Laura hesitated, then set her clasped hands on her desk. "You know, Valerie, I didn't show up at David's house the day after the party to get your potato salad recipe."

The comment was so out of the blue that Valerie didn't respond for a minute. "After I heard you didn't cook, I realized that, but I never did figure out why you came."

"Really?" She smiled slightly. "David said goodbye to me for good that night. I wanted to check out the competition."

"Me? But—"

"Please don't insult me with denials. I'm not saying you were lovers. I'm saying your attraction to each other was so obvious to anyone looking more than a few seconds at each of you. Especially when you ignored each other all night. So, I had to check you out. Make sure you would be good for him."

"We're not lovers."

"Yet."

"A crucial point, however." She leaned toward Laura. "It's *my* problem. This time I need to be the one making the deals with Senior. Anyway, David's too protective. He might interfere."

"Protective? David?" She clamped her mouth shut, then apologized. "Believe me, he never acted protective of me. So, if you needed more proof…"

Valerie wasn't sure how she felt, that she seemed to need watching over while Laura apparently did not. "When should I ask Mr. Rawling to show up?"

"I'm booked until five."

Valerie would have to find someone to watch Hannah. "I'm sure he'll agree. If there's a problem I'll call you."

They both stood. Laura gestured toward a bag on her desk. "Thanks for bringing me lunch."

"Thanks for giving up your lunch hour for me—and for your honesty. I'll see you at five."

Valerie could have stopped by the Red Rover Inn, but she didn't want to tip her hand with Senior, so she called him from her car instead. Then she contacted Aggie and made arrangements to drop off Hannah later.

Having time to kill, Valerie sat in her car, wondering how to pass the two hours until Hannah's bus brought her home. David's house was spotless. The cottage, too. He'd left no Falcon work for her. She'd shopped for groceries two days ago. There wasn't enough time to go to a movie. Dixie was working.

Her cell rang. David.

"How's it going?" she asked.

"We're butting heads."

She could hear the smile in his voice. Apparently, he liked the negotiation aspect.

"I need you to research something in the company database, then e-mail it to me." He gave her the details.

"I'm about fifteen minutes away from the house," she said. "Will that be a problem?"

"I need it ASAP."

She started the engine. "I'm on my way."

"Thanks. Everything okay?"

"Yes. Why?"

"You sound…strained."

"Just in a hurry to get the info for you."

She'd come to understand that he went silent when he didn't believe her, as if waiting for her to correct herself and tell the truth.

"I don't like to talk on the cell phone and drive at the same time, David."

"Okay. Later."

She ended the call. As she drove she wondered whether Laura was right—that she should tell David what was happening.

No. She needed to do this on her own. She'd made a mess of it the first time around. She needed to do it right and be proud of herself, knowing she could make the right decisions and carry them out.

No knight in shining armor necessary.

Just the strong man inside it.

Chapter Fourteen

David struggled to keep close to the speed limit on his way to Chance City from the airport. He was always glad to get home, but never more so than today. It seemed as if he'd been gone a week rather than not even a full day.

He pulled into his garage then headed to the house, anxious to share the news with Valerie, but music blared from the cottage, so he changed direction and moved down that path.

The door was open, but he didn't see anyone. He knocked. When no one answered, he debated about stepping inside. On the one hand, it was private space. On the other hand, the door was open. Belle hopped off the sofa and came running.

He crouched to pet his dog just as Hannah whirled into the room, dancing in circles, her expression one of utter joy. She stumbled a little when she saw him, then grinned and made two more pirouettes. "Ta-da," she said.

He clapped and she bowed. Belle barked happily, joining in.

"I think you're supposed to curtsy," he said.

"What's that?"

"Men bow. Women curtsy." He started to show her then realized how ridiculous he would look—clumsy and awkward. "Ask your mom."

"Okay."

"Where is she?"

"At the big house. We ran out of ice cream."

"Have you started dance lessons yet?"

"I'm working on it. She says maybe in the spring."

"Did you tell her about…the other day?"

Her hackles went up a little. "No, but I did everything I promised. I haven't dusted your house again."

The music changed, and she began to sway to it. "Do you like to dance?" she asked.

"Kind of. I'm not very good at it."

"My mom's a really good dancer."

He knew she was, had danced with her at the Stompin' Grounds, but he couldn't tell Hannah that. He recalled holding her close, feeling her body along his….

He glanced at his watch. "You're up late for a school night."

"Just a little. Mr. Falcon?"

"You can call me David."

She shook her head. "Mom would shoot me."

"Is she a good shot?"

She giggled. "I don't think so."

"You had a question?"

"Do you think my mom is pretty?"

"Hannah!" Valerie stood in the doorway, a bowl of mint-chip ice cream in each hand.

Hannah's gaze dropped to the ground. David was relieved not to have to answer her question but also felt sorry for her. She was a cute kid, self-confident and happy, but her mother kept a tight rein on her, especially in front of him.

"Go to your room," Valerie said quietly.

Hannah eyed the bowls of ice cream that her mother set on the kitchen counter. "But I'm hungry."

Valerie said nothing. After a couple of seconds, Hannah turned around and ran to her bedroom, shutting the door hard. Belle followed, her claws clicking against the floor. She stood outside Hannah's door, looking back at David as if begging him to open it for her.

"I'm so sorry," Valerie said the moment her daughter was out of sight. "That was rude. I'll talk to her."

"She's very…high energy."

Valerie managed a laugh. "Nice way to put it. Do you want some ice cream?"

"No, that's okay."

She waved it in front of him. "It's your favorite."

"Okay, you talked me into it."

She passed him a bowl. "I'll go check on her and be right back." She picked up the other bowl and took a couple of steps, then turned around. "I didn't even ask how your meeting went. You're home a lot sooner than I expected."

"It's good news. I'll wait here for you." He ate the ice cream as he wandered through the space, noticing the personal touches she'd added that softened the look of the room, making it lived in, not like a hotel room as before. She'd put out family photographs, a few knickknacks and fresh flowers. There were colorful kitchen canisters and towels, and a ceramic bowl filled with fruit—grapes draped artfully over the edge, and a few apples and pears.

He sat on her sofa, finishing up the ice cream, feeling like a stranger in his own property, as if he were violating her privacy. They always met up at the house, spent the most time in his office together. This was…personal. Intimate.

Sort of like this morning as he'd packed for his potential overnight trip to L.A. He couldn't remember a previous time where she'd been in his bedroom at the same time he was. Seeing her standing there by his bed, her hands folded neatly in front of her, had been a challenge to his control. He wanted to know what those graceful hands would feel like against his skin, what her hair would look like spread out on his pillow. What her body looked like, period. He knew from observation that her breasts would just fill his hands, her waist and hips were narrow and her rear round and firm. She moved quietly, efficiently, elegantly. Class. She had a lot of class.

And she kissed like there was no tomorrow.

He wished she would loosen up, though. She didn't need to be so strict with her daughter or not let him help her out when she apparently needed help. Whatever secret she'd been keeping lately couldn't be so awful she couldn't share it with him, could it?

She came into the living room just as he finished the ice cream.

"Let's go up to the house and get you some," he said, standing.

"I'm fine. Really. Anyway, I'm anxious to hear what happened."

He saw lines on her face and a tight jaw. Something had happened since he'd left this morning. But she kept her secrets to herself, and he knew that asking her wouldn't do anything except put her on the defensive.

"Nope. I feel too guilty. Tell Hannah you'll be back in a few minutes."

She hesitated, her gaze locking with his, then she turned around. A few seconds later he heard voices from Hannah's bedroom, although no distinct words, then Valerie walked beside him to the house. Belle followed, reluctantly. She probably felt she needed to stay with the overwrought Hannah.

Well, he'd maneuvered that well, he thought with satisfaction. He'd get a little bit of time alone with her. "Peterson and Koning like the idea," he said as they walked. "They'll research all those issues that need researching in such a venture, then get back to me, probably within two to three weeks."

"At which point you'll take it to Noah?"

"Yeah. I'm seeing a light at the end of the overseas-travel tunnel."

"Would you give that up completely?"

"I hope so."

The night was cool. Mid-October now, they were well into autumn in the foothills, a time of warm days and cold nights. The leaves were turning gold and brown, with just a few red scattered here and there. Intermixed with the evergreens, it made for a beautiful palette, one he'd paid little attention to for the past few years, and yet one of the reasons he'd built his house where he had.

But then, he rarely had time for any of the things he used to enjoy—hiking, fishing, bike riding. He and Joe hadn't backpacked and camped in three years.

He was aware of Valerie next to him as they climbed the stairs. Never overly talkative, she seemed extraordinarily quiet now. And the strain on her face… And her short fuse with her daughter…

Yes, something had happened while he was gone today. Something major and emotional.

"Your mother called today," Valerie said as they entered the kitchen. "She said your cell was turned off."

"As you know, I don't turn it off. I saw it was her and let it go to voice mail." He opened the freezer and grabbed the carton of ice cream while she got out a bowl.

"She was curious about me," Valerie said.

"I imagine she was."

"You never talk about her."

He got the ice cream scoop from the drawer, took her bowl and served her. He could tell she was uncomfortable with him doing that for her, which, oddly, pleased him. "I rarely even think about her."

"Why?" She put a hand to her mouth. "I'm sorry. None of my business."

"No, it's fine, and no big secret." *Unlike yours.* "She and my father divorced when I was eleven. My father retained full custody, as he had with Noah and Gideon when he divorced their mothers. My mother didn't even demand regular visitation, so I didn't see her often, but particularly after she remarried and had two more children. Every so often she starts feeling maternal for one reason or another and she'll call."

Valerie leaned against the counter and took a bite of ice cream. "Where does she live?"

"Florida." He shoved the carton back into the freezer with undue force, then pushed his hands in his pockets and made himself relax.

"So, you grew up in an all-male household? Or did your father marry again after that?"

"Fortunately he stayed single. Then he died when I was eighteen."

"Was he a good father?"

David mulled the question over. "A good father. What would that be?"

"I don't know, since mine abandoned my mother and me when I was almost two. My experience with fathers is strictly vicarious—and fantasy, based on television fathers."

"Yeah. Reality sucks."

She laughed, as he'd hoped she would. "I don't know. I've seen some good ones out there. Hannah talks about her friend Gabby's father as if he were a saint."

David took advantage of the opening she'd given him. "You said Hannah's father is out of the picture?"

Valerie went very still, then she lowered her bowl. "Her father was never in her life, but he also recently passed away, so there will never be any hope of a relationship there."

"Did you want one?"

"For Hannah, yes, of course. He wasn't a bad guy."

"Doesn't sound like a gem to me."

"There's a lot more to the story. I just found out that he

hadn't known about her existence. So, a lot of the resentment I harbored for him wasn't warranted."

"Does that have something to do with what's been going on with you lately?"

Her mouth tightened. "Yes."

He waited for her to tell him what had happened today, but, as usual, she didn't open up. "So, you've forgiven him?"

She frowned. "I hadn't thought about it, because— Well, I guess so. Mostly I feel sad that he never met her. That he never got to see what a great kid she is."

"You've been her sole support all this time?"

"Yes." A light tone, matter-of-fact. She scooped out another bite.

David watched her eat the ice cream. As soon as she swallowed, he took the bowl and spoon from her and set them aside, his gaze never leaving hers. Then he leaned in and kissed her, as he'd been wanting to since the last time, over a week ago. Her mouth was cold and tasted of mint and chocolate. She warmed quickly, both her mouth and her reaction. She wrapped her arms around his neck, pulling herself close, groaning.

It was all the permission he needed. He sought the inside of her mouth with his tongue, slid his hands down her body over her rear, drawing her even closer. She grabbed his hair between her fingers, then dragged her hands down to frame his face, all the time coming at him full force, kissing him, enticing him.

He lifted his head and looked into her eyes as he slid a hand over her breast, feeling her nipple, hard against his palm, hearing her sigh, her eyes fluttering shut.

"This is so wrong," she whispered.

"Feels right to me. Perfect, in fact." He covered both breasts, filling his palms, then he pressed his lips to her jaw and slid along it to her ear, nosing her hair out of the way. She smelled incredible, tempting. Apricots? Hot, anyway. He moved in for more.

But she pushed away after a minute, tunneled her fingers through her hair and looked straight at him. She put a hand against his lips, not letting him try to convince her to continue.

"I have to go," she said finally. "Hannah…"

One step at a time, he thought. "Speaking of Hannah, I've learned she'd really like to take ballet lessons."

Her change of mood was instantaneous. "How do you know that?"

He measured his response. "She told me."

"And in what conversation could a subject like that just happen to come up?"

He ignored the question. "I'd like to see her go for it. I'll pay for the lessons."

"If and when I determine she should have them," she said, crossing her arms, "I'll pay for them."

"You're angry that I'm offering?" he said, surprised. He'd thought she would be pleased. He knew Hannah would be. "Every kid deserves to go for their dream."

"She's not your kid, and I'm your employee," she said, closing her eyes. When she opened them she was calmer. "I know I've broken rules here with you, but Hannah has to stay out of anything having to do with you."

"Wait a minute. That sounds like you don't trust me."

"I'm talking about emotions, David. I don't want her getting close to you. Of course I trust you. If I didn't, we'd be gone." She walked away. "Good night."

After the door shut he wandered to the window to watch her until she got inside the cottage. Belle came up beside him, her tail wagging slowly. He crouched down and scratched her ears. "Well, that didn't go well, did it, girl?"

The dog closed her eyes, enjoying the affection.

"I should leave her alone, like I had been. I just can't seem to stop myself. So, maybe you can tell me what happened to Valerie today? Or are you siding with her—the sisterhood code or something?"

Belle whimpered.

"I thought so." He stood and headed toward the staircase. "Come on, girl. Let's go to bed."

But bed didn't help. He was too wound up—from his meeting with Peterson and Koning *and* from kissing Valerie.

She was right. It was a mistake to pursue any kind of relationship other than professional. He knew that. He didn't want to lose the best thing that had ever happened—

He blew out a breath. Yeah. His life ran smoothly now, thanks to her. His world was organized. His stress level was way down. Gideon had said that things would work themselves out with Valerie, but David wasn't sure he was right. Usually, having a plan in mind was a wiser course of action, something to focus on.

He hadn't planned to kiss Valerie tonight. She'd just been standing there eating ice cream, and he'd needed to kiss her. Maybe it was the strain and stress he saw in her eyes, maybe because she'd taken his away, he'd needed to do that for her, too.

He laughed at himself. "Right. That's why you kissed her. You just wanted to help. Because you've always been known for your charitable efforts."

The thought gave him pause. In the past he'd dated women who were strong, independent and self-sufficient. Not that that didn't describe Valerie, but she was different. There was something about her that made him wish she was a little less self-sufficient.

Well, how insulting could he get? He could hear her reaction to that idea, could see her eyes narrow and her mouth tighten.

He really needed to figure out why he wanted so much to take care of her.

Chapter Fifteen

"We agree to your terms," Senior said to Valerie on the phone the next morning. "When can we meet Hannah?"

"All my terms?" she asked, dropping onto her sofa. "You will visit her here, with me in attendance, until I feel she's okay to be alone with you?"

"Yes."

"You won't pay any of my debts, even anonymously?"

"I won't."

She wasn't sure she could believe him, but she had to start somewhere.

"Have you forgiven me for keeping her a secret from Wagner?" Senior asked, his voice steady.

"I'm working on it, for Hannah's sake. The harm you caused by not telling Wagner is one you have to live with, the fact he died without knowing her. And Hannah may never forgive you for it, either, you know."

"Will you tell her now, before we even meet?"

"No. I'll let her get to know you. I decided she's too young for that burden."

"Thank you for that. So. When can we see her?"

"I'll talk to her today when she gets home from school. I'll call you afterward with her reaction. The decision to meet you is hers, as we discussed."

"All right. I'll be waiting to hear from you, then. Goodbye, Valerie. And thank you."

Valerie needed to call Laura and let her know. The negotiations that took place in her office were successful because of Laura's efforts. She'd asked Valerie what she wanted, then went about accomplishing it all for her, telling her to keep quiet unless Laura directed a question at her. Valerie hadn't been anywhere near as nervous as she would've been otherwise. She knew she had the upper hand this time.

She finally felt all grown-up.

So why was she so wound up now?

She looked at the phone, knowing she needed to make another call. She dialed the familiar number.

"Hi, Mom. Got a minute?" Her heart pounded harder than it had with Senior, roaring in her ears and chest.

"Sure. The Rawlings have gone back to L.A. What's up?"

"Well, it's about the Rawlings, actually. Senior paid me a visit yesterday."

"Why?" Panic coated the word.

"He and Mrs. Rawling want to meet Hannah."

"I knew I shouldn't have given him your number. I knew it. I wasn't thinking fast enough. You said no, of course."

"Mom, as you pointed out, he would've found me, whether or not you gave him my number. And, no, I didn't say no to him." She explained how everything had come about. Her mother said nothing. She didn't interrupt, didn't ask a question. "What are you thinking?" Valerie asked into the ensuing silence.

"That it's a big mistake."

"Why?"

"He's already proven to be a liar by not telling Wagner about your being pregnant. What makes you think he'll abide by the rules you're setting up?"

"He has too much to lose if he doesn't."

"You know I'm going to lose my job because of it."

Valerie frowned. "Why would you?"

"Because the missus will want to put distance between us. She won't like us both being Hannah's grandmas."

"Well, maybe you should beat her to the punch and get yourself another job. You've been threatening to do that for years. I know you've had offers."

"Oh, well, there's a great solution. Me change my life completely so that it's easier for you. Honestly, Valerie, you are so selfish. All you care about is yourself."

Stunned, Valerie clutched the phone. "How can you say that? That's not true at all."

"You got pregnant, even after I gave you the birth-control speech. You accepted money from Senior so that your life would be easy instead of making your own way and paying for your own mistakes, like I did. You moved far away from me, even though it meant I wouldn't see you or my grand-daughter very often."

"You made me move out, Mom! You said I couldn't stay in the house, where Mrs. Rawling might see that I was pregnant. Mr. Rawling sent me to business school so that I would have skills to support myself, otherwise I would've gone on welfare. Would you have been proud of me then? I've made my own way since then. Completely. We've never been without food and shelter, even if it wasn't the best. And all without any help from anyone, including you. And it's never seemed to matter whether or not you see me or Hannah, or even talk to us. Now that you'll be in competition with Mrs. Rawling, maybe we'll hear from you more."

The silence that followed was the loudest Valerie had ever heard. She'd gone too far. Way too far.

The line clicked, then a dial tone followed, loud and accusing.

Valerie's chest heaved. She buried her face in her hands. It was all too much. First finding out that Wagner was dead, then that he'd never known Hannah existed, then Senior tracking her down, making demands. She'd countered them well, was proud of herself for that, but it was still stressful. And she had to tell Hannah today about her grandparents.

And now her mother. And her own words that would haunt her forever.

Secrets. It all came back to keeping secrets. If she'd been able to confide in her mother instead of having a secret relationship with Wagner, maybe that would've turned out differently. Oh, she wouldn't have wanted to be without Hannah for anything, but maybe there would've been a better resolution.

Then there was Senior keeping Hannah a secret from Wagner.

Secrets hurt. Crushed. Destroyed.

Now David—confusing, tantalizing, sexy David, who'd lit a fire under her, sparking flames where none had flared for a long time. Her feelings for him were a secret.

She wanted to run away from it all.

She couldn't. She had a job to do. A child to raise. Bills to pay. Her plan to create a new life for herself hadn't materialized beyond her new friendship with Dixie.

She'd also resisted meeting men and dating, and she knew exactly why.

Valerie shook out her hands, trying not to cry. She pushed herself up and paced, then headed for the door, unable to calm down. She would get to work, do physical labor today, anything that involved effort, like vacuuming. Maybe she would clean up dead leaves in the yard, even though it was Joseph's job.

David had left at the same time as Hannah left for school, an hour ago, but on his mountain bike. The last time he'd taken a ride, he'd been gone for hours. She had time to really push herself cleaning.

She almost ran to the house, trying to keep her mind a blank. She hurried through the kitchen, up the staircase and down the hall into David's bedroom. His bed was even messier than usual, the bedding jumbled and twisted, as if he'd had a sleepless night. She pulled everything off the foot of the bed, leaned over to straighten the bottom sheet.

A noise intruded. She turned around. David stood there, naked except for a towel knotted at his hips, his hair wet.

"When did you get back?" she asked, when she should've apologized and excused herself. She wasn't herself at the moment. She was Valerie, but not a person she recognized. She was wound tight, in need of a way to relax and forget.

"Long enough ago to take a shower," he said. "I pulled a muscle—or something—in my calf." He moved closer, limping a little. "What's wrong?"

She didn't want to talk about it. Didn't want to think about it. She reached out and touched her fingertips to his chest, warm and still damp.

"Valerie," he said, soft and rough at the same time.

Paralyzed with indecision, she met his gaze. She didn't know what he would see in her eyes, but in his she saw curiosity give way to desire. She didn't want to think anymore.

"Are you sure?" he asked, flattening her hand against his skin.

"No."

He smiled, sort of. He slipped his arms around her and brought her next to him. "Scared?"

"Excited. Needy." It had been building for a long time, too long, without resolution…or satisfaction.

He touched his forehead to hers. She felt his breath, warm and a little shaky, against her skin. She trembled at his tenderness.

"I want you," he said.

She wanted him, too, but couldn't form the words, so she just nodded.

He didn't waste another second. His mouth was on hers in

a flash, hot and searching. She ran her hands over his bare torso, savoring the freedom to touch him.

"You're beautiful," she said against his mouth.

He smiled. "That's my line."

"I'm not—"

He kissed her, stopping the words, scattering rational thought. He moved her toward the bed. When her legs touched it, he unbuttoned her blouse and tossed it aside. She wasn't wearing any lacy, pretty lingerie, not having anticipated such a thing happening, not owning any, regardless.

He nuzzled her neck as he unhooked her bra and let it fall to the floor. She felt it land on her feet, then a second later his hands were covering her breasts, his thumbs circling her nipples, then rubbing, teasing.

Her head dropped back.

"I knew you'd look like this," he said. "Feel like this." He moved down until he took a nipple in his mouth. "Taste like this."

Arching her back, she wrapped her arms around his head and groaned as he shifted to the other nipple. She felt his fingers slip under her waistband. The button popped open, the zipper slid down. One tug and her pants joined her bra on her feet, then he slid his hands under her panties, over her rear and squeezed. He pushed her underwear down, knelt before her to slip them and her pants over her feet. Then she was naked....

And vulnerable.

"I'm not on the Pill," she said, reaching for his towel as he stood.

He spread his arms, giving her permission with the gesture. "I'll take care of it."

Then he was naked, too, in all his exquisite glory, his beautiful swimmer's body lean and muscled, his erection flattering and tempting. She touched him, tentative for only a moment, then wrapped her hand around him, feeling him surge in her palm, hearing him release a long, low sound of appreciation and need.

He kissed her, hard and intense, changing angles again and again, demanding and bestowing, offering and taking. She'd never felt so…necessary to someone. So desired. She found freedom in his need, home in his touch. She realized her previous resistance to him had little to do with her sense of independence or even being in his employ. She'd been resisting loving him, something that had been happening slowly, steadily, since the day she'd come to work for him.

I love you. She said the words in her mind as he urged her to stretch out on the bed then lay beside her, setting his fingers at the base of her throat, then dragging his hand down her body, between her breasts, barely brushing the sides, along her stomach, across her abdomen, stopping where her thighs met. She squirmed. He took his time exploring. She opened to him, clamped her mouth before she begged him out loud, then let out a husky cry as he slipped a finger inside her. His thumb moved, too. Her hips rose. She called out his name.

"That's it, baby," he whispered. "Let it happen."

She had no choice. It was happening with or without effort on her part. He knew where to touch, where to tease, when to move, when to stop. Then when he put his mouth on her intimately, passionately, she took everything he gave. He didn't give her a moment to float back into consciousness before he was on top of her and in her and moving, filling her up, taking her high again, higher still, peaking at the same moment as he, lost in him.

I love you. Again the words came, silent and devastating. Why did she fall in love with men she couldn't have?

He sprawled on her for a while, his weight on his elbows, then rolled to his side, taking her with him, keeping her close. "I guess that had built up a while in both of us," he said.

She ran a finger around his chest. "How long for you?"

"Since I saw you in your bathing suit that first day." He toyed with her hair, sifting through it with his fingers, rubbing the ends. "How about you?"

"I don't know exactly. A long time."

He pulled her head back and kissed her, a leisurely exploration.

"Don't you have to get to the office?" she asked, feeling awkward suddenly, her problems seeping back into her thoughts, no matter how hard she tried to ignore them. Plus, he wasn't saying the right words....

"I may work from home today." He brushed his lips over her hair. "I'm not done here yet. How about you?"

She wanted to stay in his arms forever. "My boss is flexible."

He laughed quietly. Then he just held her, and she closed her eyes and let herself enjoy it.

"What's been bothering you?" he asked finally, his breath warm against her hair.

She felt her contentment die. "I don't want to talk about it while I'm naked and in your arms."

"But you'll tell me?"

"Yes," she said, making the decision. "Just not today."

He didn't say anything, but she figured he was annoyed. "I don't need to be taken care of, David."

"I figured that out."

She wanted to lean on him, though, wished she could have some burdens lifted. But she owed a lot of money, and just as she wouldn't let Senior clear her debts, she wouldn't let David, who would probably want to, as well. She'd considered asking him for a loan, with payments to come out of her paycheck at a lesser rate of interest than what she'd been paying, but had decided against that, too. And especially not now. They'd already mixed business and pleasure. There were bound to be repercussions for that.

"I want to help," he said.

"I know. And I appreciate it." She remembered Laura's reaction when Valerie had commented on David's protectiveness, how shocked she'd been. Maybe it *was* different for him this time. Maybe she meant more to him—

She couldn't think like that. She also didn't know what she was going to do now. What would their relationship be? Would he expect her to be available to him all the time now? Was their relationship exclusive or would he still date other women?

The phone rang. Valerie jumped at the intrusion. David didn't answer it, just letting it go to the machine. It was Noah.

"So, you're not answering your cell, and you're not home, either. This is getting old, David." He blew out a breath. "Okay, listen. Someone's been checking on our financial status. I need you in the office to work on this. Now." He hung up.

"That would be Peterson and Koning," David said. "Guess maybe I can't wait any longer to bring Noah in on the deal. I'd hoped—" He turned so that they were face-to-face. "I don't think I can ignore him now."

Valerie wanted him to go, anyway. She needed time to think about what came next. "I understand."

"I really don't want to get out of bed."

She smiled but said nothing.

He brushed her hair from her face. "I think you're glad to see me go."

She pressed her lips to his. "It was wonderful."

He ran his fingers along her jaw. "You're a complicated woman. When I hired you, I thought you straightforward and easy to figure out. You're not. There's a lot there."

"Good."

He kissed her long and lingeringly. She melted into him. Then he rolled off the bed and headed toward the bathroom. At the last second he turned around, catching her watching and admiring him.

"Should I call Noah and tell him you're on your way?" she asked, sitting up and pulling a pillow in front of her.

He smiled knowingly as she tried to hide her nakedness. "Too late, you know. I looked. And liked it all."

She stared back.

"Yes, that's a good idea to call him. Thanks." He disappeared around the corner.

Valerie grabbed her clothes and yanked them on, then sat on the bed to call Noah. David returned, dressed for work, as she hung up.

"He's…peeved at you," she said.

"He's about to become more peeved when he finds out I've kept him out of the loop on this project."

"Good luck," she said, not standing, not intending to walk downstairs with him and see him off, not wanting that awkward moment of whether to kiss goodbye or not. "Everything you need is on your desk."

He cocked his head. "Not going to kiss me goodbye?"

"What do you call what we did—" She pointed to the bed.

"That was hello."

Oh. So, she was being put on notice that this was just the beginning. "I know we should probably talk about this," she began.

He shook his head. "Why don't we just go with it, and see where it leads us."

"I wish it was that simple," she said. "I work for you."

"It doesn't have to get complicated, Valerie."

He was wrong about that, but there wasn't time to discuss it. "Right."

"I'll call you when I know about dinner," he said, then slipped an arm around her waist, pulled her up and kissed her until she kissed him back…and then some.

"We have to be careful," she said against his mouth. "Hannah—"

"I know. We will." Then he was gone, and she was left with regret mixed with exhilaration, satisfaction mixed with a brand-new kind of need. It didn't matter what spin she put on what had happened. Ultimately it came down to the fact that they were two healthy people who were attracted and did something about it.

Except that she was in love. And he wasn't.

Chapter Sixteen

"We can't lose," David said to Noah later in his office. "We're assuming some financial responsibility, but we have the potential to bring in a bundle."

"A loss is a loss, even when limited." Noah had gone from outrage at David's secret meetings, to stonewalling by coming up with hurdles to the success of the venture. "We have a reputation," he added.

"Not in Le Mans. In fact, it'll bring brand-new exposure to us."

"We've always been known for class and style. We cater to a limited clientele because of that."

"'Limited' being the key word. It's a new world, Noah. We need to grow and expand in order to stay competitive, but in ways that protect the company and our futures. We can't count on the sultan of Tumari forever."

"But you're talking about building race cars," Noah said. "That's risky."

"So was our business in general until recently. We're well established now. We've got a good name, a solid name, but no big name recognition. This will boost our recognition enormously. People will be talking about Falcon Motorcars. We'll get publicity like you wouldn't believe, much of it free."

"After investing millions."

"I've spent a lot of time and energy figuring this out, Noah. Then I talked to people who *do* know what will work. They think we've got a winner." David handed him a folder. "Here's your proof. The American Le Mans fan's demographics are perfect, and completely in alignment with our current buyer—the affluent 25- to 49-year-old with annual earnings well above the average. That's our market, especially for U.S. sales. We've been missing the boat there. Here's our chance to capitalize."

Noah pushed himself out of his chair and came to sit beside David on the office sofa. "I didn't understand how unhappy you've been with your job. I didn't believe Gideon when he said it."

"I can't keep up the pace, Noah. It's not like I'm quitting or anything, but I do want to oversee this branch of the company. It's my baby, my concept. Everything." David saw that Noah had calmed down. "We'll probably end up opening dealerships, because that fan will expect to walk into a showroom to buy a car with the latest innovations and technologies, ones we developed on our Le Mans car. And he'll be taking it home not just for the bragging rights but because it'll be the most amazing ride of his life."

"We'll be fully involved in all the decisions, right? We've worked too hard at building Falcon Motorcars to tarnish our reputation. If we lost business—"

"We can't lose. I'm telling you, we can't. I remember the mess we inherited, too, you know. Dad had vision but no business sense. But we're smarter, Noah. We've proven that. And we can end up with a slew of new buyers, probably young and American, all those new millionaires out there, and take the business in a whole new direction. We can hire a sales rep or two for the European market. We'll have our name all over the place on the circuit and then on the cars themselves."

"Would you move?"

David tried to get a handle on Noah. When he got very quiet, like now, he was impossible to read. Gideon could, maybe, but no one else. "No. And I'm not dropping out of the day-to-day business, just shifting job responsibilities."

"You're excited about it."

"Yeah." David couldn't even add to that. He didn't have the words. And this morning he'd made love with Valerie. Sweet, sexy, secretive Valerie. Everything in his life was unsettled—in a good way.

David pulled another folder from his briefcase and passed it to his brother. "Potential reps for overseas. Even if the Le Mans deal doesn't work out, I want to hire someone. I'd focus more on growing U.S. business. It's out there."

Noah tossed it onto his desk. "When do you think you'll have an answer from Peterson and Koning?"

"By the end of next week, probably."

"Let me look over all the details, and I'll get back to you."

Noah hadn't flat-out rejected the idea, but David couldn't gauge at all how Noah felt. He'd never had a lot of give in him, but even less since his wife died. And he ran his household like his business.

David glanced at his watch. Almost three o'clock. If he left now, he could beat the commute traffic on Highway 80. He stood. "I'm going home."

Noah nodded. "You'll be in tomorrow?"

Tomorrow was Friday. Hannah would be in school, which would give him time alone with Valerie without worries about being caught. Then he remembered, too, that next week was Hannah's fall break at school, when there would be no possibility at all of time alone. That clinched it.

"I doubt I'll be in tomorrow."

"I'm sure we'll need further discussion on this matter, David."

"Don't talk to me like Dad, okay? We're partners. I've busted my butt for this business. If I want to work at home for a day, I will." He left without waiting for Noah's response, then cooled off during the drive home. Although maybe "cooled off" wasn't exactly accurate, because the anticipation of seeing Valerie again definitely didn't have a cooling effect.

He pulled into his garage and headed for the house, then spotted Hannah sitting in a lounge chair by the pool, her legs drawn up, arms wrapped around them, head buried against her knees. He debated what to do. The fact she didn't acknowledge him made him think he should just keep going. The fact she was usually cheerful—overly cheerful—made him detour to where she sat.

He took the seat next to her. "Bad day?" he asked.

She nodded.

"Wanna talk about it?"

She mumbled something into her knees.

"I can't hear you." He almost put his hand on the back of her head in comfort, she seemed so dejected.

She lifted her head slightly. "I'm mad at my mom."

"Where is she?"

"In the cottage. On the phone. Talking to my *grandfather*."

It was the first David had heard about a grandfather. "That's bad?"

Hannah finally looked right at him. Dried tears streaked her cheeks. "He was a secret. And now I have to meet him. *And* a new grandmother."

Which must have something to do with what Valerie had been keeping to herself lately, a family drama she didn't want him to know about. "You don't want to meet them?"

"Everything was fine, you know?" she said, fresh tears welling up. "We like it here. We *love* it here," she said with more drama. "I have a grandma already. She's not lots of fun." Her voice had softened, as if Valerie might overhear. "What do I need more for?"

"Having grandparents doesn't mean your situation here is going to change. You'll still live here." At least he thought so. Hoped so. What if Valerie had told Hannah something different? What if he lost Valerie? She'd promised she would stay....

He didn't feel comfortable trying to advise Hannah when he didn't know exactly what the situation was. But he could tell her what he'd been through himself. "When I was growing up, people came in and out of my life all the time. Even my mother." He saw Hannah focus more intently on him.

"Your mom didn't live with you?"

"She moved out when I was eleven. I saw her now and then, but mostly I lived with my dad and two half brothers."

"At least you had them. I don't even have that. I want a baby brother *so bad*."

The passion in her voice made him want to smile, but he treated her wish seriously. "Then I hope you get one. In the meantime, you have grandparents. I didn't have any."

"None?"

"Nope. They all died before I was born."

"That's awful."

"I thought so, too. When will you meet yours?"

"In two days. On Saturday. Mr. Falcon? Will you be there, too?"

Her hopeful look made him wish he could be. "I don't think that'll be possible."

"But I'm scared. My mom said they're very important people. I don't know how to act."

"Give them a chance. And just be yourself. They'll love you right away."

"That's what Mom says." She wrinkled her nose as if not believing it.

"Okay, then. Two people have said it, so you know it's the truth."

"Thanks."

He finally did brush his hand down her hair. "You don't have to thank me. If you ever need anything at all, just ask. If it's within my power, I'll do it."

"Hannah." Valerie came up the path, her eyes flickering to David, questioning and welcoming at the same time. How did she manage that?

"I dusted his office," Hannah blurted out.

Valerie stopped. "What?"

"That's our secret. Mr. Falcon caught me dusting his office. He told me not to do it again, and I haven't. I promise."

David swallowed a smile. "Yes, she's kept her promise."

"He told me I should tell you, but I didn't. But now I know that secrets are bad. I'm never gonna keep a secret again." She flung herself at Valerie.

David got up, excusing himself and walking away, but hearing Hannah say, "Mr. Falcon says I should give my new grandparents a chance. So I will, Mom."

He couldn't hear Valerie's murmured response, but all seemed well.

And he'd had a hand in that.

The next morning Valerie dragged her feet about starting work, unsure of what to say to David. On the one hand, she was grateful for his advice to Hannah the day before, which had calmed her enough that Valerie could have a good conversation with her. On the other hand, now that he knew bits and pieces of the issue, she needed to tell him all of it so that he wouldn't guess incorrectly.

They'd just begun an intimate relationship. She didn't want to discuss the first love of her life—not yet—but now she had no choice.

A few minutes after Hannah boarded the bus, Valerie

finally worked up the nerve to climb the stairs to the big house. David was waiting. The moment she opened the door he swept her into his arms and kissed her.

"Good morning," she said, a little dazed and a lot aroused.

"The bus was three minutes late."

She laughed. He grabbed her hand and led her through the kitchen, then at the bottom of the staircase, he swept her into his arms and carried her up the stairs and into his bedroom. The romantic gesture thrilled her, emboldening her enough to take the lead and undress him. She tantalized him with her fingertips and her lips. He drew in air, the sound sharp, as she teased him. His fingers threaded her hair as she moved down his body, her need to touch and taste overwhelming. And his being naked while she was fully dressed seemed so much more…erotic? Intense? Definitely both of those.

But he didn't wait too long to get her just as naked, and then they landed on the bed and rolled, locked together. She loved the feel of his skin against hers from head to toe. Loved that he needed her so much but made the effort to drag out the experience so that when he finally entered her, she went into a climax instantly, arching to meet him, her head thrown back, long, low sounds coming from her.

The moment she ebbed he rolled so that she was on top. Her hair fell around her face as she rested her hands alongside his head on the pillow. He lifted up, caught a nipple in his mouth and gently pulled her lower, moving to the other side, then sliding his hands where his mouth had been and pushing her up again. His hands drifted to her hips, helping her move in erotic rhythm, until he found release, too. She loved watching him, was flattered by the absolute pleasure and satisfaction on his face.

Finally he dragged her down on top of him and held her. She settled against him, wishing it could go on and on, but reality reared its head again. She knew she had to tell him things about her life that she didn't want to bring into the relationship when it was so new and vulnerable.

David resituated her, pulling up the bedding against the chilly morning.

"So," he said. "You've been having some excitement lately."

"You could call it that." Maybe it was better this way—in bed, tucked close, where she didn't have to look at him.

"How about starting at the beginning?"

She closed her eyes for a moment, her hand pressed to his heart, which beat strong and steady. She'd gotten to know him well over the past two months, had fallen in love with him, foolishly or otherwise. Now she had to trust him more than ever.

"I told you my mother worked for a family in Palm Springs as their housekeeper."

"I remember."

"It's their vacation home, but they spend a lot of time there, often coming just for weekends, but weeks at a time, too. Wagner Rawling, Sr., whom everyone calls Senior, and his wife, Loretta, plus their son, Wagner Jr."

"I take it this story is about Junior."

"Yes, although he's called Wagner. We grew up together, sort of. He was four years older, but we'd known each other almost all our lives. As children, we played together a lot. My mother didn't like it, but the Rawlings didn't discourage it. When Wagner turned sixteen, his world expanded, and I no longer mattered to him.

"I missed him. I'd always looked forward to his visits, but he would ignore me, or worse, treated me like help. Then when I graduated from high school, he came home after finishing college and we discovered a different connection. We became lovers. I fell in love and got pregnant, but before I knew I was pregnant, he left for Europe for several months. He was supposed to return and work in the family business."

While she talked, David ran his hands over her back, soothing, making it easier to tell him everything.

"I didn't know how to get in touch with him, so I had to ask his father, who noticed the changes in my body and confronted me about it. I confessed I was pregnant. A few days later he gave me a letter from Wagner that said he'd never loved me, and had been, in fact, engaged to be married for a year. He'd apparently told his father I'd slept with several guys, and I was only looking for money."

"But?"

"He was my one and only. He'd done the seducing, and I fell as hard as any eighteen-year-old without life experience falls for a man who knows the ways of the world. His father made me a deal—he would pay all my expenses for having the baby, plus send me to business college."

"Where was your mother in all this?"

"Really angry at me for jeopardizing her job, but also telling me to take the deal, that it was more than I deserved."

David's body went taut. "More than you deserved? But—"

"Don't go there, okay?" She squeezed her eyes shut. "It's taken me years to forgive her for that. Anyway, while I was making up my mind about what to do, Wagner got married. That was the end for me. We had no contact at all, never once discussed the situation."

"DNA tests would prove paternity."

"Yes, but by then I didn't want him acknowledged as the father."

He hesitated. "You said he died."

"Recently, in a boating accident."

"And now his parents have materialized, wanting to know Hannah."

"Wagner and his wife didn't have other children. Hannah's the only tie to their son. But the worst thing is that Senior also confessed he'd written the letter, that he'd never told Wagner I was pregnant."

Valerie could feel David's outrage. His arms tightened around her.

"So, why the hell are you dealing with him?"

"Because of Hannah. They are her grandparents. Mrs.

Rawling, in particular, doesn't deserve to be shut out, since she wasn't involved. She's grieving for her only child. Hannah could help."

"You're much more generous than they deserve."

"Maybe. But when you're a parent, you think differently. Believe me, I'd like to deny them the right and keep her to myself, but I can't do that to her. You saw her yesterday. Think how she would feel if I didn't tell her, then she learned on her own later. It could cause years of estrangement and hurt between us. Better to deal with it now."

"How is—"

She put her hand against his mouth. "Shh. I don't want to talk about it anymore, okay? We won't have much time alone over the next week. Wouldn't you rather use this day to do other things?" She felt empowered suddenly. Self-confident.

And madly in love. *Mad* being the operative word. Foolish, too. One would think she would've learned her lesson about loving men she couldn't have.

But the heart wasn't so easily controlled.

So she gave him herself, everything she had to offer, and took back from him, whatever he could give, then slept in his arms for a while.

Regret could come later.

And undoubtedly would.

Chapter Seventeen

David made sure he was home when the Rawlings showed up on Saturday afternoon, in case of any fallout. He was standing on his deck when the well-dressed couple walked up the driveway, hand in hand. Mrs. Rawling seemed to be leaning on her husband, who carried a shopping bag in his other hand.

He watched the man give the woman an encouraging hug, then knock on the cottage door. The door swung open and the couple went inside. Valerie leaned out and spotted him. He lifted his hand in acknowledgment, then she disappeared.

He'd asked why she didn't schedule the meeting in a public location instead of in her personal space, and she'd said it would be easier on Hannah to be in her own environment. He supposed he saw the logic in that, but it would be easier to walk away from a restaurant than to get the Rawlings to leave her house, if things started to go wrong.

So David stayed where he was, just in case. After a few

minutes Joseph's truck came down the driveway. Grateful for a reason to get himself closer to the cottage, David went to greet his friend.

"Whose fancy Cadillac out front?" Joseph asked.

"Friends of Valerie. What's up?"

"You coming to the Stompin' Grounds tonight?"

"I hadn't planned on it. Why?"

"The Hombres are dropping in for a surprise visit."

"Surprise?"

Joseph grinned. "They want to try out some new stuff. We're trying to get a full house for them."

"It's been full every time I've been there, Joe."

"Sometimes it's slower than others. The Hombres want lots of feedback."

David shrugged. "I can't promise, but I'll try."

"Nine o'clock." Joseph headed back to his truck. "Don't be late."

"Hey, where're you going? You just got here."

"I figured a personal invite would get more people to come. I've got lots on my list," he said over his shoulder. "Maybe Valerie would like to come, too."

"I'll ask her, but I think she's going to be busy."

"Whatever. Dix'll probably call, anyway."

Then David was left waiting again and wondering. He should've talked Valerie into turning on the intercom and leaving it open for him to hear. That way if the Rawlings caused a problem, he would know.

He shoved his fingers through his hair. What the hell was he doing? He hadn't wanted to get close to her daughter, yet here he was, on guard in case either of them needed him. He'd already acknowledged the stupidity of getting involved with Valerie, but that hadn't stopped him from doing it—or wanting to continue.

He took a seat in a pool chair, watched the cottage door and waited. They didn't emerge for hours. And when they did, he couldn't read anyone's expression.

* * *

Valerie spotted David sitting by the pool when they all came out of the cottage. She wondered how long he'd been there. The whole four hours since the Rawlings had arrived?

How could Laura have thought he wasn't protective?

He walked up to them, introducing himself before Valerie got the chance. She saw him exchange a look with Hannah, who gave him an unobtrusive thumbs-up sign, drawing a small smile from him. Their silent connection and communication gave Valerie pause. Somehow David and Hannah had gotten close. She wasn't sure when or how that had happened—nor how she felt about it.

"Hannah's grandparents are taking her out to dinner and a movie," Valerie said, as upbeat as possible. Valerie had left the decision to accept the invitation to Hannah.

"And I can stay up late." Hannah looked comfortable going with her grandparents.

"We'll have her back by ten-thirty," Senior said.

Valerie decided not to walk to the car with them, not wanting to hover. She kissed her daughter goodbye and watched her leave.

"It went okay, I gather," David said a minute later.

"Yes. They brought some albums with pictures of Wagner growing up. Hannah was fascinated. It was a smart thing to do. Opened her up to them right away. They told stories I hadn't known about, of course, too." She rubbed her arms. "I don't know how I'm going to stand the wait until she's home."

"I have an idea."

She focused on him. "I'm really not in the mood, David."

He laughed. "Not that, although that would be a good way to pass the time, I think, and make you forget for a little while. No, something else. Joe stopped by to say that the Hombres are playing at the Stompin' Grounds tonight, and they want a full house for them. They're trying out new material. So, how about going with me?"

"I need to stay by my phone."

"Put your cell on vibrate and stick it in your pocket where you'll feel it. We're only five minutes from home."

"But we don't want people to know we have a relationship other than business."

"We won't slow dance. Come on. It'll keep you busy. We'll go early and have some burgers. I'll have you back by ten. Plenty of time."

She really liked the idea of having a distraction. "Okay. Thanks. In the meantime, I need to keep busy. I think the kitchen cabinets need to be rearranged."

He smiled. "I'll be in my office, if you need anything."

"You don't want to help?"

"I wouldn't be able to keep my hands off you."

Valerie smiled back.

At the Stompin' Grounds, David was trying hard to respect Valerie's need for him to keep things from getting out of hand. They'd eaten dinner, had a beer and danced one fast dance, not touching at all. The Hombres were setting up. Valerie was hanging out with Dixie and her friends in their corner.

David leaned an elbow against the bar and sipped an icy beer, occasionally looking at Valerie as she laughed and talked with the other women. She fit in. He never would've thought he would say that about her. She'd seemed so reserved in the beginning, so solemn, but not any longer. She'd made a place for herself.

He took another swig, annoyed he couldn't slow dance with her, then spotted her pulling her cell phone from her pocket, looking at the screen as she headed outdoors to find quiet. He followed.

"How did you find out?" he heard her say as he caught up with her.

"I was waiting to tell you until I saw how it went," she went on. "I'm sorry you feel that way, but this is my life. My decision... I can't talk to you when you get like this."

David moved closer, letting her know he was there. She looked up, startled. "I'll call you tomorrow.... Okay, then, you call me when you're ready. Goodbye."

She tucked the phone into her pocket. "My mother. Mrs. Rawling called her to say how thrilled she was to be sharing a granddaughter. Mom thought she was gloating."

"Do you think that's true?"

"I don't know. I kept my distance from Mrs. Rawling while I grew up. She was very formal, and a demanding boss to my mother. But then, she grew up wealthy and entitled. My mother has never liked her."

"Why'd she stay on?"

"Security. And I'm sure the fact they weren't there full-time was also part of her decision. She threatened to leave every so often but never did anything about it. She's just not a happy person, David. I'm surprised Senior didn't find a reason to fire her after I got pregnant."

"He probably figured she would tell Mrs. Rawling about Hannah."

"Oh. I hadn't thought about that. So Mom's had the upper hand all these years and probably didn't realize it." Valerie shook her head. "Ah, irony. You've gotta love it."

From inside the bar came a voice announcing the Hombres and then music began to blare. "Would you rather go home?" David asked.

She shook her head. "I want to have some fun. Let's go dance."

By the time they got inside and squeezed through the crowd to where Joseph and Dixie were dancing, the song was ending. The lead guitarist took the microphone.

"Thanks for coming, everyone. We've got a new set we've been working on. We hope you like 'em all. Before we get goin' on the tunes, however, Joseph's got somethin' he wants to say. Joe?" He held out the mike as Joseph hopped onto the small stage.

He wiped his hands down his thighs, then reached for the mike. "You all know me," he said. It was followed by boisterous response, most of it insults, making him grin. "You all know Dixie." Cheers erupted.

Dixie raised both arms and smiled, but David was also close enough to see confusion in her eyes.

"We've been a twosome since before I could drive."

"Off and on," Dixie shouted.

"Mostly on. Now, I know you've put up with a lot from me Dixie Rae, and I'm hopin' you're gonna want to put up with a lot more." He pulled a small black box from his pocket and got down on one knee. Feedback on the mike screeched for a second, then quieted down. "I love you, girl. I'm asking you to marry me and have my babies."

Dixie's hands flew to her mouth, then she seemed to pull herself together, and used her hands as a megaphone to call out, "Well, what're you doing twenty feet away? Come put that ring on my finger, Joseph McCoy."

Amid cheers and whoops, Joseph did just that as the crowd separated, making a path for him to reach her. David caught a glimpse of Valerie, her eyes sparkling with tears, her fingers pressed to her lips. Tears of joy for Dixie? Something else? Valerie had a child, but no one had proposed marriage to her, as far as he knew.

But brave Valerie hugged Dixie then Joseph, then so did David.

"I'll want you to stand up with me," Joseph said.

"I'd be honored, Joe."

The band started playing again. Joseph and Dixie took the floor. To hell with not slow dancing in front of the others, David thought. He would ask Valerie to dance. But just as he was about to, she dug into her pocket for her cell phone and pushed her way outside. He trailed her.

"I'll be there in five minutes, Hannah, okay? Just sit in the chairs by the pool... I know it's cold. Five minutes."

Valerie turned toward the bar. "Oh! You're there. They're already at the house—more than an hour early! Can you drop me off, please?"

"Let's go."

A minute later in the car she said, "So were you surprised about Joseph proposing?"

"He hadn't said a word."

"Dixie looked so happy."

"She's been very patient."

"She loves him."

David looked at Valerie's face reflected in the dashboard lights, her expression calm, as usual. "Sometimes love isn't enough."

"Love conquers all," she said.

"No, it doesn't. Love changes. Love dies."

"Not true love. True love never dies."

She'd always been so practical and logical to him, that this particular fantasy about love seemed…unhealthy. "How do you tell the difference between true love and…any other kind?"

"You can tell."

They pulled into the driveway. He didn't know whether to be glad that the trip was over and the conversation was ending, or if the conversation should continue so that he could get her to see she was deluded to think love could last forever. It couldn't. He'd seen it fail too many times to believe that. It barely lasted beyond the honeymoon stage for most people.

"A while back you told me they were meant for each other," Valerie said serenely, quietly.

"I think if anyone can make it, Joe and Dixie can. After all, they've had fifteen years to figure it out. Generally people don't know each other a year before they make a lifetime commitment. No wonder relationships fail."

She patted his hand, a slight smile on her face, just as he came to a stop in front of the garage, deciding to park the car later. She pulled open the door and hurried up the path to the pool. Hannah met her halfway.

"Did you have a good time?" Valerie asked.

"I ate lobster!"

Valerie slid her arm around Hannah's waist and walked to where the Rawlings were waiting. "Did you like it?"

"It was good. And they bought me a bracelet. See?" She held out an arm, displaying a circle of sparkling pink gems.

Real? David wondered, coming up next to them.

"It's beautiful. You need to tell your grandparents good-night."

David heard tension in Valerie's voice. Did Hannah?

"Good night," she said politely. "Thank you."

Mrs. Rawling hugged her, although Hannah kept her arms by her sides. "We'll see you tomorrow."

Hannah looked into Valerie's eyes then hurried off. Some kind of drama was happening, he decided.

Everyone stood silent until Hannah shut the cottage door.

"That bracelet is too expensive for a child," Valerie said.

"We have a right to buy our granddaughter gifts," Senior replied harshly.

Belle growled. Everyone turned toward her. David hadn't even known she was there.

"It's okay, girl," he said. "Go lie down."

She looked up at him as if she didn't want to obey, then moved a few feet away and sat, but didn't put her head down.

Valerie turned back to the Rawlings. "Children her age lose things. They don't understand the value."

Mrs. Rawling stepped in. "We impressed upon her that it was valuable and she should be careful with it."

"What's valuable to an eight-year-old—" She stopped, seemed to slow herself down. "Never mind. A bigger issue seems to be that you made plans to see Hannah tomorrow without talking to me first."

"Hannah brought it up, not us," Senior said, then looked at

his wife. "But Loretta and I did want to ask a favor. We understand Hannah has vacation from school next week. We'd like to take her to Lake Tahoe for a couple of days, if you don't mind."

Valerie crossed her arms. "Where would you stay?"

"We have friends who own a home there. They're not using it at the moment. I assure you we'll watch her every minute."

"I'll think about it. I'll call you in the morning and let you know my decision."

David admired her. She was holding her own with the couple, not seeming at all intimidated.

"We enjoyed our evening very much," Mrs. Rawling said. "She's quite a girl. High spirited, but sweet. I see a little of my son in her, in her eyes."

The woman's tone set David on edge, so he could only imagine Valerie's reaction. Hannah was a miniature of Valerie, including her eyes, both in shape and color.

"She's just Hannah," Valerie said. "My mother said you called her."

"I thought we should talk, yes." Her chin went up. Senior slipped an arm around her waist. "The situation is a little... awkward, don't you think? I was trying to make her feel at ease."

David would've ended the increasingly uncomfortable conversation right then, before it escalated, but it wasn't his place. Valerie would only accuse him of interfering. Fortunately Senior took charge.

"We need to go, my dear. Valerie, we'll be looking forward to your call in the morning."

The man was slick, David decided. He wished Gideon was there to take a better measure of him. But David knew for sure that Valerie needed to be careful of Senior and his power and pull. Should David warn her? Would she accept advice from him about it?

Probably not.

His option was to keep tabs. That much he could do.

Valerie didn't move until the Rawlings were out of sight, then she faced David. "I need to get inside and talk to Hannah."

"I know." He cupped her arm. "Are you going to let them take her to Tahoe?"

"I don't know yet. I don't trust them, David."

Okay. Good. She'd keyed in on it, too. He relaxed a little. "Trust your instincts," he said. "Good night."

For a moment, just a moment, he thought she was going to kiss him. She leaned toward him then suddenly turned away. He waited until she was inside before he climbed his stairs, Belle appearing from where she'd been banished to accompany him.

"You're worried, too, aren't you, girl?"

Belle barked once.

"We'll both stay alert, then. Between us, we can take care of them."

It was the last thing Valerie would want, to be taken care of. *Tough.* In this matter she had no choice. She'd been under his protection since the moment he hired her. And Hannah was part of the package.

He would protect his own.

Chapter Eighteen

For the second morning in a row, David awakened with Valerie in his arms, although she was still asleep this time. They'd slept late each morning since Hannah had gone to Tahoe. It had been an incredible couple of days, even with Valerie's tension never letting up. If anything, her stressed emotions had made her more passionate, more intense, more needy. They never spoke about what would happen next, how their working relationship would be impacted.

David's hope was that everything would continue as it was. Life was good. Perfect, in fact.

She stirred sleepily.

"Good morning," he said against her temple, this time smelling lemons in her hair.

"Morning." Her hand rested on his chest.

He covered her hand with his. "Sleep well?"

"Yes. And Hannah comes home today."

"You've missed her."

"It's the first time we've been apart for more than a few hours. But I've had other things to occupy my mind." She tipped her head back and smiled at him. "She sounds fine on the phone. I just need to see for myself."

He was about to take her mind off it when the phone rang. He picked it up.

"David, this is Ron Peterson. Can you make a meeting today in my L. A. office?"

"Are we finalizing things, Ron?"

"It depends on how this meeting turns out."

"I'll check on flights and get back to you." He hung up and stared at the ceiling, his heart racing. "This is it."

"They okayed the deal?"

"I should have an answer today. Last meeting, I hope."

"Then *lots* more meetings," she added, a smile in her voice. "I'm happy for you."

He hugged her tight. "Your help was immeasurable."

"My pleasure. Now, do you need me to get an airline reservation for you?"

"Yeah, thanks. Let me call Noah first and see if he wants to go, too."

Valerie threw back the covers and got out of bed. He wasn't in such a hurry that he couldn't take a minute to admire her as she pulled on her robe, not blushing like the first time she was naked in front of him, but not trying to tease him, either.

Natural. He liked that about her.

"I'll start the coffee," she said.

He nodded then reached for the phone.

A couple hours later he set his garment bag and briefcase by the kitchen door. He would pick up Noah, who was taking his first trip since his wife had died. He'd agreed to it only because Valerie had said she would stay at Noah's that evening, giving his nanny time to drive to Sacramento for a class at the university she took twice a week. Valerie had just gone to the cottage to pack a few items. After the Rawlings dropped off Hannah, she and Valerie would head to Noah's.

The phone rang. He saw the number was Valerie's cell, which she'd given Hannah to use.

"Hey, kiddo, what's new?" he asked.

"Mr. Falcon," Hannah said in almost a whisper.

He pressed the phone to his ear. "What's wrong?"

"Is my mom there?"

"She's in the cottage. Do you want me to get her?"

"No. You said I could tell you if I needed something, remember?"

He squeezed the phone tighter. "I remember."

"I heard my grandparents talking when they didn't think I could hear them."

David's entire body went on alert. "Okay."

"They were talking about me, how I would stay with them a lot, like all summer and stuff. Maybe more."

David relaxed. "It's all right, Hannah. They can't make you do that unless you want to. And your mom wouldn't let them, either."

"But, Mr. Falcon, I also heard them say how Mom had beer on her breath that night you guys had to come home early. My grandfather said something about an unfitted mother. Do you know what that means?"

And so it began, David thought. He *knew* the Rawlings couldn't be trusted. Hell, even Belle had known that.

This needed to be stopped before it got started.

"Mr. Falcon?"

"Yes?"

"You can fix it, right?"

"I will fix it. I promise you."

"Will you tell my mom?"

"After I fix it."

"She's not gonna like that. I promised I wouldn't keep any more secrets."

"I know. But we don't want to upset her, okay? Let me check on things first. Can you do that? Just for one day, Hannah?"

"Oh, here they come. Bye."

The line went dead. David knew the Rawlings planned to drop off Hannah at the cottage then take their private plane home to L. A. The timing couldn't have been more perfect.

The kitchen door opened and Valerie came in, smiling, anticipating her daughter coming home, and also happy in a way he hadn't seen before. He didn't want to see her unhappy again. Or worried. Or scared.

He kissed her goodbye, a promise in the embrace to protect her. No one would burden her ever again.

"What's going on with you?" Valerie asked her daughter late that evening as she tucked her into bed in Noah's guest room. Hannah had acted strangely all day, clinging to Valerie's side, not wanting her out of sight.

Hannah pulled the blankets to her chin. Her eyes were wide and serious. "I can't tell you."

She'd never seen her daughter like this. "What do you mean you can't tell me? No secrets, Hannah, remember? Is it something to do with your grandparents?"

"I can't tell you, Mom. I told Mr. Falcon."

"Mr. Falcon?" Stunned didn't begin to describe Valerie's reaction. "Telling me what's bothering you is much more important than a promise to Mr. Falcon."

"It's my grandparents," she blurted. "They want to take me away from you."

"What?" Fury burst inside her, red-hot and instantaneous. "How do you know that?"

"I heard them talking. They thought I was asleep."

"And what does Mr. Falcon have to do with it?"

"I called him, and he said he would take care of it. I knew he could fix it. I knew it." She pulled the blankets even higher so that just her eyes were revealed. "He said we would tell you tomorrow, after he fixed it," she mumbled under the covers. "Don't be mad."

Valerie didn't want her to be afraid of telling the truth, ever. "Honey, it's okay. I promise, it's okay. You did the right thing by telling me."

"But I don't want Mr. Falcon to get in trouble, Mom. He's my…friend. You know? He's really nice to me. Like a—" She stopped for a moment. "Like a dad," she finished, almost whispering. "My dad."

No! When had her daughter started fantasizing about David being a father to her? How had Valerie missed that? The other day she'd realized they'd talked and were friendly, but more than that? Did David know how Hannah felt?

How could he get her hopes up like that? He didn't want a wife and family, he'd made that clear. It was one thing to have a relationship with an adult woman who knew what she was getting into, but a child?

"Everything will be okay, Hannah," she said to her worried-looking daughter. "Just go to sleep."

"You'll come sleep with me?"

They had to share the guest room, but Valerie wouldn't go to bed until the nanny, Jessica, got home from Sacramento.

"Yes, I'll sleep here." Not that Valerie expected she would sleep. "I have to wait up for Jessica first."

And when her cell phone rang later and she saw it was David, she let it go to voice mail without a moment's regret, as well as the next three times.…

Valerie wandered to the kitchen window when she heard a car coming down Noah's driveway. She looked at her watch—11:00 p.m.

The vehicle came into view. Not Jessica's car, but a truck she didn't recognize. Floodlights lit up the yard, and she spotted Gideon Falcon. Valerie unlocked the back door as he climbed the stairs.

"Something wrong with your cell phone?" he said as a greeting, stopping in the open doorway.

So. He'd been sent to spy. She crossed her arms. "Not that I know of."

"Getting reception okay?"

"Last I checked, yes."

"Noah's landline working?"

"Yes."

He frowned. "Then you're in trouble."

"Why?"

"David's been calling you for hours, as you must be aware. Everything's good here?" He stepped into the kitchen and looked around.

"Noah's children and my daughter are asleep. You're welcome to check on them."

His brows rose at her snippy tone. "So, the even-tempered Valerie has a temper, after all. My little brother tick you off?"

She walked to the sink and filled a glass of water, not liking how easily he'd figured her out. "You could say that. Were you sent to check on me?"

"Yes, although I didn't get the message until five minutes ago as I was driving home from Sacramento. Does he know what he did wrong?"

"I'm sure he does."

"I'm guessing he doesn't know it made you angry, however."

"He should, but he can be oblivious."

Gideon grinned. "Yes. So, you're waiting to bang him over the head with a pan or something?"

She clamped her mouth shut. Why was she talking to Gideon about David, anyway? She was usually so good at keeping her own counsel. "I don't even want to see him," she said, shocking herself that she'd spoken the words aloud.

Another car made its way down the driveway. "I don't know how you're going to escape it." He looked out the window.

"You mean David is coming *here?*"

"If you'd answered your phone, you would've known that. Never mind. It's the nanny."

Ooh, she hated how calm Gideon was, and how entertaining he thought the situation was.

Jessica breezed in. "Am I late for a party?"

"More like a showdown," Gideon said.

"Please stop. This is private," Valerie said.

The young woman looked from one to the other then shrugged. "I'm going to bed. Thanks so much for filling in tonight, Valerie. And for listening to me."

"Did you make a decision?" Valerie asked, moving closer.

Jessica nodded. She left the room.

"Well, I can guess what that was about," Gideon said. "I imagine Noah will be looking for a new nanny. Again."

Valerie didn't confirm or deny his statement. "You can head home now," she said. "As you can see, everything is under control."

He leaned against the kitchen countertop, his arms folded. "And miss the fireworks? No way."

"I'm not a violent person."

"Good thing. David grew up amid daily battles between our father and his mother. He doesn't tolerate fighting."

"I've noticed he's very patient," she said, grudgingly giving him credit for that.

"That would be news to me. All I know is, he doesn't fight."

Another car approached. "Frying pans are in the cabinet under the cook top," Gideon commented, slanting a look her way, challenge in his eyes.

She heard someone take the steps in a hurry. Then the back door flew open.

David stopped just inside the door. "You're okay."

"Of course I'm okay." She took a sip of water, noticed her hand shook.

"Why didn't you answer your phone?"

Noah came in behind David and nudged him forward so that he could shut the door.

"Your children are fine," she said to Noah. "Jessica just went to bed. I'm sorry you were worried."

"Me? Not me." He and Gideon exchanged a look. "You could've called and let David know all was well."

Gideon raised his hands. "I just got here."

"Did you seal the deal?" she asked Noah, avoiding looking at David.

Noah nodded. Tension filled the room like a snorting, pawing bull getting ready to charge.

"Apparently we need to talk," David said evenly.

"Not tonight." If she could delay until tomorrow, when she was calmer, more in control—

"Tonight. Now," he said. "Either here or outside."

She felt the gazes of all three brothers on her. "Outside."

David opened the door and waited for her. She walked past him and down the stairs, not stopping until she found a spot out of earshot of the kitchen.

"What's going on, Valerie?"

"Like you don't know."

He closed his eyes briefly, as if digging for patience. "I don't know."

"You don't respect me at all. You don't acknowledge me as an adult woman capable of taking care of myself and my child." *Because my daughter wants you to be her daddy. Because I'm stupidly in love with you.*

He frowned. "I do respect you. I do acknowledge that you are competent."

"Then why didn't you let me handle the Rawlings in my own way?"

His jaw twitched. "How did you find out?" he asked quietly.

"Does it matter?"

"I guess not. Valerie, I just wanted to help."

"I retained a lawyer. She was handling everything. I didn't

need your help, David. You had no right to act without discussing it with me."

"Sometimes it takes a man-to-man discussion to get things done."

"Is that what happened?" She clenched her jaw. "You had a *man-to-man* with Senior?"

"There will be no custody question, ever. He won't be pursuing anything beyond occasional grandparent visits."

Relief almost drowned her, rooting her in place. "That was all he was ever going to get."

"You don't know men like Rawling. I do. Whatever your lawyer—Laura, I'm assuming—set up, Rawling and his *team* of lawyers would find a way to tear apart. I made sure he wouldn't."

"Should I thank you? Okay, thank you." Her tone didn't reflect her words. "But you also involved my daughter in a secret, one that caused her a great deal of anxiety. How am I supposed to feel about that?"

"I am sorry for that. I can see it was a mistake."

How could she counter his apology? He'd left her nothing to say. "Maybe I should look for another job." She saw hurt flash in his eyes before he shuttered it, his jaw turning to granite.

"You're never going to find a job that pays as well, that'll allow you to pay off your debts."

Ice ran through her blood. "What do you know about my debts?"

"My company runs a credit check on every potential new hire."

"Why?"

"It speaks to character, Valerie. A lot of companies do it."

She hated that he knew how much debt she had. Hated it.

"Look, you told me about the sexual harassment claim," he said. "I knew it was tough for you to find another job. I'd be maxed out, myself, if I were in the same situation. I didn't hold it against you."

Was he really that dense? He couldn't see how condescending he was being?

"And as long as you're already mad at me," he said, "I guess I should tell you that I had payroll put a direct deposit in your checking account, enough to pay off your debts."

"What? Why? I don't want your—"

"It's a loan, not a gift. You can pay it off with interest, *low* interest. We'll make automatic deductions from your paycheck. You determine the amount."

"Why didn't you talk to me first?"

"I wanted to surprise you. I thought it would make you happy. Bring you some relief."

She had a hard time staying angry about it, since she'd considered asking for a loan herself. It's just that he was so…autocratic.

What a mistake she'd made, getting involved with him intimately while working for him. Yet another gross error of judgment. She should've learned by now.

How could she stay with him?

"You're wrong, you know," she said.

"About which thing?" He almost seemed to sigh.

"I could get another good-paying job. Right here. Jessica told me she's quitting. Noah pays extremely well."

"Noah wouldn't hire you."

"Why not?"

"Because I would tell him not to. He's my brother, Valerie. That counts for a lot." He moved closer to her. "Don't quit."

Tears burned her eyes and throat. As idiotic as it was, she loved him. But Hannah was hoping for something that would never happen. Valerie could deal with the pain and disappointment. Hannah couldn't, shouldn't have to.

"I don't know what else to do," she said finally.

He reached out to stroke her hair. She jerked back. He moved closer, made a soothing sound, touched her cheek for just a moment. "Let's go home."

That tiny touch caused an earthquake of reaction inside her. She ignored it. "Hannah's asleep."

"I'll carry her to the car."

No. Nothing paternal. Not now, not ever. She shook her head. "I'll drive her to school in the morning from here. It's what we planned."

"And heaven forbid we should deviate from a plan."

She took a step back from him, hearing frustration— anger?—in his voice. "I'm not *that* strict."

"Yeah. You are."

That stung enough that she didn't have a comeback. "If you have more to say, say it now. This seems like the time to clear the air."

There was a long pause. "I have nothing to say."

He doesn't fight. Gideon's words rang in her head.

But he could apologize.

Would that make the difference? she wondered. Would that be enough? It didn't change the fact that Hannah would only get hurt if they stayed.

"I'll see you tomorrow." She headed back to the house, jogged up the stairs, ignored Gideon and Noah as she strode through the kitchen, then joined Hannah in bed, where she didn't sleep a wink all night.

David followed more slowly. He shut the kitchen door and faced his brothers.

"You obviously didn't kiss and make up," Gideon remarked.

David glared at him.

"What? Kiss? *What?*" Noah said. "Are you crazy? You got involved with her?"

"It takes two to tango."

"You're her boss," Noah said.

"You think I wanted this to happen?" He kept his voice low, but it shook. "It's the last thing I wanted."

"What's she mad about?" Gideon asked.

"I sort of interfered in some business of hers."

"Sort of?" Quiet descended for several long seconds. "Did you apologize?" Gideon asked.

"No."

"Why not?"

"Because I'm not sorry. I handled something she couldn't handle on her own."

"Are you sure?"

He hesitated. Was he? He thought over his confrontation with Senior Rawling. "Yes."

"Sometimes it's incumbent upon us men to apologize for things we don't think need apology," Noah said. "To keep the peace."

"She was wrong to be angry," David stated, annoyed. "I was protecting her. And her daughter. They're in my charge." He saw his brothers exchange looks. "Well, they are. You would've done the same thing."

"Doubtful," Gideon said.

"Yeah," Noah agreed.

They were playing with him, but he wasn't in the mood for it. "Oh, shut up."

Both men laughed.

He walked out.

David wished he'd driven the Falcon. He needed to put the top down and feel the cold October air against his face. He yearned for the feel of the powerful two-seater under him, zipping along the straightaways, taking the curves, tight and fast. He wished he could get lost.

But since he'd taken Noah and their just-in-case suitcases to L.A. with him, he'd had to bring the SUV, so he drove straight home, garaged his car and went upstairs to let Belle out. At least someone was happy to see him.

He followed her downstairs, turned on the pool lights, then sat in a lounge chair. Belle trotted over, laid her head in his lap and nosed his hand.

"How was your day?" he asked, scratching her ears. She wagged her tail. "Mine was good for a while. Then it wasn't."

His gaze landed on the dark cottage. After a minute he walked to it, unlocked the door and stepped inside. Belle didn't wait for him to flip the lights on but went directly to Hannah's room. When she returned a few seconds later she whimpered.

"I know how you feel," he said, standing in the middle of the great room, his hands in his pockets, the emptiness bombarding him. "I don't see how she can be mad at me for protecting her, do you? Isn't that the job of those who are stronger? To protect the weak?" He sighed. "She wouldn't like being called that, weak. She's not. She just can't handle a man like Senior. Shouldn't have to."

David sat on her sofa and opened a photo album sitting on the coffee table. Hannah, from the day she was born, to this year's school picture. The photographs were taken in a variety of settings, many of them apparently places where they'd lived, small, orderly rooms filled with ancient furniture. From garage sales, maybe? Thrift shops?

Hannah smiled in every picture. In a few, she posed in a tutu. In those shots she beamed. He smiled back.

He set the album aside, wandered into the kitchen, opened the refrigerator. Spotless, and filled with healthy foods many in plastic containers, labeled and dated. He peered at one, spaghetti and meatballs, made just the day before. He remembered how good it tasted. The freezer held mint-chip ice cream.

Belle trailed him into Hannah's room, the walls decorated with posters of ballerinas. He didn't know anything about that world and guessed they were famous dancers. She was young to have such a big dream. He wished Valerie would let him pay for lessons. To delay meant—

He shut down the thought. Her daughter. Her choice.

The door to the adjoining bathroom was open, and he went in there next, could smell perfume or soap, he didn't know which, that fruity fragrance he'd never quite identified on

Valerie. Something feminine and heady. Then he continued into her bedroom.

Neat as a pin. She hadn't added anything but a couple of framed photos on the dresser. He moved to look out the window and realized he could see the pool area clearly now that the plants were tamed. He'd swum in the nude many times since she'd come. Had she known? Had she watched? Looked away?

"Belle, come," he ordered quietly. They went up to the house, headed for the staircase to his bedroom. He stopped at the family picture wall, focused on a photo of his father. "You messed me up, big-time," he said, jabbing a finger against the glass. He found the one of his mother. "And you, even more."

An ache settled in his chest as he climbed the stairs. He glanced at the bed. Had it been only this morning that he'd woken up with Valerie, sated and content? What a difference a day made.

He didn't bother to get undressed. He wouldn't sleep.

Belle walked to her doggy bed but didn't lie down. She barked once.

"I know. I'm confusing you. Sorry."

Sorry. Such a simple word. Why couldn't he tell Valerie he was sorry he interfered? He'd apologized for making Hannah a conspirator. Why was the other so difficult?

Was Noah right? Should he just keep the peace, no matter what? Is that all it would take? He knew what would happen if Valerie left. His life would descend into chaos again, even without all the trips to Europe. He'd be sleeping single in a king-size bed once more.

His life…. He shoved his hands through his hair. His *entire* life would revert to the old ways.

And if he apologized? What then? Peace. Order. Valerie in his bed, in his arms. Hannah dancing around the pool, making Belle happy, making everyone smile.

After a few seconds of staring at his empty bed he retraced

his steps. He dragged a dining room chair into the hall, placed it where he could see the photos of his mother and father, and then carried on a long debate with them, getting a lot out of his system, comparing himself to his father, comparing Valerie to his mother.

Then he analyzed Valerie, dissected their every conversation. He looked beyond his appreciation for her as a housekeeper and assistant to the woman at her core. He dug into his own soul, was honest about himself *with* himself, the most honest he'd ever been.

By morning he knew what he had to do. And it didn't involve apologizing.

Chapter Nineteen

"**M**om?"

"Hmm?" Valerie pulled up at Hannah's school the next morning. She was exhausted and trying not to show it.

"Please don't be mad at me."

Valerie loosened of her grip on the steering wheel to put her hands on Hannah's shoulders. "I'm not mad at you. Why would you think that?"

"You're not talking to me." Her eyes welled. "I promise I won't keep a secret again. I promise."

"You did nothing wrong, sweetie. Absolutely nothing. I'm just really tired this morning, that's all. I'm sorry you thought I was mad. I'm not."

"Are you mad at Mr. Falcon?"

How could she answer that? "We talked it over last night. It's okay."

"You're not going to quit, are you?"

"Oh, Hannah." She couldn't lie to her daughter, couldn't

tell her that they would be staying, when she didn't know that for sure herself. "I can't promise something like that. Life is full of surprises."

Hannah searched Valerie's eyes. "Did Mr. Falcon talk to my grandparents, like he said?"

"Yes, he did. Everything is fine now. You'll only visit when you want to, and for how long you want to."

"Okay." Her relief roared through with the force of a tsunami. "Mr. Falcon is so nice."

"Yes, he is."

"I like it there, at his house. It's home, you know?"

Valerie gathered her close. "You have a good day." She watched her beautiful daughter until she was safely in the building, then, emotionally drained, headed for Laura's office, having called her earlier.

"You have news?" Laura asked as Valerie took a seat.

She filled Laura in on what David had done. "He decided on his own to handle everything with the Rawlings. The upshot is that there will be no custody issues, not now, not ever."

"What'd he do?"

"He didn't share the details, but he implied I shouldn't worry my pretty little head about it."

"That annoys you," Laura said.

"I'm glad it's taken care of, but he went behind my back to do it. He even involved Hannah."

"David isn't known for patience. He's action oriented, solution oriented."

"I'm learning that."

"Valerie, you know that David's mother left when his parents divorced, don't you?"

"He told me. My father did the same thing, although I was barely two. So?"

"Right. No wonder you're both so pigheaded," Laura said, sitting back.

"Geez, Laura. Just when I'd come to like you."

Laura never took her eyes off Valerie. "His mother abandoned him. Your father abandoned you. Hannah's father abandoned you, too, or so you thought. Neither you nor David will admit you need each other, because you're scared. And pigheaded."

"I don't need you to—"

Laura put up a hand. "I've had a lot of experience with this in my practice, and here's what I've learned. People who've been abandoned have a hard time forming primary relationships. It's a little different for you because you have a child, which is your primary relationship, but how many serious boyfriends have you had since Hannah was born?"

"None," she admitted quietly.

"Why?"

"I never really trusted anyone to—"

"To stay," Laura said, finishing her sentence. "Right? You figured they would leave."

After a moment Valerie nodded.

"David feels like that, too. If a relationship gets serious, he's outta there in a flash."

"We don't have a relationship."

"Don't insult me."

After a moment Valerie stood. Laura followed suit. They shook hands. "Thank you for everything, Laura."

"You're welcome."

Valerie wanted to suggest lunch sometime, but couldn't decide if she wanted a friendship with a woman David had been intimate with. Wouldn't that be too weird?

She left Laura's office and headed toward her car, then saw Dixie coming toward her, not looking like a happy bride-to-be should. In fact, she started crying the moment Valerie said hello.

"What's wrong?" Valerie asked, alarmed.

"Joey."

"Is he hurt?"

"He won't set a date." She pressed her fingertips to the corners of her eyes, then straightened up and shook her head, her hair dancing. Her expression changed from hurt to angry. "I don't know what I expected. He's stalled all these years until he knew I wouldn't take much more. Now it's a new stall."

"What's he afraid of, do you know?"

"No. It's a McCoy family curse affecting the males only. His sisters are all married, but he and his brothers won't commit. I don't get it. His parents had a happy marriage, were good role models. My parents have a good marriage. He shouldn't be gun-shy."

"How much slack are you going to give him?"

"Not much." She looked at her watch. "I'm late for work. Thanks for the shoulder."

"Anytime." Despair gripped Valerie. If Joseph and Dixie couldn't make it, who could? What would David say about it? "See?" It wouldn't take more than that one-word question. He'd be right. One more nail in the marriage-and-family coffin.

Her stomach in knots, she pulled into the garage later, relieved to see David's truck was gone, therefore so was he. She'd just walked into the cottage when her cell phone rang. Senior. Great. Just what she needed.

"Hello?"

"I didn't appreciate your sending your henchman after me. We could've solved this between us."

Valerie dropped onto her sofa and tossed her purse aside. "Not to my satisfaction, I think. And you've got some damage to undo. Hannah told me she overheard you and Mrs. Rawling discussing her. It scared her. I'm not sure she's going to be comfortable with you now."

A beat passed. "I didn't know that. Wait. Hold on."

He covered the mouthpiece and spoke with someone, then Mrs. Rawling came on.

"Valerie, dear, you have my word that we won't interfere.

It was a dream, that's all. The dream of parents who wished for their son back. You don't have anything to fear from us. And we'll make sure that Hannah knows it."

Valerie believed her. "That would be good."

"We'll call later to arrange another visit."

"All right."

"I have to say, I'm really going to miss your mother. She was an excellent housekeeper all these years. But it's probably for the best."

Valerie was shocked but didn't want to let on that her mother hadn't spoken to her. She hung up, waited a second then called her mother.

"So, what's new?" Valerie asked. "Quit any jobs lately?"

"How did you hear? It just happened twenty minutes ago."

Valerie wanted to keep the conversation light, not rock the already shaky boat. At least her mother was talking to her. "It's in the ethers. So, tell me about it."

"It's Mrs. Cullen, do you remember her? She's asked me for years to come work for her. This seemed like the right time. I needed a change. You were right, you know. The kind of natural competition for Hannah between me and the missus wouldn't have been healthy for any of us. But you were wrong when you said it didn't seem to matter if I saw you or my granddaughter. It does matter. Maybe I haven't been good at showing it."

Relief made Valerie go weak. "We'll all make a better effort, then. I miss you, Mom."

"As soon as I'm settled, maybe you'll come for a visit?"

"Yes." They talked a little longer. Although Valerie was grateful for the shift in their relationship, she didn't confide about her relationship with David. When she hung up she debated whether to go up to the house and see what needed to be done.

See if he left her a note or something…

The rumble of his truck pulling into the garage paralyzed

her. She panicked. She could hardly catch her breath, her heart thundered so loud.

Would he come to her? Continue their discussion? Had he thought about it overnight and decided she should leave, after all? That she was complicating his life way too much?

Her hands knotted together, she waited. And waited. And waited. He never came. Never knocked on her door.

When she couldn't stand it any longer, she left the cottage. The moment she saw the yard she stopped. There were pots of purple flowers everywhere, pansies mostly, but mums and asters and some she couldn't identify. She stood and stared, then she saw David on the kitchen deck, watching her.

"You're crazy," she called up to him.

"Maybe. Probably."

Her throat ached. "Is this your way of apologizing?"

"No."

She didn't know whether to laugh or cry, so she groaned in frustration. She'd hoped he would make her decision easier. He hadn't.

"Don't move. I'm coming down," he said. Within a few seconds he was standing in front of her. "I had a sleepless night," he said. "One filled with revelations. I exorcised ghosts. I faced my own demons."

He gestured toward the garden. "And this is the result. This is not my way of apologizing but of telling you I love you."

Was there a word stronger than *stunned? Shocked,* maybe? *Staggered?* She put her face into her hands.

"It's my way of saying please stay," he said, his voice rough and yet so tender, emotion spilling out of him, drifting over her.

He was saying some of the words she wanted to hear, but not all. She was tempted to let it go, but she thought it would set a precedent between them, one where he would always dominate, not include her as a partner. She put her shoulders back. "You're not going to apologize?"

"I didn't do anything wrong. I love you, Valerie. I will protect you with my life. That means sometimes I'll do things you won't like, but they'll always be for your own good. For your protection."

She laughed shakily, coming to more of an understanding of where he came from, where he stood, what his personal rules were. "That's some ego you lug around with you," she said, making light of things because she wanted more from him, much more, and was afraid to show it.

He waited. She finally slipped her hands into his. "I love you, too."

He squeezed her hands almost to the point of pain. "You'll marry me."

There. The magic words. Joy burst inside her. "Yes. Oh, yes."

He kissed her, a deep, lingering merging, warm with promise. "You'll let me adopt Hannah," he said against her mouth.

All her dreams were coming true at the same time. She nodded, her eyes filling. "Hannah seems to think you would make a good father."

"I happen to think she's right. I love that kid. She snuck into my heart. I can't tell you when, but it happened. I think I'd like to have a couple more." He drew a long breath. "That's another revelation I had during my sleepless night."

"I didn't sleep, either." She couldn't stop smiling.

"How fast can you put together a wedding?"

She toyed with the top button of his shirt. "I'm pretty efficient, you know."

"I've learned that."

"But you told me not too long ago that people should know each other better, longer, before they get married. Did you change your mind?"

"Yeah." He brushed her hair from her face and pressed gentle kisses all over her face, leaving her wanting, not satisfying her need by kissing her lips. "When it's right, you know it. A wise woman told me that love conquers all."

The distinctive sound of the school bus approaching made them move apart. There was no time to celebrate by making love. Later, though. Tomorrow, the first of thousands of tomorrows. He took her hand. "Let's go tell our daughter."

* * * * *

Don't miss the next book in the WIVES FOR HIRE *mini-series,* The Single Dad's Virgin Wife, *this October from Mills & Boon® Special Moments.*

Mills & Boon® Special Moments
brings you a sneak preview.

In The Bad Son *Beau McCain has become a*
successful lawyer, held the family together, mended
fences and watched while others found love...
Now it's his turn!

Turn the page for a peek at this fantastic new story
from Linda Warren, available next month in
Mills & Boon® Special Moments!

Don't forget you can still find all your favourite
Superromance and Special Edition stories
every month in Special Moments!

The Bad Son
by
Linda Warren

IN THE WESTERN SKY, an orange sun sank slowly toward the hazy net of trees low on the distant horizon. It reminded Beau McCain of a large basketball sailing toward a basket. Bam. Three points. The light was gone and a shadowy dimness crept over central Texas.

He gazed through the beam of his headlights, a slight grin on his face. He'd been playing too much basketball with his brothers. He changed lanes and shifted uncomfortably in his seat. The grin faded. He was returning to Waco after visiting a law firm in Dallas where he'd been offered a senior partnership, an offer he had no intention of refusing.

It was a drastic move. Living all of his forty-two years in Waco, except for a law internship in Dallas, he had his own firm practicing family law and was doing quite well. His personal life was the problem. All because of Macy Randall. He was tired of waiting for her to see him as more than a friend.

At his age, he wanted a home and a family and he had to finally acknowledge that wasn't going to happen with Macy. He had to move on, start a new life and forget her. Moving to Dallas was a big step in that direction.

Taking an exit off I-35, he turned by a McDonald's then onto the street leading to his subdivision. He and Macy lived next door to each other and Beau had known her all her life. She'd lived down the street when they were kids. He was eight years older, but he was a sucker for those big blue eyes and her sad little stories. Single-handedly, she was trying to save every animal on the planet.

Macy was a neonatal nurse who worked nights and Beau had babysat her strays more than once. She was never going to love a man as much as her animals. Beau wasn't sure she saw him as anything more than a very good friend. She cried on his shoulder, told him her problems, but not once in all the years he'd known her had they progressed beyond friendship. He kept waiting, though. Like a lovesick fool, he kept waiting.

Not anymore.

Beau McCain was moving on.

He turned onto a cul-de-sac that housed several condos. When he'd bought the place, he'd no idea Macy lived next door. She'd married and moved away to Dallas, but now she was back—without a husband. He'd asked her about it, but in the last seven years she'd only said the marriage hadn't worked out. They talked about everything else, but her marriage was a subject she avoided.

He remembered her wedding vividly. He, his younger brother, Caleb, and their parents had attended. Though he'd acted like a normal friend, all the while his heart had been breaking.

Everyone in the neighborhood knew the scrawny, curly-haired girl who was always searching for a home for the endless array of animals she rescued. When Beau returned after his internship, the scrawny girl had turned into a leggy beauty with alabaster skin he'd never noticed before. But he knew where the freckles were on her nose, even though makeup hid them flawlessly.

Following the divorce of her parents, he'd become her confidant, her friend. That was his first big mistake. The next thing he knew she was engaged—someone she'd known in college and had met again. Beau had never told Macy about his real feelings and he never planned to. Their lives went in different directions, then a short two years later they were living next door to each other and the cycle started again.

His brothers teased him all the time about Macy and her ability to wrap him around her finger. He was too good for his own well-being—that's what his brothers said. But that's not how he felt. His father, Joe McCain, had called him "the bad son" because when Beau's parents had divorced, he chose to go with his mother. His brother, Jake, stayed with their father and spent years estranged from the family.

Joe McCain was a jealous, abusive man who drank heavily. When he did, he became angry and mean, and hit Althea, their mother. When Althea became pregnant with their third son, Caleb, Joe accused her of sleeping with Andrew Wellman, a man from their church. He said the baby wasn't his and beat Althea until she was black and blue. His mother knew she had to get out or risk losing her unborn child.

But Althea hadn't counted on Joe spreading his lies to their oldest son, Jake. When the sheriff came to take them away, Jake refused to go. It broke Althea's heart, but she left one of her sons behind. She tried and tried, but Jake remained steadfast in his loyalty to his father.

Beau saw his father from time to time as a kid, mainly running into him by accident. Joe had refused any contact with his younger son. On those rare occasions, Joe never missed a chance to tell Beau what a bad son he was and how disloyal he was to his own father. Those words stayed with him all his life, but he never changed his decision. It only instilled in him a need to prove his father wrong—to prove he was a good son.

As a kid, he grew up wanting Jake back in his life— and Althea's. When Joe passed away, Beau went to the funeral, determined to make contact with his older brother. Jake resisted at first, but Beau never let up. He kept talking and visiting, wearing Jake down, and he didn't stop until he brought Jake and their mother back together. They were a real family now. Even Elijah Coltrane, a son Joe had with another woman, was a part of their big family.

Eli and Caleb were Texas Rangers and Jake ran the McCain farm. Beau knew from an early age that he was going to be a lawyer. Since his parents' divorce, he'd become passionate about keeping families together. He was good at negotiating and working out problems. This was his life's work.

Caleb had just married and was ecstatic. Jake had a wife and a family, and Eli was also married. He and his wife Caroline were expecting their first child. Beau wanted a bit of that happiness—with his own family.

His friend, Jeremiah Tucker, known as "Tuck" to the family, was also still single and the same age as Beau. Tuck was Eli's foster brother and the McCain brothers had accepted him as one of their own. Since Tuck and Beau were the two single sons in the group, they'd become good friends.

Beau started to call Tuck to see if he wanted to commiserate over a beer, but he decided it would be best to go straight home. It had been a long three days and he had to tell his family about the job offer.

And he had to tell Macy.

© Linda Warren 2006

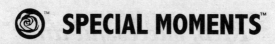 SPECIAL MOMENTS™

Single titles coming next month

HAVING TANNER BRAVO'S BABY
by Christine Rimmer

Tanner Bravo was the type to settle down, free-spirited Crystal wouldn't hear of it. Now that Crystal is pregnant, will Tanner have his way after all?

HER FAVOURITE HOLIDAY GIFT
by Lynda Sandoval

Colleen Delaney would never forget her one night with Eric Nelson. Now the irresistible lawyer was going head-to-head with her in a high-stakes case. A meeting under the mistletoe seems inevitable...

HITCHED TO THE HORSEMAN
by Stella Bagwell

Mercedes had come home to the ranch she loved, not to get involved with a heartbreaker. Yet Gabe called to something deep within her, making her yearn to build a future with him.

THE DADDY PLAN
by Karen Rose Smith

It was a big gamble for Corrie to ask her boss if he'd father her child. But she absolutely didn't expect sceptical Sam's next move – throwing his heart in into the bargain...

On sale 21st August 2009

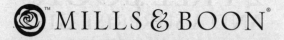

2 FREE BOOKS
AND A SURPRISE GIFT

We would like to take this opportunity to thank you for reading this Mills & Boon® book by offering you the chance to take TWO more specially selected titles from the Special Moments™ series absolutely FREE! We're also making this offer to introduce you to the benefits of the Mills & Boon® Book Club™—

- **FREE home delivery**
- **FREE gifts and competitions**
- **FREE monthly Newsletter**
- **Exclusive Mills & Boon Book Club offers**
- **Books available before they're in the shops**

Accepting these FREE books and gift places you under no obligation to buy, you may cancel at any time, even after receiving your free books. Simply complete your details below and return the entire page to the address below. You don't even need a stamp!

YES Please send me 2 free Special Moments books and a surprise gift. I understand that unless you hear from me, I will receive 5 superb new titles every month, including a 2-in-1 title priced at £4.99 and three single titles priced at £3.19 each, postage and packing free. I am under no obligation to purchase any books and may cancel my subscription at any time. The free books and gift will be mine to keep in any case.

Ms/Mrs/Miss/Mr _____ initials _____

Surname _____

address _____

_____

_____ postcode _____

Send this whole page to: Mills & Boon Book Club, Free Book Offer, FREEPOST NAT 10298, Richmond, TW9 1BR

Offer valid in UK only and is not available to current Mills & Boon Book Club subscribers to this series. Overseas and Eire please write for details.. We reserve the right to refuse an application and applicants must be aged 18 years or over. Only one application per household. Terms and prices subject to change without notice. Offer expires 31st October 2009. As a result of this application, you may receive offers from Harlequin Mills & Boon and other carefully selected companies. If you would prefer not to share in this opportunity please write to The Data Manager, PO Box 676, Richmond, TW9 1WU.

Mills & Boon® is a registered trademark owned by Harlequin Mills & Boon Limited.
Special Moments™ is being used as a trademark.
The Mills & Boon® Book Club™ is being used as a trademark.